FROM THE ASHES OF GODS

EIGHTH CIRCLE BOOK 1

KATERINA SPEERS

For mom. I miss you, lady. I hope I make you proud.

CONTENT WARNING

Please note this book contains subject matter that may be difficult for some readers, including discussion and/or description of death, torture, violence, profanity, and sexual situations.

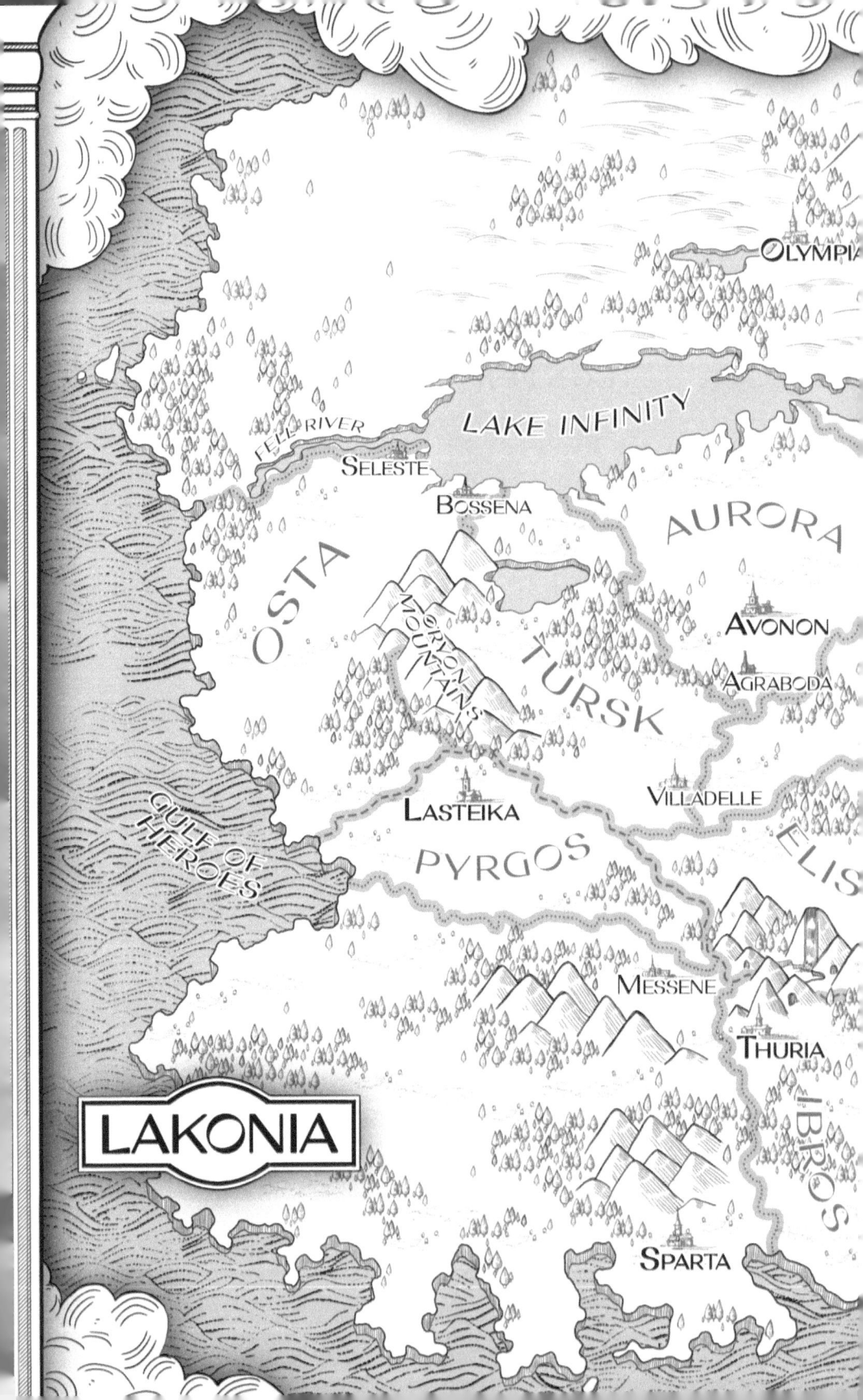

OLYMPIA

FELL RIVER

LAKE INFINITY

SELESTE

BOSSENA

OSTA

AURORA

MORVONIS MOUNTAINS

TURSK

AVONON

AGRABODA

GULF OF HEROES

LASTEIKA

VILLADELLE

PYRGOS

ELIS

MESSENE

THURIA

BROS

LAKONIA

SPARTA

CHAPTER ONE

A curse wasn't enough to deter Terena Luca. She would stop at nothing to find her parents, and the fabled artifact she hunted now was worth the risk if it led her to them.

She'd tracked the legend to Agraboda, the once beautiful city decimated by a plague now lost to time. Terena was grateful to find the ruins undisturbed centuries later, feeling in her bones what she sought was still there.

Terena lifted her hand, shielding her eyes against the late afternoon light that glinted off the scattered remains of marble columns.

It'd be dark soon; they'd have to stop for the night.

"Can we please just admit defeat already?"

The whining plea came from her right, and Terena craned her neck to see her brother standing atop a ledge. He posed to look like the horned beast with large fangs and half a leg—the rest wiped away by time—from the wall beneath him.

She tossed a pebble at him. "It's here," she called back.

Terena wiped her brow and returned to her work. She dropped a red cloth into the marked off area before stepping outside of it and looked back up at her brother. "This would go a lot faster if you helped, Croak."

Croak waved her off. "I'm here, aren't I? I just don't think *it's* here."

Terena pursed her lips, stretching out two more markers, then stepped inside the area and dropped to her knees. She ran her fingers over the cold stone, wiping away some debris and dirt with a small brush. "It's here. For the thousandth time, it's here."

Croak mumbled something she didn't care to hear and dropped from the ledge. Terena heard his shuffling steps as he came close.

"Maybe you got it wrong this time."

A corner of her mouth lifted, but Terena just shook her head.

"You know, it *has* been known to happen," Croak said.

When she still didn't reply, he came closer, bending over and sneering. "Even the all-knowing and fabulous Terena Luca can be wrong."

He rose to his full height and Terena glanced up to see him throw back his head, dark brown locks shifting in the breeze. He raised his arms up, his fur-lined cloak flapping back as he bellowed to the sky, "O how the gods wept the day Terena the All-Knowing's power of foresight failed her and she did not find the Towel of Destiny! Now mankind is doomed to never seeing its dirty likeness ever again!"

"It's not a towel, idiot," she replied with a grin, shaking her head again.

"A doily?"

"A shroud."

"Shroud," he said, stretching out each letter until the word was barely recognizable. "Sounds weird."

"You're weird," Terena grumbled, then sat back on her heels, her hands at her hips. "And not helpful!"

She reached out and pulled her tool bag closer, blowing on her icy hands before rummaging inside. Pulling out a few markers, she tossed them at him. "Be helpful and mark some areas on the other side of the square. If you can find—"

"This is boring!" Croak yelled up to the sky, dropping his arms with a swoop as he stomped in a circle behind her. Terena sighed and closed her eyes, shaking her head once before turning back to her work.

"Why the fuck would the shroud be here, anyway? And why does Duke Aurora want someone's death laundry?"

Terena smothered a grin; she did not want to encourage him. "I don't care why he wants it," she called out. Her brother continued his stomping dance. "I care for the coin he's paying me to find it."

"Aye, all right," Croak mumbled. Terena busied herself once more with pressing her fingers into the ground, searching for gaps or a seam, something that would reveal a hiding spot large enough—

Her brother yelped a second before a loud crash sounded behind her. Terena jumped to her feet; her brother disappeared beneath a cloud of dirt, billowing up to hide his whereabouts. Terena surged toward where he'd been standing, batting away the dust, coughing as she screamed his name.

Dropping, her knees cracking on the ground, and she cursed, pain shooting up her thighs.

Terena got down on her belly and slithered forward, feeling her way to where she'd last seen him, her hands finding the edge of a hole. She peered into the darkness.

"Croak!"

The dust settled, and she swiped at her eyes, blinking against the grit.

"Are you all right? Croak!"

A groan drifted up from the hole and a long time later, the dust cleared enough for her to see her brother's lanky form sprawled in the dirt below.

"Fuuuck," he cried, his voice cracking on a whimper.

Terena hung her head, a sigh of relief escaping her mouth. "Are you hurt?"

He whimpered. "Not at all," he answered, his voice an octave higher. "Just having a lay down."

"Stay there," Terena called down. She heard his weak laugh.

"I have rope in my bag. I'll be right back."

She turned away, scrambling for the bag she'd left near the walled area she'd been working in. Turning it over, she let the contents drop onto the ground.

No rope.

She turned, eyes darting around until she remembered she'd left it tied to her saddlebags on her mare, Nyx.

Terena yelled out to her brother to hold on as she ran for her horse, cooing nonsense words at the black beauty, and tugged the rope from where she'd secured it.

Her brother shrieked curses at her.

Terena knelt over the hole and peered down at Croak, sitting up now, covered in dirt.

"Can you see anything in there? Is it a room?"

"It's dark, Ren, I can't see shit."

"Tie this around your waist and I'll pull you up," she called down.

"Fuck's sake," he grumbled, but grabbed the rope, wrapping it around his waist. He made to rise, then stopped.

"Come on, let's go."

Her brother continued to look off to his left. He held up a hand to her for silence. "Wait."

Croak stood slowly and untied the rope. His neck stretched out as he squinted into the darkness.

"Are you kidding me now? What can you possibly see down there?"

Croak flapped his hand at her and took a step. After a moment, he looked up at her. "I think it's a tomb."

Terena stilled. In all her research, there'd been no mention of anyone being buried in the palace. Or under it. The royal family lay buried in the crypt beneath the Temple of Gaia, which was a mile from where they stood.

"Croak," Terena called again, "is it a tomb? Do you see—"

"Just... give me a *second*, woman!"

Terena rolled her eyes, dropping her hands to grip the lip of the hole, and waited.

"Ah!"

Terena leaned forward, trying to see into the gloom below.

"Hey! Drop a torch, will you?"

Terena hung her head, then nodded. "Aye, all right."

She rose and turned back to her bag, grabbing the torch, flint, and steel. She struck the flint with the steel until it sparked, lit the torch and brought it over to the hole.

"Here it comes," she yelled down and dropped it.

Croak leaned back toward the opening, yipping when he tried to grab the torch mid-flight and failed. He hissed when it cracked against his long fingers, letting it fall to the ground.

"Idiot," Terena said.

Croak flapped his injured hand and grabbed the torch with the other. He held it high and awkwardly gave her his middle finger.

He moved back out of sight. Long moments passed before she called out. "Well?"

No answer.

"That's it," she mumbled to herself as she rose, wiping her hands on her leather leggings. She strode off toward the nearest column and wrapped the rope around it before tying it off. "Don't know why I'm even waiting. I need to see this for myself."

Terena dropped into the hole, shimmying down the rope, a dim glow at her back. She turned when her feet hit the ground and saw her brother holding up the torch.

Her mouth dropped open as she took in the small chamber. Words covered the walls. Terena's head swam for a few seconds, vertigo overcoming her whenever her visions matched her reality. This chamber, the ceramic tiles at her feet. The writing she couldn't quite make out in her visions.

It was the same as in the vision.

Another wave of vertigo hit her. She held out her hand to steady herself but Croak grabbed her arm in a practiced way. Putting her hand to her forehead, she breathed in and out a few times.

Her head cleared, and she opened her eyes once more.

"I'm fine, Croak."

"So, we're here, right? This is what you've seen?"

Terena nodded slowly.

He whipped the torch around, almost hitting her in the face. She cursed and grabbed the torch from him.

"Did any of your research mention a walled-in room like this?"

Terena turned slowly. He was right. She lifted the torch to the opening.

"Sealed off," she whispered. None of her research said anything about what she was looking at.

"Tell me *this* is what I think it is," Croak said excitedly.

He lifted his chin toward the wall to his left.

She moved forward, holding the torch higher as she exhaled. She smirked at him. "If you're thinking this is orichalcum—"

"Ori—! Are you serious?"

Terena stepped closer, lifting a hand to run across the words written there.

"And here I thought we wouldn't find anything fun," Croak said. He unsheathed his dagger and began chipping some of the ore out of the wall.

"What are you doing?" Terena asked him, her lips pulled back.

"*I* have to tell *you* how valuable this shit is? I'll sell it to Benson. Or maybe save it for some rich asshole in Metilai."

"Shit, I didn't bring anything to write with," Terena muttered, patting her pockets. She usually kept a small notebook and charcoal on her, but hadn't thought to unpack it while they'd searched for the shroud.

"Can you go up and grab it?"

Croak didn't bother to look at her as he stuffed some of the ore into his pockets. "What? *You* do it."

"Croak, really? It's in my bag. Hurry and bring it back."

He grumbled, stuffing more of the orichalcum into the pockets of his pants and sheathed his dagger before stomping off toward the rope. She didn't bother to watch him make the climb, instead taking a step closer to the wall, tracing the words written in Ancient Greek. Wonder filled her as she read the story of the shroud and the power it was rumored to have.

The power to bring back the Olympian gods.

Cold shot down her spine, and she shivered.

Terena swung the torch to her right, eager for more. Shuffling forward a few steps, she read the names of the royal House of Galaneas, the last family to rule Agraboda, but no other mention of the gods.

She continued further, stopping when she spied something shadowed. The wall beveled deeper than the previous two. She'd missed it at first because of the shadows. As she drew nearer, the light revealed a small, wide table flashing in the light of the torch.

Terena took two steps closer and saw the table was pure gold with a gilded, oblong box sitting on top. She moved the torch closer and read the words above the box in the ancient language.

Defiling the tomb has proved our undoing.

Learn from us.

Forgive us.

The stories on the walls were of the fall of Ostapolis and King Selenas of Agraboda taking the shroud from Faybhen's tomb.

Upon his return to Agraboda, the king presented the shroud to his wife as a gift.

The queen died that night. The king and their son a week later.

And someone had put the shroud in this sealed off chamber beneath the palace with a warning.

Terena wasn't sure why, but she knew her visions of this place and the shroud weren't meant to lead her to her death, despite what it had done to the city and its people.

She opened her mouth and sighed as she reached out a trembling hand and lifted the top of the box.

Tucked inside and folded neatly was a plain, white cloth. She touched it, her fingers tracing lightly over the linen.

Her heart raced.

Found you.

CROAK MUMBLED AS HE CLIMBED THE ROPE, PULLING HIMSELF OUT OF the hole and stretching out on the ground beside it. He yanked his cloak around him, the chill of the stone beneath him seeping through to his wool tunic. He closed his eyes and took a deep breath.

When he opened them, confusion made him blink.

"Ren," Croak called out as he slowly sat up, eyes darting around. "Terena!"

Terena came to the opening and held up the torch. "What?"

Croak didn't answer. Rising to one knee, his hands stretched out to feel for the ground.

"Wait, what's going on up there? Why's it so dark?"

Croak shook his head, turning. His gaze narrowed. "I don't know, but this is not natural. I can't even see my own fucking hand!"

He slowly unsheathed his sword.

"We've been down here maybe five minutes," she called up.

Croak searched frantically for anything that would tell him he hadn't gone mad.

A minute later, he heard Terena grunt and moan. She tossed the torch up and he jumped when it landed an inch from his boot. She pulled herself up from the hole, cursing, then snuck closer to him and drew her dagger from the center of the shoulder guard she always wore.

He frowned over at her. "You're loud, you know that?"

"Do you see anything?" she whispered.

Croak shot her a baffled look. With heavy sarcasm, he said, "No, Ren, I can't see in the dark. Can you?"

She scowled at him, then turned to light the torches closest to them, creating a small ring of light in the pitch black.

It was better than nothing.

Croak swallowed.

He turned around just as an arrow whizzed past his shoulder, tearing his cloak.

They ducked, stumbling around until they found cover. To their left, shouts sounded out of the darkness.

Croak gasped and looked up as three men appeared in the air, shouting as they landed in front of them. Their heads were covered in black and masks covered the lower half of their faces, scimitars raised high as they rushed at Croak and Terena.

Croak lifted his sword and feinted left as one attacker barreled toward him. He came back and thrust down with his sword, catching the man above his hip as he stumbled past.

"Fucking Magi?!" Croak shrieked, looking around frantically, searching for his sister.

He caught sight of her fighting two Magi. She blocked one with her sword on her left while the other she kept at bay with her dagger. Terena dropped to the ground to kick out the legs of the first Magi.

Croak surged forward with a roar, launching into the air. The Magi closest turned and kicked out, his foot catching Croak in the face and he whirled, falling and rolling on the ground.

To his right, Terena lifted her sword, bringing it down to cleave the wrist of the Magi she fought. She quickly twisted as she dropped to her knee and gutted him with the dagger in her right hand.

Scrambling back, Croak gasped as the last Magi approached, lifted his scimitar, his dark eyes hard.

"Ren!"

The Magi swung down. Croak raised his arm but the Magi jerked forward, dropping his scimitar and landing in front of Croak. Cursing, Croak bolted up, his sword aimed at the Magi, who was now on his knees clutching his shoulder.

When the Magi bent over, Croak saw Terena's dagger embedded to the hilt. Wiping his face with the back of his sword hand, Croak looked down at the Magi and yanked down the cloth covering the man's face.

"Why'd you attack us?" he asked, panting, his sword pointed at the Magi. "Now your friends are dead and it's all your fault."

The man was still on one knee, his trousers torn from where he'd fallen. He clutched at his bloodied shoulder.

When he lifted his gaze, his nostrils flared and eyes burned.

Then he shifted his eyes to Terena.

"It is you," the Magi exhaled, his accent thick.

Terena lifted an eyebrow.

"You should not have come for the shroud. You are not ready."

Croak dropped to his haunches, twisting his wrist so his blade was perpendicular to the Magi's throat. "What shroud?"

The Magi barely glanced at him, annoyed, before he nodded at Terena. "Do you know what this means? If you take it, it begins again."

"What begins? What do you mean?" Terena asked, hands splayed as she took a few steps closer.

The Magi looked off to his right and his eyes widened slightly. He licked his lips and looked wild-eyed at Terena.

"I'm usually dead by now," he mused.

"What's that now?" Croak frowned.

The man dropped his chin. When he looked back up at Terena, his dark skin was pale beneath a sheen of sweat. "You must kill me."

Terena scoffed, shooting a look at Croak.

"Take the shroud and go north this time," the man pleaded. "Do not go to Metilai. You will die there."

Terena stilled. "What?"

"Take the shroud and go north," the man said, his voice almost manic now. "You've searched your whole life for him. You can get the Twins later. Go north. Now. *You have the shroud.*"

"I don't understand." Terena bit out. "Who—"

"Please let this be it," the Magi mumbled. He glanced off to his right again.

The right side of his lips lifted beneath his thick black beard, but his eyes looked sad when he turned back to Terena.

"Who are you talking about? What does the shroud—"

"Please," the Magi whispered as he looked up at the black sky.

He mumbled something in a language Croak didn't know. He looked up at his sister, her face ashen.

The Magi leaned forward so fast, Croak had no chance to react. The man grabbed Croak's wrist and tugged it forward, slicing his neck on Croak's blade.

Croak stumbled to his feet, falling a few steps away, and cursed.

"What…," Terena whispered, drawing out the word as she gawked at the dead Magi. They both watched him slump to the ground, blood soaking into the worn marble beneath them.

"What the fuck?"

Croak's pulse thundered in his ears. He blinked, then looked around as the area all around them became brighter.

Croak nudged Terena a few times before she glanced at him with a frown.

He pointed to the sky.

All around them, stars appeared, as if something heavy and unnatural had dissipated. The full moon glowed. The sounds of the night drifted toward them, and Croak took a minute to calm himself.

"What just happened? What the fuck with everything just now?"

Terena barked out a laugh and lifted both hands to her head, strands of black hair matted to her face. "No idea."

She brought a hand down to her mouth and shook her head. Her hazel eyes remained fixed on the dead Magi.

"What did he say?"

Terena looked out at the now moonlit square.

"Ren. What was he mumbling there?" Croak asked again, taking a step toward her.

Terena turned her head as if in a trance. Croak waited, his breath held.

After a long pause she said, "'The shroud, the heir, and the weapon. Only then will they return.'"

"What's that mean? Does that mean something to you?"

Terena looked at him and didn't speak for a long time. Croak's bones ached from standing so stiff.

"I hear a voice. In my dreams. I don't know if it's me." Terena shook her head and pushed the heels of her hands to her eyes. "Sometimes I think it is, but I don't... I heard those words before. It was ringing in my head over and over the last time I dreamt of the shroud."

"The shroud, the heir, and the weapon, huh? Think these three were protecting the shroud?" Croak asked.

"Aye."

"So... what weapon? Have you seen that in a vision?"

Terena shook her head.

"What about an heir? Think he was talking about your father?"

Terena's eyes snapped to him, her face tight. "Who else could he have meant?"

"Makes sense," Croak said with a shrug. "Baba said he found you up north at Hekate's temple."

"I don't think he's the heir, though."

"It's frozen up there now. Has been for over a year." Croak said, wiping a hand over his face. "How would we even get there?"

Terena didn't answer.

After a long pause, he asked, "You got your fancy blanket, then?"

Terena twisted her lips. "Yes, I have the shroud."

"Can we get out of here now, please? Thank you. Also, I'm taking his scimitar."

Croak grabbed the Magi's weapon, then turned and headed for his saddlebags, snatching them up as he mumbled to himself. He heard Terena follow a few seconds later.

"Hey," she called out and snapped her fingers a few times.

Croak arched an eyebrow when he turned to her. "Really?"

She nodded to her left.

He looked over, then narrowed his eyes when he saw a shadow on an overlook a hundred yards away. "Could be an animal. Or a rock."

Terena's dark brows furrowed, and she made a face. Redoing her ponytail, she asked, "Remember how he kept looking over that way? The Magi? It was weird."

Croak shrugged and turned away dismissively. "This whole thing was weird."

"We were just attacked by Magi. Guardians of the temples of Olympian gods." She shook her head in wonder. "Why are they even out here? We're nowhere near Lakonia."

"Out drinking maybe and took a wrong turn? This one for sure was drunk or something, the way he was talking. I hear they drink a lot of keikon, so..." Croak shrugged, referring to the hallucinogenic drink the southern priests favored to bring them closer to the gods.

"Next time don't kill the man we're trying to get answers out of," she said reproachfully.

Croak's brows shot to his hairline. "Are you fucking with me?"

"A little more care next time. That's all." She went back to cleaning up the area of her markings, stepping gingerly over the fallen Magi as if they were decorative art in these ruins.

She didn't notice the mulish look he threw her.

Croak scoffed, shaking his head. "Unbelievable."

Terena looked back up and planted her hands at her hips. She gestured to the shadow again. "You don't think it looks like it could be a man? Watching us? It's still there, whatever it is."

"Well, real smooth pointing at him then," Croak said as he turned, blowing on his gloved hands as he walked toward his horse, Cerberus. He dropped the saddlebags over the horse and turned to Terena. "Thank you for all of this, by the way. Enjoyed myself, immensely. Near-death experiences are exciting."

"Wait. You're mad at me?"

"Let's go. Seriously. I've had a bad fucking day."

Terena laughed, incredulous, but she hefted her saddlebags over her shoulder and followed. "We've had the same day, you idiot." She pulled herself up on Nyx and tugged on the reins to turn her.

"If he is with them, it doesn't seem to matter we know he's here. He's not doing anything to come closer."

"Then let's leave him to his business and be about ours. Which is getting the fuck out of here," Croak called out as he led the way.

CHAPTER TWO

Croak hadn't spoken one word to Terena since they'd left Agraboda. Didn't stop her from prattling on about 'her find'. He burned to tell her it was *his* find, and now she was conveniently forgetting that fact while going on and on about Galaneas this and Faybhen that.

"...that's why I need you to pretend, all right?" Terena was saying.

He didn't reply. Just huffed a sigh of relief as he sited the city gates in the distance.

They'd reached Avonon, the seat of power in Aurora.

"Okay?" she asked again, her sable ponytail swinging over her shoulder when she turned to look at him. "Come on, it's important. Just go along with everything I say."

Croak shrugged, but said nothing. Out of the corner of his eye, he watched as she looked at him for several seconds before turning away. *Good*, he thought. *Let her stew.*

The guards at the gate moved forward as Croak and Terena pulled up. Croak rested an arm on the saddle horn, watching his sister pull down her hood. Despite being the Royal Tracker and all that entailed, she preferred simple traveler's clothes of leather leggings and a plain tunic under a leather jerkin. The shoulder guard she wore was found in an armory a few months ago in Tursk. Her black leggings and jacket were dust covered and stained with blood from the Magi; he imagined he looked much the same.

Terena spoke with the guards and one of them nodded before looking up to wave at someone in the guardhouse above.

Terena dug her boot heels into Nyx's soft belly and the horse snorted, trotting forward. Croak clicked his tongue and his mount, Cerberus, followed.

This time of morning, the streets of Avonon bustled with activity, the shops open and the market off to the far right already teeming with people ready to haggle.

Croak followed Terena as she moved off the main thoroughfare and down a back street on the left. It was much quieter the further away they went from the shopping district. The duke's castle loomed large in the background.

When they reached the gates to the road leading up to the castle, the guard waved them through without a word. Croak touched fingers to his imaginary hat at the man, earning a vulgar gesture in return. Croak put his hand up to his chest as if mortally wounded.

They dismounted in front of the grand double doors, a stable boy racing forward to take Nyx's reins. He hollered behind him at another boy he called 'Arthur', whose little legs pumped furiously. He stopped next to Croak with labored breaths. Croak handed him the reins, and the boy took hold with a shaking hand.

Croak bent down and grabbed the boy's other hand, pressing a coin into his palm. "You're doing fantastic, Arthur," he said and ruffled the boy's mousy brown hair. "Keep up the good work."

The boy beamed up at Croak and stood taller as he walked off, with Cerberus, a gentle giant, following behind.

Croak crossed his arms at his chest, leisurely following Terena up the steps.

"Mistress Luca, always a pleasure."

The silky voice belonged to the biggest snake Croak had ever met. Danilos of the Offeni, Duke Aurora's steward and a general pain in the ass, clutched his hands in front of him as he simpered. "I trust your journey was…fruitful?"

Terena gave him a curt nod. "Is His Grace available?"

"He heard of your arrival, of course, and made room in his schedule to see you," the steward said, his bald head dipping low.

Croak snorted.

Terena ignored him and placed a hand atop the cloth covered box she held under her right arm. "Wonderful. I think he'll be pleased with our visit."

"Indeed," Danilos murmured, his greedy eyes narrowed on the box she cradled. He gestured with a grand sweep of his too-thin arm and Terena preceded him into a cavernous hall where courtiers mingled, occasionally sending them dismissive glances that had Croak blowing kisses at them around his middle finger.

They didn't have any time to look at the castle, which was a shame —this was the first time they'd been inside. They weaved their way through the idle nobles, which wasn't difficult as three of the duke's personal guard showed up to escort them into a receiving room.

As the large gilded doors opened, Croak glimpsed the duke, the young royal strutting forward with a stupid grin on his face to greet them.

Or rather, to greet Terena. Croak was pretty sure the duke hadn't noticed his presence.

He wore a long velvet jacket in yellow with a dark blue sash across his chest and a silk shirt beneath, the long lace cuffs peeking through the sleeves of the jacket. The Aurorans favored short silk or satin breeches ending at the knee with silk stockings and ornate shoes with more jewels on them than the emperor's crown. Even after being conquered, they refused the fashion of the Heylisian Empire.

He stopped in front of Terena and held out his arms.

"The gorgeous tracker returns triumphant!" Duke Aurora remarked as he rubbed his hands together. He dropped kisses on either side of Terena's face, then lifted a dark blond eyebrow at her and added, "She does, doesn't she?"

"She does indeed," Terena said with a smirk. She made to hand the box to Danilos, who had snuck up to the duke's side, but Aurora swatted at the man's hands and took the box himself.

He let the cloth covering the box fall onto the floor without a care; the steward dropped swiftly to pick it up as Aurora ran a hand reverently over the gold, his dark eyes round as saucers.

No one spoke as the duke turned and strode toward a large mahogany table near the back windows, papers and maps strewn atop ignored when he placed the box down gently.

He made to lift the lid but paused and said, "Are you certain—"

Before he could finish, Terena stepped to his side and said in a low voice, "Not only am I certain, but when you see the shroud, you'll know."

Croak rolled his eyes at the duke's barely contained excitement. His hands trembled as he reached for the lid, lifting it back slowly. His mouth fell open, and he put a hand to cover it, shooting a look at Terena before he reached inside and lifted the cloth as delicately as if he handled the emperor's balls.

The room was silent while everyone beheld the cloth—ordinary, if you asked him—but Croak knew these idiots would never say so. Duke Aurora let it unfold as he held it aloft, his dark blue eyes sparkling when he saw what Terena had meant. The shroud had a barely visible outline—a face or something. Croak couldn't tell, nor did he care to.

With a snap of his fingers, Duke Aurora summoned one of his lackeys to clear a space on the table. The duke laid the shroud across the cleared space and ran his long fingers over it, closing his eyes.

"I can feel its power," he muttered, his blond head tipped back.

Croak sniggered.

Terena jabbed an elbow into his side. He snapped his head to her, surprised she was even there. When had she moved?

"I apologize I don't have a formal letter of authenticity drawn up yet, Your Grace," Terena said, idling closer to the royal as she clasped her hands behind her back. "We came straight here upon finding the shroud in the ruins at Agraboda. But I'm happy to sign it if your steward will do the honor of creating the document."

Danilos practically went boneless as he bowed and scrapped his willingness to do so. Duke Aurora nodded dumbly, still transfixed by the shroud.

"Wonderful," Danilos simpered. "I shall get it completed momentarily. In the meantime, might I suggest refreshments for Mistress Luca in the solarium while she waits? They are being laid out as we speak."

Again, the dismissive nod from Duke Aurora and Terena thanked the steward, turning back to Croak and gesturing with her head. He fell into step beside her and tossed over his shoulder, "The Mistress's brother also appreciates your hospitality, Your Grace." He shot a look at the steward. "Looking forward to those refreshments, Danny."

TERENA FOLLOWED A SERVANT DOWN THE LARGE HALLWAY TO THE solarium. She'd never been to Castle Surraine before, having only been in Aurora a handful of times and only seeing the duke and his steward when they visited the duke's sister or the emperor in Metilai.

Marveling at the decadent beauty, Terena openly gawked. She glanced back, a smile lifting a corner of her mouth at her brother's gaping face, his eyes huge while his head swiveled.

Aurora had only been under the empire's rule for the last ten years, so many of the trappings of the once-independent kingdom were everywhere, from the extravagant decor to how the servants treated the duke. Henri du Surraine, the second Duke Aurora, inherited the title after his father died from injuries sustained during the Battle of Coloin, a failed rebellion to take back his throne and kingdom from Emperor Solon.

"Not to sound... completely gauche," Croak said to the servant's back, "but what does it cost to clean this place?"

Terena grinned.

Ahead of them, a group of men rounded the corner, and Terena's grin faded. She narrowed her eyes at them as she slowed. One of the duke's guard was escorting a tall, broad-shouldered man—a warrior—

so out of place amongst the foppish courtiers around them. Terena told herself that's why she was staring at him.

It wasn't at all to do with the graceful way he moved or the way others turned their heads to look at him as he strode past.

The style of his short-cropped brown hair, tipped with gold, was unusual for the empire and caught the light from the tall windows he passed, accentuating the strands of gold and copper. He also had the beginnings of a beard, as if he had been traveling and could not shave.

The only thing the men of Heylisia hated more than short hair was facial hair.

His head was bent toward the guard who was speaking, two more large men at their backs. He wore silver plates at his shoulders with matching bracers and greaves. The rest of his outfit comprised dark brown leather, his weapons belt bare. A cape of deep red, pinned at his shoulders by silver clasps that looked like miniature shields, rustled as he walked.

As they neared, Terena continued to study the warrior, but couldn't place him, and she knew almost everyone worth knowing.

Lifting her eyes to meet his, their gazes locked. Time stilled. Eyes of a light, clear blue pierced her soul.

Her heart stuttered. Something squeezed in her chest—almost to the point of pain.

A memory—only a flash of something—swept by her so fast she thought she'd imagined it. Still, she couldn't shake it. It almost felt like... she knew him.

But that wasn't right.

She'd never seen him before.

The man broke off first, dropping his gaze to the ground and then quickly past them, as if he hadn't been staring at her, too.

Her skin was too tight. Terena's lips twisted, and she clutched at her belly when something shifted within.

Terena squeaked when Croak shoved her from behind.

"You're holding up the line."

She punched his shoulder, then turned and walked faster, her face in flames.

"Ouch!" he whined. Then, "Do you know him?"

"Who?"

"Who? Are you hard of seeing?" Croak snorted. "Wait. You really didn't…? Of course not. What was I thinking?" He shook his head and jogged to catch up to her. "Next time I see Lerek, I'll congratulate him. Anyone that can ignore *that* kind of man has to be in love. Ah, I need a moment."

She punched him again. He hunched up and she punched him once more.

"Had your fun?" she asked as Croak rubbed at his arm. "Now, what is it? I saw three men being escorted by the duke's man. Same as you. What of it?"

Croak's face scrunched. "Well, if your world wasn't pink with unicorns and rivers of starlight, you'd have recognized the colors, at least."

She frowned.

"The uniform of the men? The one's in back, I mean. The one in front—that's got to be Daris Antonius," Croak said, still massaging his shoulder where she'd hit him.

Terena froze.

The servant ahead of them cleared her throat, hands folded in front as she eyed them pointedly. Terena lifted a finger at the woman before turning back to look up at her brother.

Then she looked past him to the empty hallway. "Those were Liodari? You're sure?"

Croak arched a dark eyebrow. "I know those were Liodari. And— I've never *seen* him before, but the description was enough that as soon as I saw *him*," he jabbed a finger down the way the men had gone, "that was definitely Commander Daris Antonius."

Terena stood there a moment longer, thinking.

Was that the feeling that overcame her? Was she recalling a flash of seeing the man before but couldn't place him?

She liked that thought a lot better than the one that had invaded when they'd locked eyes. Her face heated as she shook her head, forcing the thought from her mind.

No.

She must've seen him before, although she was sure she'd have remembered.

She took a couple steps toward Croak, laying her hands on his shoulders, absently. "They are Liodari." A moment passed before she whispered, "What are they doing here?"

Croak shrugged and grabbed Terena's shoulders, much as she'd done to him, and shook her once before letting go. "No clue."

She frowned at him but turned back to the waiting servant, motioning the woman to proceed.

"We can't leave without finding out," she said in a low voice, head bent close to Croak.

He slid his eyes to her and pursed his lips. "Distraction?"

"Definitely."

"Chaos?"

Terena snorted. "A little less, please. I need to be able to hear them unseen, not have them find me on their way to help with whatever you caused."

They entered the solarium at last. It was a beautiful room, she had to admit. The air was too humid for her tastes but she saw how relaxing it would be to honored guests of the duke.

The woman pointed out the refreshments being laid out by servants at the main tables to the right of a large fountain that graced the center of the room. Next, she motioned toward the reading nook nestled in the back and mentioned it as a favorite of the duke's. Finally, the woman gestured to an area on the far left, which was where Duke Aurora's mother took her tea when she visited.

All were available for them to enjoy as they awaited the conclusion of their business.

As soon as she left, Terena motioned with her head, leading Croak to the reading nook. She stopped and looked over his shoulder at the servants setting down cakes and sandwiches or pouring drinks.

Satisfied they wouldn't be heard, she hissed, "We'll get some food, and as soon as I pick up my drink, I'll go toward the front of the fountain. You see me there, that's when you...," she waved her hands at

Croak, "do whatever you're gonna do. Get me at least ten minutes. Hopefully less. Good?"

Croak winked. He turned on his heel, chin high as he flourished his elbow at her. When she linked their arms, Croak said loudly, "My dear and beauteous sister, of *course* we'll get you some food! I know you're hungry, dear. I think even the duke can hear your belly growl!"

Terena barked a laugh and let him lead her to the tables laden with all kinds of small treats.

A servant floated close and proffered a plate, which Croak accepted graciously. He took his time and made a show of picking out only the most delectable pieces for his wondrously lovely sister.

Terena smiled and wandered toward the fountain. Another servant held a tray of wine, bending low in offer as she passed. She took a glass and thanked him, glancing at her brother, who was still reviewing the selections.

Terena cleared her throat, loudly, as she neared the front of the fountain.

Before she could turn to give him a look, a deafening crash sounded behind her and she jumped. Terena whirled, then moved around the fountain's stream to see her brother collapsed on the floor, the table broken beneath him, food pooled around him in a mess of sugar, meats, and plates.

She had a second to gape before she whirled toward the entrance. The servants lunged for her hapless brother.

Hunching her shoulders and keeping her gaze lowered, Terena wound around the way they had come, slowing at the corners. She wasn't sure where they'd gone after they rounded the last corner, but she guessed it might be to an audience with His Grace, so she strode back toward the receiving room.

Moving along the wall, she slowed when she neared the guards in front of the double doors to the room. They stood open as she passed. Glancing inside, she saw no one. Terena moved past the room.

If they aren't there, she thought, *they'd be in his private rooms. A study.* Terena frowned. She didn't know this castle. How would she—

"...and tell His Majesty we eagerly await his visit once the—"

Terena stopped short as she heard Danilos's voice.

She shot a glance around, heart thudding as she sought a place to hide.

The voices drifted closer, and she knew she had seconds to run or be caught where the steward had obviously not left her.

Terena doubled back and dove for the first door she saw, lifting the latch and ducking inside. She pushed the door so only a crack remained, leaning her head against the cool stone as she willed her breath to calm.

The voices stopped close enough to the door she had a moment of panic. But they didn't come in, only stopped as a rough, accented voice interrupted the steward's sniveling.

"He will not be coming."

Terena turned her head slightly, honing in on the voice. She hadn't heard him speak before, but somehow she knew—*knew*—that voice belonged to the commander.

Daris Antonius.

Moving slowly to peek through the crack, Terena smothered a curse when she could see nothing other than the steward's robes and clutched hands.

Someone moved in front of her line of sight and blocked out the light. His voice rumbled again and Terena ducked back, away from the door.

"...again this way. Not until after the war."

She had no idea what that meant. There was no war.

What else had changed in the three months she'd been gone? Why was the Commander of the Liodari, the elite legion of Lakonia's army, currently visiting a duke of the Heylisian Empire?

The last time she'd been in Metilai, talks between the empire and the southern nation of Lakonia had broken down and Emperor Solon, furious with the foreign king, had mobilized his legions for war.

Was Duke Aurora some sort of intermediary? Had Solon tasked him with reviving peace talks while she'd been gone?

Talks must have broken down again if the Commander of the Liodari was now speaking of war.

Unless…

Terena frowned as she tried to pick up more of their conversation. She doubted Aurora would be so dumb as to have sided with Lakonia against the empire.

Duke Aurora was young and ambitious, true, but he had also seen firsthand what happened to those who opposed the emperor. And his sister was currently residing at the White Palace in Metilai as one of the Tasters. Terena was certain that alone would forgo any ambitions he might have to restore his birthright and kingdom.

"A shame, but of course we understand," Danilos was saying, and Terena peeked out to see them all move past.

"With Lady Annalise at the prince's side, may we request of you…" his voice faded and Terena waited several seconds before pulling the door open another inch, then another, until she was satisfied the hallway was clear. She slipped from the room and latched the door softly behind her.

It wouldn't do to come upon the steward and his guests, so she waited. Satisfied she'd waited a good amount of time, she sauntered back toward the hall leading to the solarium, only to pull up short.

Commander Antonius stood alone with his men, the steward nowhere in sight.

Terena blinked at the commander, then at the other two men, all of whom now looked at her, eyes narrowed. She made to move past them, nodding in greeting as she walked.

"Ah! Mistress Luca! Mistress!"

Terena winced when she saw Danilos running toward her. Well, as much as he *could* run in those robes. He waved his hands frantically. "Master Croak—"

"I was looking for the… er…," Terena started to say, then shot a look at the commander. Cursed herself when her cheeks heated.

"Oh!" the steward exclaimed, his face blotchy as understanding dawned. He looked torn between running toward the mess her brother had created and helping her with her obviously delicate needs.

"You are Terena Luca."

It wasn't a question, but Terena turned to the commander after he'd spoken and gave him a reserved smile. She cocked her head quizzically. "Have we met?"

"Please, Mistress, do follow me and I'll show you—" Danilos said, reaching out to lay a hand on her arm.

The commander stepped closer, making Danilos take a step back.

Terena didn't move.

He towered over her, his light blue eyes narrowed with no trace of what had passed between them earlier. Maybe it had been one-sided.

A muscle in his jaw feathered. "I have not had the pleasure, no. But your reputation precedes you."

Terena huffed a breath, a corner of her mouth lifting as she pretended an irreverence she was far from feeling. Her throat became hot. "Well. Don't believe everything you hear. Unless it was good! Then, of course, it's all true."

She even tossed in what she hoped was a saucy wink.

Dear gods.

He didn't respond, his eyes still locked on her. What was he thinking?

"Mistress," Danilos prodded, his voice high.

The commander blinked, his full lips pressed in a tight line. He shot a glance at the steward and she noticed for the first time three thin scars along his left cheek disappearing beyond his ear.

He straightened, relaxing a bit. "Emperor Solon's Royal Tracker. I heard you're remarkably gifted at finding lost treasures of the gods. That's quite a talent."

"It's a living," she said with a forced laugh.

"Indeed," Danilos replied through gritted teeth. He cleared his throat. "Indeed, Mistress Luca was the one who found the Shroud of Faybhen."

Daris Antonius snapped his eyes back to Danilos, who held his gaze a moment before the steward turned to Terena.

"And once you're done with... your... well," Danilos coughed. "The document is ready for your signature."

Before she could stop herself, Terena turned back to the commander and blurted out, "You're far from home, aren't you?"

She watched those cerulean eyes gutter, his handsome face a blank, polite mask as he regarded her.

Terena's chest quaked, but she plowed on. She gestured at him and his men. "What business does the Liodari have with Duke Aurora?"

Danilos looked as if he'd expire any moment. The steward wiped at his forehead, all but squeaked and panted at her to please allow him to show her—

"I'm afraid that's not something I can share," the commander replied in a silky voice.

He lifted his eyes to the steward and then motioned to someone behind Terena. She didn't dare turn away to look.

"Of course," she whispered.

"If you're staying for dinner—"

Terena blinked. Her heart missed a beat. "Unfortunately, I'm not staying." She jerked her thumb behind her, loosing a fake laugh. "Other clients; meetings and such."

"There you are!"

Terena stifled a curse and closed her eyes at her brother's bellow.

She heard his exaggerated stomping as he closed the distance between them, his clothes a medley of stains, and took a step away from the commander. She chanced a look back at him to find his gaze still on her. Assessing. And something else.

Danilos wrung his hands and hissed at her. Terena smiled at the steward and turned back to the commander, intent on getting away.

She muttered some pleasantries and pivoted to face Croak when the commander grasped her elbow.

The touch shocked her and she gaped at him. He leaned in, eyes thoughtful. "It was a pleasure to meet you, Terena Luca."

She nodded, giving him a brief smile as she tugged her arm free before walking swiftly away toward her brother, Danilos at her heels.

"WELL?"

Terena tucked her thumbs into the straps of her shoulder guard, not bothering to turn to Croak when he spoke.

"Well, what?"

Croak scoffed. He lengthened his stride to keep up with her. She may be shorter, but her steps were much more purposeful than Croak's ever were.

When they exited the castle, Terena turned toward the stables. The small boy, Arthur, was running a brush over the only part of Cerberus he could reach. Croak's lips widened in a slow smile.

He shot Terena a look. "Did you learn anything from the fabulous Commander Antonius?"

Terena slowed as she neared Nyx. She tossed a couple of coins at the older boy that brought her mare forth. She grabbed the reins and whispered something to her horse.

Croak planted his hands on his hips. "You ignoring me, now? Is that what you're doing? Fine."

"What?"

Croak crossed his arms. "What."

She blinked at him.

He sighed. "Commander Daris Antonius? That tall drink of water you were going to spy on while I made a fool of myself? Not to mention my soiled clothes. The only clean ones left after Agraboda. Or was my performance for naught?"

Terena inhaled, her head rising in understanding. "Oh. Not much. Just... strange."

"Explain."

She put her face close to Nyx and nuzzled her nose. Croak rolled his eyes and waited.

"Ren."

She looked at him over her shoulder. "He knew me," she said, more to herself than to him. "He said it was because of my reputation. I don't know if I believe that. And get this: he didn't introduce himself. At all."

"Well," he scoffed and lifted a hand at her, "he *is* Daris Antonius.

You'd be hard pressed to find anyone on the continent that wouldn't know him. Except you, apparently."

She turned to Croak fully, her brow furrowed. "When I asked him what they were doing meeting with the duke, he shut me down. Quickly."

"Interesting."

Terena shrugged and moved to mount Nyx, but then turned, leaning forward.

"Hey," she said, her voice low. Croak sauntered closer.

"Have you heard anyone mention anything about a war?"

Croak's brow shot up. "A war? No."

Terena frowned. "I overheard something about a war. Antonius was saying something about not being able to come back to Heylisia until after the war."

Croak made an obvious show of looking around at the peaceful castle yard. "I mean, Solon is always provoking Lakonia, but even he wouldn't go against Altos and *that* guy. Did he say anything about who was at war?"

"No. I only heard bits and pieces. Obviously, none of it made sense."

"And my performance?"

"Your finest yet," she assured him with a quick grin.

Croak tried not to look as pleased as he felt. They made their way through the yard and out of the gate into the city.

An hour later, they were outside the city's eastern gate and Croak pulled up alongside Nyx.

"What were you pretending about, by the way? What was I supposed to go along with?"

Terena flashed him a wolfish smile. "You didn't notice the shroud?"

Croak shrugged. "What about it?"

"It wasn't the Shroud of Faybhen."

CHAPTER THREE

Terena and Croak reached the port town of Laurica a fortnight later. The weak evening light barely broke through the heavy mist and rain. It didn't seem to bother anyone; there were masses of people everywhere she turned. This close to the northern border, towns were sparsely populated, having lost many to the warmer climes of southeastern Elis over the last year.

With her hood up and head down, Terena navigated the puddled streets, passing the dressmaker's shop, heading for the blacksmith's stalls.

Sudden shouts and running feet sloshing through the street behind them made Terena turn her head.

Croak came up behind her. They watched as shadowed figures danced in the rain. Angry shouts and cries of pain rang out. She took a step closer. Bodies rushed past them.

Croak grabbed her arm. "Don't."

Terena frowned. She heard more screams and cries. Soldiers yelled and someone moaned; Terena could just make out a slumped figure on the ground.

The mist cleared enough for her to see three soldiers surrounding the pitiful lump lying still in the street. Two others huddled together nearby, weeping. One soldier backhanded a man who'd stepped forward.

A girl rushed to his side while another soldier grabbed up the figure on the ground. He shouted something at another soldier, and the two hefted the limp person between them, dragging their burden away.

The other man reared up once more, only to be cuffed again for his troubles, the girl wailing and clawing at him to stay down.

"I'm goin' in," Croak grumbled at her back.

Terena didn't follow. Her jaw hurt, and she released a breath.

"You coming?"

Terena said nothing. Striding through the rain, she yanked the soldier who'd backhanded the man by his hair, her other hand holding a dagger to his throat.

"Drop him. Now."

The soldiers holding the unconscious man froze. The man she held squirmed, trying to get loose from her hold, but she tightened her grip on his wet hair and he yelped.

"Do it now," she said again.

The one to her right—much younger than his friends, with a scar running across his lips—peered closer at her, then gasped and looked at the other soldier.

"Luca," the other one, a bald man with a heavy brow, sneered and spat on the ground. "Your father's not Captain of the Imperial Guard anymore. You don't want to interfere. We're here on the emperor's orders."

"I won't say it again."

"We have orders," the young one said, glancing desperately between her and the bald soldier.

Terena's response was to dig the tip of her dagger deeper. The soldier screeched obscenities. "Fucking do it, Connor!"

Pushing the man he held to the ground, Connor, the bald soldier who had spat at her, warned, "The general will hear of this." The other soldier let go with more care.

"Peleon knows how to find me."

When the soldiers stepped back from the unconscious man, she dropped her hand and shoved her captive toward his friends. "Fuck off. Now."

The girl rushed to the man's side as she and the other man, much older and in no fit shape himself, tried to revive him.

Terena sheathed her dagger and strode back to the blacksmith's where her brother waited. He leaned against one column framing the entrance, arms crossed at his chest and rain dripping from his sodden hat as he frowned over at her.

Terena dropped her chin and closed her eyes. She could still hear the wailing of the girl and the whimpers of the old man. Feeling satisfied those folks would no longer be bothered, she turned back to Croak and followed him inside.

Benson the Blacksmith didn't have a door. A tarp stretched out at the entrance as an awning. It was only to be used in bad weather, protecting the supplies and weapons and work areas in the front.

For the last year, the tarp had remained.

The shop comprised a few different stalls, remnants of the previous marketplace there two decades ago. He had modernized them with an addition in the back where the forge stood.

Down the center, the corridor led back and deeper into the bowels of his hellish shop. Terena's face and neck beaded with sweat. Steam danced everywhere and the sounds of hissing sent up fresh bursts of vapor in its wake.

Tools of his trade lined the walls, along with the finished and unfinished works of his labor. He had an apprentice, Mello, who skulked around with a stoop Terena thought owed more to his height than his having to bend over often for his work. The man was close to seven feet if he was an inch, and the low ceiling was no friend to him.

"Where is your master?" Croak asked the giant after he'd yanked off his hat. Mello didn't look up from his work. Instead, he grunted something and motioned with his left shoulder.

Croak moved past him, mumbling. Terena followed down a ramp leading to a room in the back. Much wider than the front of the shop, the room had a large forge in the center, anvils and various sized molds on either side.

A long workbench with a couple of old stools made up the far wall. Leather aprons set on hooks to the right where the master blacksmith stood.

"Your order, good sir," Terena said as she dropped a large satchel on the workbench along the back wall.

Benson grunted but did not look up. He yelled for Mello, and the big man lumbered over.

"Grab the payment for the Nesky contract," he said.

Mello blinked, turning without a word and went back out to the front. Benson struck his hammer down twice more on the blade he held against the anvil, then lifted a hand to his brow. Covered in soot and grime and sweat, he smelled worse. "Expected you weeks ago," he said.

"Trouble with the weather. The road through Coleta was blocked with snow, so we went south through Belle Forest."

"Commotion outside," Croak said as Benson continued to work.

The older man turned and set the blade in the fire. "Didn't 'ear a commotion bein' back 'ere and all," he said with a sigh. He pulled the glowing steel out of the fire and brought it back to the anvil. "But, aye. Commotions gettin' real regular just lately."

"Lots of soldiers out there."

"Aye," he grunted, going back to his work.

"Any reason for it?"

Benson shrugged. "Another one o' those commotions I's tellin' ya bout."

"Is that commotion related to anything specific?" Croak prodded.

"Reckon they're lookin' for gods."

"Ha!" Croak quickly hid his grin behind his hand. He looked over at Terena and mouthed *sorry* at the look she gave him.

"No such thing as gods anymore, old man," Terena said, staring daggers at Croak.

"Must've forgotten," Benson remarked. He dropped the hammer to wipe at his sweaty forehead. "A thousand years since they roamed, now stirred up all over again."

"Those were the general's men," Terena said as she stared at her fingernails. "Is he acting on orders from the emperor or is it his own mania driving him now?"

"Ye'd know better'n me."

"When did they come?"

Benson shrugged, wiping his hands on his leather apron. "Two nights, mebbe?" He nodded at her with narrowed eyes. "Think it might 'ave somethin' t'do with the new king?"

Terena snapped her head up. "New king?"

"Ya 'ear nothin' 'bout the new king in the northern provinces?"

"No, nothing," she said.

"Where y' been? A hole?"

Croak snorted. "Not far off."

Terena glared at him until he ducked his head.

"I 'ear tell he's recruitin' now. Lookin' fer strong arms an' payin' well."

"Reckon he needs trackers?" Croak asked with a grin.

"Was tole' specially trackers."

Terena glanced over at Croak. He watched her and shrugged as he picked dirt out of his fingernails with something he'd picked up from the table.

"What's he need trackers for?"

Benson wheezed out a chuckle and struck the blade once more. "Who the 'ell knows? Why's 'e lookin' for strong arms? What the 'ells 'e want to be king of that shit pile anyways? All mysteries o' the world, far as I'm concerned.

"But rumor's he's rich. And every day I 'ear tell o' the refugees makin' their way toward the border. Sure ya passed some on the way 'ere." He pointed his hammer at her. "Could be work for ya there. Steady work. Better work than 'ere, that's no lie."

Terena folded her arms and frowned. "I saw you last month, and you said not one word about any of this. When did all this happen?"

Benson dropped his hammer. He turned and grabbed a filthy rag off one stool and scrubbed his face with it before balling it in his fist at his waist. "I seen ya four moons ago at the least an' much has 'appened." He gave a mock bow. "As y' see. More folk an' now soldiers to boot. Tensions w' the royals, talk of war with Lakonia bruin', folks goin' north to get away from the emperor's reach."

Terena glanced at Croak at Benson's mention of war. He returned her look, his lips pinched. "Now his men are 'ere, lots of fightin' an' wailin' an' fear," Benson continued. "Speakin' for m'self, mostly mercenaries in 'ere, looking for anythin' I have on 'and afore headin' north. Reckon the soldiers using the gods as an excuse. Reckon the general's 'ere to put the mercs in chains afore they flee north an' fight against 'im."

"That could be," Terena said, rubbing at her chin. "Have they rounded up many? Do you know where he's keeping them?"

"Not sure, but he's taken over Atton's Bathhouse. 'im and 'is men."

"Ask any of them anything else about this new king before they were taken?"

"Asked one of 'em what gives, an' was tol' the king was recruitin'. 'King', I says, 'didn't even know they *had* a king up there.' And then he says, 'aye, a king an' richer than Solon.'" Benson paused, one hand on the hammer and the other on the blade as he looked over at her. "Another came jus' two days past, grabbed up the last o' me longswords. Said they'd finally finished th' bridge at Thalos and he was on his way to make his fortune."

"Good luck to him, then," Croak muttered. "Most like you'll never hear from that one again."

"Most like, specially seein' as 'ow 'e got snatched up last night. Suspicion of 'idin' a god, what they said." Benson shook his head. "Not sure 'ow they knows that cause 'e sure as 'ells was travelin' alone. The others they jus' plain ain't givin' excuses for why they gone."

"And what of Duke Ravos? Is he helping find gods?"

"Ha!" Benson hawked and spat on the ground. "That turd won't even come out 'is castle. No word from 'im since Peleon's men arrived. One good thin', that. Oh, an' his tax collectors 'aven't been 'round either."

"Don't think that debt won't come due," Croak mumbled.

Benson nodded, and with a sigh he shoved the blade back into the forge. "I knows it, young 'un, I knows it. But we've got more jus' now t' think on than what's owed to the empire."

"His Excellency must be worked up if he's delayed the taxes in favor of a gods hunt."

"Aye. And he sent th' cleric, as well."

"What?" Terena pushed away from the wall and dropped her arms. "Christos is here?"

"Nah," he said. "The younger."

"Orry!" Croak cried out with a laugh.

"Aye. Scared of 'is own shadow, that one."

"So, Orry is cover for their gods hunt story while they're looking to round up anyone going to find this new king?"

Benson shrugged and mopped at his forehead, leaving a filthy trail. "Sounds 'bout right."

"What do you know about him?" Croak asked.

"The new king? What I said."

"Where'd he come from? How'd he become king?"

"Boy, ya askin' me like I's an ol' woman sittin' round 'er knittin' folk. I ain't."

"You didn't ask?"

Benson turned a baleful glare at Croak, who lifted his hands.

A few seconds later, he looked up as if recalling something important and pointed his hammer at Terena. "Someone came in askin' 'bout ya." He shook his head. "Late last week. Came in fer weapons but asked 'bout trackers. Named ya."

Croak cursed. "Really, Benson? You just remembered?"

"My brain ain't young an' full o' nothin' like yers," he grumbled.

"Asked for me by name?"

"Aye."

"What'd you tell them?" Terena asked.

He shot her a glare. "I didn't tell 'em nuthin' bout ya."

Terena arched an eyebrow.

"I tole them I'd let 'em know if I 'ear anythin' when theys come back for th' orders theys placed."

"When are they expected?"

"End of th' week. Told 'em dawn on Saturday, they'd be ready."

"Mercenaries?"

"By th' look of 'em."

"They say anything else, Benson?" Terena asked as she slid a coin toward him on the workbench.

"Aye, said 'e was lookin' fer trackers. Said th' king had need of 'em. Then asked after Terena Luca."

Terena glanced back at Croak, who was busy rolling a coin between his fingers.

"I'd planned on leaving straight from here."

"Eh, 'tis a few days. 'Ear 'em out and then decide." Benson thunked the hammer on the sword. He huffed, straightened, and cracked his neck. "Ye can stay 'ere if'n the soldiers is what bothers ya."

"I'm needed in Metilai."

He snorted. "Yah, yer needed in Metilai."

Croaked snickered and Terena shot him a dirty look. "Where're they staying, you know?"

Benson shook his head. "Why the shit would they tell me? Easily found out by wanderin' to the usual holes." He lifted his head and grinned with a lift of his chin at Croak. "He sure as rain knows those venues."

Terena pushed away from the table to stand and stretch. She turned to leave. "I'll try to be back at week's end."

"Aww, will 'is high and mighty lordlin' be done wi' ya that quick? Shame."

Croak barked out a laugh that turned to a yowl when Terena punched his shoulder as she passed.

"If they're rounding up the mercs, how are you getting them their orders?" Croak asked.

"Been using the temple as the drop."

Croak snorted. "You serious?"

Benson shrugged. "Seemed like a good 'nuff spot theys wouldn't be watchin'. So worried bout gods but they's not lookin' in theys own house."

"Take care, Benson," Terena said. "If they're locking up mercs, they might have eyes on you."

"What for?"

"For supplying them."

Benson grunted and went back to work. "No one's been 'round yet and Mello's keepin' an eye out."

She nodded and turned to leave. Croak fell in behind her.

On the way out, Benson's giant of an apprentice came through the doorway. He held out a black pouch and Croak took it with a muttered thanks. The man turned back the way he'd come. Terena followed, calling out a goodbye as she passed, but Mello only lifted his head and stared at her dully before going back to his work.

As they exited Benson's shop, Terena pulled up her hood and paused under the awning to watch the rain. It had lessened its fury in the time she'd been inside.

The earlier crowd had dispersed, now slinking under awnings or in doorways, anywhere away from the soldiers still patrolling the main street. No signs of the young girl and old man.

Croak came up beside her. Terena walked to where they'd tethered their horses and rummaged in her saddlebags.

"See if you can find Orry," she said as she pulled out a small bundle wrapped in oilcloth. Croak looked down at her, brown eyes narrowed and arms crossed at his chest. "Give him the shroud and tell him to keep it somewhere safe. I'll get it from him when we head north." She handed the bundle to Croak, who took it and shoved it inside his jerkin.

"What about the mercs Benson mentioned?"

Terena sighed and rubbed at an ache on the back of her neck. "If you can manage, find out what they know of the northern king or why they're looking for trackers. And why they asked for me."

"Anything else, Your Majesty?"

Terena twisted her lips. "I'll try to be back at week's end."

"And then what?"

Terena shrugged. "Then we head north."

CROAK WATCHED TERENA DISAPPEAR IN THE RAIN. PULLING UP HIS collar, he ran out into the street to the buildings on the other side, cursing the rain as it seeped down his neck and into his tunic to soak him. He kept to the sidewalks and cursed whenever he hit a puddle.

Even in the rain and the gloom of dusk, he knew this town inside and out.

At the end of the street, he saw a group of soldiers huddled near the entrance to Atton's Bathhouse and recalled their conversation with the blacksmith. Quickly doubling back, Croak took the back alley.

He was close to his destination when the rain turned to a drizzle. He sighed and slowed his pace.

"Awww look at the raggedy rat the cat done drug in, eh?"

Croak lifted his head to frown at the slag leaning against the door to the back entrance of the brothel. Melissa had the worn and haggard look of many of her profession and she was only twenty, if that.

He grimaced and stopped, one boot on the step leading up to the house of pleasure. "And yet still a sight better than the rats calling on you, right Mel?"

The whore pursed her lips and spat at his feet, some phlegm landing on the tip of his boot. He frowned and toed it in the mud as she cackled. He put his hands on his hips and lifted his chin at her. "You gonna let me pass?"

"Not wit' out a big fat kiss I ain't," she said with a wide grin to show off her rotting front teeth.

"As tempting as that offer is, every single time you make it, I'll pass. With regret."

She cackled again. "You young 'uns always turn yer noses up at the packagin', but experience has ya sniffin' round in the end."

Bile rose in his throat and took a moment before responding. "Charming, Mel. As always. 'Young 'uns,'" he mumbled. "You realize we're of an age." He cleared his throat and winced at the tang still at the back of it. "Just a question, if you don't mind?"

"Nothin's free, even questions," she said and hitched up her skirt to scratch at a rash on her thigh.

Croak closed his eyes as a shudder passed through him. "Uhm, just curious. Any gents visiting from out of town?"

"Our whole bidness is out of town gents."

"Bidness?"

"Ya ye fool!" she spat. "Bidness. How we's make a livin'?"

"Ah yes, bidness. Of course." Croak smiled thinly. "Any chance any of those gents going north?"

"Lots of folk headin' north just now. Ye blind as well as stupid?"

"Right," Croak said with a frown. "Know of any waiting on weapons from Benson? They'd be big fellas, swordsmen? Mercenaries? Here until Saturday. Two of them, traveling together."

Melissa narrowed her eyes and crossed her arms over her big breasts.

Croak waited.

Melissa lifted a pale eyebrow at him. Croak sighed and dug into his breeches for a coin. He flicked the silver at her and she snatched it out of the air with one big paw.

"Saw a one such as fits that descriptin'." She nodded down the street. "Had hisself a good time wif Jana then off to grab some food at Nathaniel's."

"Just the once?"

"Well, one's all I's seen," she answered.

Croak looked down the street, then back at Melissa. "A pleasure, as always."

She grunted in response and he tipped an imaginary hat at her, then strode off down the street, his pace more leisurely now the rain had settled to a fine mist.

He knew it could turn into a downpour at any moment, but for now, he enjoyed not having to run from awning to awning like an alley cat.

Benson was right; Laurica was busier than Croak had ever seen it.

He shot quick glances at the people he passed on his way to the tavern but noted mostly families, more than likely refugees, trying to return home by the looks of them.

More than a year had passed since the first quake had shaken the ground beneath his feet. Weeks afterward, they'd heard stories from those running south, fleeing the devastation wreaking the north, decimating the land.

No armies, no war.

This was the work of Gaia, the superstitious northerners claimed. The old Titans stretching their limbs, reminding them they were still around a thousand years later.

After the earth shook, there were months of freezing temperatures in the north stretching as far south as Lindeloris, snow falling so heavily it buried entire villages. Then swirling cones of air ravaged cities, tearing through them like a sword through the neck.

In Laurica, the rain started shortly after and hadn't stopped since.

Croak jogged up the walkway on the left, passing shops selling everything from hats to feed and tack. At the end of the cobbled street, a large stone structure stood with wooden doors and glass windows. The glass was thick and glazed in patterns of fish and water. A few men mingled outside and more streamed in and out. Business was good.

He slid past a couple men in front of the doors and swung one open, apologizing to the two as they shot him a look. Inside, the heat was almost as oppressive as Benson's.

Croak caught his breath and almost heaved as the smell of unwashed bodies mixed with alcohol and food hit his nostrils. He fished a kerchief from his breast pocket and held it to his nose, breathing deep of lavender while he took in the packed tavern.

The tables were all filled and people stood who hadn't found seats, holding their plates or bowls as they conversed. A harried barmaid rushed past, holding a large steaming bowl in each outstretched arm.

Croak shouted a greeting at the girl, but laughter drowned out his words. To his right, a large man guffawed so sharply, it startled Croak and he moved off to the left, darting toward a clearing before anyone filled it.

Croak was as tall as he was thin, but even he had to stand on his toes to get a decent look around. The barkeep and owner, Nathaniel, shouted something across the room, his good-natured grin hidden beneath his bushy chestnut mustache. At a nearby table, men lifted their tankards in salute and shouted back to him. Croak wound his way carefully through the throng toward the bar.

"Oy!" he yelled and thumped the bar top. The man next to him grumbled and gave him a frown, turning back to his drink. Nathaniel had his back to him, speaking with someone on the other side of the bar.

Croak moved further along the bar, waving his arms when Nathaniel finally turned his way, but the big man bent over for something and turned back without glancing over at Croak.

Frustrated, Croak looked around.

His eyes settled on the wood beam next to the man to his left, where a large bell hung.

"Mate," he said to the man next to him. The man turned a baleful look at Croak, his big brows low and his mouth turned down. He didn't respond.

Croak cleared his throat. "See that bell there?" he asked, pointing to the bell attached to the beam on the man's left. "You ring it and get old Nathaniel there to come this way, I'll give you," here he dug into his pants and pulled out two coins which he showed to the man. "I'll give you this."

The man looked at him a moment longer, then grunted. He turned and lifted his hand to the bell and punched it with his fist. A roar went up across the tavern and Nathaniel swung his head around with his arms raised high and then pointed at them with a yell.

"Someone wants to buy you all a round, lads!" his voice boomed across the already raucous mob. His smile split his thick cheeks.

Croak smothered his own grin, ducking behind another patron as the man looked around at the many faces smiling back at him, his eyes blinking and his face dumb.

"What you mean?" he grumbled.

"You rang the bell, lad," Nathaniel laughed and threw a dirty rag over one shoulder before folding his tattooed arms. "That means the next round's on you."

"I didn't—"

"You did."

The man shifted his body up off the bar and turned to find Croak had slid back and through the masses. He turned back, almost desperately eyeing the expectant faces all around. "I don't—"

"You do."

The man gulped as Croak wound his way closer to Nathaniel, his face wreathed in smiles as he clapped several patrons on their backs as he passed.

The man stood now, puffing his chest out as his mouth opened and closed like a trout. While the crowd cheered, he grumbled back into his drink.

Croak rapped on the bar top. "Nathaniel."

The barkeep glanced over his shoulder, realizing who it was. He turned and leaned back against the counter stacked high with dishes, his massive arms crossed over his even bigger chest. "Well, look what the stinking alley cat dragged in."

Croak dropped his chin and shook his head, grinning. "What is it about me and alley cats?" He winked at Nathanial. "Who woulda thought the civilized, settled life would suit you so well?"

"Aye," the big man grunted. He narrowed his eyes at Croak. "And what you be needing this time? A barrel to hide inside? Sack of coins to pay off a debt?"

Croak gasped and put a hand to his chest. "You wound me, good sir."

"If only it were mortal."

"You haven't seen me in months and this is how you treat a friend?"

"Friend?" Nathaniel scoffed. He flipped the dirty rag off his shoulder and wiped the bar top, forcing Croak to move away. "Your friendship almost cost me an arm."

"Ah!" Croak said. "And yet if it weren't for me, you wouldn't have this fine establishment and the living that goes with it."

Nathaniel's mouth dropped open. "You cheeky shit! 'Twas reward for my service to Solon I owe this living. Ain't nothing to do with your scrawny arse."

"And yet who whispered in Solon's ear you deserved the living?"

"Again, naught to do with you," Nathaniel snorted. "And if she were here with you, I'd thank her as I always do."

"But she's not here, so might I suggest you thank her through me?"

"You are a snot, aren't you?"

"We all serve a purpose."

"And where's your better half?"

"Off to Metilai."

Nathaniel nodded, then ducked beneath the bar to bring up two tankards. He filled each and passed them down to the men waiting on Croak's right side. He turned back to Croak with a lift of his eyebrow. "And she left you here? You two have a falling out?"

"Hardly," Croak said and leaned his arms on the bar. "I'm on an important mission."

"Huh."

"Reconnaissance."

Nathaniel resumed wiping down the counter, jabbing his hand against Croak's elbows, compelling him to step back.

"Important stuff, really," Croak said. "Which is why I've come to you, my good friend."

"What's she need?"

Croak waited until Nathaniel put the rag away and turned to filling more drinks. "You see any men 'round lately, heading north?"

Nathaniel snorted and shot him a glance. "Every man in here is heading north."

Croak pursed his lips and glanced around. "Right," he said, his voice low.

After several seconds watching Nathaniel go about his work, he rapped on the bar. "Any asking around about Terena? Was told a couple mercs were waiting on some gear from Benson and looking for her."

Nathaniel was scrubbing a tankard with a different, equally filthy rag. He paused, considering. "Maybe."

"Ah!" Croak motioned with his hand for Nathaniel to continue. The big man sighed and put one hand to his hip, the other holding the tankard at his side. "Had a man earlier ask after your sister and mentioned looking for trackers. Not sure if he's still around."

"Earlier... today?"

Nathaniel shrugged, wiping the tankard again. "Aye. Morning. One of the first in here. Sat at that back table. Strange, it was. When the soldiers came in midday looking for some poor unfortunate, that man never once moved, though the rest of my patrons cleared out right quick. Saw them have words with him but left empty-handed."

"He was alone?"

"Aye. Joined a bit ago by another big brute."

Croak followed Nathaniel's gaze but a sea of bodies stood between him and where Nathaniel's chin had pointed.

"Back there?" he asked.

"Wasn't keeping track of them, mind," Nathaniel grumbled. "But aye, they were back there and for a while, too. Lost sight of them when the dinner rush came in. I ain't seen them in a good hour. Might ask Moira. She's been here all day."

Croak turned to see the slight barmaid as she weaved her way through the crush of bodies, hands filled with empty tankards, stopping here and there as voices called out with more orders. He watched as she nodded absently, then slowly made her way back to the bar.

Croak made room for her as she dropped off six empty tankards and sagged against the bar with a tremendous sigh.

"All work and no play makes for a dull girl, Moira," he said.

She gave him a disgusted look. "Child."

Croak laughed. "You seen a couple mercs been here all day?"

Moira ignored him as she wiped a limp strand of blonde hair out of her face. Her cheeks were pink with exertion and she had a fine sheen of sweat on her brow and upper lip.

She leaned forward and shouted some orders at Nathaniel, who nodded and set to work. When she grabbed the tray, full tankards sloshing ale, she turned back and set off through the horde.

Croak followed.

"C'mon, love!" Croak wheedled, yelling over the noise. He kept close to her back as patrons moved to fill the space behind her.

She set three tankards down on one table and moved on to another. Croak stuck close, waiting.

Moira turned and bumped right into him. She shoved at his chest with her free hand, the drinks in her other spilling out onto the table to her right. Men bellowed, but she paid them no mind as she deftly lifted the tray to save the drinks.

"Yor botherin' me is botherin' our guests!" she spat at him as she turned toward her next destination.

"All's I need is a quick answer to a tiny question!"

She huffed and dropped another tankard onto a nearby table. "I seen many folk. Obviously."

"Couple of mates heading north? Maybe staying the week to take in the many beautiful sights of Laurica? Asking about trackers? Been here all day, according to the big boss."

"Only ones I can think of sitting over there," she said with a sigh and a half-hearted tilt of her head over her left shoulder. "Been sittin' there since I got here."

Croak squeezed her arm in thanks and shot past her, wending his way around the gathered patrons, until finally he was at the back of the tavern.

Crowded, but with space enough around the table for Croak to make a smart smack of his heels and a bow low enough to please Emperor Solon.

When he rose, he noticed with a slight slip of his smile the table had only one occupant, rather than the two he'd expected. Glancing around, he pasted a big smile on his lips.

"Ah, good sir, might I join you for a pint?"

As he made to sit, Croak froze. Something sharp poked at his side.

"And who the fuck are you?"

CHAPTER FOUR

"And who the fuck are you?"

Rydon of Decu leaned in close to the thin man who had approached their table. Gabriol, his lieutenant in their former life, sat back, a broad smile on his bearded face. He lifted his tankard and saluted Rydon before taking a long swig.

The thin man in front of Rydon stiffened, but otherwise showed no fear. In a full tavern with so many unaware or preoccupied, it would've been a simple thing for Rydon to stab the man and carry him to a far corner with nary a glance from the patrons. Instead, the man turned his head enough Rydon saw the smile on his face. His eyes crinkled, genuinely amused.

"I see I have the right men," he said, shooting a quick glance back at Gabriol. "If I may buy you both another round, I'd be happy to tell you who the fuck I am."

Rydon looked across at Gabriol, who shrugged. He bellowed for the barmaid and gestured for more ale. The tired woman acknowledged him with a nod as she wove through the tables away from them. Gabriol kicked the chair next to the thin man with his boot.

"Sit, then, friend. And tell us who you are," he said, his voice high for a man of his size.

The man—boy, really—inclined his head and put a pale hand to his chest. He had the nerve to wink at Rydon over his shoulder before pulling out the proffered chair and plopping down onto it with a loud sigh.

He slapped his knees. "Well," he said, with another big huff as he moved his gaze between Rydon and Gabriol. "I have been looking for you two everywhere."

"And why would you be looking for us?" Rydon growled. He sheathed his dagger and pulled out the seat next to Gabriol, eyes narrowed on the stranger. His clothes were travel worn but of fine material, so he must have some wealth. He had the sharp straight nose and almond-shaped eyes of the Heylisian noblemen from Metilai but carried himself comfortably amongst rougher folk such as were in that tavern. Rydon was certain the boy was anything other than the guileless fool he pretended.

"Before we get to that," the boy-man said and slapped at his chest with his right hand, inclining his head slightly, "I am Croak. Twenty years as of two moons ago. I live with my sister—well, she lives with me, of course." With that, he winked again at Rydon.

"What else? Oh! I am recently arrived in Laurica though this is not my first time. I am not originally from Heylisia, but I have sworn fealty to Emperor Solon, of course. I am fond of the carnivals of Paladia in Osta and had hoped they'd catch on here, although that's not likely because, let's face it, few dwarves venture east of the Oryon Pass. I break into a disgusting rash if I eat rattleberries and I have had one song written of me after a rather magnificent duel in Ermanel. I believe owing more to the cuckold than sword skill.

"No wait," here he paused and muttered something to himself, his chin lifted as he squinted at the ceiling, one finger up and tracing something unseen. "Yes!" he shouted with a thump on the table, making Gabriol blink stupidly over at him. "Yes, I recall now. It *was* my sword skill that was immortalized by the bard, although a sword of a different kind, yeah?" He laughed and then exclaimed as the barmaid appeared with their ale. He held out both arms, offering profuse thanks to the barmaid he knew by name.

When the wench left, the young man lifted his tankard in salute. "And just lately, I am arrived in the lovely town of Laurica once more to hear friends tell of a new king, up in the savage lands of the north, who might be in the market for some hired hands."

Rydon blinked at the young man, who regarded them both as if they were all old friends.

Gabriol leaned forward, blue eyes flashing. "Croak, is it?" At the young man's enthusiastic nod, Gabriol pursed his lips. "You talk too much and look too stupid for us to give a shit about what you've heard. What we give a shit about is why you are here seeking us out."

The young man, Croak, shifted his dark brown eyes back and forth between them. "Were you not listening? I just told you!" He took a swig of ale and smacked his lips. "New king, mercenaries." He motioned with his tankard at both warriors. "I wish to join you, good sirs! To seek my fortune in the north. Hire out my sword, if you will."

Rydon steepled his hands and stared across at the young man. "And who says we are heading north?"

Croak snorted. He wagged a finger at Rydon. "I am not as stupid as I look, gentlemen. You, for example," he said, pointing at Gabriol. "Going by your braided fair hair and the tattoos I see peeking through your tunic, I'm guessing, Roison? You're from Rois, aye? I met a man from Rois once. And you," he said, turning away from Gabriol's surprised face to squint at Rydon. He stroked his hairless chin. "Judging by the amount of earrings in your ear and the bones dangling from the leather at your neck, I'd say... Decu?"

Rydon's eyes widened, shooting a scowl at Gabriol's laughter.

"How'd I do? Did I guess it?" The young man asked, his face earnest as he looked between the two men.

"I'm Gabriol, and yes, I'm from Rois. This is Rydon of Decu."

"Ha! Gabriol! Serendipitous! That's my name!" the young man cried with a grin, pounding his fist on the table.

"I thought you said your name is Croak." Rydon growled.

He shrugged. "Croak's how I'm known, but Gabriol is the name my mother gave me. Gods keep her soul safe."

"How'd you know where we're from?"

"I'm good at shit like that. I'm good at a lot of things. And I have many friends who look out for my wellbeing, and part of that wellbeing is my employment status, of which I am, currently, in between jobs."

Rydon continued to glare at him. Croak shrugged. "I asked around about the new king and was told a couple of mercs were heading north. He's looking to build an army, aye? Thought I'd join you and make some coin."

Gabriol laughed. It was a hearty bark of laughter, causing the younger man to startle, but he covered it up with an uncertain chuckle. He raised his tankard once more.

"And what gave you the impression we'd let a weasel such as you join us wherever the fuck we're going?" Gabriol asked.

Croak shrugged. "I am an adventurer such as yourselves. I wish to see the world. Meet beautiful women. Get blooded in battle, fighting alongside the right and righteous."

"Are you daft?" Gabriol asked. "Or blind? Have you not seen the Imperial soldiers rounding up men?" He glanced at Rydon with a half smile. "Suppose we hand this one over, boss? Think they'll give us silver for him?"

Rydon smirked. "I think they'd laugh in our faces if we told them this scarecrow was heading north to fight for the new king." He leaned across the table, brows furrowed. "If you are sworn to Solon, why would you want to pledge to the northern king?"

Something about this fool was off, and yet he could not put his finger on it. He was most assuredly alone. Anyone calling him a friend would've made themselves known by now. The young man neither glanced about nervously for intervention nor seemed to play for time.

"Ha!" Croak snorted. "That man! Do *not* get me started. I have given him years of my life and he keeps leaching more off me every day."

Both men looked wide-eyed at the young fool, waiting.

"I am sick of being taken advantage of! I want to work for someone who knows my worth, who values my loyalty as well as my sword arm. He has made a fool of me for the last time!"

Rydon and Gabriol exchanged a look.

"I am a freeman," the young man went on, lifting his arms and face to the ceiling. "Well, as free as a man is without employment."

Gabriol looked over at Rydon. "And what kind of employment would that be? What's your trade?"

"Much as yourselves, as you see."

Rydon laughed, his grin stretched wide enough to hurt his cheeks.

He leaned forward so fast the boy startled. Rydon's grin faded and his eyes narrowed. "We're mercenaries, fool. And you are not."

"Ah, but I am indeed! And you will see the truth of my words when we reach the new king."

"We?"

"Of course! I wish to travel with you. Me and my companion."

"Companion?"

"Did I not say?" Croak laughed and wiped his mouth. "It is indeed your lucky day, my dear fellows. Along with my brilliant company, you also get the sword of my traveling companion, who is a mercenary, such as yourselves—*ourselves*."

Rydon frowned, making a show of looking around. "And this friend is where?"

"Oh, she's on an errand. But we'll see her at the end of the week. Just in time for us to head north!"

"You're not going with us," Rydon said, his face impassive. He motioned for the barmaid and looked back at the young man next to him. "We travel alone. Always have."

"We can pay our own way, if that's what troubles you," the boy replied, leaning forward. "And we can, well, *she* can—my friend, that is —she can be of much use to you if fighting breaks out. She's a warrior."

"I don't care," Rydon said, his voice low and menacing, "if she's Athena reborn. We travel alone."

"Best you leave, young Croak, 'fore Rydon makes it difficult for you to leave," Gabriol said as he stared pointedly at the young man. "And don't let us catch you hanging about or next time we won't be as nice."

Croak looked from one to the other and shrugged. "No bother, my new friends. No bother at all. I predict the next time fortune smiles on you with my presence, you'll be the ones seeking *me* out. My companion's a tracker."

He rapped the table with his knuckles and stood so swiftly his chair fell over, knocking into the back of a burly man's legs. The young man slithered into the crowd, leaving the angry patron to growl at Rydon and Gabriol.

Croak hummed as he sauntered down the stairs and out of the tavern onto the back alley. He winced and put a cuff to his nose, the stench of urine and rotted food overwhelming. He strode away quickly and turned onto a quiet street, away from the town center, winding his way up into the more gentrified area of Laurica.

Despite the hour, Croak saw five Watchmen within a minute. The people in this part of town enjoyed a much more attentive guard than the merchants. Here, there were not only influential citizens to be guarded, but great wealth, or as great a wealth as those living in central Laurica could claim.

Croak walked as if he belonged, nodding to a Watchman he passed.

The crown jewel of this district was the Temple of Sassia, who, like many of her generation, was martyred by a god during the Immortals War, but not before she saved a dozen children from the fiery rage of the gods by squirreling them away in the basement of an alehouse. Sassia's temple stood over that blessed tavern.

Boasting two large oak doors with intricate scrollwork and polished brass handles the length of a man's legs, the temple itself was only two stories, modest by temple standards today. Still, it had the beautiful detailing and gilded buttresses the modern temples adopted. The white marble was greyed in some areas but had none of the mildewed crevices Croak had seen in the capital. Here, Sassia enjoyed a humble but clean and expensive home, owing to her patrons' attentiveness and the priests' avarice.

Croak pulled on one of the door handles as the skies opened up. The door swung open easily with only a slight whoosh as if Sassia herself had let out a sigh of expectation.

Croak swallowed.

The interior was a dance of shadows, the dim illumination coming from the tiny candles lit throughout the chapel. There were no pews here, only the marble floor reflecting the shadows and light so it seemed the surface of water.

The illusion carried the eye toward the altar, where a large marble slab lay beneath the life-sized statue of Sassia. Behind the statue, large domed windows depicted Sassia in stained glass going about her many kind deeds.

Croak stepped slowly toward the statue of the heroine and removed his sword belt, letting it drop to the ground at his side with a clatter.

"You are lucky she did not strike you down as soon as you entered!"

Croak jumped a foot. He clutched his chest and let out an unmanly squeak as his eyes searched out the body that went with the voice.

At last, a chuckle sounded to his left, and he frowned, seeing the man come out of the shadows. "You are a toad," Croak said at last.

Ormano Parador, a cleric under the High Cleric Christos of Metilai, grinned like a buffoon. He stopped close enough Croak could have wrung his neck if he'd wanted. Instead, he slapped his friend on the arm and frowned.

Ormano grabbed at his arm as if wounded, then laughed again and wrapped his plump arms around Croak. "Wait," Orry said as he pulled back, his nose wrinkled. "Did you shit yourself?"

Croak shoved away as his friend laughed. "I could've killed you, you know."

Ormano guffawed and jumped back a step as Croak made to hit him again. "With what? You're unarmed."

"I am not without resources, as you well know," he grumbled. He snatched the lapels of his jacket and yanked them down to right himself.

Orry's smile did not waver. "Aye, true, but she's not here, is she? Your 'resources'?"

"Oh, you are hilarious."

"And right, as always," Ormano said. "So? What are you doing here? Not a place I'd ever thought to find you."

"I'm looking for you, you idiot," Croak said.

Ormano lifted an eyebrow. "How'd you know I'd be here? You know what? Doesn't matter." He punched Croak lightly in the arm. "I missed you. Where's Terena?"

"Off to Metilai," Croak said and crossed his arms. "Left me here on an important fact-finding mission."

"Busy work to keep you out of trouble, you mean?"

"Leave off," Croak grunted. He strode toward the ledge of the sanctuary and sat on the first step. "The better question, and the one I've come up here for, is, what are *you* doing here?"

"I was volunteered. By Christos," Orry said with a shrug. "Came with General Peleon. I was looking for your sister, actually, and hoped I'd find her here. In Laurica, I mean." He gave Croak a smirk and took a seat beside him.

"Your intent was correct, but your timing is abysmal, as usual. She's already set off. Left me behind to deal with some ruffians."

"Gather gossip, more like," Ormano smiled. "So she's gone, truly? Well. I can't go back yet. I'm to wait for Prince Lerek and his convoy to arrive, and then we travel north together."

"North?" Croak said, instantly alert. "Well, that's a weird coincidence."

"Why?"

"Terena's coming back; end of the week. We're to accompany a couple of mercs north to find work under the new king's banner."

"Coincidences abound, my friend. We are to the new king as well. Ours is a diplomatic mission."

Croak crossed his arms at his chest and lifted his chin. "So then, why are you all here ahead of Lerek?"

Ormano pulled a face. "Imagine it's to thin some of the herd, as it were. Too many folk in Laurica now. Can't have the prince and his retinue ride through with so many risks present. Too much of a tactical headache. We brought the horses and provisions, too, as they'll be taking the ferry from Gall. Emperor wants as few people to know about the convoy as possible."

"They would've found out, regardless."

"Aye. Maybe. But hopefully not until after we've gone."

"And why are *you* going? You hate travel and you hate the cold."

"All truths. I'm going for the same reason I'm looking for your sister. And the same reason I suspect she herself wishes to head north."

"She's curious to see what the king wants with trackers, is all."

"He's interested in trackers, huh? That may be what the king wants, but you know your sister better than that," Orry chided softly.

Croak was silent.

"It's there, Croak," Orry said as he leaned closer. "It has to be. And with the new king's appearance, it all but confirms—"

"It's bullshit."

"No," his friend said as he grabbed Croak's wrist. "No, Croak, it's not bullshit. It has to be where we find the portal. Terena always thought it'd be in the north. And she is right. The veil to the Olympians is—"

"A myth! The gods were killed in the Immortals War! There are no gods left!"

Orry swore and pursed his lips. "You and I both know that's not true."

Croak hung his head and stared at his boots. "I know."

"Then what's bothering you?"

Croak snapped his eyes to his friend in disbelief. "You have to ask?"

"Croak—"

"They will *kill* her if they find out," Croak hissed, leaning close enough to see the gold flecks in Orry's brown eyes.

"Not if we find the portal."

"And you think this new king will help her do that?"

"It can't be coincidence, Croak. Everything that's happening?"

"Why now, though?" Croak asked himself out loud.

"What does Ren think?"

Croak pulled a face. "I know you know what she thinks. You two are thick as thieves every time we see you. I'm with her when she writes to you and I'm the one she has run to the Sergeant in every town to send off notes to you on every trinket we find. I sent one off before we left Aurora, so I'm assuming that's how you knew we'd be here."

He leaned in and narrowed his eyes, pointing his finger at Orry. "What I want to know is, what does," he waved his hand and blew lip bubbles, "a thousand year old mystery have to do with my sister's real parents?"

Orry wiped at his nose. "We've always been told the mortals killed the gods. But what if they didn't? What if they banished them instead, to another realm? A realm that can only be accessed using the Shroud of Faybhen?"

"Why would anyone have lied about that?"

Orry looked at him as if he was dense. "Why else? If anyone knew the truth, what's to stop someone from bringing them back? Can you imagine having the Olympians reign over mortals once more? I can think of at least one person who would not like that idea much."

Croak snorted. It had been a millennium since the Immortals War and in the centuries that passed, much had changed in the region, with power over most of it in the hands of Emperor Solon and the Heylisian Empire.

"I've found some interesting texts in the archives," Orry went on, his brown eyes thoughtful. "It seems many were not in favor of outright killing the gods. They feared angering the Titans. I found a journal at the monastery in Mount Athos detailing a meeting between King Justinian and Hekate. She proposed banishing the Olympians into another realm using a portal only she could create. And so Justinian agreed, but had history changed to say the Immortals were killed and that's what's been passed down through the ages."

"Ah ha!" Croak slapped Orry's knee. "So how do you know the book you read is the truth?"

Orry smiled in that pompous way that grated on Croak's nerves. "Because a priestess devoted to Hekate, who was present when the bargain was made, wrote the journal."

"Great. And you just found it, huh?"

Orry shrugged. "Only found it through one of Terena's visions. Someone definitely didn't want this particular bit of dirty laundry found."

"Speaking of dirty laundry," Croak said and dug inside his jerkin to pull out the oilcloth covered bundle Terena had given him. "Terena said to give you this."

Orry took the bundle and unraveled it, only to gasp and cover it back up quickly.

"This is the shroud!"

"Aye."

"Why is she giving it to me?"

Croak's brows furrowed. "I thought you'd know."

Orry shook his head. "Your sister's note said she'd found some-thing in Agraboda. I didn't realize it was the shroud. Did she find anything else?"

"Some writing I didn't understand. In the chamber *I* found where the shroud was hidden."

"*You* found?" Orry asked with a wink.

"Yes, man, *I* found it! Did she mention in the note she sent we were attacked by Magi?"

"What?" Orry exclaimed and leaned back. "No, she didn't! Did you not read the note you sent me?"

Croak shrugged. "I never read the notes."

Orry ran a hand over his face. "Magi. Incredible." He shook his head. "What were they like?"

Croak looked at him sideways. "Fucking terrifying. Everything turned black. It was like fighting in a void. Which is something else you should ask Terena about. They came out of nowhere, screaming and brandishing scimitars. Oh! I took one; I'll show you, but I left it back at Benson's. Thought it might attract some unwanted attention."

"Well, at least now we can all go north together!" Orry said happily.

Croak rose with a loud groan. "Fantastic," he said, grabbing his sword belt and fastening it.

"Wait! Where are you going?"

"Going to get a drink, Orry. Want to come?"

"I can't," Orry grumbled. "Peleon wants me to stay close to the bathhouse. He only let me out because I was coming here."

"Fine. I'm off, then."

"Well, where are you staying? Where shall I find you?"

"Find me at the inn on Pitts Lane. Or leave word with the blacksmith."

"This is exciting, isn't it?"

"Thrill of a lifetime," Croak called out as he held up his hand, giving Orry his middle finger.

CHAPTER FIVE

"**G**et up!"

Sonah Yahn gasped, springing up in bed as cold water sloshed over her head. She sputtered, then yelped when the drapes snapped open and light beamed into her dark chamber like rays from Hades's eyes.

"What the fuck?" Sonah screeched. She wiped at her eyes as she was yanked from her bed. The sound of bedding being ripped off and dumped somewhere behind her was the only response to her query.

The grip on her forearm gave her some insight as to who had started her day so rudely, but the question remained. Sonah was sure she had two hours left of sleep before she had to wake.

"Language!" Lady Maranou, her Matron, hissed. "Prince Lerek is breakfasting early today. You are to be in the dining room by half-past five, so you are already late."

"Why so bloody early?" she whined as two more maids set about dropping a day dress over her head and tugging at her arms and waist to fit it dangerously tight.

Sonah groaned and glared at her torturer, Lady Maranou. "Couldn't you just bring me his dish and send it back with word I did not die?"

Lady Maranou scowled at her as the others dropped quick curtsies and left.

"The last time you did that, I was pulled into an uncomfortable audience with His Excellency I do not wish to repeat. Now," she said, turning Sonah by the shoulders so her back was to her, "pretend to be a young lady worthy of your family's name and do your duty."

Sonah rolled her eyes as the older woman pulled her hair back roughly to plait it, securing it in a bun at the nape. She followed the matron out into the corridor, making faces at her back all the way down the stone steps of the Diamond Tower and across the courtyard separating the guest chambers from the rest of the palace.

It was still dark, and Sonah had to rub her eyes to stay awake. The early morning mist still hugged the walkways and turned the topiaries in the courtyard into ghosts.

The palace was more awake than usual at this hour. As they walked, a flurry of activity surrounded them as servants rushed about.

The low buzzing of voices and occasional barks of laughter drifted out to greet them as they entered the large room where the emperor and the royal family entertained their honored guests. Today, it was Crown Prince Lerek who filled his father's seat, laughing at something Lord Galen, the son of Duke Ravos, was saying. The firstborn sons of the realm crowded the table, chatting and laughing, and largely ignoring her entrance behind Lady Maranou. A line of ladies stood against the west wall and turned to stare at her.

Sonah's heart plummeted as Prince Lerek looked up and, with the most beautiful smile, greeted her warmly. His coppery brown hair hung to his shoulders in soft, shiny waves and his brown eyes danced as he raised his arms.

"Ah, there she is at last! Lady Sleepy, come, please, so we may eat our fill and ready ourselves for the journey!"

The other lords thumped the table and called out, joining the prince with shouted greetings. Sonah cheeks pinkened, but she squared her shoulders and lifted her chin, refusing to return any of their smiles.

Sonah looked at Lady Maranou over her shoulder. "Journey? What journey?"

The older woman pushed her forward, and Sonah tripped. She caught herself on the back of Lord Arron's chair and the man whooped as he caught her wrist, steadying her.

A rush of blood flooded Sonah's face and chest and she mumbled apologies while continuing toward the head of the table.

"If I'd known you'd planned a hunt at this ungodsly hour, I wouldn't have kept you waiting, Your Highness," she said with a deep curtsey as she reached Prince Lerek's side.

He stood and hugged her good-naturedly, earning a frown from Lady Maranou and a deeper blush from Sonah.

His show of easy familiarity always made her feel awkward, especially in front of the other nobles, even after seven years.

"We both know you still would've been late, Lady Sleepy, but I'm glad you're here." Prince Lerek gestured to someone over her right shoulder and Sonah turned to see a servant bring a platter of meat, bread and cheese, while another came around the prince's left side, setting down a cup of ale. The servants bowed and stepped back.

"And it's not a hunt, Sonah," he continued with a grin. "We're to the north, to see the man who styles himself king of that wasteland."

She started. Looking over at him, she furrowed her brow. "Oh."

Lady Maranou loudly cleared her throat. Sonah shot her a sour look as she took the cup of ale. Lifting it to her lips, she noticed the expectant looks around the table.

"Bit early to be poisoned, I think, but let's see," she muttered and took a healthy swig of the bitter brew. She almost heaved, hating the taste—especially first thing in the morning—and set down the cup. She then selected a few bits of meat and chewed on it as she placed some cheese into a bit of the bread and stuffed it in her mouth.

Still chewing, she nodded in appreciation to the prince, motioning how wonderful and un-poisoned his breakfast was. Some snickers sounded around the table, and she saw Prince Lerek look across at the others with a small smile dimpling his left cheek as he winked.

When she was done, she lifted her skirts and moved toward the far wall where the other ladies waited.

The expectant glances from the lords bounced off her unnoticed while Prince Lerek took up his cup and sipped. There was a roar of applause when he lifted his cup toward Sonah with a small tilt of his head.

Sonah dropped her gaze and made herself appear bored. This ritual had been going on since she was ten. Being the center of attention for the short time it took to taste his food was agonizing, worse so because the other ladies always sneered at her for it, believing she relished the eyes of the prince and other lords upon her.

Quite the opposite; Sonah loathed attention of any sort. And it made her life at the palace difficult.

"When will you be ready?"

Sonah started as Lady Annalise, standing beside her, smacked her wrist. Her mouth opened when she noticed the way everyone was looking at her. Sonah turned to the prince, who was watching her as well.

"Your Highness?"

"Lady Sonah is ready whenever Your Highness is ready to depart," Lady Maranou said, her voice carrying over Sonah's mumbling.

Sonah threw the woman a questioning look. Of course, Lady Maranou didn't bother to look at her charge.

"Good," the prince said, setting down his ale. "You can ride with the Ladies Merina and Tollis."

He must've seen how that news sat with her, because he gave her a wry smile. "I apologize for the inconvenience, Lady Sleepy. Blame my father. Luckily, we do not leave until midday. So, you have some hours yet to ready yourself."

"But—"

Sonah flinched when Lady Maranou pinched her arm behind her.

"Is something amiss?" the prince asked.

Sonah's cheeks burned as she looked at the prince, then around the table. Some lords looked at her while others spoke amongst themselves, but it was enough to make Sonah want to vanish into the marble at her feet. She cursed inwardly, knowing the comments she'd get later from the other ladies.

"Your Highness—"

"Lerek, for goodness' sake, Sonah."

The heat in her face threatened to make her faint. "Lerek," she choked out, "I appreciate the kind invitation, but I—"

"Not exactly an invitation, Sonah," Prince Lerek said, arching a dark eyebrow at her. "I am going, so of course you must as well. I apologize for the late notice, but this is official Imperial business and when the emperor gives an order, by the gods, we all must jump."

"Yes, of course. But, you see—"

"She will be waiting in the courtyard, Your Highness," Lady Maranou said, grabbing hold of Sonah's arm and squeezing. "We will leave you, so we may pack."

"Your Highness," an Imperial Guard came in then and handed Lerek a note.

Lady Maranou paused and Sonah yanked her arm free. They waited in silence as Lerek smiled down at the missive before he folded it and slid it into the inside pocket of his coat.

"You've been given a reprieve, Lady Sleepy," Lerek said with a glance at her. He picked at the food on his plate and added, "We now depart on the morrow."

Sonah perked up. Maybe she'd be able to get those extra hours of sleep after all.

She'd barely smiled at the news before Lady Maranou grabbed her arm once more and led her from the room.

"Lady Maranou, please!"

"We have plenty of work to do before the morning," the matron responded, her grip tightening.

"Yes, of course, but I had other things planned for the day, you know. Wait. How long am I going to be gone, exactly?"

"Your duty is to the prince."

"But he never travels outside the empire," Sonah whined. "Why now and who is this godsdamned new king, anyway?"

"You ask too many questions! And how many times have I warned you about your language!" Lady Maranou hissed at her, tugging her so close, some spittle hit Sonah's cheek. "This is an important opportunity for you!"

Sonah wrenched her arm away and vigorously wiped at her cheek. She continued to stomp toward her chamber, huffing as she took the stairs with more than her usual vigor. "Perfect. Pray, enlighten me."

"I've heard the emperor wishes Prince Lerek to marry from amongst the firstborn daughters of the realm. Since all of you ladies are already here in your capacity as Tasters to the firstborn lords— and prince, of course—you, being Prince Lerek's Royal Taster, should be the one he chooses. And now you have significantly fewer competitors for who knows how many months!"

Sonah stopped so abruptly Lady Maranou slammed into her back with a squeak of surprise. Sonah turned around, gaping, and for once the color drained from her face to leave behind cold sweat.

"My nose!"

"What are you saying?" Sonah asked in horror.

Lady Maranou rubbed at her thick nose and glared up at Sonah on the step above. "My nose!"

"Oh, hang your nose, Sybil!" Sonah hissed, turning once more to stomp up the last few steps before turning toward her room. "I have no wish to marry Lerek, and I won't be forced to perform any function other than that of Royal Taster, which is the only reason I am even here!"

Lady Maranou followed further behind, her voice nasally and muffled when she responded. "Well, I have already sent word to your father, so you'd better do all you can to gain the prince's interest. You've seen how quickly the ladies are working to secure time with him. So if the Ladies Tollis and Merina are traveling with the prince's retinue, you'd better believe they're going to try to win his favor. And so shall you."

Sonah stared at the matron as if she'd grown a third eye. "You wrote the—you wrote to my father? Already?"

"Of course," Lady Maranou said with a sniff. She strode toward the trunk at the foot of the bed and rummaged until she found the buried riding habit Sonah hadn't worn since the hunt last autumn.

"Oh, gods above, this is filthy!" Lady Maranou said and threw a nasty look at Sonah before bundling it up in her arms. Since riding wasn't a particular favorite pastime of hers, Sonah had forgotten all about the mud caked on her riding outfit.

"I don't know if it'll be ready by the morning, but I'll have it washed and we'll see. Remember to wear the fur lined wool cloak too. Where did you leave your gloves? You'll need those too. It's still cold up there."

"We're going by carriage. What's it matter?"

Sighing, the matron gave her a disgruntled look in response.

Now, as Lady Maranou carried the dress out, dried mud cracked and fell to the floor, following in a sad trail after the grumbling woman.

Alone, Sonah lifted her hand to her chest, forcing deep breaths to calm herself. Of all the ridiculous, no, *inconvenient*, things to happen.

Prince Lerek was like an older brother to her. She had no romantic feelings toward him whatsoever and she knew from their limited conversations he had no such feelings for her, either. Besides, he was in love with the Royal Tracker, Terena Luca.

Now, *she* was someone Sonah admired, and not because she was that rare breed of beauty that was also kind to other women. She was also… free. Some of the greatest homes in the realm and beyond welcomed her because of her profession, and Terena Luca answered only to the emperor, traveling the continent with her brother.

Sonah sighed and rubbed at her eyes. What she wouldn't give to be so free. To travel and see the world without men telling her what to do.

Or forcing her to taste food that could be poisonous.

Or making her pretend to be Duke Ovenno's daughter, Sonah Yahn.

It had been some months since Terena was last in Metilai. The view of the city as she rode closer to the western gate had always been one she loved, and she often paused at the very spot she now passed to admire the ethereal beauty of the capital city of Metilai, the beating heart of the Heylisian Empire.

In the last year, however, the rain and overcast skies had cast a pall over the city. It dulled the magnificence of Metilai and the gleaming bright white of the aptly named White Palace. The stunning spires of the palace were now hidden, and the jeweled brilliance of the buildings making up the largest city on the continent lackluster.

The main gates were guarded on either side by a statue of the first Emperor of Heylisia, Alexandros, and the Heylisian hero, Calix, who —according to the historians of the empire—had gravely wounded the Olympian god, Zeus, leading to their downfall. Built by Emperor Brotis three centuries ago, the statues were well over a hundred feet tall.

Terena guided her mare to the left of the White Palace and entered through the northern gate. Dismounting, she led Nyx toward the stables, passing the training yard where a flurry of activity caught her attention.

"I got 'er, Ren," Ozi, the stableboy, yelled as he ran up to her. He gently took hold of the reins, cooing nonsense to Nyx.

As he led her away, Terena called out to him.

"Ozi." She looked back out at the yard and motioned with one hand. "What's the ruckus?"

"Emperor's sending a convoy north to meet the new king."

"Really?" she said, more to herself. She pulled out a coin and tossed it to the towheaded boy. He caught it and grinned at her before turning back to the mare.

Terena looked out over the bustling courtyard. She spotted an older man with long grey hair secured at the back of his head in a neat bun, calling out orders as he strode across the yard and started toward him.

"Captain!" she called out. "Captain Cortis!"

The man turned his head but did not stop. When he saw her, his craggy face lit up with a grin. She caught up to him, matching his stride with some difficulty.

"You're leading the convoy," she said, more to confirm what the boy had said than anything else.

"Aye," he said, flashing her a wink before stopping for a word with one of his men.

Terena waited until he'd finished and turned back to her before she said, "Let me go with you."

Startled, he paused. He looked down at her with a frown. "Do you know where we journey?"

"North?" she said, "To see the new king."

He narrowed his dark green eyes at her. They were the only attractive thing about him. "Indeed." He turned to face her, his thick arms folding at his chest. "When did you get back?"

"Just now," she said. She let out a deep breath and gestured to the commotion in the yard. "When do you leave?"

"The morning, most likely," he said with a frown. He scratched at an old scar running the length of his throat. "Lucky you arrived when you did. Would've been gone already, but the emperor delayed us. Wanted a word with the prince."

"Which one?"

"The eldest," he grunted. "Prince Lerek."

Terena couldn't hide the spontaneous smile breaking out on her face. She nodded and dropped her gaze. "Of course. So?" she asked the captain again. "Do you have room for one more?"

He looked at her for a moment. "For my part, aye, we could use someone like you on this errand," he said, his voice gruff. "But you must first speak with the emperor. Get his blessing."

"Aye, of course."

"Find me in the morning, if he allows it," he said with a nod. Before he took off again, he placed a hand on her shoulder. "We'll wait for you."

Terena watched as the captain strode off. She looked around the courtyard once more before turning toward the eastern wing of the palace, wondering how quickly she could get an audience with His Excellency.

CHAPTER SIX

"Mistress Terena Luca."

Terena strode into the emperor's throne room after the herald's announcement. It was larger and more quietly elegant than Duke Aurora's, with white and gold decor throughout. Beautiful portraits of past emperors adorned the walls. Portraits of the empresses, of course, were conveniently absent.

Other courtiers milled about, but as she made her way to the center of the room, she caught sight of Lerek on the dais to the right of the emperor. She dared not show any emotion as she met his gaze; her face a careful mask, but something inside of her softened at seeing him after so long. His hair was longer than she remembered, now falling below his collarbone in soft waves, the light in the room picking up copper highlights when he tilted his head in silent greeting. His dark brown eyes flashed as he gazed at her, and Terena's breath caught. She lifted a corner of her lips in response, then turned her attention back to the emperor.

Xoran, Captain of the Imperial Guard, stepped up next to Emperor Solon, his scarred hand on the hilt of his sword as he looked at her with his usual sneer. Xoran tolerated her because her father, Lorence Luca, had been his captain before his death at the Battle of

Alloras five years ago, but the man had never liked her and made no secret of the fact.

Emperor Solon watched her as she stopped a few feet before the dais and bowed low. She kept her gaze on the marble, looking at her reflection while she waited for his command.

"Rise."

Terena straightened and clasped her hands behind her back. Her eyes picked a spot on his prominent forehead and remained there. The emperor regarded her behind dull brown, down-turned eyes. His Imperial robes seemed to hang off him, though he was not a small man. It was just his frame was not commanding, and his clothes seemed to know it. The white did not do his olive skin justice, unlike his son, and yet he preferred the color to any other that might suit him better.

"Mistress Luca, you have uncanny timing," the emperor said, his voice carrying across the marbled room. His steward, Salorus, to whom he'd been speaking before her entrance, bowed low and stepped away.

"Your Excellency."

"I trust by now you've heard of the convoy I'm sending to the north?"

"Aye, Emperor."

"Good," the emperor said and stood. He stepped off the dais, his movements elegant, unhurried, as he came closer. He stopped a foot away and folded his arms across his chest. "Stay a moment. I need a word alone. Everyone else, out. You too, Xoran."

The captain didn't like that at all, less so when Terena dipped her chin and gave him a pointed look, but he walked off the dais, his gold and green cape snapping as he strode past her.

"Should I stay, Father?"

"No," Emperor Solon said with a sigh. "You may finish preparing, but see me again before you leave in the morning."

Terena shifted her gaze then and looked at Lerek. He bowed and took his leave. As he passed, close enough his arm brushed hers, he murmured a greeting. She nodded in return.

The sound of the doors closing behind him echoed in the room. Terena kept her eyes fixed on the throne, but sensed when the emperor walked off to her left.

He had gone to the southern facing wall, a large tapestry depicting the fall of the Olympians taking up the bulk of the space. The emperor's hands folded at his back while he gazed at it. Terena wasn't sure if he was thinking about what he wanted to say, but for her part, she wished he'd get on with it so she could leave and find Lerek.

"As I said, your timing is impeccable. I'd hoped you'd return before they departed, but my messengers returned without word of your whereabouts until this morning."

He turned at last. Terena saw new worry-lines as he furrowed his brow. He was not handsome like his twin sons, Lerek and Isher; they inherited their good looks from their mother, the Empress Adanna. But their height was their father's.

He sighed, his eyes small in a face dominated by his forehead.

He regarded her steadily when he asked, "You've heard of the man who calls himself king in the northern provinces?"

"Aye, Excellency."

He nodded. "You'll have heard, too, he is building an army. Encouraging men to join him with the promise of riches. We've had reports of many with and without experience heading north. Some have left the legions. General Peleon has told me, despite floggings and a few hangings, men are still leaving our armies in secret, working with smugglers who are getting paid by the new king's men to bring *my* soldiers over the border in Osta."

Terena hadn't heard, of course. What made no sense was how fast this was all happening. Again, she thought of her conversation with Benson in Laurica. She'd been in Elis and then Aurora for the past few months, but surely she should have heard something.

"Emperor Solon," she said, "I concede I've been gone longer than I expected, but I've only now heard of this new king. Do—"

"Then you've heard all you need," the emperor interrupted. "I have a different matter of concern."

He paused and bowed his head. The silence stretched as he seemed to struggle with how to proceed. Terena felt a prickle of unease.

"You're aware some of our provinces have been... restless? The dukes dislike my legions at their borders. They believe a war with Lakonia is unnecessary. And now the northern king is making them even more outspoken about the need for peace."

Terena shifted uneasily. "I've not heard, no, Your Excellency," she lied. She and Croak couldn't help but notice the tensions as they'd crossed the empire these past few months.

"I understand Duke Aurora contracted you to find him a relic," he said after an uncomfortable pause.

Terena stiffened. "Aye."

"And you delivered this relic to him recently?"

"As always, Your Excellency is well informed."

The emperor lifted an eyebrow. "Do you know why the duke wanted the Shroud of Faybhen?"

Terena's face was carefully blank as she answered. "No, Your Excellency."

He paced in front of her, stopping a few feet away. Terena was certain this was the closest he'd ever gotten to her in her whole life, but she wouldn't quail before him.

"But you know what the shroud is."

That wasn't a question, she knew, but still she answered. "Aye."

"And you thought fit to deliver—to a man who is openly dissatisfied with his sovereign—what is essentially a weapon? The power to bring the Olympian gods back to this realm!"

Shit.

Terena swallowed, keeping her eyes on the throne as she opened and closed her mouth a few times before saying, "That is a myth, Your—"

"Do not *dare*," he hissed as he snapped forward, his face so close to hers, the heat of his breath was on her cheeks. "Do not dare to lie to me!"

It took everything she had to stay calm and continue to stare at the throne while he seethed.

"Every ruler that has stood where I stand now has understood one thing above all! Since the Immortals War, we must do everything in our power to ensure gods never darken our world again. It is why the gods that remained on the continent were killed. There are no more in all of Elysium because they are dangerous to mankind.

"We let the people worship the Titans, aye, and some worship the mortal heroes, which we also allow. We built temples and priests and clerics for them because we know faith is power."

Emperor Solon stood so close to Terena she trembled at his nearness.

"But *I* control that power," he snarled. "I let them have their religions. Their holidays. *I* tell them who to worship. And the moment someone comes along and threatens my control of that power, I strike them down as I have my entire rule! The only reason you're not in the dungeons for your incredibly *stupid* actions is because I still have need of you. Do not think for one second my son's feelings for you protect you from me."

Terena could feel his stare burning into the side of her face, and yet she dared not turn her gaze to his.

"You will leave in the morning before Prince Lerek and the convoy depart. You will go to Aurora and you will *bring that fucking shroud to me!*" He roared so loud she flinched and backed up a few steps. Her calm facade cracked, and she shook as her eyes flew to his for a moment before snapping them to a spot over his right shoulder.

"Yes, Majesty," she whispered.

Silence settled around them, but Terena dared not look elsewhere. Her face flooded with heat as she stood there, hands clasped at her ramrod-straight back while she waited.

A minute passed before he moved, and Terena chanced a quick look at him. Turning away, his hands moved to clasp at his back.

"I do not need to remind you, you will not speak a word of our conversation to anyone," he said as he turned one last time to look at her, his dark eyes narrowed at her.

"Including my son. If you dare say anything, I will ensure those words are your last."

Terena swore she saw a look of disdain on his cold, plain face before he turned away and called out over his shoulder with a wave of his hand, "You're dismissed!"

TERENA WALKED SWIFTLY UP A FEW FLIGHTS OF STAIRS AND TURNED down several corridors until she reached the small private garden where she and Lerek usually met.

The Winter Garden was at the top of the Diamond Tower. Before it was converted into accommodations for palace guests, the tower was solely for the empresses and their courts. But Empress Adanna had preferred staying with her husband and sons in the Royal Tower, so had allocated the beautiful rooms to the honored guests and the Tasters.

Terena entered and spotted Lerek immediately, sitting on the stone bench in front of the statue of the goddess, Nyx. He wore the flowing white pants with matching silk coat he usually preferred, gold epaulettes at his shoulders the only adornment, preferring to wear jewelry over detailing on his clothes. A year ago, he would've foregone the shirt he now wore beneath the coat, but now his wardrobe always included multiple layers.

He was frowning, lost in thought as he played with a bracelet on his right wrist, pulling it off and on again. As she neared, her heart flipped to see it was the one she'd given him a year ago for his Name's Day.

The first time he'd kissed her.

As if he'd heard her thoughts, he looked up, his lips curling in a soft smile.

"You look smug."

Lerek stood, his smile growing. "How can I not? My lady has returned."

Terena laughed. She watched as he slipped the bangle onto his wrist before pulling her into his arms. She went readily, her face turned up to his for a kiss that snatched the breath from her lungs. He tightened his grip, deepening the kiss, then trailed his lips down her neck.

Terena shivered, her breath coming fast and hot when his hands dropped to her waist. Her eyes closed and she let out a small laugh.

"You've missed me."

"Let me show you how much," Lerek said, then scrunched his nose. "But first, you need to bathe, my love."

Terena let out a noise of protest and twisted to get out of his embrace.

"That's what you have to say after months apart?"

He laughed and tugged her hand to pull her back. "I missed you. Of course, I missed you. But I have a meeting shortly. I figured you'd want to freshen up and then we could…" He leaned down once more and kissed her neck. When she moaned, he tightened his embrace.

"I stink, remember?" she whispered, although she dropped her head back so he had more access to her neck. He obliged by leaving soft kisses along the column down to her shoulder. She shivered and pushed at him.

"Lerek," she protested.

Lerek pulled back but did not release her. "All right," he said with a sigh, then winked at her. "To be continued this evening."

"Tell me what you know of this northern king."

Lerek blinked. "Ever the romantic." He released his hold on her and sat back down on the stone bench, tugging her hand so she sat next to him. "What do you wish to know?"

She shrugged. "Don't you find it odd one minute no one's heard of him and the next soldiers are leaving their legions and mercenaries are flocking to the northernmost cities of the continent, all intent on fighting under his banner? I've not been gone long enough for anyone to become so strong the emperor sees fit to send his heir in a convoy to treat with him."

"I wouldn't say I'm going to treat with him, exactly," Lerek said as he played with her fingers.

"Then why go?"

Lerek dropped his gaze to their joined hands. She stilled at his hesitation. Terena sighed loudly and rose.

A long, uncomfortable silence stretched between them. Terena dropped her eyes to her hands. She knew there were things he couldn't tell her. Political things she knew the emperor did not want her or anyone knowing, but it still hurt when Lerek pushed her away like this.

"Forget I asked," she whispered.

Lerek stood and reached for her hand. She let him take it, threading his fingers in hers. "What did my father want?"

"It's a secret."

He snorted. "Really."

Terena lifted her eyes and smirked. "I'll share my secret if you share yours."

He narrowed his eyes. "We're playing games now? Is this what you want?"

She shrugged. "I think it's interesting you would have me break my vow to your father, my emperor, and yet you don't seem inclined to do the same."

She wandered off toward the statue of Cronos across from their alcove. "What I *can* say is I leave in the morning for Aurora."

"Fine," he said and strode toward her. He settled his hands on her hips. She turned her face up to meet his gaze. "I don't want to fight with you. We have some time together, that's enough for me. For now."

She smiled, and he kissed the tip of her nose. "Will you do me a favor?"

Terena lifted an eyebrow and waited.

"When you've finished your business in Aurora, don't go north. Stay in Aurora."

"Why?"

Lerek dropped his chin, and she swore she saw him frown before he pasted on a smile. "I have a surprise for you."

"A surprise for me in Aurora?"

"Aye."

"What?"

Lerek smirked. "It wouldn't be much of a surprise if I told you. Trust me, you'll like this surprise."

Terena groaned and pulled away, but Lerek grabbed her chin, forcing her to look at him.

"Do you love me?"

"Aye."

He bent his forehead to hers. "Stay in Aurora, then."

"Fine. But you owe me."

Lerek smiled wolfishly. "I do indeed, my love. And happy to repay as you see fit."

CHAPTER SEVEN

Clutching the note a servant had slipped into her hand while she was on her way back to her rooms to change for dinner, Sonah stopped in front of the doors to Prince Lerek's rooms. She tapped her foot while enduring the Imperial Guard's scrutiny before he opened the door and let her inside.

The antechamber was cool, the early spring breeze wafting in from the terrace on her left, and she smiled in greeting at an Imperial Guard just inside the room. He did not respond, staring at her with a stoic mask, and she rolled her eyes and strode toward the terrace.

Sonah shivered and folded her arms, hunching her shoulders as another chill breeze whipped her blonde hair off her shoulders. Looking around, she saw light from the fire pit to the right where the pergola's white silk curtains floated. Squinting, Sonah saw Prince Lerek and straightened, taking a deep breath before proceeding toward him.

Pushing aside one of the billowing curtains, she stepped into the relative warmth of the pergola. Sitting on a large, cushioned wooden chair near the crackling fire, Prince Lerek stared into the dancing flames, arms resting on his knees. Uncertain, Sonah stood awkwardly and cleared her throat.

"Ah," Prince Lerek said with a smirk when he looked up and saw her. "Little Changeling."

Blinking, Sonah's mouth hung open for a second before she launched forward, arms out and screeched, "Isher!"

The prince stood in time to catch her, Sonah's embrace making him almost fall back into his seat as he laughed. He squeezed tight before pushing her back and lifted a hand to her face, tucking a lock of blonde hair behind her ear as he grinned at her.

"Been a while," he murmured, and she laughed, hugging him again.

When she finally let go, she swatted his shoulder. "What are you doing here? I thought you were Lerek!"

"I just got here," he said, retaking his seat. Sonah looked around before moving to a seat nearby and pulled it close to Isher. Sighing, she sat and gazed at him while he settled back.

"I'm waiting for Lerek," he added.

"Does he know you're here?"

Isher shrugged. "I sent him a note this morning."

Sonah opened her mouth and made a noise. "So it was *your* note he got at breakfast," she said, snapping her fingers and pointing at him. "That's why we didn't leave."

"What are *you* doing here? Not that I'm not glad to see you, Little Changeling," Isher said with a wink. Sonah blushed, loving the nickname he'd given her when she first arrived at the White Palace because of her different colored eyes. She had been self conscious of them, one brown and one green, when she'd first come to court, the other ladies making fun of her for them. But Isher loved them, exclaiming how unique they made her, which made the other ladies jealous, especially since Isher showed so much interest in her. It wasn't in a romantic way, Sonah knew, but in a cherished, younger sister way, making her feel loved and protected.

Sonah sighed and opened her fist, the crumpled missive in her hand. "I've a note saying Prince Lerek was to have drinks in his rooms before dinner, so... here I am."

"A Royal Taster's duty never ends," Isher said with a trace of disgust. "Thank the gods he's the heir, Sonah, because I'd run you ragged."

Sonah laughed and ducked her head to hide the flush of color in her face. "It's too bad we're leaving in the morning," she groaned. "It would've been nice to see you for more than a few minutes."

Isher leaned forward and rubbed the back of his neck. "I think you'll be seeing a lot more of me soon, Little Changeling."

Sonah's eyes widened. "Truly? The emperor will allow you to come back?"

The harsh laugh greeting her words made Sonah startle. "Let me come back? No. I doubt my father would let me, but I see some changes coming."

Sonah's brows furrowed, but she didn't dwell on his words for long. Looking around, she saw the wine decanter and crystal goblets on the sideboard and cocked her head at Isher. "Well, I supposed I should at least do my job and taste the wine before he gets here. I need to get going."

Isher inclined his head and motioned with his hand, smiling at her as she rose and went to the decanter, pouring herself a glass. She arched an eyebrow at him, shaking the decanter in question.

"Of course," he said with a laugh, and she poured a glass for him.

Taking both goblets, she walked over and handed him his wine, then tapped her glass against his. Sonah took a long drink, closing her eyes and savoring the sweet taste.

"How long do we wait until you're dead?" Isher joked with a grin.

She scowled at him and set her glass down on the rim of the fire pit. "So, you never said why you're back. Are you going with us to see the new northern king?"

Isher made a face. "Lerek wrote to me about the trip north, but it was Serephina who told me to come home. Apparently, I'm a surprise for my brother."

"That's weird," Sonah said. Lady Serephina was the emperor's second wife, and she disliked Lerek and Isher, mostly because they were ahead of her own son in the line of succession.

"Aye," Isher said with a deep sigh and stretched. He shrugged and took a sip of his wine. "I think she's trying to get on my good side. Anyway, I wanted to make sure he'd still be here, so I sent him the note. It'll be good to see my mother, too."

"The empress has kept to her rooms in recent months," Sonah said, lifting sad eyes to the prince. "It'll be good for her to see you."

Isher nodded and looked down at his goblet.

"Will you still be here when we get back?"

Isher stared at her for a few long seconds before he nodded. "Aye, Sonah. I'll still be here."

"Good," she said and stood. The blood rushed to her head, and dizziness swamped her vision for a moment and she snapped her hand out. Isher bolted from his chair and grabbed her arm to steady her.

"Are you good? Was it the poison?"

"Ha ha," she muttered. "I think I stood up too fast."

Isher released his hold, his eyes still on her, and she gave him a quick smile. "Tell Lerek I was here, and the wine is fine?"

"Aye, Little Changeling."

Sonah nodded and turned to leave, then turned back and gave him another hug, her arms tight as she rested her head on his chest. Going up on her toes, she planted a kiss on his cheek. "I'll miss you, but I'm glad you'll be here when we get back. I'll see you soon!"

Isher grabbed her face and dropped a kiss on her forehead, then stared into her eyes for a few seconds. Sonah frowned, but then he tweaked her nose and she jerked her head back.

"Ugh, stop!" she said, pulling away.

When she made it to the terrace doors, she glanced over her shoulder to look at him one last time and caught him still standing, his gaze sad as he watched her.

A chill went down her spine, and Sonah had the feeling she was missing something, something important. She shook it off and left, hurrying through the antechamber and out the door as if chased by ghosts.

TERENA PACED THROUGH THE WINTER GARDEN, PAUSING NOW AND then to sit on a stone bench, only to rise and pace again.

She glanced over at the doorway for the hundredth time, wondering where Lerek could be.

Only once had he failed to meet her: when his father had unexpectedly fallen ill, eating some spoiled fruit. The palace had been in an uproar; half the kitchen staff put to the sword before the Royal Physician had announced the fruit was bad, not poisoned. They executed the fruit vendor that afternoon.

Terena cursed and strode toward the exit, nodding as she passed two Imperial Guard and took the stairs down four flights and across the walkway, where another flight of stairs led up to the royal residences.

The upper gallery was silent. Terena stepped out into the hallway and listened. As she strode across the hall and down the corridor leading to Lerek's rooms, she frowned.

There were no guards about.

Lerek's personal Imperial Guard, Alexi, was always outside the prince's rooms. Terena had caught him sleeping more than once during a night shift, but it wasn't late enough for him to have already fallen asleep.

And she'd never seen him not at his post.

Terena looked around, then reached for the latch, lifting it slowly and pushing the door open. The silence beyond was not reassuring at all.

Terena unsheathed her dagger slowly, pushing the door wider, and slipped inside. She closed the door behind her, her eyes adjusting to the dark, darting around the large foyer.

As she turned to step into the room, she saw a guard lying on the floor on the far side of the door.

Terena held her breath as she hunched down, her hands sliding up to the guard's neck to feel for a pulse. She gasped, snatching her hand back when she felt the slippery slide of blood. Glancing around, Terena moved carefully through the antechamber, stopping beside a plush chaise where someone was sitting facing away from her.

As she stepped closer, her eyes narrowed, and she leaned in to see a guard slumped half on and half off the chaise. The smell of copper hit her nose as she kneeled, hissing at him to wake up, but he didn't so much as twitch. Terena lifted a hand and pushed at his shoulder roughly. He slumped over and Terena's heart skipped.

Alexi.

Terena reached out, running both hands over his body. Something warm and wet covered his armor.

She pulled her hand back, sliding the pads of her fingers together, the coppery smell filling her nostrils. Terena leaned forward, her arms flying across the guard's chest to his neck, where the blood pooled thickly at the collar of his uniform jacket. Blood roaring in her ears, Terena rose slowly and glanced around the room once more before stepping toward the open terrace doors.

Outside, she paused, straining to hear. Nothing but silence and the gathering darkness greeted her. Her grip tightened on her dagger as she stepped up onto the upper terrace. Lerek's garden terrace surrounded a pergola wreathed in white silk curtains billowing slowly as she neared. The cool night air did nothing to ease her overheated skin. Beyond the swaying silks, she could see the dim embers of a dying fire.

The silence was thick in her ears and she blinked owlishly at her surroundings. As she parted the silks, Terena stared dumbly around at the scene. Lerek lay on the ground in front of the settee, wearing the same clothes he'd worn earlier, a dark stain marring the white silk, his arms stretched out wide. Looking across, her eyes landed on another figure, her eyes widening. Lerek's twin, Isher, was half lying on an armchair across from Lerek, an empty glass near his fingers shattered on the stone. Another guard lay on the ground face down near his feet.

Terena rushed to Lerek, her hands trembling badly. She whimpered incoherently as her hands groped his chest, his face, feeling something sticky she couldn't see but knew by the coppery scent what it was. She put her head to his chest, her cheek in the wetness on his shirt. He was so still, his skin like ice.

She couldn't hear his heartbeat.

Terena drew her hands back in horror, then stared at them like she'd never seen them before, covered in blood.

Terena sat there, mouth opening and closing.

"Please... please," she whispered, over and over, her shaking hands reaching once more for her beloved as she moved them frantically across his body, begging him, pleading with him. "Please!"

A movement across from her startled her, and she fell back, her ass hitting the stone hard, jarring her out of her stupor. She looked up to see Isher mumbling and working to sit up. At last, he lifted his head and stared back at her. As their eyes met, he blinked at her.

"What are you doing here?"

Terena stared at him, then back down at Lerek.

"What did you do?" she whispered. Isher's eyes widened as he stared at her.

"WHAT DID YOU DO?!" she roared as she sprang to her feet.

"Wait!"

Fire raced up from her belly, along her arms and up her chest. Her vision tunneled. She flung out her hands and roared.

Blinding light filled the terrace. Isher screamed as he rose in the air and crashed against a pergola beam, his head cracking loudly against the wood. Terena's hands lifted higher, her left hand curling as if to choke him. Isher struggled against the force holding him against the beam, his legs kicking wildly as he clawed at his throat.

There were shouts and running feet behind her, but Terena was focused only on Isher. She tightened her fingers and was rewarded with fresh, guttural sounds from Isher. Hands pulled at her, nails gouging into the skin of her arms, leaving bloody welts, but Terena did not relent. More hands pulled at her and she lost her control of Isher. He crashed to the ground.

Terena turned with renewed rage and shook off the hands holding her in place and whipped out her arms. A great force whooshed from her hands, arms glowing bright white, and three guards flew across the terrace. Two more guards rushed forward, followed by three others. Swords held high, they ran at her, yelling, but she snapped out her left hand, curling her fingers. The two guards closest to her dropped to their knees, hands clutching at their throats in agony.

She was about to turn her attention to the others when something cracked against her head and she fell atop Lerek's body.

Terena held her eyes open long enough to see her love's dead eyes staring back at her.

CHAPTER EIGHT

Sonah sighed, following behind Lady Maranou as she whispered with Lady Serle, Matron to Lady Tollis. Usually when they strolled after dinner, Lady Maranou walked beside Sonah, freeing her from having to converse with any of the other ladies.

Tonight, however, it seemed the events of the day—the delay in departing for the north, Terena Luca's arrival and most recently the arrival of Prince Isher—was too much fodder for gossip Lady Maranou could not ignore.

A commotion near the palace reached them and Sonah looked up. She thought nothing of it until she saw an Imperial Guard rush over to Captain Cortis, who had been standing near a few guards at the bottom of the steps to the lawn. Sonah watched as he then motioned for three others to join him.

The captain then turned his head every which way, his gaze finally landing on Sonah and, even across the distance, his eyes locked on her. She slowed her steps and frowned, staring back. A second later, he strode toward her, his face like thunder.

Something uncomfortable slid down Sonah's chest, and she took several steps back, clutching her cloak.

Lady Maranou turned, noticing at last something was amiss, and made to step in front of her, but the captain pushed her aside as he snatched Sonah's arm, his grip so hard it made Sonah's knees buckle.

She cried out, even as Lady Maranou shouted in protest, and dragged Sonah along until two Imperial Guard reached them. The matron's shouts and even Lady Tollis's cries did nothing to stop him.

"Take her down to the dungeons and place her in a cell," he bit out, dropping her arm to grab a fistful of her blonde hair, shoving her at the two guards.

Sonah saw stars, the pain on her scalp draining the color from her face, her mouth dropping open.

As the guards led her away, dread washed over her and she dug in her heels, screaming for Lady Maranou as the guards tightened their grip, almost lifting her as they carted her off.

Sonah could hear the matron somewhere behind her, yelling at the captain, at the guards, at everyone as more voices shouted behind her.

When they burst through a side door into the palace, Sonah paused her screaming for a heartbeat as she saw the chaos around her.

Servants ran as if they were headless chickens, some wailing or hugging others who sobbed uncontrollably. Others looked angry or frightened.

Frankel, one of the kitchen boys she'd befriended last summer, spotted her and she called out to him for help. The look he sent her was so filled with hate, Sonah could only gawk as he launched himself at her. He screamed obscenities at her as other servants and guards grabbed him, Sonah's own captors hauling her off in a direction she'd never gone, through a door she never knew existed.

She sobbed as her confusion and terror mounted, dragging her feet as they pulled her along, bruising her arms with their grips. Sonah begged and cried, but still they half-dragged, half-carried her toward some unknown destination.

Sonah had no idea what she was saying, nonsensical words pleading with her captors while they dragged her down a stairwell, the steps turning from marble to stone as the surrounding walls became damp.

Down and down they went, Sonah tripping a few times during the descent, her knee hitting the stone so hard the shock of it arced up her leg. She looked down through blurry eyes to see blood trailing down to her foot, her stockings and dress torn.

When they reached the bottom at last, Sonah gasped for air and looked up, still crying and screaming for help she soon realized would never come.

For the room they had brought her to was one she'd heard spoken of so rarely she'd assumed it was only a legend.

As her vision cleared, she saw a large man standing in the far corner of the room, his face blank and his eyes dead. Dressed in black, he had a leather apron over his jerkin, and his long, thinning grey hair pulled back so his sallow cheeks appeared more hollowed out.

He looked like Death.

The man watched as two guards shoved her into a wooden chair in front of what looked like a stone altar, tools or she knew not what strewn about, as if someone had dumped it all in a rush.

One guard kept a hand clamped on her shoulder, but Sonah was too frightened to move. She continued to plead and cry, asking them to send word to Prince Lerek when the other guard turned, his face red with violence, and backhanded her.

The slap was so vicious, her head snapped back and the world went black.

ORMANO HAD JUST FALLEN INTO BED WITH A CONTENTED SIGH WHEN someone pounded on his door, jolting him upright. He clutched the thin covers to his chest at another round of thwacking, louder and harder.

"Cleric Ormano!"

Orry scrambled from the bed and lunged for the door, yanking it open as he gaped at the offender.

The young guard's face was red and his eye twitched as he bit out, "We need to leave immediately. There's been an attack at the palace."

He turned without another word, leaving Orry to gawk at his

retreating back. Ormano shook his head and leaned out into the hall-way. "What sort of attack? What's happened?"

The guard didn't bother to turn around, his answer carrying across the dark hallway and into Orry's heart. "The princes. An attack on the princes."

Slamming the door shut, Orry burst into action. Snapping up his meager belongings, he shoved them into the small pack he'd brought with him.

Hurriedly tugging on his pants and robes over his light undershirt, Orry did not bother to fasten the hooks and loops to secure his robes as he hefted his pack across his shoulder. He yanked open his door and fled down the hallway and stairs until he reached the foyer.

Chaos greeted him.

He paused long enough to take in the soldiers moving about quickly and efficiently, shouting at each other with instructions or requests. Orry's eyes darted around, his mouth opened slightly as he eyed the organized frenzy. He darted out of the path of one soldier barreling right at him, and made himself as small as he could, despite his girth.

Orry squeezed past soldiers, wending his way toward the open double doors of the bathhouse entrance, and spied the general holding court outside. More shouts and orders erupted all around him as men gathered horses, some of them already leaping onto their backs and thundering down the cobblestones.

Orry's eyes were round as saucers as he made his way to the general. The man's usually ruddy face was even redder, his lips curled and snarling as he barked at the men closest to him. A path opened up as the men separated and Orry clutched at the pack strap across his chest as he leaned toward the general, cowering slightly as General Peleon pulled himself up to his full, considerable height.

Orry swallowed, hoping his voice wouldn't betray him as he tried his best not to show this man any fear. "What's happened, General?"

Peleon looked down his long nose at Orry, his lips thinned to a tight seam. "We make for Metilai. Someone's made a move on the princes."

"A move?" Orry asked, wincing as a soldier bumped into him from behind and barreled past. "But Isher's in Ermanel."

"He was at Metilai," came the gruff response.

"Is Lerek—are the princes all right?"

The general called out something to the soldier who appeared behind Orry. Orry whipped his head around, but the soldier was already gone, his strides carrying him past a group of men.

Orry turned back to the general who had turned away, his long legs crossing to the horses closest to them.

As he made to mount, Orry caught up to him, panting, and laid a hand on the general's arm. "Please," he gasped, "what of the princes? Are they all right? Is Lerek... Isher..."

General Peleon yanked his arm out of Orry's limp fingers and sneered down at him before mounting his stallion.

He tugged on the reins to turn away, then looked down at Orry, his dark brown eyes burning.

"Prince Lerek is dead."

CHAPTER NINE

Ormano's heart thundered in his chest for most of the backbreaking ride back to Metilai.

They had commandeered the ferry to Gall. Horses awaited them at the harbor and Orry was bone tired and heartsick by the time they raced through the gates of the White Palace.

The mood was dark in the courtyard. Soldiers everywhere. He yelped as someone grabbed his arm, the soft flesh instantly yielding to the general's iron grip. Orry lifted terrified eyes up to the tall man, whose face was like Death. He stumbled along as the general strode to the left of the courtyard, never pausing even as Orry struggled to keep up. By the time they'd reached the doorway leading to the bowels of the palace, Orry was gasping for air.

The dungeons were the worst in the empire for a reason. This was the last stop unless you were one of the lucky few sentenced to death.

From the dark, cold stone walls dripping with water and grime to the rats scurrying between legs and chairs, beneath filthy straw piled in the corners of the cells or inside old tin waste pails, this was a place not concerned with anyone's well-being.

Ormano fumbled inside his robes until he found the small ball of fabric, lifting the lavender scented kerchief to his nose and stumbled through the archway of yet another corridor. He held out one thick hand and accidentally slapped at General Peleon's back. He mumbled his apologies and smiled wanly back as Peleon's dark face scowled at him through the gloom. The older man's frown deepened, but he turned back, proceeding deeper into the disgusting catacombs.

"Well?"

Orry jumped at Peleon's barked demand.

General Peleon let out a huff and motioned Orry ahead of him. Orry did not need further prodding.

"All he wants is a yes or no," the general said. Orry's steps were slow, and he looked everywhere, shrinking more into himself the deeper into the catacombs they went. The darker it became, too, with torches spaced out at longer intervals, the sounds of their steps echoing and empty, adding to Orry's misery.

"Who, lord?"

"Who?" the general snapped. "Who do you think, you cockroach? The emperor!"

Orry winced and dug the kerchief harder against his face. He closed his eyes and gave a half shake of his head. General Peleon continued to frown.

"The accused?"

The general stopped a few feet behind him and Orry floundered along without light. He stopped and turned, taking a few tentative steps back toward the dim light of the general's torch, as if waiting for something to pop out and snatch him.

General Peleon lifted the torch in front of his face and the flash of hatred Orry saw on the older man's features made him cringe back as if he'd been hit in the face.

"She's in here," the general sneered.

Orry blinked, his eyes swiveling in the direction he'd indicated. Another black hole, hollow and deep behind thick iron bars. Orry looked back at the general. "She?"

"You can sit out here and question her," Peleon continued as if Orry hadn't spoken. He turned and motioned to someone behind him, and a young soldier came forward quickly with a chair. He dropped it at Orry's feet, the echoing clang shearing across Orry's already heightened nerves.

Before Orry could nod his thanks, the soldier scurried off. Orry grabbed the chair back with shaky fingers, adjusting it on the ground with great attention and careful consideration.

At last, he sat down—even that process taking exaggeratedly long as he fought to grasp hold of what was happening.

"General, if I may—"

"Is she a god, yes or no? That is all the emperor requires." General Peleon turned to leave, then paused. "Do not go inside, whatever the provocation. God or not, she is a trained killer and will snap your neck before she is even aware of who you are."

Ormano's hand flew to his throat, and he worked his mouth for several moments. General Peleon turned once more to leave.

"Wait!" Orry shrieked. The sound bounced off the stone and back at him. He winced. He pasted a smile on his face and said, "Lord, I beg you. I do not understand why I was summoned."

The general frowned. "High Cleric Christos said you are the most learned when it comes to the gods. Are you not?"

Orry laughed, a nervous reflex. "Of course, yes, but—"

"Then you know why you are here. We have a murderer, at the very least. A god at the worst." He loomed over Orry, his eyes filled with such loathing, Orry cowered. "And before you render your decision, know that before she was apprehended, no less than five of the Imperial Guard swore to Captain Xoran she used some sort of power on them, as well as Prince Isher, when she tried to kill him. There hasn't been a god for centuries and the emperor wants it verified because he plans a public execution. So. We await your judgement."

The general turned sharply, shoved the torch into a sconce and left, his boots clipped and loud before fading away, leaving Orry alone.

Orry wiped a hand across his mouth and looked back into the darkness where General Peleon had been. The light from the torch danced around, but mostly, the gloom won. Orry glanced back at the cell where General Peleon had mentioned a prisoner—a woman—was being held. Leaning forward in his seat, Orry stretched out his left hand, but it barely touched the torch. He tried again, leaning until the chair was on two legs and finally grabbed hold. He held it in front of him, hoping he'd see something.

"Hello?" he called out weakly.

There was quiet shuffling in the darkness, jealously hiding whoever was in the cell.

He tried again. "Hello?"

Orry heard a sigh and then the sound of metal hitting the iron bars as a bruised and bloody hand wrapped around the iron.

"Ormano?"

TERENA WAS STARTLED AWAKE. HER BODY STILL ACHED, BUT AT LEAST her head was not pounding as much as earlier. She turned her head slowly. Satisfied her nausea had gone, she moved her head some more, looking around to get her bearings.

It was dark. She must be in the dungeons. She'd only seen them once when she and Croak had gone exploring, quickly hustling out as the Royal Inquisitor rounded a corner and scolded them for being there. Terena was glad to have Croak with her; the Royal Inquisitor was a terrifying man in social settings but alone in the dungeons is something she didn't want to imagine.

Now, she wouldn't have to.

He'd been the first to question her after the guards had beaten her before dragging her down to this cell. He'd taken the fingernails from her right hand first. Terena recalled every second of that, but nothing after. She'd woken to see the Royal Inquisitor sitting in his chair, watching her with his soulless eyes, his face mild as if he was about to have dinner.

Terena closed her eyes and willed the nausea to settle. She didn't think she'd ever forget what happened next.

Heavy irons banded her wrists. From the pain that arced down her right arm, she was sure it was broken.

As she maneuvered up, Terena pushed her bottom along the ground and up against something. She pulled her broken limb to her lap, cradling it with her left hand. Crying out, she lifted her hand to see blood crusted where the tip of her smallest finger should have been. The chains rattled as she shook.

Breathing slowly, she could hear more chains rattling somewhere off to her right and mutterings and whimpers closer, but could not tell where either came from. It did not matter. She could do nothing but sit and wait and hope her body recovered enough before her jailers came down to interrogate her some more.

She must have fallen asleep again. When she next woke, a dull light danced around the gloomy area beyond the bars. Having slumped over while she'd slept, Terena moved her shoulder on the dirty stone floor, sliding her hip up to pull her leg under her. She gasped as a sharp pain raced up her leg to her hip and she almost passed out. Terena lay back against the ground and gave in to tears again.

"...and question her."

Terena's eyes flew open. She tilted her head toward the bars of her cell, sure she'd heard something, someone. A sharp clatter followed, and she winced.

Voices again. One soft, timid... familiar? The other voice she knew, beyond doubt. His words were short and clipped in his high nasal pitch, so at odds with the harsh countenance of the man she'd had to suffer while in the emperor's employment. His brother, General Peleon, was not someone you'd easily forget.

"We await your judgement," General Peleon was saying. Terena heard his boots echo in the cave as he walked away.

She shifted again, slithering closer to the bars. She blinked—one eye so swollen she couldn't open it—until the film over the other was gone and she could see torchlight wavering closer.

"Hello?" the timid voice said at last. Terena stared out, and the torch moved again. The faint outline of a cowl became visible, then a silver chain, then the pinched, round face of an old friend. She reached out a shaky hand and wrapped it around the iron bar in front of her.

"Ormano?" she whispered, hopeful and incredulous.

The torch arced to her right as her friend pitched forward, grasping the bars in both hands. She smiled to see his face, then started crying.

"Terena!"

Her eyes closed, and she sobbed, succumbing to the aches tearing through her body.

"Terena, please," Ormano said, his voice low and urgent. "Please stop this now. You need to help me, Terena! You need to tell me what in hells is going on!"

Terena's sobs turned to mewling sounds, and she hated herself for the weakness taking over. She'd never been so hopeless in her life and was sure the grief crashing over her now would finally break her.

"Terena! Focus! We haven't much time," he hissed, his voice pleading.

She opened her mouth on a gasp and opened her eye. Only the dark of the ceiling greeted her, so she turned her head to look at her friend.

"I..." she muttered something, then sniffled and coughed.

"Focus!"

"He's dead, Orry," she whimpered, her voice breaking.

"Gods, Terena," Orry's mouth opened as he stared at her in horror. His eyes watered. "Your face..."

She coughed again, the tang of copper in her mouth. "Lerek is dead. And I—"

"I know, love, I know. I'm so sorry," he whispered. "They told me, but... how? Did you... oh, Terena. Did you kill him? Is that why you—"

"No!" she snarled, her voice sharp and almost normal for the first time. It cost her, though. Her body screamed in protest. She cradled her sore head, wincing when she moved her broken arm.

"Terena?"

Something tugged at her sleeve. The wave of nausea passed, and she turned to Ormano.

"Terena, please, are you awake?"

"Barely," she whispered back. She heard his sigh of relief and felt again the slight tug on her filthy tunic.

"Tell me as much as you can," he said, his voice louder and desperate. Terena fought to keep her eye open.

"He's dead, Orry," she said again, her voice breaking on a sob.

"What happened?" Ormano demanded.

Terena opened and closed her mouth several times. At last she said, "I don't know. I... he was to meet me, and he was late, so I... I searched for him, Orry."

"Where was he? Where did you find him?"

Terena choked back more tears. She sighed. "On the terrace. His rooms. Isher was there. I didn't know he was back. It looked like they'd been drinking, but..."

"But what, Terena?" he asked after a long pause. His voice was softer now, soothing.

"He was just... lying there." Her mouth trembled so badly she clenched her jaw tight to still it. When she was sure of herself once more, she continued. "I went closer and saw him on the ground and when I bent down I saw... there was so much blood, Orry. What that bastard did to his own brother!"

She spasmed with a coughing fit, her body crying out in protest, and she was helpless with it. She didn't care. Nothing mattered anymore.

Her coughing turned into sobs, and she was choking on the phlegm and tears. She didn't care.

Ormano stretched out a hand and although she was too far to reach for it, his nearness calmed her. Orry said nothing for a long time.

"Terena," he said at last, "did you kill Isher?"

She laughed. It was not a cheerful sound. She lifted her left hand slowly and wiped at the snot over her mouth. "I'm not sure. I hope so. They caught me before I could."

"What did you do?"

Here she paused. She squinted her good eye against the darkness of the cell, trying to see beyond, into the past, into that moment when she had Isher in her hands.

Then she remembered.

"I never touched him," she said, her voice barely above a whisper. "And yet I choked him. I remember the feel of his throat as it strained against me. His body quaked, fighting me." She turned her head to her friend. "But I never touched him, Orry. I never touched him. How can this be?"

Ormano's hand froze between the bars.

"Terena," he began, then cleared his throat, "Terena, when the soldiers came for me, they didn't tell me anything about why they were seeking me. We came straight from Laurica, and General Peleon brought me here.

"I asked, several times, but instead of answering me, he told me to find out if you are a god." He scoffed. "I did not know it was you I was to question, Terena, and other than finding out if you are a god, Peleon said nothing more."

He snapped his fingers and hissed at her when she turned her head away, "Who's spoken with you? Gods, you look like shit. Was it the Royal Inquisitor?"

She whimpered and muttered something, but couldn't form words. It took several tries and lots of finger snapping from Orry before she said, "Get me out of here."

"Get..! Get you out of here?" He laughed, and it sounded more like a squeak. "Peleon thinks you killed one prince and were close to killing the other! You are not getting out of here, Ren. Best you can hope for is they believe me when I tell them you most assuredly are not a god!"

"Are you sure?" she whispered back.

This time, when he laughed, it sounded hollow. "You don't have adamantine chains on, so they can't seriously think you are."

She scoffed.

"Now is not the time for your games, sweetheart," Orry said. "The palace is looking to hang you and here you are jesting."

"Orry," she said, exasperated at yet another round of finger snapping when she closed her eye. "Remember when we went to Forasa, when they were inducting the new priest there?"

Orry stopped snapping and sat silently. She almost smiled.

"We raced up the mountain," he whispered.

"Yes," she said, and this time she allowed herself a small lift of her lips as she recalled the laughter and then the sheer terror.

"Isher's horse startled at something," Orry said. "I don't remember what. He would've fallen down the side—"

"If I hadn't grabbed his arm."

"Indeed," he said.

"How did I catch him?"

Silence. Then, "What do you mean?"

Terena sighed. "How did I catch him, Orry? He went over the edge. I was still on my horse when he fell."

"Well, you—hmm. I don't remember the details, Ren. We were children. I remember him going over and you on your stomach pulling him up. And then Croak and Lerek were there, too."

"You know, Orry," she whispered and turned her head back toward the ceiling. Tears slipped down her temples. "You've always known."

He was silent for a time. Somewhere deeper in the catacombs, someone screamed and metal clanked. Terena heard Orry shift, his sandals scrapping the stone floor.

"You're right. I wondered at first. Of course, I did. When I first met you and Croak, you and I were eight years old. A year later, you were... different. You were suddenly so interested in myths. In the gods. The Olympians. Then Croak—that idiot!—slipped once when we were older. Right after you'd become a tracker. I asked him why you didn't want to be a Lady. After all, your father was Captain of the Imperial Guard. All you had to do was look pretty and nab a husband. Croak laughed and said you had no interest in that. He said being a tracker would help you find your birth parents." Orry smiled as if recalling that moment. "We only talked about it one time, and he never came out and said it, but I knew. And he knew I knew, but I swore to him I would never say anything to anyone about it. And I never have. No one knows Lorence wasn't your real father."

He reached over and gripped one of her fingers. "Why do you think I became a cleric? It was the best way I knew to help in your search."

Terena dropped her forehead against the bars and cried. He leaned forward and kissed her hair.

"But this is not the place for such revelations, Terena," he said at last, his voice rough. He cleared his throat. "I will, of course, tell the general and the emperor himself you are *not* a god, only a particularly strong female whose years of training have certainly rendered her stronger than the prince. Peleon said five guards have sworn you used... powers on them, but I will stand by my word as I am the expert and they are brutes."

"And what of Isher? He'll have told him his version as well. You would contradict him?"

Orry snorted. "Again, who is the expert? Besides, he could've been drunk, or smoking, or both. In fact, I'll ask to go see the terrace. Hopefully no one's disturbed anything there, yet."

Terena shifted, trying to sit up straight. As the pain arced up her broken arm and bruised leg, Terena cried out, but managed to prop herself against the bars to face her friend. "Yes, please. Go up there as soon as you leave here. If you're stopped, tell them you need to inspect where I was to determine if, in fact, I had used any powers."

"Why the hells would I say that? It will only—"

"I need your eyes!" she hissed and then winced as white hot pain wracked her aching body. When she could speak again, she said, "I need you to tell me every detail of what the terrace looks like. Smell the glasses and the wine if there's any left. Look for signs of a struggle near where Lerek was found. And see if you can find Sonah Yahn. She would've been there as well, to taste his wine. I don't know how long she might've stayed, but she should know something. I need to piece together what happened and I need your help to do that. Will you do that for me?"

Orry was silent.

"Orry? Can you do that?"

"Aye," he whispered. "Aye, of course, Ren. Of course I will."

She sighed and closed her eyes. "Thank you."

She heard him shuffle and knew he was leaving. He did not speak as he took a few steps further away, but then stopped. "And if it's as they say? That you—"

"I did not kill him, Orry," Terena said.

She turned her head and narrowed her eyes at him. "I loved him. I did not kill him. But if Isher did, I will kill *him*."

SONAH SHIVERED IN HER SHIFT, THE ONLY CLOTHING THEY'D ALLOWED her after they'd stripped her of her dress, stockings and shoes. They even took the ribbon from her hair. Wiping her nose on her wrist, she sniffed again, no longer caring.

She stared down at the top of the table. Sonah had cried off and on for hours, having seen or heard no one since they dumped her in this room.

Sonah looked up, chancing a look around the small room. Blinking away the tears, she realized she was in the maids's dining room.

She huffed out a sigh, and it hitched as she swallowed, so glad she was back in the palace proper and not...

The door opened, and she stiffened, dropping her gaze to her lap. She might not be in the dungeons anymore, but she sure as hells was not being cared for as befitting her station. She had a good idea she'd done something terrible, though she did not know what could be so bad, this was the consequence.

"I am sorry they brought you to the dungeons," a silky, high-pitched voice called out, and Sonah shook. Hearing that voice directed at her made Sonah quail.

The general sat across from her, but she still wouldn't look up at him. "Captain Cortis was overzealous."

Silence.

Pretend he isn't there. Pretend this is a dream.

"You went to the terrace? With the princes?"

Sonah didn't respond.

Something clattered on the table, and Sonah jumped. She looked across the table and saw the general had dropped his dagger on it. She lifted wide eyes to him. Cold, blank eyes stared back.

"Were you with the princes, yes or no?"

"No."

"No?" The general scowled. "Lady Maranou said you were called to Prince Lerek's rooms that evening before dinner."

"Aye," Sonah said, blinking in confusion.

"Then why did you lie when I asked if you were with them?"

Shaking her head, Sonah opened her mouth. The general leaned forward, startling her.

"Only Isher—Prince Isher was there."

He nodded. "Good." He leaned in, dark eyes narrowed. "And did you drink the wine? You tasted it before Prince Isher, aye?"

Sonah nodded. "Aye."

"And yet," Peleon bit out, "Prince Isher says he was drugged. And Prince Lerek must have been, too. Now, Prince Lerek is dead, along with his guard. Their throats were slashed."

Sonah's head snapped up, mouth hanging open. She tried several times to say something, but her throat wouldn't work, her lips opening and closing uselessly as tears gathered behind her eyes.

"Where were you?"

"Prince Lerek is dead?"

"Where were you?"

"What?"

"Where were you? Where did you go after the terrace?"

"I—" Sonah stopped, eyes searching the tabletop for an answer.

General Peleon slammed his hand on the table and Sonah jumped.

"Who are you working with?"

"Please…"

"Who did you let into the prince's rooms?"

"I didn't!"

"So, *you* killed the prince? His guard?" the general sneered.

"No! Of course not! I—"

"You are going to be executed," General Peleon said, as if announcing he was going fishing in the morning.

Sonah's eyes swam with tears, dread slowly washing over her chest. "But I didn't... I didn't do it. I didn't do *anything!* Please. Please, where's Lady Maranou—"

"You will die. You and that traitorous bitch."

Sonah couldn't breathe. Her chest hurt and she tried sucking in air, but her throat closed up. She hurt all over, was cold and terrified, and now she couldn't breathe and would drop dead right there.

General Peleon stood, sheathed his dagger and walked to the door. He lifted the latch and swung the door open wide before turning back to her. "In the morning, I'll give you one last opportunity to confess who conspired with you. Who you're protecting. If you do, I'll make sure the emperor grants you a quick death. If you don't, you'll be drawn and quartered, along with Terena Luca."

CHAPTER TEN

C roak groaned and turned over, pulling the thin blanket over his head against the sunlight shining on him. He heard shuffling nearby, but didn't bother to look. He'd left money on the table and hoped the blanket would forestall any conversation.

Eventually, he heard the soft click of the door as it shut.

He must not have left the correct amount; a moment later, banging almost cracked the door, and he jumped out of bed in confusion and fear.

"What the hells is all this about, eh?" he shouted as he rummaged around the room for his pants. "If it's wrong, tell me how much I owe—"

"Croak? Open the bloody door!"

Croak paused with his shirt half on and frowned. "Benson?"

"Aye, it's bloody Benson, y' fool! Open up, quickly!"

Croak mumbled profanity under his breath as he hitched on his pants, padding to the door in bare feet. No sooner had he unlatched the door than Benson the Blacksmith burst through, slamming it shut behind him. His eyes were wild and his face ashen.

"What the—"

"Listen to me boy," Benson rushed ahead, reaching one shaky hand to paw at Croak's shoulder.

"Well, you—"

"Listen!" Benson hissed. He wiped a hand across his mouth and Croak could not remember a time when he'd ever seen Benson in such a state. He shook from head to toe and looked as white as a corpse.

Benson took a deep breath. "Yer sister's been arrested."

Croak blinked. "What now?"

"She's been arrested, boy!" Benson said, his voice breaking. "She—she—on suspicion of murderin' Prince Lerek."

Croak's mouth dropped open as the blood drained from his face. He sobered up quickly. "*What?*"

Benson nodded his head repeatedly, wringing his weathered hands. He wiped his mouth again and continued. "An' fer th' attempted murder of Prince Isher."

Croak's knees buckled, and he dropped to the wood floor. "Wha—"

Benson rushed over and grabbed Croak's arm, shaking him. "No time for that, boy! They mean to try her an' execute 'er in two days!"

Croak shook all over. His mind tried to make sense of what the old smith was saying but he couldn't make his mind keep up. He fought through the haze of booze to focus on Benson's words.

Lerek dead.

That was unreal enough. But that Terena had killed him was too much for him to process.

His head throbbed and Croak hunched over, his forehead resting on the cool floor as Benson continued to shake him. He mumbled something at the old man, hoping to get him to stop, batting at his beefy hand ineffectually.

"For Sassia's sake, son! Get yer arse up! Wash yerself an' I'll 'ave Ditta bring ya up some mulled cider an' bread. Soak some of that ale outta ya."

Croak moaned and fell over onto his side. Eyes closed against the painful light, he heard the old man rise and grumble his way out of the room. He inhaled deeply, trying to steady the pounding in his head.

Lerek dead.

Terena accused.

Lerek dead.

Soft, muling cries turned to heavy sobs, wracking Croak's body. He curled into himself, drawing his knees to his chin as he ground his head into the floor.

"Come now, come now," Benson said a short time later. His rough voice, for once, sounded almost soothing as he bent his big frame low and scooped up Croak's limp body like a baby.

He carried him the few steps to the bed and Croak realized someone else was in the room. Shuffling sounded on the other side of the bed and someone whispered to Benson. The old man replied, but Croak was too broken to care. He let the old smith prop pillows behind his head and shift him about without protest.

"Bring me that cup," Benson said and Croak caught sight of a slight arm as it crossed in front of his blurry eyes. Something was at his lips and the old man murmured to him, but a fresh wave of memories assailed him and he succumbed once more to despair.

"Lerek," he sobbed, that one word making Benson stiffen and stop his ministrations.

"I know," Benson answered, and tried again to coax Croak to drink. He turned his head away and tried to raise a hand in protest.

"Come, now, y' must at least try," Benson cajoled. He heard the rustle of fabric to his right and then a soft voice saying something about more cider and a bowl of fresh water. Benson muttered a response and before long, they were alone.

The bed gave as Benson sat and braced his arm across Croak, bringing his face uncomfortably close to his.

"Listen, now, shhhhh, shhhh," Benson crooned and slapped gently at Croak's cheek. "Y'must push this down, far down now boy, so as y'can focus on yer sister."

Croak turned his face away and sniffed back snot.

"Boy, I ken how y' feel, I do," Benson said, his voice softer than

Croak had ever heard and perhaps the reason it pierced through Croak's fog. "Ye must think of yer sister. Terena. Terena is th' most important thin' right now. An' ye must get 'er free."

Croak focused on the old man's lips as they moved in a litany: *Think of Terena. She is all that matters now. Get her free, boy.*

"How?" Croak whispered, his voice breaking. "How do I free her and I don't even fucking know what's going on?"

He raked his hand through his hair, sobbing anew and Benson's big arms folded over him. "I'll give ye this one moment. This one moment only, boy. Get it all out. But ye need t' get goin' soon. Get t' Metilai an' find out where theys keepin' her."

Croak dug his head into the crook of the old smith's arm, wiping his nose on the man's tunic. "How the fuck am I getting her out, then, Benson?" he shoved absently against Benson's embrace. "If you'll recall, she is the clever one of our duo."

"Go to the harbor, see if any of th' mercs headin' north can be 'ired for a few days. If ye can get two or three ye can give 'er a chance. The rest she'll make sure of 'erself, ye know it."

Croak wiped his snot on his sleeve while his mind raced at Benson's words.

He looked about the room, unseeing, instead envisioning the escape he could mount with muscle to help.

"When's the ferry to Gall?" he asked at length.

Benson shrugged and rose from the bed. "Runs every day at six bells."

Croak dug the heels of his hands into his eyes and took a deep breath, heaving it back out and bolting from the bed. He moved with purpose, gathering his things, then tied his cloak on.

As he strode for the door, he glanced back at Benson. "Thank you, Benson."

Benson grabbed his arm as he reached for the latch. "I'll 'ire a boy to bring yer 'orse to Metilai. Just mind ye catch th' ferry in an 'our if ye want t' reach 'er in time, aye?"

Croak nodded and swung the door wide, all but running down the corridor.

CROAK STUCK TO THE BACK ALLEYS AS HE MADE FOR THE HARBOR. THE streets were packed with refugees and merchants, and he heard news of Lerek's death everywhere he passed. He got snippets of information as he strode purposefully toward the boardwalk.

If possible, it was even more crowded than the city streets, the piers packed with all manner of humanity. The small port city was experiencing a boom it was not ready for and the amount of time it took Croak to reach the boats was testament to how quickly the political landscape had changed even this tiny town.

He pursed his lips, looking out over the sea of sailors and slaves and businessmen and taxmen and anyone else who could find some way to earn a coin. His eye caught on two swift moving forms.

Croak narrowed his gaze, and his mouth opened. He spotted the Roisan first—Gabriol—his big head of blond braids and even bigger body giving him away as he plowed forward. He had strapped on his hauberk and looked a giant in the daylight, pushing at the inflow of people all around as if they were nothing more than annoying gnats.

Croak froze, watching him before he shifted his gaze to the smaller but no less powerful figure of his friend, his red beard and the earrings glinting a path up his ear, marking them both as the men he'd met at Nathaniel's.

"Mother fu—!" he muttered then tore a path through to the mercs, uncaring and unheeding of the curses and screeching in his wake.

"...FUCKER," GABRIOL MUTTERED, HALTING IN THE MIDDLE OF THE street. Rydon smacked into him. Voices of various dialects sounded all around him as he leaned forward to yell into Gabriol's ear.

"What the fuck!"

"Yeah, that's what I say," Gabriol said and nodded toward someone making their way through the press of bodies. Rydon followed his gaze and cursed anew under his breath.

As the lanky young man from the tavern came toward them, Rydon stepped in front of Gabriol with his arm stretched in front of him.

"Wait! I need—*oof*," Croak doubled over as Rydon planted his fist into the young man's stomach.

"What did I say," he hissed in Croak's face, "What did I say would happen, Croak? Did I not say you'd regret crossing paths with us again?"

Croak spit and shuddered, lifting his head enough Rydon could see the deathly pallor in his cheeks and puffiness of his eyes. He frowned and held the young man by the shoulders as he appeared to be about to faint.

"Please," he whispered, over and over, hanging his head. Rydon looked over at Gabriol with a frown, and his friend shrugged. Rydon shook Croak, trying to peer at his face.

"What's happened?" he asked.

Croak shook his head and Rydon had the uncomfortable feeling the young man was about to cry. He quickly pulled him off to the side and away from the jostling of sailors and merchant traffic to a building near the boardwalk where there was more privacy. Croak stumbled along, wiping at his mouth and nose.

When they reached the building, he thrust Croak against the wall and held a hand to his chest to keep him upright. "Speak."

Croak took several long seconds composing himself. When he raised his face, Rydon could see resolve. He knew what he risked in seeking them out and yet sought them out anyway. The man was either a glutton for punishment or in some serious trouble.

"I need your help. I will pay, of course, but we need to leave quickly. For Gall."

Rydon raised his brows and cast a quick glance at Gabriol, who stepped closer. "Gall?"

Croak nodded. He squared his shoulders and almost seemed as if he could stand on his own again, though Rydon continued to hold fast to his chest. "As I said, I will pay, and even pay for passage north when we're done, but we must leave now."

"What's in Gall?" Gabriol asked, shifting so they were shielded from view.

"First, I must secure your agreement. I will pay you two hundred silver if you agree, and another three hundred if we succeed."

Gabriol lifted his hand to his mouth, eyes wide as he took in the sum, but Rydon pushed in closer. "And what do we need to succeed in?"

"I need your agreement," Croak said, his bloodshot eyes never wavering from Rydon's.

"Young man, I can see whatever's happened is serious indeed, and if you're offering that sum, it must be dangerous as well." He frowned and took his hand away, leaving Croak to sway for a second before he stiffened his spine.

Rydon glanced at Gabriol and put his hands on his hips. "I can't, in good faith, lead my man into a situation without first knowing what we're getting into." He motioned with his hand. "Come, tell us what you need and I'll give you my answer."

Croak's face twisted and Rydon had a moment's sympathy for the youth's dilemma. He softened his face, deciding to help him out. "Does this have anything to do with the news out of Metilai this morning?"

Croak's head swiveled between the two as Gabriol crossed his arms at his chest. He looked back at Rydon and pursed his lips. Then gave a quick nod.

"All right," Rydon said with another glance at his friend. "How does Prince Lerek's death involve you?"

Croak opened and closed his mouth several times and then cursed. "Lerek...," he started, his voice breaking. "The prince was a friend."

Rydon and Gabriol exchanged glances once more.

"You wish to avenge him?" Gabriol asked. "General Peleon will have that well in hand, boy."

The muscles in Croak's neck jumped. Rydon motioned again with his hand as he would to a child, his face softened by the youth's obvious despair. "Speak now, young Croak."

"Yes, I wish to avenge him," he snarled as he looked at Gabriol, then turned his gaze back to Rydon. "But that must wait. My sister's been accused of the crime and I wish your help to secure her release."

Rydon looked over at Gabriol, who shared his shock and almost laughed. He quickly masked his sudden interest with curious politeness and shrugged. "Her release will be difficult to secure, Croak. If she killed the prince, she—"

"She did *not* kill him!" Croak said so vehemently, spittle flew from his mouth. His cheeks colored and his eyes filled with a rage Rydon knew all too well.

"And you're sure of this how?"

"She loved him," Croak whispered, his lips trembling.

Rydon did not dare look at Gabriol, instead nodding his head at Croak. If he knew the prince well enough to call him by name in mixed company, then Rydon was sure the sister was indeed the woman he and Gabriol had been sent to find.

Without giving himself away, he pursed his lips as if in thought. At last he said, "For the sake of argument, let us agree your sister did not kill the prince. How do you propose we secure her release? She'll be in the dungeons, guarded by the Imperial Guard. Most likely she's been questioned too, so in no state to—"

"I know the palace inside and out," Croak hissed as he leaned forward aggressively. Gabriol made a move toward him, but Rydon raised a hand to stop him. "She's a tracker. I know the northern king is looking for trackers. You are as well. You're looking for Terena Luca, my sister. That's why I sought you out in the first place. Help me rescue Terena and you'll be richer for it. On my honor. "

At the mention of her name, Gabriol turned away and Rydon dropped his gaze to the ground so Croak would not see his smile. When he'd composed himself, he lifted his head and nodded grimly at the young man.

"So, securing her release as rescue, not negotiation?"

Croak gave another curt nod.

"Very well, Croak. We will help with your sister's rescue. But the price is four hundred silver now, and another four when we escape. Deal?"

Gabriol almost gave away the game as he looked at Rydon in shock. Rydon did not dare take his eyes off of Croak. He knew the difficulty of the young man's position, but he did not wish to make him suspicious by immediately agreeing to rescue the tracker without at least haggling over the price.

Croak nodded curtly, then straightened his jerkin. "We are agreed. How quickly can you be ready?"

Rydon spread his arms and smiled grimly. "We are ready now, young lord. Gather your things; we leave anon."

CHAPTER ELEVEN

Terena sat back against the cool stone and closed her eyes. She'd awakened not long ago but wasn't sure what time of day or night it was. The meals were sporadic, and between beatings and sleep, she hadn't kept track of time.

The general had yet to come and see her. Part of her thought it a blessing—maybe he'd believed Ormano's assessment and hadn't bothered to check for himself.

Voices drifted nearby and she moved into a crouch, her one good eye blinking in the dimness of the cell. As they neared, she heard whimpers and sobs, scuffling on the floor as if something—someone —was being dragged.

Terena moved closer, reaching out with her bruised left hand and lightly grasped an iron bar. As she peered out, she saw two Imperial Guard dragging someone between them, the small figure slumped over. General Peleon appeared behind them and Terena jerked back, careful to stay out of his sight as she watched.

The guards dropped their burden into the empty cell across from hers and one of them locked the gate before moving back. The general sauntered closer to whatever poor soul they'd dumped in there.

"Your father's been sent for, but according to his steward is in

Ermanel," the general said. Terena leaned closer. "I fear he won't make it in time for your execution, but we'll make sure your body is prepared for when he arrives."

The general paced in front of the cell, his head down, thoughtful. "Of course, I will tell him I gave you every opportunity to confess your co-conspirators, and you refused. I can only assume that means someone you love is involved, so perhaps I'll detain your father when he gets here."

No response from the figure shadowed in the cell. Terena couldn't make out any movement at all.

Long seconds passed before the general shook his head and made to leave. The figure rustled in the rushes on the ground. Thin arms came into view as pale hands grasped the iron bars.

"Please, I beg you," the person whimpered and Terena startled.

Was that a girl? Gods, he put a child down here? She sounded as if she was ten.

"Please," the voice sobbed again, "I am not conspiring with *anyone!*" That last was screamed at the general, a face finally appearing through the bars.

Terena's blood drained from her face.

Sonah Yahn.

They had Sonah Yahn in a cell.

"You were with both princes when it happened. Prince Isher confirmed for us you did, in fact, taste the wine before either of the princes drank it and then you left."

Terena's eyes narrowed.

So. Isher had survived her attack.

"He claims he was drugged," the general continued, "has no memory of anything after that until he was attacked by Terena Luca."

At this, Peleon looked over his shoulder at Terena's cell. She let him see the hatred that burned on her face when she stared back.

"Is that who you're protecting? Did Terena Luca put you up to this?"

"Terena wouldn't do that," Sonah said, her voice weak, her forehead against the bars of her cell.

Sympathy speared through Terena when she saw the bruise marring the young woman's left temple, how pale she was. "She loved Prince Lerek. She would never harm him."

"And yet she attacked Prince Isher!" Peleon's voice boomed as he pivoted, his eyes boring into Terena's, his face thunderous. "He begged her to stop, but she tried to kill him." His eyes narrowed when he spoke again, directly to Terena. "The guards heard her, ran to help their prince while she brutally attacked him!"

"No," Sonah said, her voice firm. The general snapped his head back to her, crouching down so his body blocked her from Terena's view.

"Yes!" he hissed at her. "Yes, she attacked him. My men were there, and the prince confirmed it. When he finally woke up after what she'd done to him!"

Peleon threw Terena a scathing look before turning back to Sonah. "If you don't confess, you will die alongside her. And your father will stand trial for putting you up to this."

At first, only silence met the general's harsh words.

Then, a soft laugh.

Terena blinked.

Sonah's laugh turned louder, until it was a hysterical cackle. Full bodied and harsh, she laughed until the general rose.

"My father," Sonah said between bouts of laughter, then laughed even louder. Peleon motioned to one guard, and the man stepped forward to unlock the cell. As he heaved open the door, Peleon lunged inside and dropped low, viciously landing two quick punches on the girl.

Terena winced when the laughter abruptly stopped. She flinched again as another punch landed. Sonah only grunted, silent at last.

"I can't wait to see you pulled apart tomorrow," Peleon snarled down at her, then stood. He spat at the ground or on Sonah—Terena couldn't tell—before striding out of the cell. The guard surged forward to close and lock the door.

General Peleon didn't bother to look at Terena as he strode out of the dungeons, the guards following behind.

Terena waited a minute more, listening after their departure—silence broken up by the quiet sobs coming from Sonah's cell.

"Sonah," she called out.

No response.

"Sonah."

The crying stopped. Terena heard rustling as Sonah shifted. A long moment passed before she shuffled back to the bars and Terena saw her peeking out, her eyes blinking as she glanced around.

"Hello?"

Her soft voice cracked and Terena closed her eyes. "Sonah, it's me. It's Terena."

"Terena?" Her voice was so hopeful Terena felt a pang in her heart.

"I'm across from you."

She saw Sonah look in her direction so she held out her bruised hand through the bars and waved. "It's me, Sonah. I'm here."

Sonah saw her and the moment she did she started sobbing anew.

"Sonah, please," she said soothingly. "Honey, I know, I know."

Her words only caused the poor girl to cry harder.

Terena listened to her cry a little longer.

"Shhhh, Sonah," she crooned, "honey, listen to me, please. Can you do that for me?"

She watched the girl as she nodded, closing her mouth and with an effort Terena knew was difficult, she controlled her hitching breaths and wiped at the tears on her cheeks.

"Good," Terena soothed, "good. Take your time, Sonah, take your time. And when you're ready, can you tell me what happened? Where they've kept you since... since that night? Anything at all?"

The girl nodded again, exhaling raggedly. Terena smiled at her, then the girl opened her eyes to meet Terena's gaze.

"I don't know what happened," she said, her words a whimper. She shuddered, her next words stronger. "I was walking outside with Lady Maranou. It was shortly after dinner."

Terena nodded encouragingly.

"We heard noises near the courtyard entrance, then a guard came running out to speak with Captain Cortis and then they dragged me away." She wiped at her lip and winced.

"Someone hit me. Hard enough I don't remember what happened after that," Sonah said and sniffled. She wiped her nose on her wrist. "At first they brought me down here. I don't know how long. When I woke up, I was in the kitchens. You know, the room where the female servants take their meals?"

Terena nodded.

Sonah closed her eyes, her face crumpling. "The general came in and started questioning me, asking me all kinds of things that made no sense. Who was I working with? Who told me to drug the princes?" She sighed and wiped at her eyes. "I didn't know what he meant. No idea why I was even there. I begged him to tell me what was going on, but he got angrier and angrier. He wouldn't let me see Sybil, Lady Maranou. Wouldn't—"

"Sonah, breathe," Terena said, her voice firm.

She watched as the girl took big gulps of air, nodding her head as she tried to control herself.

At length, Terena asked, "Are you okay to go on?"

Sonah nodded.

"Good," Terena said softly, calm. "All right. Let's go back to when you last saw… Prince Lerek. Was Isher with him?"

Sonah shook her head. "Prince Lerek wasn't there. Only Isher."

Terena started. "What? Are you sure?"

Sonah nodded. "Aye." She sniffed. "I thought it was Prince Lerek at first, though."

"Was anyone else there?"

"No."

"No guards?"

"There was one at the door, as always. And another just inside the room."

Terena nodded. "And Alexi?"

"He wasn't there."

But he was there when Terena was in the room. There had been three dead guards. The one near the door; Alexi on the settee. The third on the terrace near Lerek.

Terena frowned, thoughtful for a few moments, then lifted her gaze to Sonah.

"Good, Sonah. Can you do me a favor? Can you tell me if Isher had already been drinking?"

The girl tilted her head but didn't answer. Terena watched her as she waited.

After a long pause, Sonah shook her head and said, "No, I don't believe so. I walked in and saw Isher—Prince Isher," Sonah corrected herself and lifted her eyes to Terena in apology, "and I went over and hugged him. I didn't know he was even in Metilai until I saw him. Anyway, then I drank some wine, and we chatted a bit and then I left. Oh! Before I left he hugged me but... he looked so sad about it."

A short silence filled the space between them while Terena thought on what Sonah had shared.

"And you weren't sick at all? Afterwards, I mean. Didn't feel dizzy or tired?"

"No. Nothing. It tasted like it always does. I was fine. Well... I was dizzy at one point, but I think it's because I stood too fast. Right before I left."

Terena caught on that for a second and filed it away for consideration later.

"Only one decanter?"

"I wasn't paying attention, sorry," Sonah said. "Did you know Isher grew out his hair?"

Terena looked over at the girl. "What?"

"It was weird," Sonah said, almost to herself. "I know it's been a while since he's been to the palace but... I always thought... anyway, he had it long. Like Prince Lerek likes to wear it. They looked more alike than ever. I mean... obviously."

Terena frowned. In all the years she'd known the princes, she'd never seen Isher style his hair anything like Lerek's. He prided himself on his individuality. When she recalled the events of that night, she didn't remember Isher looking different.

"Anything else you remember?" she asked after a pause.

Sonah shook her head.

"Was it... do *you* remember? What happened that night?"

Terena hung her head.

"I'm sorry. That was stupid."

The silence stretched before Terena heard Sonah shift, the rushes beneath her rustling as she moved to lean her side against the bars, then she hung one arm out.

"Your father will come for you, Sonah," Terena said into the quiet. "He'll come, and you will be spared. The emperor can't afford to have such a powerful ally as an enemy by executing his daughter."

Sonah snorted.

"It's true," Terena said. "He needs your father. Now more than ever. He's about to commit his army in the south. To attack Sparta. Solon's been planning it for a long time. There's a legion in Elis right now. And now there's a new king in the north. And with Lerek murdered..." Terena grabbed hold of the bars with her left hand and leaned out as far as she could. "Your father's support is crucial to him —Solon needs his army. He wouldn't risk breaking that alliance because you didn't get sick from the wine. There could be a thousand reasons you weren't affected. Your father will come, you'll see. And they'll have to free you."

When Terena stopped speaking, she heard it.

Crying.

"Sonah?"

The girl continued crying, occasionally sniffling and wiping at her eyes and nose.

"Have faith," Terena urged.

Sonah huffed a laugh. "That's not—" she sighed, swallowing. "He won't come, Terena. Because he's not my father."

Ormano could not recall a more wretched week.

Not only did he have to watch as the general's men rounded up those poor souls in Laurica for gods knew what fate, he'd also lost a great friend in Prince Lerek. He'd been one of the few who treated him like a person and not a cleric, or worse, a second son only tolerated because of his knowledge of the gods.

Now, as he sat scribbling away in his bedchamber above the palace temple, he was sure the week would end with him bearing witness to another of his childhood friends losing her life.

Something sounded behind him and Orry turned, his eyes darting around the shadows hiding from the fire and the flickering flame of his candle.

Nothing.

He frowned, turning back to his writing. He'd been researching the powers of the gods when they'd first appeared—or rather, when the first records of their appearance had been documented by poets and bards, and much later, by scholars and historians.

He'd read most of these already, when he'd first begun his religious studies. At the time, he'd done so to pass the exams and impress his professors. Now, it seemed much more relevant to what had happened with Ren and the powers she seemed to manifest more and more.

Another sound interrupted him, closer this time. Orry turned fully, his quill raised as if he might use it as a weapon. After his search again yielded nothing out of the ordinary, he was about to turn back when something struck him in the head.

He howled, slapping his palm to his injured temple only to cause further injury. He whimpered and twisted, casting about for the offending party. His eye snagged on something near his feet and he bent lower.

A pebble.

What?

He bent to retrieve it when something sailed through the window and connected with the top of his head.

"Gods!" He sprang to his feet and rushed to the window, intent on screaming his displeasure at whatever foul person thought it was funny to annoy—and physically harm!—a cleric.

When he saw Croak waving at him from the narrow walkway, Orry blinked. He rubbed at his head and leaned out of the window.

"What in Gaia's good name are you doing? You hit me twice!"

"What do you think I'm doing?" Croak hissed. "Obviously, I'm trying to get your attention!"

Orry's lips turned down. "Well, why wouldn't you just come *in?*"

"I'm trying to be stealthy," Croak said in a loud whisper.

Orry rolled his eyes. "Well, get in here already! You look conspicuous."

He moved back into the room and headed for his door when he heard a thump and then a scraping noise coming from outside the window.

Surging back toward the window, Orry leaned out in time to see Croak climbing the wisteria vines. He'd planted his left hand on the window ledge when his foot slipped. Orry lunged for him, grabbing hold of his hand, grunting with the effort as Croak's legs flailed before finding his footing again.

He pulled back and Croak thrust his chest over the ledge, the air whooshing out of his lungs as Orry fell onto the wood floor.

Croak slithered the rest of the way in as Orry scooted back along the floor until he'd grabbed hold of his chair and lifted himself up.

Croak lay sprawled on his belly.

"Imbecile! I have a perfectly good door and a sturdy staircase you could've used!"

"Can't," Croak said, his voice muffled with his face on the floor. "City Watch all over, looking for me."

Orry blinked. "What? Since when? I haven't heard—"

"One of the men I'm with heard them," Croak said as he lifted himself up off the floor. He dusted off his breeches and stood, hands on hips. "Said I'm being sought for questioning."

Orry shook his head. He pulled out his chair, motioning Croak to take it and moved to sit on his bed. He watched his friend as he plopped into the chair. His face was flushed, but he couldn't tell if it was from the climb or nearly falling.

"Have you seen her?"

Orry didn't bother asking who he meant. "Yes, of course. Almost as soon as I arrived. She's being kept in the dungeons." He hung his head before continuing. "She's been worked over, Croak." He lifted pained eyes to his friend. "She's in terrible shape. The Royal Inquisitor."

Croak closed his eyes for only a second. When he opened them again, there was resolve in them as he sat forward, bracing his forearms on his legs. "What are they saying? What did *she* say? All we've heard is crazy shit I will not believe unless I hear it from you."

Orry splayed his hands. "It's not good, Croak. They have her because she attacked Isher. At first they thought she'd killed the guards and Lerek too. Maybe they still do. The general hasn't said. They're also holding Sonah Yahn."

"Sonah? Little Sonah Yahn?"

"Aye," he said, "they think she drugged the princes and let in whoever it was killed the guards and Lerek." Orry wiped a hand over his face. "I saw her too, poor thing. She looked terrified, with no idea of what's going on. Or what's going to happen to her on the morrow."

"What do you mean? They won't execute her," Croak scoffed. "Ovenno will—"

Orry shook his head. "No. Her father's in Ermanel. He won't make it in time. The girl is to be executed alongside Terena at dawn."

Croak gaped at him. "But… that will start a war! At the very least, the royals will gather and protest! The dukes—"

"He doesn't care," Orry interrupted. "The emperor doesn't care. He's in a rage, I tell you. He's out of his mind with grief. He wanted both of them killed on the spot but General Peleon convinced him to allow him time to question them. Especially after what Terena did to Isher."

"What do you mean? What did she do?"

Orry steepled his hands and gazed across at his friend. "Apparently, Ren attacked him without ever touching him. She did the same to the guards."

Croak looked at him expectantly when he didn't elaborate. He motioned with his hands. "How? What's that mean?"

"According to Isher—and a few of the guards that were there—she used some kind of... power. Somehow, she choked him, elevating him several feet off the ground."

"Ren's strong for a woman," Croak grumbled.

"No," Orry said, shaking his head, "No, you misunderstand. Croak, Isher and the guards all said she was nowhere *near* him when she did it. She was standing by Lerek. Well away from where Isher had been sitting. When the guards came in, they saw her with her arms raised as if she were choking him, and there across the way, high up on one of the pergola columns, was Isher, flailing against invisible hands!"

Croak stared at him in horror he tried to mask by ducking his head. "They lie."

"Croak." Orry frowned across at his friend. He spread his hands. "All of them? I mean—I know it sounds absurd. Nothing like that has happened in close to a thousand years! When the last of the demigods were killed."

He was silent, hoping some of what he had shared was sinking in. He dropped his chin, then lifted his eyes once more to his friend. "Also... I talked with Ren. She said—"

"Stop."

"Remember the time—"

"Stop. Orry."

Orry pressed his lips together and leaned back.

A long time passed before either spoke.

"I wish we had the luxury of time, Croak, but," Orry shook his head. "I need you. I need your help to free her. They're going to make it a public execution. Not only is she being charged with murder and treason, but she'll be executed as a god." He shook his head when Croak leaned forward with his mouth open and forestalled him. "Listen, I gave my judgement she is not a god — if she was, she'd have manifested powers to free herself. The fact she cannot heal after the tort—sorry... anyway. It didn't matter what I said. I'm certain Peleon changed my judgement to suit his purposes."

He looked across at Croak, his mouth screwed up in frustration. "They won't let me back in to see her." Orry reached out to Croak. "I hope you've thought of a way to get her out of this, Croak. Because tomorrow she is going to be executed. I hope you have a plan to rescue her. Her and Sonah Yahn."

Croak's head snapped up. "*Both?*"

Orry scowled at him. "You honestly think I'd let another innocent be sacrificed because of the emperor's grief? Ren said it too. We have to get them both. And we have a few hours to come up with how. So," Orry sighed and slumped his shoulders. "What's the plan?"

Sonah looked across at Terena Luca's cell. Despite the shadows, Sonah managed to see the bruises on Terena's face and body, with one eye swollen shut. Blood crusted her lip, and the hand hanging out of the bars was caked in blood and swollen.

The good eye stared back at her. "Who's not your father?"

Sonah sniffed and wiped at her nose with her wrist. "Duke Ovenno. He's not my father."

Terena didn't respond. Sonah closed her eyes and dropped her gaze to the middle of the room. "I feel strongly he is not coming because he doesn't want to, not because he's not at home. I'm not his daughter, so it's a good possibility you're not dying alone tomorrow."

"We've known you for years, Sonah," Terena said, her voice harsh. "If you're not his daughter, who are you, then? What's your real name?"

Sonah looked across at Terena, resigned. "Sonah is my real name. But Yahn is not."

Terena scoffed. "Lie."

"Truth," Sonah said. "I'm an orphan. Left on the steps of the Lethe Monastery seventeen years ago. They only ever called me 'Sonah'. Duchess Ovenno came to see me there, I was told, and my plight moved her so much she visited every year on the day I was brought there."

Sonah shrugged. "When I was nine, the abbot took me to see Duke and Duchess Ovenno. A year later, on the tenth anniversary of my arrival, they presented me to Emperor Solon as Sonah Yahn. I couldn't even tell you if they *had* a daughter, but I guess they must, because I was expected. I didn't understand half of what went on that day. Only that I wouldn't be going home to the monastery." Sonah bent her head, her eyes glazed as she recalled. "I remember seeing my new room. Being presented to Sybil—Lady Maranou. I met the other girls the next day and gods, I remember *that* day very well, too."

"How did you let it go on?"

Sonah lifted her eyes to Terena, blinking a few times to settle her focus. "Before he left, the duke said he would have the abbot murdered if I said anything. That man raised me," she whispered. "I told myself I could do this. For him."

A long silence pressed in. Sonah lost herself in her thoughts, then took a breath and said, "I'm scared."

Terena said nothing for so long, Sonah thought she might not have heard. Didn't matter. Didn't stop it from being true.

"I am too."

Sonah's eyes welled.

"Why is this happening?" She hated how weak she must sound to this woman whom she admired.

"I don't know. There are too many things it could be. But each time I think it must be this one," Terena laughed, gesturing to Sonah with her hand, her voice bitter as she said, "I find out something like *that*."

"I only said it because you looked like, you know, hopeful," Sonah grumbled. "I didn't want you thinking we might get out of this because of the duke."

"I understand it though," Terena said, as if she hadn't heard Sonah. "I don't know any duke—any father—liking the idea of giving over his firstborn daughter to be the Royal Taster for the Crown Prince. Duke Ovenno doesn't have a son, though. So either he didn't want to give up his daughter and played a dangerous game by placing you in her stead, or—"

Terena looked up, her jaw slack.

Sonah stared at her, caught between fear and resignation.

"The general asked you about conspirators," Terena said. "Did he say anything else about that? Did he mention any of the royals?"

Sonah shrugged one shoulder as she leaned into the bars. "Maybe? I was mostly crying. Pleading my innocence. Fat lot of good that did."

"Did he ask about your father at all? Did he say anything about him at all you remember?"

"Other than he wasn't in residence when the general wrote to him of my arrest? No."

Another silence. Sonah felt the weight of the day. The week. Her eyelids drooped.

"The duke is planning a coup."

Sonah arched an eyebrow. "What?"

"It makes sense," Terena muttered, and Sonah sat up straighter to focus.

"What now?"

"The duke doesn't need to come; you said it yourself. And if he's not in Ovenno and can't come in time to save his daughter, the emperor executes you and now," Terena laughed, "Now Duke Ovenno has a reason to go to war. Wait, no. No. The emperor still holds the other heirs. And their daughters. He wouldn't risk that if they are allies."

"Maybe he just wanted to save his daughter," Sonah said.

"Someone knows."

"Hmm?"

"Someone knows," Terena said, "about you. He's being set up. And the others won't believe him because the duke doesn't have a child at stake anymore. He doesn't have an heir, and he switched his daughter with a fake. It's not a coup, it's a diversion."

CHAPTER TWELVE

The silver and pink of encroaching dawn made Croak quicken his pace. He made a face, cursing as his foot slid again in the muck near the river while he made his way toward the sewer grate near the western wall of the city.

He had a small window to make it inside and up to the walkway leading out to the garment district of Metilai. From there, it was about a five minute walk to the city square, where the execution was to take place.

Croak reached the grate at last, grimacing when his hands slipped on the slimy bars. A shudder coursed through him. He wiped his hands on his breeches, laced his fingers together and flipped his wrists until his fingers cracked while he twisted his head sharply to either side and cracked his neck.

"You got this. You got this," he whispered to himself as he wrapped his hands once more around the disgusting bars and pulled. He heaved twice more before the grate gave. He held his breath as he pulled it to the side and dropped down into the sewer.

"I swear to the gods you are the only person I'd ever do this for, Ren," he said, striding as quickly as possible through the sludge. He gagged. "Maybe Orry. Dunno. Might have to think on that one for a bit."

A few minutes later, he heard sounds overhead and peered up through the grates as he passed them, trying to gauge where he was. More turns and more sludge. The contents of his stomach almost came up several times as he rushed through the sewage until he came to the bend leading up to his destination.

The stone steps appeared up ahead on the left and he ran the last few feet, climbing the steps two at a time until he reached the iron door. He shoved it open enough to look out. Once he was sure no one was about, he eased the door open, cringing as it squealed.

Not daring any more horrendous sounds leading anyone to find out what had caused it, he slipped through the narrow opening and shut the door behind him.

It was much too early for any of the shopkeepers to be out and about, which gave him enough privacy to navigate the streets and back alleys to the square. He ducked behind a building close enough to the open area and gawked at the scene.

A dais had been set up on one side of the square with a throne and chairs on either side of it. Tiered stands had been erected on the other three sides, already filled with spectators. A large area in the middle lay empty while City Watch stood as a barrier at the foot of the stands.

Croak moved closer, sticking to the side of the building. He had no idea where Rydon and Gabriol were, just that they'd meet him in the square when Terena and Sonah were brought out. He frowned, thinking back on the conversation last night when he'd casually added they'd be rescuing not one but two treasonous damsels. While Gabriol had cursed and blustered, Rydon had simply moved on to adjusting the logistics of their plan.

"What am I doing here?" he asked himself, his voice a singsong. "I'm going to get myself killed, along with my sister, that's what I'm doing here."

Croak dropped his chin and rubbed at his eyes with his right hand. His nose wrinkled. "Oh, for fuck's sake," he groaned as he sniffed his fingers and smelled the shit on them. He wiped his eyes with the sleeve of his tunic.

He heard shouting and a commotion on the other side of the square, where a mob of spectators had formed. He moved out and got up onto his toes, hoping to see what was happening. His pulse thrummed in his ears as he saw the first of two Imperial Guard riding toward the square. More guards appeared in a procession and finally, a cart with bars and two huddled figures inside rounded a turn to stop near the dais.

The people in the stands began throwing things at Terena and Sonah, both wearing only shifts with their legs and feet bare, the stained clothing hanging pitifully from their bruised and battered bodies.

Croak put a hand to his stomach as bile rose at the sight of his sister. Terena leaned against the bars of the cart and clutched at Sonah's hands, her right arm hanging limp at her side. One side of her face appeared mangled, and tears slid down his face before he realized he was crying.

He walked forward out of the cover of the building, pulling his hood up as he wended his way through the masses, becoming thicker the closer he came to the stands. Edging close to where the guards were now dragging the girls, Croak looked around.

High Cleric Christos came forward, followed by High Penitent Paros, the emperor's personal priest and seer, and Ormano bringing up the rear.

As they assembled on the dais, General Peleon strode forward, one hand on the pommel of his sword. His thin, hawklike face was stark as he stopped in front of the throne. Captain Xoran of the Imperial Guard moved to stand at his side, his swarthy countenance sneering.

The people quieted as trumpeters trilled out short bursts. The herald came forward next and stepped smartly to the front of the dais, calling out, "All Hail, Solon of House Angeloi. Emperor of Heylisia."

Croak stiffened as the emperor emerged. His white robes swirled around him, the large gold crown glittering with pearls and rubies atop his shoulder length raven hair. He strode to the dais without a word and everyone sat once he'd taken the throne.

Croak frowned. Where was Isher?

General Peleon frowned down at Terena and Sonah as the guards roughly placed them before the dais. Terena didn't move fast enough for one guard's liking and suffered a vicious kick to her left leg. She landed hard on hands and cried out as her broken arm gave out, the side of her face cracking against the ground. Sonah lurched for her and was rewarded with a backhand by another guard.

The crowd erupted, roaring their approval, and Croak shook, his hands balled at his sides. Furtively, he scanned the surroundings, hoping to spot Rydon or Gabriol, both of whom had disguised themselves as Imperial Guard, but all of them wore bronze helmets obscuring much of their faces.

Croak's stomach pitched as he watched a guard yank on his sister's arm to lift her up and the black clad executioner stepped forward with a rope. He tied it around her wrist and motioned for another guard to take the other end. Croak closed his eyes as they tied another rope to her right wrist.

When her ankles were tied, a guard stood at her back to keep her upright.

She was barely conscious.

Croak was now at the front of the spectators.

General Peleon raised his arms, and a hush fell over the square.

"Terena Luca," General Peleon's harsh, high-pitched voice rang out across the yard. "You are charged with treason against the empire, the murder of Prince Lerek, and the attempted assassination of Prince Isher. Additionally," he paused and moved his gaze over the crowd who seemed to lean in closer. "Additionally, you have been found guilty of hiding your true nature, for which there is no redemption in the laws of the empire and in the laws of man."

He turned and faced Terena. Her head hung as she stood with the help of a guard. Croak's heart was in his throat, waiting for the announcement that would seal her fate.

"You are a god, and the penalty for that alone is death."

The people exploded and Croak cringed against the renewed frenzy at the general's words. He fought to stay at the front as everyone pushed their way forward. Imperial Guard and City Watch rushed out to stop the masses from storming the square.

Peleon smirked down at Terena and opened his mouth to speak again, but Terena lifted her head at last. Croak's mouth hung open, but he could only see her profile from his vantage point.

"You," she said, her voice barely a whisper, but as soon as she spoke, the square fell silent.

"You," she said again, louder, "You do not know what's coming for you."

Gasps from the spectators sounded all around, and Croak took a step closer, putting him within reach of one guard. His heart thundered so hard against his ribs he became faint.

"You think you can kill *me?*" she yelled, and the guard at her side stepped back. Terena stood on her own for the first time since he'd seen her.

"You think you can kill a *god?*"

The blood drained from his face as his sister screamed at the general.

Terena lifted her arm, and all hells broke loose.

RYDON STOOD AT TERENA'S SIDE WHEN SHE LIFTED HER ARM, WHITE light illuminating her veins as it raced to her fingers. A pulse of something he'd never felt before rushed out, slamming into the general and everyone on the dais. Their bodies flew to the ground, and the spectators cried out.

Rydon lunged for her when she fell. All around him, people ran in the ensuing chaos, the guards helpless to stop the stampede. Rydon ripped off his helmet and reached down with his dagger, slashing at Terena's bindings. He surged forward as someone dropped to his side, but he looked up in time to see Croak.

"We need to go! Now!" Rydon roared. "Gabe!" he yelled, not bothering to turn to look for his man. "Get the girl!"

Gabriol grunted in response and Rydon turned to the dais to see Peleon and Xoran and the remaining Imperial Guard shuffling their royal burden toward a waiting carriage.

A cleric darted out from under one guard and ran down the steps of the dais toward them.

"No!" Croak shouted, lunging to grab Rydon's arm when Rydon sprang at him, intent on gutting the man. "He's with us!"

Rydon froze and frowned down at Croak, then looked back at the cowering cleric, his face ashen and eyes wide as he stared back at Rydon.

He grunted, bent down and, as carefully as he could, lifted Terena Luca's broken body into his arms. Croak fussed over her for a second before Rydon snarled at him to move.

"We have maybe ten seconds before the guards reach us," Gabriol called out, breathless as he rushed past, the frightened girl, Sonah Yahn, in his arms. The look of terror on her face gave way to tears when she caught sight of both Croak and Terena.

Croak, to his credit, narrowed his eyes and turned, no trace of fear on his face. Striding forward, he cleared a path through the mob. Rydon rushed to follow.

"What now?" Croak screamed over the noise. Rydon heard Gabriol swear behind him and several people cry out.

"We move!" he yelled back and shoved Croak aside to barrel through the crowd.

CHAPTER THIRTEEN

"Would you fucking move?" Croak fumed, shoving Orry in the back as he stopped again to retch. Croak's heart was pounding so hard he thought it might burst. He didn't need to worry about Orry, too, while they all fled for their lives.

Orry mumbled something and started moving through the sewer once more.

Croak grabbed his arm to haul him along. "I've puked twice now. You didn't see me stop, did you?"

Gabriol looked over his shoulder at them, Sonah Yahn a limp doll in his arms. At least she was in better shape than Ren.

Croak swallowed.

"You boys all right back there?" Gabriol called out as he turned back to the front.

"Fantastic," Croak bit out, groaning as Orry once more stumbled through the shit at their feet.

Rydon was well ahead of them, despite carrying Ren's unconscious body. They had made it through the worst part, according to him— although, personally, Croak thought going through the sewers twice was worse.

Getting past the Imperial Guard and the City Watch as they made their way through the streets of Metilai was what Rydon and Gabriol had been most worried about. But with the chaos breaking out after Terena's spectacular performance and the crowds helping to shield their escape, they'd made it to the sewer entrance in the garment district much faster than they'd expected.

But they weren't safe yet.

"How's she doing?" Croak called out.

Rydon didn't answer for a bit, and Croak looked up, scanning ahead to Rydon's back.

"She's still out."

"Alive, though, right?" *Please be alive.*

"Alive," Rydon called back.

The relief washing over him was short-lived as Orry retched, his knees buckling.

"What a dramatic little shit you are! Seriously, how much did you eat this morning?" Croak groaned as he hauled his friend back upright. Some of the puke flew onto his tunic and Croak gagged. "Oh, my gods."

"Here!" Rydon stopped, stepping back a bit to let Gabriol get in front.

He set Sonah on the ground. Croak had left the grate on the grass, so Gabriol pulled himself up to make sure it was clear.

Sonah leaned heavily against the wall as Croak neared with Orry in tow. He saw the sweat on her forehead as she closed her eyes. He whipped off his cloak and draped it over the girl's shoulders. She looked up at him with haunted eyes, clutching the cloak tight around her.

"You're doing great, Sonah," he said, touching her arm. Her hair hung in limp, dirty clumps, shielding her face when she turned away. Croak moved closer to Rydon, hoping to get a better look at his sister when Gabriol's head appeared.

"Clear," he said. He held out his arms as Rydon shifted Terena, transferring her to Gabriol. After Gabriol pulled Terena out, Rydon hoisted himself up and out of the sewer, then leaned back down. "Croak, you're next."

"What about—"

"Easier to help the others if you're up here too."

"Good thinking," Croak mumbled. He reached up to clasp Rydon's outstretched hand, yelping when he was yanked up.

"Sonah."

Sonah was already waiting below the hole, and reached up when Rydon poked his head down.

Croak moved to help her. Moving her a few feet away to where Gabriol was settling Terena, Croak dropped to the ground beside him. "Easy, easy."

"Cleric, come on," Rydon urged. Croak ran back and dropped beside Rydon.

Orry stumbled over and stretched up his arms. Rydon lifted him out, with Croak pulling on his friend until he was up on the lip of the hole. "You gotta lose some weight, brother," Croak groused.

Rydon stood and strode over to scoop up Terena in his arms. Croak let out a long breath and raked his hands through his hair.

Gabriol had his arm around Sonah, water trickling down her chin onto Croak's cloak. She must have gotten a drink from the creek. Orry, too, was now standing, his hands wet as he wiped water from his mouth.

Gabriol whistled, and a boy of around ten came out of the woods across the water, holding the reins of a pair of horses. Rydon crossed the creek with Gabriol close behind, lifting Sonah over the water. Croak went to Orry to see if he needed help. Orry shook his head, patting Croak on the shoulder, and they both crossed the stream.

"What the fuck? Only two horses?" Croak whined.

"Another boy is waiting with horses a mile that way," Rydon answered, gesturing somewhere to his left. You know the woods near Baldana?" Rydon asked Croak as he mounted his horse. Gabriol then lifted Terena high enough Rydon caught her and positioned her in front of him in the saddle. Croak's lips thinned when he saw she was still out.

"Croak?" Rydon prodded.

"What? Yes. Yeah, I know them. Just past Dawn Lake."

"Right," Rydon said with a quick nod. "You and Orry meet us there. Stick to the trees until you get your horses and do not, whatever you do, do not take the Greek roads. They'll have soldiers all over them."

Gabriol leaned down and motioned for Sonah to take his hand. Her lips parted but didn't say a word as she took his hand and mounted behind him.

Rydon turned his horse and rode off, Gabriol right behind him.

Croak watched them take off, then turned to Orry. "Just us now, kid."

Orry bent over and puked.

SONAH WASN'T SURE HOW LONG THEY RODE BEFORE STOPPING AT THE edge of a lake. She looked across at Terena, still unconscious in the arms of the big man who had helped Croak in their rescue.

Gabriol, the other man, swung a leg over his horse, then reached up to help Sonah dismount. He was taller than his friend, his dark blond hair braided and pulled back in a leather tie, blue eyes flashing up at her as he gently settled her on the ground. When he lifted his hand to drag across his mouth and short beard, she noticed he had rings on almost every finger.

Sonah loosed a shaky breath and wiped her sweaty palms on her tattered chemise, cheeks flaming. She tugged the edges of her borrowed cloak tighter around her and walked on stiff legs toward Terena.

"Is she..." Sonah couldn't finish her question, but when she lifted her eyes to the other man—Rydon, Croak had called him—he gave her a grim smile.

"She lives," he said, his voice deep and rough.

Sonah nodded, glancing back to see Gabriol coming back after tethering his horse.

"We rest until her brother arrives," Rydon added gruffly. Sonah watched Gabriol reach up to take Terena from Rydon's arms.

He carried her to the water's edge and laid her gently on the ground. Sonah cradled her arms at her chest and hunched down at Terena's side.

"Get my cloak from my saddlebags, would you?" Rydon called out to Gabriol. When the man came back with the folded garment, Rydon tucked it around Terena's body.

"Are you a friend of Terena's? I'm sorry, I haven't seen either of you before at the palace," Sonah said. She reached out and slipped her hand into Terena's, careful not to bother the crusted wounds of her missing fingernails. Her eyes welled as she took in the damage to the woman's poor body.

"We hope to be friends," Rydon said. He crouched down next to Sonah and looked at Terena.

Sonah looked over at him. "How do you know her?"

Rydon gazed at Terena for a few more seconds before turning to Sonah. "We met her brother in Laurica. He promised us coin to help his sister."

Sonah's eyes widened. "Oh! I thought you were Imperial Guard. You're mercenaries then?"

"Aye."

She looked up at Gabriol. "It must've been a lot. I don't know what he offered, but for my part, I've only my thanks to give." Sonah fidgeted, only now realizing she was alone with two large warriors and no friend in sight. She scooted closer to Terena.

"Have no fear, girl," Rydon said, his voice low as he clapped a large hand on her shoulder, making Sonah fall over onto Terena's arm. She shifted quickly so she wouldn't cause Terena any pain.

"So what now for you both?" Sonah asked, more to kill time than any genuine curiosity. She hoped Croak and Orry found their way to them soon.

Gabriol came to their side and Sonah looked up to see him looming over her, arms crossed at his chest, bracing his weight on his left side.

"We were going north when the boy found us," he said. "We'll have to wait until she's better."

Sonah blinked up at him. "You plan to stay with us, then?"

Rydon shared a look with Gabriol, then grunted his assent. "Until we can head north. The king there has charged us with bringing him trackers."

Sonah's mouth dropped open, and she glanced between the two men. "You're... you're going to sell her?"

"What? No!" Rydon scoffed, affronted. "No, of course not. The king asked us to find her and recruit her."

"Recruit her? For what?"

Rydon shook his head and rubbed the back of his neck. He looked flushed. "Don't know. But it's not to harm her."

"How do you know?" Sonah asked, narrowing her eyes as the color continued to creep up his neck. That wasn't a good sign.

"I trust him. He's a good man."

"No one's heard of him before. No one even knows his name," Sonah muttered. "I was to be part of the convoy the emperor was sending north to meet with him."

Rydon turned and gave her a frown. "Aye? What for?"

Sonah shrugged. "Diplomatic stuff. Private, empire stuff."

"Ah," Gabriol said with a smirk. "Worried about the man's rise to power in such a short time?"

"I don't know. Maybe. I... didn't want to go. We were supposed to leave... that day. I prayed to Gaia for something to happen, so we wouldn't have to." The blood drained from her face and she felt sick. "Do you think she heard me? Is that why Prince—"

"Don't be foolish, girl," Rydon grumbled. He reached out a hand and laid it on Terena's forehead. Sonah inched away so he wouldn't accidentally brush against her.

He shot her a look of irritation. "Those gods don't bother with mortals. Prince Lerek's death was nothing but the scheming of men with a grudge against the empire."

Sonah ducked her head. "Sorry."

"Don't be sorry," he said. "I'm the one who should apologize. You're a young girl, raised to believe the gods are good. Some are. Most aren't. The ones you pray to, though, don't give a shit about us either way and wouldn't lift a gods damned finger to help. No way for you to know that."

"How do *you* know that?"

Gabriol chuckled. Rydon shot him a look. "That's a story for another time," he said.

Sonah didn't press.

"Do you have family?" Gabriol asked, his voice soft. She turned to look up at him. "Is there somewhere we can take you after...," he motioned to Terena with his chin.

Sonah dropped her head. She caressed Terena's thumb with hers. "No."

"No? No one? Croak said you're the Royal Taster. Your father must be one of the dukes."

Sonah's face flamed. "You would think, but no."

She snapped her head up at him, shifting as a thought came to her. "May I travel with you? I mean, with all of you? I won't be a burden, I promise. I'll... I can gather wood and start a fire, I can wash your clothes—"

"Child—"

"I'm not a child," Sonah said vehemently. "I'm seventeen years old. I spent the last seven years in the White Palace as a glorified prisoner, tasting food for Prince Lerek, knowing any day I could die if someone decided to kill him by poisoning his meals. And guess what? They did. I spent the past week being questioned by the scariest men alive, spent some of that time in the catacombs they use as dungeons beneath the palace, terrified they would torture me like they did Terena and the rest of the time dreading today because I knew we'd die."

Sonah angrily wiped at her tears, her mouth set stubbornly as she glanced between Rydon and Gabriol. "I think I've earned the right to be treated as an adult by both of you. I'd appreciate if you don't condescend to me."

"You're right," Rydon said. He laid a hand on her forearm. His touch was warm, and it brought her a small measure of comfort. "You're right. Apologies again. It's been a long time since I've been around someone your age and it's made me awkward."

Sonah gave a small nod and mumbled her thanks.

They were silent for a while, Sonah lost in her thoughts, with no particular desire for further conversation. Sometime later, to her horror, she started breathing too fast, thoughts of that morning and how close she'd been to having her body ripped apart overcame her. Her chest squeezed tight and she panicked.

Wide eyed, Sonah's gaze darted around, for what she didn't know but when she caught sight of Rydon, her breathing became more shallow. She reached out and grabbed his arm, digging her nails into the skin of his forearm. He said something she didn't hear, her pulse exploding in her ears and she thought she might faint.

Rydon pulled her to him and wrapped his big arms around her, pressing her to his chest, holding her head against him as he rocked her. She calmed and her breathing slowed.

"We leave you alone for one minute!"

Sonah heard Gabriol curse, and she jerked back from Rydon, who let her go even as he observed her.

She scrubbed at her eyes, still gulping for air. She hadn't heard the horses, nor Croak and Orry as they arrived, but when she looked behind her, she saw Croak's grin fade as he looked at her.

"Gods, Sonah, I'm sorry. I'm an ass, I—"

"If she knows you at all, she knows you're an ass," Rydon snapped.

"Did anyone follow you?" Gabriol asked, still standing over Terena as he glanced over his shoulder at Croak and Orry when they ambled over.

Orry set himself down at Sonah's side with a loud groan, giving her a sympathetic smile, almost making her cry again. He seemed to sense it and moved closer, putting an arm over her shoulders.

Croak went to Terena's other side and dropped to a knee as he pressed a kiss to his sister's forehead.

"Has she woken at all?"

"No," Rydon answered.

"So, what now? They'll be combing these woods next," Croak said.

"Should we take a ferry at Lios? We can be across the Bay and into Elis by tomorrow night." Orry replied.

"No ferries. At least not yet," Rydon said. He dropped onto the ground, stretching out one leg and pulled his other knee to his chest. "The general will have men watching the ports nearby. And she's in no shape to travel, so first we need to find someplace to shelter for a night or two before we decide our next move."

"You don't have a plan, then?" Croak asked, scowling across at Rydon.

"I'm not from here," Rydon said, scowling right back. "We helped rescue them, but now we must rely on your knowledge. Gods help us. So tell us, young master, where can we take your sister until she's well enough to sit a horse? And remember, we have all the empire looking for us, so make it good."

Croak ran a hand over his mouth but didn't answer.

The silence was deafening. Sonah squirmed and glanced up at Orry.

"What about Lethe Monastery?"

Orry blinked at her. "What about it?"

Sonah looked around at the others, then lifted a shoulder, her eyes dropping when she realized they were all watching her.

"I... spent some time there. Before the White Palace. I know the abbot there. He and the monks would take us in."

"Where's this?" Gabriol asked, shooting a look at Croak before turning back to her.

"It's in Ravos," Orry said. "Twenty-five miles or so northwest of here, near the border of Ermanel. How did you come to spend time there?"

"They will take us in? Are you certain?" Rydon asked Sonah. She was grateful not to have to answer Ormano.

"Aye," she said, nodding as she pulled out of Orry's arm. "Abbot Malis knows me. He will keep us safe."

"Even if the empire comes knocking? Or, more to the point, threatening death to anyone harboring us?" Gabriol asked, arching an eyebrow at her.

Sonah lifted her chin. "They would protect us with their lives. But I don't expect soldiers to go there. They wouldn't know to."

Orry looked at her quizzically, but she ignored him. Only Terena knew of her past and she didn't think it was something she should share with these men, not until she could be sure of them.

She did not fear Croak, and she was fairly certain Ormano would do her no harm, but... the less she shared, the better off she'd be.

"Just over the border, then?" Gabriol asked, breaking into her thoughts.

She opened her mouth to answer when Orry said, "A day's ride, maybe more if we need to go slower for Terena."

As if his words pierced her subconscious, Terena stirred. Croak leaned forward, his face close to hers as he whispered her name.

Terena said something, her lips moving as her good eye fluttered and she raised her left hand to her brother. He took it gently, holding it to his chest as he leaned closer.

"Terena, I'm here. I'm here and you're safe. So is Sonah."

She tried to say something again, but it was so soft no one caught it.

"What was that, Ren? What did you say?" Croak asked, his voice sweet as if speaking to a baby.

"Your... your..."

"Aye? Aye, it's me! It's me, Ren."

Terena pursed her lips and her brow furrowed. Then she swallowed and opened her good eye.

"Your breath stinks."

CHAPTER FOURTEEN

They spent the next week at Lethe Monastery while Terena recovered.

Sonah had been right. The monks welcomed them as soon as they had seen her. Abbot Malis had embraced Sonah so tightly, Croak had cast a look at Orry, both of their eyebrows in their hairlines.

When they'd gotten Terena settled and one of their healers to tend to her many injuries, the abbot had requested their presence in his private room. It was bare, as Croak had expected, but had a wonderful view of the pretty courtyard below.

"Do you have any news from Metilai, Abbot?" Rydon had asked, getting right to the meat of it as Croak closed the door behind him. Rydon and Gabriol had declined a seat so Croak had as well, standing as they did with arms across their chests. Sonah had taken a seat on the tiny couch across the room, looking as if she'd done so hundreds of times. In fact, she looked so at home in this place, Croak wondered again how she knew the monks.

"We heard what happened, if that's what you mean," Abbot Malis said as he took a seat at Sonah's side. Orry took a seat in an arm chair by the desk. The abbot looked out at each of them. He had kind eyes, set deep in a thin face lined with fine wrinkles at the corners of his eyes and mouth. Croak imagined he was older than Rydon, although he wasn't great at guessing someone's age.

"And what's happened?" Rydon pushed.

Sonah took hold of the abbot's hand. Rydon shot a look at Gabriol that clearly showed they were wondering at the relationship, same as Croak.

"First, the sad news of the prince's murder," Abbot Malis said, casting a sympathetic look at Sonah. She dropped her gaze to her lap. "Then of course the escape of the two thought to have carried out such a heinous crime, although," here, the abbot had squeezed Sonah's hand, "we did not believe a word of it. And we thanked Gaia for sparing Sonah." The abbot then looked up at each of the men standing before him and, with his heart in his brown eyes, bowed his head. "We thank you, as well."

Croak had shifted uncomfortably. The conversation then turned to Terena and her injuries, sleeping arrangements, and how long they could stay before Terena was well enough to travel.

The abbot had said no one from Metilai had come to their doors, and if anyone from the empire bothered to seek them out at the monastery, the abbot assured them he had a place for them to hide.

The question Croak had been asking himself was, why?

He'd just left Terena's sick room, happy her color had returned when he caught sight of Sonah sitting with a monk in the courtyard. As he moved a few steps closer, he saw her wave brightly at two monks walking across from her.

He frowned and leaned against a pillar, watching her.

"You thinking the same thing I'm thinking?"

Croak glanced to his right to see Rydon sauntering over, his thumbs tucked into his sword belt. He was wearing clean breeches and a white tunic and, for the first time since he'd met him, didn't look as menacing. His red beard was trimmed neatly and even his hair was tamed and tied at the back of his head.

"Are you thinking it's been a couple of weeks since you've had sex and maybe taking a chance and going into town is not a bad idea?"

Rydon snorted. "Are you ever serious?"

"I've got plenty of time to be serious when I'm old like you."

Rydon arched an eyebrow at him then turned to look out at the courtyard. "Don't be any more ridiculous than you already are. I was talking about Sonah."

"What about her?"

"She's familiar with the monks here. I know she claimed she was here when she was younger, but I'm curious how the daughter of a duke would've become so attached to the monks of a monastery in Ravos."

Croak shrugged. "I've known her since she was ten and this is the first I've even heard she had any knowledge of a random monastery in Ravos."

"How's your sister?"

Croak shifted. "Much better. Asking when we can head north, of course."

"Well, we can't do that yet. We need—"

"Master Croak! Master Rydon! Quickly!"

A monk by the name of Daniel was huffing his way toward them and Croak looked back out at the courtyard to see Sonah running to them, her face a mask of terror.

"What's happened?" Rydon demanded. Gabriol and Orry came around the corner with another monk escorting them, the monk's face pale and pinched.

"Heylisian soldiers are here," the monk said breathlessly as he caught up to them. When the others came close, he looked up anxiously at Sonah. "Abbot Malis is with them now, but he wanted me to find you."

Gabriol cursed, and Rydon shoved past Croak toward Terena's room. Croak had a second to look at him before he turned back to the monk. "Where do we go?"

"We anticipated something like this since your arrival, so if you'll follow me, I can hide you until they've gone. If you need to leave, the packs we've gathered for you will be with you and you can go from there."

Sonah grabbed hold of Orry's hand and they all followed after

Daniel, Croak lagging behind long enough for Rydon to come through the door. Terena was secure at his side, her face a kaleidoscope of colors from the bruises, but standing for the first time since they'd rescued her.

He came up on her right and helped Rydon carry her along.

Croak's heart raced as they moved into the corridor leading to the dormitories. They turned left down some steps and then into a much darker hallway.

"How are we—"

"This passage leads to a spring behind the olive grove," Daniel said, holding up a torch. "Stay low once you're outside. They should not venture through the grove, but if they do, go left and you'll see the forest. You can lose them in there."

At last, they reached the door leading to the outside and the spring Daniel mentioned. Just beside the door was a pile of what looked like potato sacks.

Daniel turned back. "I will be back as soon as they're gone. If I'm not back within the hour, take those and leave," he said and pointed to the sacks. Sonah embraced him. When she let go, Daniel went back inside and shut the door.

Croak helped Rydon ease Terena onto the ground and Sonah dropped to her side, hugging her gently.

"It's so good to see you up," Sonah said, her smile bright but tinged with worry.

"Thank you for taking good care of me," Terena said and laid a hand on Sonah's cheek.

It was true. Once the healer had tended to her injuries, Sonah had stayed at Terena's side, feeding her, bathing her and brushing out her hair. Croak had walked in once to find her plaiting Terena's hair, the two speaking in low voices and giggling.

He was thankful to have Sonah with them, even if it was under shitty circumstances. Maybe because of them.

An hour later, Daniel still hadn't returned and Rydon was pressing them to leave. They had gathered their supplies when the door opened below them.

Daniel reared back in fright when he saw Gabriol and Rydon with their swords drawn.

"It's me! It's me!" He squeaked as he stopped at the top of the stairs, dropping the torch. Sonah swooped down to grab it.

"What news?" Rydon demanded, sheathing his sword.

Daniel took a moment. "You're fine for now. They weren't the emperor's men, though. Well, not entirely. They were Duke Ovenno's soldiers. They were looking for Sonah, aye, but they were looking for Mistress Luca as well."

Sonah swung her head to Rydon, wide-eyed. "I didn't think the duke would come for me!"

"Ovenno's your father?" Rydon scowled at her, and Gabriol cursed. "Why are you running from him?"

Croak moved between them. "Can you please focus?" He turned back to Daniel with an arm out. "What else? Did they bring news from Metilai?"

"Aye, that they did! They told Abbot Malis that, during your escape, the firstborns escaped as well. The soldier speaking with the abbot said it would be safe for Sonah and Mistress Luca to return with them to Ovenno. But the abbot made it clear he hadn't seen Sonah and did not know who Mistress Luca was, other than the rumors of her treason, that is."

"Did they believe him, Daniel?" Sonah asked, grabbing the monk's hands.

"Aye, they did. After they searched the monastery, of course. We had to pretend one of the monks was ill to account for the medicines in Mistress Luca's room."

"I love Abbot Malis," Croak muttered and raked a shaky hand through his hair.

"But the abbot said to tell you he doesn't believe the duke will be satisfied, and fears he'll return himself. Abbot Malis suggests you take the packs and leave forthwith. You endanger yourselves if you stay."

"We endanger you all as well," Rydon admitted, then gave Daniel a curt nod and clapped his hand on the man's shoulder. "We thank you,

Daniel. And please thank the abbot for us as well. We hope to repay you all someday for your kindness."

Daniel looked fondly at Sonah, pride shining in his eyes. "There's no need, Master Rydon. It was enough to see this young lady again. You've grown into a fine lady, Sonah. As we knew you would."

Croak and the others looked on with obvious curiosity as Sonah blushed and hugged the monk once more.

"I've had Temple and Simeon bring your horses to the woods. You won't miss them."

"*Our* horses?" Croak asked. He'd been relieved when he'd found the boy with Cerberus and Nyx waiting for him and Orry after their harrowing escape from Metilai. He vowed to go back with Daniel if they weren't the ones the monks had fetched.

"Aye, your horses," Daniel confirmed with a smile. Croak grabbed the man's shoulders and gave him a squeeze.

With a final wave to them all as the others said their farewells, Daniel turned and went back down the steps to the tunnel.

Terena woke with a start. She shifted and looked down, the soft folds of the cloak she slept on clutched in her fists. It took her a moment to recall where she was. No rats gnawing at her feet as she tried to sleep. No buckets of water being thrown on her to raise her from unconsciousness for more questionings or beatings.

She glanced around, the fire casting a glow around their small camp, and she relaxed enough to settle back into her cloak.

Avoiding any towns or villages, they had been traveling west through Ermanel for a fortnight, mostly sticking to the wooded areas.

"They'll have expected us to head for Helster Lake, so they'll have the port towns between Thalos and Vesala watched. Although, who knows what's happening in Ovenno these days. Or the empire, for that matter." Rydon said when he caught Terena watching him. He was sitting in the same spot as when she'd fallen asleep, so she doubted he'd gotten any rest.

Terena stared at the fire, thinking. "We keep heading west, then."

"Aye," he said, and poked at the fire with a stick. It crackled and sparked and they both gazed at it for a few seconds.

Terena propped herself on her arm.

"To Tursk," they said at the same time.

Terena narrowed her eyes.

"And then north to cross the lake at Bossena?" he asked. His smile deepened.

"Is this your plan or mine?" she grumbled. She moved to sit up straighter, taking care not to reawaken any of her aches. Galloping across the countryside had not helped.

Rydon chuckled and looked over at her. "Your brother told us of your emergency escape plan should anything… untoward… happen."

Terena stared at him mulishly, but did not respond.

"Don't blame the lad," he said with a shrug, then gazed back at the fire. "He had no choice, obviously. And you'll agree this was an emergency."

"How do you happen to be in my brother's company?"

Rydon sighed. "He sought us out in Laurica. At your direction, as I understand it. Needed help with the rescue and all. Promised us a fortune." He shrugged. "You know, the usual."

Terena snorted. "Of course. And the fortune is why you agreed, is it?"

"Why else?"

"Indeed," she said.

They were silent for a while. Terena lowered herself back onto her pallet with a sigh.

"We cannot take the Greek roads."

"Hmm," Rydon said in assent.

The fire crackled and Terena listened to its music for several minutes. "You were never heading north," she said at last.

Rydon made another sound. "Yes, and no. We're heading that way. Eventually. Not before we had you."

Terena stiffened. "Had me?"

Rydon shrugged, still gazing into the fire. "That's no longer necessary, is it?"

"That's a matter of perspective, I suppose," she said. "Who are you?"

Rydon stared at her. "I was sent to find you," he said at last.

"That is no answer."

"I'm a mercenary. As is Gabriol. That is the truth."

"And who sent you?"

"I'll get to that shortly, but I must beg a question before I answer. It will... affect what I share."

Terena barked out a laugh. "Indeed!"

"Come. One question, and I promise I will tell you anything you wish to know."

The silence thickened as she thought on his words. Curiosity got the better of her.

"All right, then," she said with a lift of her chin. "Ask."

Rydon shifted his weight and turned toward her, leaning his arms against his knees as he regarded her. "Are you a god?"

Terena was stunned by the question, blinking at him for several seconds. "What?"

Rydon gestured at her with his palm up. "You have powers. We've seen it. You know this," he said, his lips pressing tightly together. "But there are stories too of the... gifted, being able to use god powers." He splayed his hands. "Magic, yes? The powers the gods bestowed on some of their favorites. But the king asked for you specifically and tasked me and Gabriol to find you. So my question is, which are you? God or gifted?"

"I am neither," she spat.

"Aye, and I am the next emperor of Heylisia. All right," he said with a huff. "Ask me your questions. Might make more sense why I asked mine."

Terena cocked her head. "Who sent you to find me?"

"His Majesty, the King of Olympus."

Terena blinked. "King of Olympus. Tell me another."

"No word of a lie," Rydon said with a wry grin.

"Ambitious man. Does this king have a name?"

Rydon ducked his head. "He asked me not to say. He wishes to tell you himself."

Terena scoffed. "You promised to tell me anything I wished to know."

"I apologize," Rydon said with sincerity. "I am sworn to him and he specifically impressed upon me not to. You'll see why when you meet him."

"Because I'll know him?"

"Aye."

Terena's pulse raced. "And what does he want with me?"

"I did not ask, of course," Rydon said with a shrug. "But I assume it has something to do with the others he's looking for."

"Others?"

"Aye. He has more men like me and Gabriol—mercs—searching for people. Specific people."

"And we have something in common, I assume."

"You assume correctly," Rydon said. He leaned closer and pointed a finger at her. "They are all rumored to have powers such as you have exhibited."

Terena snorted. "I told you, I have none."

Rydon's lips thinned. "Terena, you may not recall, but I was standing next to you in Metilai. You used your powers in that square. It was actually timely. You covered our escape with the chaos you created."

She looked at him with a blank expression, and he waved a hand dismissively. "Look. I know the other marks—the people he's searching for. We all talk, you know. Us sell swords. So I know who the others are His Majesty wants found. They have powers. And according to the guards back at the White Palace, you used powers on them as well, and on the prince, Isher. They swore it to a man. Ask your cleric."

He rose and tossed the stick he'd been playing with into the fire. He walked toward her and stopped as he passed. "Deny until your face turns blue, goddess," he said with a mock tip of his hat, "But I am not buying."

CROAK TURNED OVER, MUMBLING IN HIS SLEEP. HIS HEAD WAS BLESSEDLY quiet, and he'd been able to fall asleep as soon as his head hit his folded up coat. Now, as he flung his arm wide, it smacked something that cursed. A second later, a hand clamped hard on his mouth, hot breath on his forehead.

"Fuck, Croak!"

His eyes bulged wide as he tried to see his assailant. He bucked at the weight atop him, which made the figure curse and press down harder.

"Croak, stop! It's me!" Terena hissed.

Croak stopped and shook his head. Terena lifted her hand away and moved back enough he could see her face.

"What the fuck?" he wheezed.

She got off him and shoved at his chest before looking around the camp. Ormano, Sonah and Croak had stayed close to the fire, bedding down on rolled up coats, one of them having draped a cloak atop Sonah, while Rydon and Gabriol had gone further out, taking turns on watch. Croak glanced across the fire to where Orry and Sonah lay asleep.

"What are you doing?" he hissed at Terena as he sat up.

"What do you know of the mercs?"

Croak made a face. "Honestly? This couldn't wait until morning?"

"No, it cannot," she hissed back. "Tell me everything from the moment you met them."

Croak huffed and leaned up to see over her shoulder. There was no movement beyond the flames. Both were still asleep.

"I went looking for them like you asked," he whispered. "Found them at Nathaniel's and tried to get them to let us join them or what not and they kicked me out the table. Hadn't spied them again until a few days later when Benson brought me news of your arrest." He gestured with his hand and sighed. "I needed their help with your escape. They agreed, for a price of course. Had to give them half my orichalcum."

"They wouldn't have anything to do with you until you offered them money for help with my escape? Someone charged with being a god and the murderer of the Crown Prince? And nothing about that struck you funny."

"Honestly sis, only you would think any of that crossed my mind in that moment when all I could *think* about was getting you out of there!" This last he all but yelled at her.

She reached out and grabbed his flailing arms, shushing him. When she was sure Croak had calmed, she let go of his arms and sat back.

"Gods, Croak," she mumbled. "I get it. Sorry." They were quiet for a time.

"The shorter one told me he was sent to find me. Not a tracker. *Me*." Terena said.

Croak lifted his head and looked back at her. "Aye, Benson said that back in Laurica. What of it?"

"That doesn't seem strange to.you?"

Croak looked at her, incredulous. "Are you joking?"

Terena ignored him and instead asked, "Did he tell you if he's a god?"

"Who? Rydon?"

Terena smirked. "The northern king. Calls himself the King of Olympus."

"Oh, that's rich," Croak said, then narrowed his eyes at her. "You don't think... it's not Zeus, is it?"

"I don't see how it can be. Whoever it is also told the shorter one he doesn't want me to know his name. Not until he tells me himself."

"Ominous."

"Indeed. And is specific about those he seeks."

"Oh, he has a list, does he?"

"According to the shorter man—"

"Rydon."

"What?"

"His name's Rydon," Croak said. "The shorter man. The other one with the permanent scowl to go with the permanent stick up his ass is his man, Gabriol. Not sure of their relationship otherwise, but I see deference every once in a while."

"So they have—"

"Gaia's blood!"

Croak and Terena whipped their heads across the dying fire to see Ormano dusting off his robes and grabbing at his cloak to stomp over to them. He sat down with a grunt, struggling for a bit as he tried to cross his legs. He gave up after three failed attempts. Sonah hadn't moved, huddled beneath the cloak.

"You two are jabbering loud enough for the dead to hear, let alone Masters Rydon and Gabriol!"

Terena shushed him. "Oh, so you're best friends now? Masters, indeed." Terena said as she scooted over to allow Orry to settle closer.

"Hardly," he said with a frown. "They may not have said it, but I know noblemen when I see them. Even if they're not from Heylisia. We had the opportunity to speak while we stayed at the monastery. And it was their plan that saved you, mind, so I'd be more civil in future."

"Civil?" she laughed. "They came here seeking me out for a man who was no one and nothing a few months past!"

"And yet, if their aim was to kill you, they need not have lifted a finger to help you," Orry said.

"Fine! Then what's their play?"

"Well," a voice said over Terena's shoulder, making them all jump. "I was thinking we head as you'd planned but further west, to Osta. There, we can use the Greek roads and head north."

Orry gasped and Croak reached out to grab hold of his sword. Terena simply sat there, staring over Croak's shoulder at Rydon.

He smiled at having surprised them and loped over, bending slowly to one knee near the group.

"Solon has men there," Terena snapped. "His soldiers are deserting to go north so he'll have men there to stop them."

Rydon shrugged. "A lot has changed. He no longer has deserters top of mind. He'll be looking for you."

"So what do you suggest?"

"If it were me," Rydon said as he shifted, "I'd pull those men back. Further east to Vesala. Men to cover the other ports north. And the places where you could find sanctuary. They will choke those towns first before they look west," he continued.

They were quiet a moment before Terena spoke. "But we'd have to go through the Pass or go south through Elis which, I'm telling you right now, I will not do. The empress's family rules in Elis. At best, we lose three days."

"We'll be going through the Oryon Pass," he confirmed. "And you'd better get used to the possibility it might take longer than that, even." He gazed at Terena, then looked over his shoulder at Sonah's sleeping form. "You and Sonah are wanted for the murder of the Crown Prince of Heylisia. And you specifically, for being a god. There's no one in the empire won't be looking for you. Remember Duke Ovenno's men at Lethe?"

Croak stiffened, and he saw Terena flinch.

"You are not going north anytime soon," Rydon finished, his voice rough, but Croak saw the sympathy in his emerald eyes.

Silence thickened around them, broken only by the pop of the fire.

Rydon leaned forward and started drawing in the dirt near their beds.

"If we get to Osta without issue, we head north to Seleste. We can cross safely there. "The river is still frozen over, and Seleste is the furthest west we can still cross on horseback," Rydon said, casting a look at Orry. "By then they'll have assumed either they missed us, lost us or were looking in the wrong place."

"I thought you didn't know this area," Croak said suspiciously.

Rydon shrugged. "I lied. Mercenary."

Croak looked over at Terena, who sat looking at the ground.

"And when we get to the north?" he asked. "I assume there's a plan for that as well?"

"There is," Rydon said with a sigh. He glanced at Croak before turning his gaze to Terena. "The king wishes to meet us at Olympia. They have rebuilt the palace there. Once we cross Fell River, there will be no need to worry about pursuit. I doubt the emperor will send men across."

"You do not know him," Terena said, lifting her head at last. She narrowed her hazel eyes at Rydon, and Croak could tell by the set of her mouth she was angry, although he wasn't sure if it was at the mercenary or their predicament or, more likely, herself.

"Aye, that is true," he said with a shrug. "But in the unlikely event he sends men north, they will not return."

"And how can you be sure of that?"

"Because the king is like you, lady," Gabriol said. He had quietly approached as they'd talked and now stood behind Croak, his thumbs hooked at his waist. They all turned when he spoke.

"What do you mean, like me?"

Rydon looked at Gabriol, then back at them all. "He is a god."

CHAPTER FIFTEEN

They'd been traveling for a week when Ormano fell ill. He blamed it on the food they'd bought from the small inn at Portia in western Ermanel.

When he fell off his mount a couple of days later, he could no longer hide his illness.

Croak pulled up Cerberus and jumped off, hurrying to crouch next to Orry.

"You're burning up!" he snapped after he'd settled his palm on Orry's forehead.

"What's the matter?"

Croak turned his head as Rydon pulled up alongside. "He's feverish," he said, his lips pulled tight as he looked back down at Orry's huddled form.

"Let's get him up." Rydon dismounted and reached down to lift Orry gently off the cold ground. "We can do nothing for him out here. We're a few hours' ride from Nosam. 'Tis small, but it has an inn."

"What's going on?" Terena pulled up and hopped off her horse before anyone could respond. When she saw Orry being held by Croak and Rydon and looking like death as he moaned with every step, she shot forward, quickly grabbing her brother's shoulder as they labored to lift Orry onto his horse.

Croak moved and transferred Orry's weight to Terena, while Croak mounted Cerberus. They lifted Orry's mostly dead weight, grunting and shifting as Croak pulled and held the reins at the same time. Cerberus moved, adding to their burden, but Croak handled him masterfully and he settled enough for Croak to heave Orry the last few inches.

"Will a delay hurt us?" Croak asked when they rode off. Orry let out a groan, shifting painfully against Croak's thighs.

"A day or two would not, although we gamble the longer we are in one place," Gabriol called out. He rode alongside Croak, Sonah in front of them, while Terena and Rydon led the way.

"I have money to bribe the innkeeper and his staff, if that is the worry."

Gabriol shrugged. "It is *a* worry, of course, but it is not the only worry. How ill is your friend? Does he require a surgeon? How many others will notice us traveling through and will remember an ill man and his companions?"

"I cannot know the answers, Gabriol. You know as much as I."

"My point is, we cannot know the danger until we know those answers."

"I am not… that sick."

Croak patted Orry again. "Go to sleep, little one. Let the adults speak."

"Sleep, cleric," Gabriol called out. "We'll see how sick you are soon enough."

THE INN AT NOSAM WAS SMALL AND COULD BARELY BE CALLED AN INN. It had three bedchambers, and the main hall had only one table with a small bar in the corner. The innkeeper had his fists planted on his fleshy hips as a sleepy maid led them up a creaking staircase at the back.

They settled Orry in the first chamber they came to, Croak and Rydon taking care to be gentle while Orry moaned and panted. Terena pressed a coin into the maid's hand and whispered something to her. The young maid nodded and bobbed a curtsy before scuttling back down the stairs. Croak pulled the meager covers over his friend as Rydon pulled out a chair from the corner for him.

"Here, mistress," the diminutive maid said as she appeared once more in the doorway. Terena motioned to Croak, and the maid shuffled in, handing him a bowl of water and several washcloths. As he smiled and thanked her, she ducked her head, her face flushed bright red. She bobbed another curtsy and hurried out as quick as a sparrow.

"You've a way with the ladies, boy," Gabriol said with a smirk. Across the room, Rydon grinned at him.

"It is a gift I am cursed with," Croak said with a sigh. "Maybe *I'm* a god." He dipped a washcloth into the cool water and wrung it out, then placed it on Orry's head. "Do not be fooled by the long, gangly body and lack of muscles, good sir. I am a madman in the bedroom. And the ladies know it," he said, turning to Sonah with a wink.

Sonah choked, and Gabriol grinned across at Rydon.

Croak looked up when Terena pushed away from the doorframe. She was still weak herself; the bruises on her face still visible, but she stood as straight as ever.

"I am to bed as well," she said. "Come, Sonah. You must be exhausted, too." The young woman sighed and mumbled her agreement as she slumped out of the room. Terena nodded at the men and left without waiting to hear their responses. Croak looked over at Rydon.

"Come!" Croak said with forced joviality and stood. "Let's leave the weakling to his rest and we will find food, ale, and women. Not necessarily in that order, eh, Gabriol?"

CHAPTER SIXTEEN

Rydon looked out over the small town as he sat crouched on the thatched rooftop of the stables. It was the quietest part of the night, and the darkest. The torches along the pathways were dim and cast so little a glow, they almost made it harder to see.

A bird call made him glance across. He spotted Gabriol on the ground near the gates to the village. He used the bird call to signal back and saw Gabriol's shadow move away and melt into the night.

They had been in Nosam two days already, and the cleric was no better. He had argued with Terena earlier about leaving him there. No surprise she had refused to listen, and had walked away childishly. He was not used to having his word challenged. He'd been told this was a simple assignment. Find and escort.

Now they were stalled in a country of their enemies, being hunted like game.

And if what the cleric had told him that first day was to be believed, they needed to get to the north and behind the protection of the king as quickly as possible.

The bird call sounded once more, except this time Gabriol added two short whistles. Their signal for danger.

Rydon crouched as he padded across the rooftop. Dropping to the ground, he scurried to a doorway opposite. He saw nothing and heard nothing, so he slid out, hugging the wall of the building at his back, remaining low when he came to the street.

He heard it then.

To his right, the bushes rustled and he strained his eyes to see three or four shadowy forms glide through the streets, weaving past a row of buildings in front of him where Rydon lost sight of them. Blood pounded in his ears as he moved after them, staying far enough back he went unnoticed.

When they entered the inn, his blood dropped to his feet.

He broke into a run, using the bird call. He unsheathed his sword, hearing the shouts and screams as he entered the doorway. Rydon flew up the stairs, taking the first man out with a slash to his knees, stabbing him through the chest as he fell backwards.

Another soldier on the landing turned and rushed him with his sword raised high. Rydon dropped to his knee and stabbed up with his sword, catching the man in the gut.

Rydon looked up into the hallway to see Gabriol fighting another soldier. He heard two others inside the room where they'd put the cleric. He shoved the dead man off his blade and staggered to his feet.

As soon as he reached the doorway, a piercing cry cut through his head, and he lurched back against the wall. Rydon slid to the ground. The shrieking noise in his head nearly deafened him and he brought his hands up to his ears. He looked to his right and saw Gabriol huddled on the ground. Rydon saw his lips open and move, but he couldn't hear what he was saying.

Like a man under water, Rydon turned his head back toward the cleric's room. He lifted his body like a man much older than Rydon's years. He ached everywhere.

Rydon made it to his knees. Crawling to the doorway, he stopped and leaned against the doorframe. The cleric was on the bed, hands to his ears and gasping. Terena stood at the end of the bed, looking down at something. Rydon leaned in, trying to get a better view. Someone lay dead at Terena's feet.

Something shook him. Rydon looked over his shoulder and saw a hand. Looking up, he saw Terena silently screaming at him. She grabbed his shoulders and screamed. Spittle landed on his nose.

"—thing?"

He swallowed. In a whoosh, sound returned. His ears popped, and Rydon's eyes went wild as they took in his surroundings.

"—r anything? Rydon!"

He turned toward the sound, toward Terena. She shook him again. He focused on her mouth.

"Can you hear me? Can you hear anything?"

"I can hear you," he whispered.

She sighed and hung her head for a second. "Get up when you're ready. I'm going to get Croak. Where's your man?"

Rydon turned toward the hall and pointed, his hand dropping back down at his side.

"Good," she muttered and stood. He heard her moving about the room but his eyes were closed as he concentrated on breathing.

At last, he opened his eyes to see her lift the cleric. With one hand braced at his waist, she hauled him around the bed. The girl, Sonah, was beside her, hunched over as she clutched a bundle to her middle, her face ashen.

"Wait," he whispered, but Terena was already moving past him and out of the room, the girl at her heels. He looked around dazedly, regarding the dead man near the foot of the bed, his black clothing giving no clue to his allegiance. Blood pooled beneath him. Rydon looked up, hearing Terena saying something in the hallway before their footsteps receded.

It took him a few minutes to stand. He was still weak, but he had to find Gabriol. With some difficulty, he stepped into the hall and saw Gabriol sitting up against a wall, eyes closed. His steps halting, Rydon sighed and leaned against the wall next to his friend.

"What happened?"

Rydon shook his head, then immediately regretted it. A thousand sparks shot across his eyes and his head throbbed. He took a few seconds before responding.

"I don't know, but the girl seems unaffected. Pale, but otherwise fine. Terena too."

"And the cleric?"

"Alive," Rydon answered. He opened his eyes and looked down at Gabriel. "You?"

"Alive. Croak?"

Rydon warily looked around the empty hallway and slumped his shoulders. "Terena's going to find him. We're leaving as soon as you're ready."

With a groan, he pushed away from the wall. He walked like an old man, his body still aching from whatever that blast was earlier. He was still foggy when he reached the common room downstairs. The innkeep huddled outside the door with the maid clutching at his apron. They startled when he coughed, then jumped out of his way, eyes down. He didn't pay them any mind as he walked past and out into the darkness.

To his right, he heard the sounds of feet scuffling and low voices. As his eyes adjusted, he saw shadows moving. He walked toward them until he could make out their voices.

"And don't stop until you get to Villadelle," Terena was saying.

The other shadow jumped on the horse and pulled on the reins. As Rydon came to stand by Terena, he watched Croak's horse gallop away, leading another horse with what he assumed was the cleric atop.

Terena stole a glance at him. "You all right?"

Rydon continued to stare off into the distance after the horses. Long seconds passed before he turned his gaze to her.

"That was you."

"What was me?"

"That blast," said Rydon, his teeth gritted as he turned his body to face her. "Whatever that was, it was you."

Terena didn't answer, but he caught the gaze she flicked up at the girl. Rydon turned to look at Sonah, but her head was down. He looked back at Terena, frowning at him before striding away.

Over her shoulder she said, "Croak will meet us in Tursk, but we ride for Pyrgos."

"We?"

"Aye," she snapped. She turned and walked right up to stand close enough her hot breath fanned his cheeks. "If you and your man want to live, we ride for Pyrgos. We can go north from there to meet Croak. We've a few days before word gets back we escaped again."

"And what about the innkeep? The maid?"

She didn't reply right away, turning instead to the frightened girl and spoke to her in a low enough voice he couldn't hear. The girl nodded, her hands still shaking, but she straightened and went to the stables.

Terena turned back to Rydon, eyes narrowed. "I've plans just now for him. When I'm done, we tie them up. Should give us until at least midmorning before someone stumbles across them."

She strode toward the inn as Gabriol appeared at the door. Terena walked past without acknowledging him.

Rydon wiped a hand down his beard and cursed. He looked down at his hands and frowned to see them still trembling. He threw another curse before striding after Terena.

"You all right, lord?" Gabriol called as he caught up to him.

"I'm fine," he snapped.

"Did you find Croak?"

"Aye," Rydon said curtly. "Rode off with the cleric. For Villadelle."

"What's going on?"

Rydon shouldered past his bewildered friend without answering. Gabriol followed but did not pester him for a reply.

By the sounds coming from the kitchen, Rydon didn't need to guess where Terena had got to. He lifted the curtain to the room and stopped, watching as Terena stuffed a rag into the mouth of the maid, stifling her screams.

She looked up as they appeared, but continued her work. She rounded the chair where the fat innkeep sat, her lips pulled down as she unsheathed her dagger. At the sight, the maid fainted, and the man struggled anew. His gag shook with the force of his shouts, muffled behind the dirty fabric. Terena watched him for a few seconds more, the blade pointed at the man's cock.

"You are not very hospitable for an innkeeper," she said at last. The man's face was blotched, making the pock marks along his cheeks stand out. His eyes bulged as he struggled to move. "I'm of a mind to tell all my friends never to visit Nosam. The service is terrible."

The man's muffled shouts were in vain and he struggled some more, his face mottled an ugly red.

"Where's your messenger?" asked Terena.

Rydon looked at her, then back at the innkeep. After a moment, she pulled out the rag so he could speak.

"Go fuck yerself!" he screamed, a stream of saliva catching on his lips and the stubble on his chin.

Terena dropped to a crouch, her dark hair bouncing over her shoulder in the leather tie she liked to wear up high. The blade tip pressed deeper into the folds of the man's trousers. He yelped and tried to scoot back, but he was tied well.

"I don't have time," Terena sighed. "I wish I did. I do like to fuck myself, especially after waking up in the morning. Right before I wash. Great way to start my day."

She looked over at Rydon, hazel eyes flashing. "But no, not today. Today, instead of fucking myself, I was rudely awakened by men sent to kill me. And my friends." She tutted, patting the man's britches with her blade. He let out a low moan.

"Now, we try again." Her voice was soft and menacing as she leaned in closer to the man, her blade once more threatening his manhood. "Where's your messenger?"

"I don't—aaaah!"

The man's scream tore through the room and Rydon's skull. He winced and lifted his hands to his head as he stared daggers at Terena. She paid him no mind as she dug the blade tip deeper into the man's crotch. He howled and whined and blubbered, then nodded his head and told her all about the man he'd sent off to the emperor's men.

"Where can I find this man? Lefren, is it?"

More crying before he answered. "If he's back, he's at 'ome. Back of th' village near th' stables. His place has a green awning."

Terena turned to look at Rydon, one eyebrow lifted. He scowled at her, then turned to leave. She stood and grabbed hold of his forearm, stalling him, making a show of stretching before sheathing her blade and looking around the room.

"Well then. My friends and I will take our breakfast on the road." She patted the innkeep on the shoulder as she moved past him to rummage in the cupboards and drawers, pulling out food and folding items into towels. "Don't take this the wrong way," she said, her voice sweeter than he'd ever heard her use before. She continued to gather foodstuffs, walking around the kitchen. "I don't trust you to make meals up for us, so I am taking the liberty of doing so myself. As you know, I cannot trust your hospitality. Not after all this!" She laughed and lifted her hands up.

It was not a pleasant sound.

"Rydon," she said before tossing a couple of bundles at him. He fumbled to catch them as she tossed the last one over her shoulder. "You good?"

He nodded, his face mulish.

She strode past the innkeep, then turned back. Grabbing up the rag, she shoved it in his mouth. She slapped him, hard, when he protested and moved his head all over, struggling against her.

Rydon moved out of her way as she strode from the room. He stood for a moment, watching the portly man crying, his head limp. The maid had awakened some time during the whole business and was silently crying beside him.

Rydon had done a lot of bad in his life, he freely admitted. But something about this sat wrong with him. True, the man had sent a message to the emperor, but they were fugitives. Wanted for the slaying of a beloved prince. This man knew nothing more about them than that.

Rydon spat and followed Terena.

DAWN WAS ALMOST UPON THEM. THEY HAD TO LEAVE, SOON, BEFORE the village woke. Terena stalked down an alley behind the tavern and out onto the street dead-ending at the stables. She stopped and looked for the house with the green awning.

"Do not do anything reckless," Rydon hissed over her shoulder. She hadn't paid him any mind, feeling the heat of his anger on her back while they'd walked. Instead, she focused on the man who had stolen into the night and almost gotten them all killed.

"Get our horses ready," she replied. She spotted the house to the left of the stables, the green awning washed out in the pre-dawn gloom, but it was the only one in the area with any awning at all. "I hadn't thought you so squeamish, mercenary," she added before striding across to the house.

Rydon grabbed her arm and swung her around. Quick as a snake, Terena lashed out, grasping his throat, squeezing her fingers enough his chin popped up.

"You have strange ethics, lord. Do not stand in the way of my justice."

"You will make the emperor's claims true if you continue down this path," Rydon snarled at her.

"Terena, please," Gabriol pleaded, coming up to Rydon's side. "We came to your aid at significant risk. Do not let it be in vain. We must leave. Now."

Terena continued to scowl at Rydon before dropping her hand. He took a step back, and she caught the look of disappointment in his eyes before he turned, his hand to his throat, and headed for the stables. Sonah stood there, anxiously watching them.

Terena cursed, but decided against going after the man who'd brought the emperor's men. Against her better judgement, she followed Rydon. Gabriol brought up the rear reluctantly.

The shadows were fading, so they made fast work of saddling the horses. Terena hitched her food bag to the saddle, then tugged on the reins, walking Nyx out into the street. The others followed close behind.

As they neared the back gate, a man emerged from the house with the awning. Terena and the man locked eyes, and she cursed when she saw recognition.

"Alarm!"

At the man's shrieking, they rode away. Terena swore, pinching her lips in frustration. She knew she should've taken care of that weasel.

Damn Rydon!

She rode hard down the path leading out of the village, then turned sharply left when they came out onto the Greek road heading south.

A small copse of trees came into view on the horizon and Terena dug her heels in, urging her mount faster. They tore across the valley as the sun rose ever higher. She leaned low, whispering words of encouragement to Nyx, praising the mare when they finally reached the woods. She slowed, waiting for the others to catch up.

"You ride like Artemis," said Gabriol, his words labored as he panted. She turned as they pulled up beside her, Gabriol wearing a grin that almost made him handsome. Rydon still scowled.

"I let him live because of you and now we need to work much harder to disappear!"

"Oh, this is *my* fault," Rydon scoffed. He jumped off his horse and spat. "You've been reckless since the moment we rescued you! And what thanks did we get, huh? You've been surly and ungrateful ever since we found you!"

"I am being hunted like an animal for a crime I did not commit and *you're* the wounded party?" Terena, too, dismounted and strode to stand toe to toe with Rydon. "My lo—my prince was murdered, and I blamed for it, but of course, let me stop and thank you properly." With that, she hauled back and punched him.

Sonah gasped and stepped back, bumping into Gabriol. Terena had a moment's satisfaction as Rydon's head snapped back, his eyes wide with shock. Blood flooded his cheeks as he roared and came at her, Gabriol's solid form stepping between them, stopping him.

"You will both get us killed," yelled Gabriol. His face, too, was beet red, his blue eyes narrowed, and shot them both a disgusted look. "*You* are children scrapping and *we* are fugitives on the run! So we must *be* on the run! Now!"

He shoved them both, hard, and left them panting behind him. He mounted his horse and turned it as he looked down at them. "Get your shit together, both of you. Kill each other when we reach the north. Until then, we need each other."

Terena smothered a curse before striding off toward her horse. She mounted and rode away. She heard the others behind her as she leaned low over Nyx, urging her faster.

CHAPTER SEVENTEEN

A hawk soared above. Terena followed it with her eyes, up and up. Just then, clouds separated to reveal a building, a temple perhaps, columns gleaming so bright in the sunlight it hurt to look at.

Terena squinted, hoping for another glimpse of the temple. Her breath caught tight in her chest as another cloud passed, blocking the sun's rays before obscuring the view of the building and the surrounding lush greenery. She held her hand to her forehead, shading her eyes. Her mouth dropped open as she realized there was no way to get to the top.

She looked around. There was no path to be found.

"How do I get up there?"

"Do not think on that now," a voice at her shoulder said.

Terena frowned. "How will I find you?"

"Look up again. See the temple. See the mountain. You will find me."

"WE NEED TO BE OFF, TERENA," RYDON SAID.

Terena sat up with a jolt. Sonah sat back on her heels, startled. Terena reached out to her in apology, then looked around and noticed they had packed away their camp. Gabriol set his saddlebags over his horse as he arched a dark blond eyebrow at her. Sonah too, was watching her curiously and Terena shifted to see she was still wrapped up in her cloak, her saddlebags as her pillow.

"What?"

"How can you still be asleep? We've already packed everything," Gabriol said.

Terena rubbed at her face, realizing she'd been dreaming.

Usually her visions were only images, pictorial clues leading her to treasures or artifacts left behind by the gods. Breadcrumbs she hoped would one day lead her to her parents.

The voice she'd heard, however, was new.

Terena stood, frowning as she thought more on the vision she'd just had. It had been a woman speaking, that was certain. But she didn't recognize the voice and none of what she'd said made sense. She focused instead on the mountain and the building she'd seen. A temple.

The frustrating thing was, whenever she'd had these visions in the past, she had resources at her disposal to find where those clues led. Now, in the middle of the continent with no books or Orry to help her decipher the visions, she was stuck.

"I'll be ready in a minute," she grumbled, fastening her cloak and grabbing her saddlebags. "Would you mind putting this on Nyx while I piss?"

Rydon snorted and grabbed the bags from her. "As you wish, my lady."

Terena mumbled her thanks and strode off a good distance. She and Rydon had formed a tense truce after fleeing Nosam. A day later, she'd even apologized for hitting him, to which he'd complimented her on the viciousness of it. He had then apologized for not letting her silence the messenger when they'd had their chance, agreeing leaving him alone made it more dangerous for them. She'd accepted his apology and soon they'd fallen into a more amicable mood.

Finishing her business, Terena made to turn back to the others when pain shot through her belly. It was so sharp and sudden, she doubled over.

She shut her eyes and breathed through the pain when a voice went through her head.

Find me.

Terena exhaled and blinked. Instead of seeing the surrounding woods, she saw the mountain from her vision. She dropped to a knee, gasping for air when her chest tightened.

Find me.

And then she saw it. The temple. So white it looked like a beacon. Gilded pillars and large brassieres with fires licking at the sky. Sitting atop a mountain with no clear path up to the top. A straight column of earth and stone and trees, as if the trees themselves held the mysterious building aloft.

Pain shot through her gut once more.

She heard rustling in the trees but she couldn't straighten, could do nothing but gasp as the pain receded.

Find me.

"Terena, are you all right?" Sonah's worried voice sounded a second before the girl rushed over, bending and taking hold of Terena around her shoulders.

Terena nodded, her hands clutching her belly. Sonah helped her straighten, keeping hold while Terena took in big gulps of air.

"You look green," Sonah said, and Terena's lips lifted at the sound of Sonah's distaste.

"I just threw up," she said.

Sonah looked down and yelped, her soft leather boot in the mess.

"Gross, Terena, gods," she moaned and stepped away. "A head's up next time, please."

"Of course," she said.

"Are you in pain? It's only been a few weeks since... anyway, even though you look better, you're still recovering. You should rest more."

"Nonsense," Terena said with a sigh. "I'll be fine. I... I need a minute."

"You were gone awhile," Sonah said, more to fill the silence than anything. "The men worried, so..."

"Mother hens," Terena said with a smile. She straightened fully and patted at Sonah to release her. The girl did so but slowly, eyeing Terena as if she were a babe taking her first steps.

"What do you think Croak and Orry are doing right now?" Sonah mused as they began walking back to the others.

"Well," Terena said, her voice stronger now, "knowing Croak, he's probably sleeping off a late party with one or several women. And probably in Orry's room."

Sonah laughed, a pretty blush rising in her cheeks. Her green and brown eyes flashed at Terena. "I bet he tells the women how his poor sick friend is a cleric and never been with a woman. I can just see Orry's face."

They laughed as they reached Rydon and Gabriol.

"That was one hell of a piss," Rydon remarked. He mounted his horse and looked down at them.

"What's funny?" Gabriol asked, leaning on his saddle horn.

Sonah smiled up at them, and Terena winked at her. "Just thinking about what Croak and Orry might be up to."

"I haven't known your brother long," Gabriol said as he watched Terena mount Nyx. "But I'm betting he either spent the night at a brothel or had the brothel brought to his room. No, the cleric's room."

Sonah's cackle warmed Terena's heart as they rode off, her smile widening at the thought of seeing Croak soon.

THE PARTY HAD BEEN A GOOD IDEA IN THEORY, BUT NOW CROAK HAD the burden of getting the girls to leave his room.

Well... Orry's room.

It had taken him the better part of an hour, but Croak herded the women along, their slow progress making his mood sour even more. He offered more coin if they moved faster and was rewarded when they quickened their efforts and left.

When Croak finally closed the door behind them, he looked around at the mess left behind with a weary eye. Orry had slunk out during the night to sleep in Croak's room. He hadn't taken too kindly to being awakened by Croak and four of the women he'd convinced to join him from the nearby brothel. Yelling at Croak over the sound of the women's laughter, Orry had stomped from the room.

Croak did his best to straighten the room before giving up. He grabbed up his breeches from the floor and hunted until he found his tunic, rumpled and stuffed in the corner behind the bed, before leaving the room. He walked next door and rapped on the door to his own room, listening for Orry.

When his knock was met with silence, he used his key to open it and slipped inside. Orry lay sprawled on his back, one leg on the floor, an arm flung over his eyes and his mouth wide open, snoring.

Croak groaned and walked over to the washstand next to the armoire. He splashed cold water on his face and gasped, blinking away the sleep as he fumbled for the towel on the bar beneath.

Walking over to his bed as he dried his face, Croak looked down at his friend, noting the color back in his cheeks and the easy way he breathed. Well. As much as he could tell around the snoring.

He snapped the towel against Orry's leg and his friend jumped.

"Wha.."

"Rise and shine, gorgeous," Croak said as he walked over to his bag, rummaging inside for a clean shirt. He sniffed at one, immediately tossing it back inside in favor of another. He reached back and tugged off the soiled one he wore and put on the new one.

Orry had moved to sit at the edge of the bed, his head in his hands.

"How'd you sleep?" Croak asked, eyeing Orry with a frown.

Orry grunted, then lifted his red eyes, blinking up at Croak owlishly. "Much better after I came in here."

Croak grunted. "But you missed a hell of a party."

Orry grimaced. He rubbed a hand on the back of his neck and sighed. "Breakfast?"

"If you're feeling up to it," Croak said as he regarded his friend. "I can bring something back for you."

"No," Orry said and then moaned as he rose slowly. "I feel much better this morning. I'll go with you. Besides, we need to find another inn today."

"Right," Croak mumbled.

Villadelle was large enough they could stay hidden from anyone searching, but only if they moved around. They'd stayed at this inn for the past two days, so Croak had scouted out the next inn they would move to, this time with a room large enough for both of them.

When Orry finished getting dressed, they gathered their belongings and ate in a tavern on the other side of the city. Croak watched Orry, but other than a bit of fatigue, he seemed much better. He no longer had a fever and his appetite was back.

Croak leaned back, stretching, his gaze wandering around when he saw a group of men cross outside the window. Leaning forward, he frowned as they passed, noticing the gold and white of their uniforms.

Heylisian soldiers.

"Fuck," he said under his breath. He rose, his chair scrapping back loudly on the wood floor, and he nodded across at Orry. "We need to go."

Orry looked up at him in confusion. "I'm not—"

He leaned down, his hands braced on the table as he hissed at Orry, "Heylisian soldiers just passed outside. They could double back any second. We need to get the fuck out of here now."

CHAPTER EIGHTEEN

"We should be in Tursk by midday," Rydon called out, glancing over his shoulder at them. Sonah didn't bother acknowledging as she sat slumped in her saddle.

"Once we get there, we can rest for a few hours and set off after dinner. We should start traveling at night from now on," he continued.

"Have you travelled throughout the continent?" Terena asked as Nyx walked slowly behind Rydon's mount.

He glanced at her over his shoulder and shrugged. "Aye. Been all over. I'm a mercenary."

She nodded, thinking. "Have you ever seen a building like... a temple or a large monastery atop a mountain?"

Rydon looked back at her again, this time holding her gaze. "I've seen many temples across the continent. And aye, many have been atop mountains. The priests and priestesses feel closest to the gods on those mountains."

Terena pursed her lips. "This one would be unique. The mountain isn't," she shrugged, "but the temple wouldn't be accessible."

He arched an eyebrow. "So, how did they build a temple up there?"

She looked away in frustration. "Never mind."

They continued on in silence, the sounds of the forest filling the space around them as they travelled.

After a while, Rydon slowed his horse until he was beside Terena. "Unless you mean the sanctuary at Messene?"

Terena turned to look at him. "What?"

"What you asked earlier, about a temple on a mountain?"

She frowned at him.

"There's a temple atop a mountain in Messene. The priestesses there call it a sanctuary. Only way to get up there is to be invited."

Terena slowed Nyx to a halt, staring at Rydon. Ahead of them, Sonah turned and called back as Gabriol slowed his horse as well.

"What's going on?" Gabriol called out.

Terena held up a hand but did not take her eyes off Rydon as she asked, "You've seen this place? The sanctuary?"

"Aye. In Messene."

"Messene," Terena said, dropping her eyes to her pommel in thought.

"South of here, though," Rydon added.

Gabriol walked his horse to them and paused, his gaze swiveling from Rydon to Terena. "Why've we stopped?"

Rydon didn't respond, instead leaning over his saddle as he frowned over at Terena. "We don't have time—"

"We have to go," Terena said, finally looking up at him. Rydon pulled back at the look on her face and shook his head.

"We don't have time, Terena," he bit out.

"Gabriol," Terena said, ignoring Rydon. "I need you to go to Orry and Croak in Villadelle. Please. Tell them where we're going and meet us there if Orry can travel."

"That is south, Terena," Rydon said again, flashing Gabriol a dark look. "We are going north. We grab Orry and Croak on the way and we cross at—"

"We have to go to Messene," Terena said, her voice brooking no argument. "I can't tell you why, not yet. But I need you to trust me. I have to go to that sanctuary."

"Did you forget the part where I said you have to be invited?"

She knew he was irritated, but she didn't care. He could be as irritated or angry as he wanted, but she had to find the woman from her vision. She'd had another one the night before, and the woman's voice filling her head all night made her sleep restless.

If she went north before finding the woman—who might be in Messene in that sanctuary she also saw in her vision—she might not get another chance to do so. At least not for a long time.

And, somehow, Terena knew what she might find at the sanctuary would bring her closer to finding her parents.

At the very least, why she had the powers of gods.

NIGHTMARES FROM THE LAST NIGHT SHE HAD SEEN LEREK BESIEGED Terena when she tried to sleep. She couldn't get the image of his lifeless eyes staring at her while she cried over his chest, out of her head. And then the confrontation with Isher. The way her mind had shut down and her body had taken over on instinct.

The rage that had filled her.

The helplessness.

Soft hands rested on her shoulders, a whisper in her ear. Terena moved, quick as lightning, lashing out her hand to grasp the slim wrist above her shoulder.

When Sonah cried out, Terena's eyes snapped open, and she huffed out a breath. She dropped the girl's wrist and scrambled to sit up, ducking her head and quickly wiping the tears from her cheeks.

"I'm sorry," Terena said in a low voice.

"I heard you crying," Sonah said after a few seconds. She was sitting on the ground next to Terena, her knees pulled up to her chest. "I just wanted to... I thought you might—"

"I'm fine," Terena mumbled, pulling her cloak tight around her body.

"You're not fine," Sonah said with more firmness than Terena had heard thus far from the girl. She looked up at her.

"You've been through a lot these last few weeks, not to mention you must be…" Sonah shook her head. "You lost someone, Terena. Someone you loved. I loved him, too. Not like you, of course," she scoffed, wiping at her nose and Terena realized the girl was crying too. "Lerek treated me like a person, not his Royal Taster. I mean, I know he probably did that for Isher. But even Isher could be a wretch to me sometimes." She sniffed. "Lerek was… he was special. And you loved him. Of course, you're feeling like this. I can't imagine…"

Terena said nothing. For a long time, both women were silent, each lost in their own thoughts.

Sonah shifted and brought her hand out to touch Terena's knee. "If you need to talk, I am here. I know we don't know each other well, but you saved me, Terena. You and Croak and the others. You didn't have to. And I know it was a great risk and I know I'm slowing you all down and I am pretty useless with weapons and I'm miserable with a horse. But I am a good listener. And it breaks my heart to see you going through this alone." She shifted closer and Terena let her. Sonah pushed back a lock of blonde hair falling out of her braid, then laid her hand on Terena's and squeezed. "You're not alone. I'm here with you and I'm your friend."

Terena's eyes welled up, and she reached out and squeezed Sonah's hand, tugging her close so the girl fell forward into Terena's arms. The hug was awkward, but Sonah didn't protest as Terena wrapped her arms around the girl's slight frame, squeezed once, and let her go. Sonah sat back, crossing her legs as she watched Terena with a soft smile.

"Thank you, Sonah," she said and wiped away a few tears. "And aye, you are useless with weapons and a horse. But we've time to rectify both while we're waiting out the emperor and his thugs before we can travel north again. So tomorrow, we'll start your training, yes?"

Sonah pulled a face. "I was being nice. You don't have to be so cruel."

Terena laughed, and for a second she marveled at how genuine it was, how glad she was of Sonah's company. "You've been an idle lady for too long. Time to toughen you up."

Sonah grumbled as she stood and walked back to her own pallet. Terena bedded down once more, smiling as she heard Sonah's grumbling continue until she had fallen back asleep.

CHAPTER NINETEEN

The journey to Messene took more than a fortnight, and most of that due to traveling unpaved roads or through woods to stay hidden. Terena missed her brother; this might be the longest she'd been apart from Croak since they were children.

She hoped Gabriol had found him and Orry.

They arrived well into the evening, and Terena was surprised to see the small city alive with the bustle of people. There was music everywhere, a cacophony of song and shouts and laughter everywhere they passed.

A far cry from the tension filled provinces they'd travelled through since their escape.

Sonah glanced around nervously, her hands gripping the reins tight as she kept her horse close to Terena's side.

As they made their way slowly through the main square, they stopped many times when people stumbled drunkenly into their path. Rydon began yelling out at the bystanders, clearing a path as Terena and Sonah followed close behind.

After ensuring their horses were cared for at the stable yard, Rydon led them toward an inn recommended by the stable hand.

Terena didn't worry any of the Heylisian soldiers or Imperial

Guard would be lying in wait, especially in Lakonia, but she did cast a wary gaze around as they entered the inn and Rydon negotiated for their accommodations.

"You and Sonah have the room at the end of the hall on the second level. I'm going to walk around a bit. See if I can get any news."

Terena watched him leave, then motioned to Sonah as she led the way up the stairs. She was worried the girl would keel over from exhaustion, but she followed without protest, dropping onto the bed as Terena closed the door to their room.

"Are you hungry?" Terena asked, her voice soft as she regarded the girl's prone figure. Sonah grunted, but Terena wasn't sure if that was assent or not. She waited all of three seconds before moving closer, pushing back a lock of Sonah's hair from her face. She smiled when she saw Sonah was already asleep.

Terena sat at the edge of the bed, letting out a long exhale, and closed her eyes. She was tired, but not enough to sleep. Maybe some food would help.

She looked back at Sonah before rising and leaving the room, locking the door and headed downstairs.

Thirty minutes later, she was sitting at a table at the back of the inn, a half-eaten plate of lamb and rice on the table as she finished the last of the bread and ale. She ordered another ale and stared out the window.

The door to the inn opened and Terena looked up to see Rydon's wind-reddened face as he came in, shutting the door softly behind him. She sat up, waving to him when he caught her eye. He raised his eyebrows and came over to the table, taking the seat opposite hers with a big sigh.

"Hear anything?" Terena asked.

Rydon was about to speak when the innkeeper came over with two tankards of ale.

"Figured you'd want one too, lord," the man said in the common tongue, his accent barely there. "Can I get you a meal? No more lamb, I'm afraid, but I've bread and cheeses, some figs, if you're hungry."

Rydon thanked the man, accepting the bread and cheese offered and waited until he'd walked back to the kitchen before answering Terena.

"You were right," he said, flicking a glance at her with a raised eyebrow as he pointed to her lamb. She shrugged and shoved the plate toward him. He grabbed her fork and speared the meat, chewing on it as if he hadn't eaten in days.

Terena waited patiently.

"You were right," he said again after swallowing. "Duke Ovenno never went to Metilai. When the emperor issued a warrant for his arrest, Duke Ovenno sent an announcement out to the provinces of their secession from the empire. Three other provinces also declared independence from the empire. Heylisia's preparing for war."

Terena sprang forward, her hand shooting across the table to grasp Rydon's forearm. "What provinces? And are they still looking for us?"

Rydon nodded, taking a drink of his ale. "Aye, still looking for us, unfortunately, but only near Metilai and only as far west as Ermanel. Aurora, Ravos and Tursk also declared independence and are readying their armies. Ermanel's still holding out, but they have soldiers posted at their border, so it's real fucking lucky we got out when we did. No word from Osta or Elis but—"

"Elis won't secede."

Terena sat back as the innkeeper brought Rydon's food.

"What of the firstborns? Is it like the abbot said? That they escaped?"

Rydon nodded once and popped a piece of cheese in his mouth. "Gone. From what I gathered, the young royals all disappeared during your execution."

Terena's mouth hung open, and she sat back in her seat, staring at Rydon.

"They were long gone by the time the emperor sent the warrant for Ovenno."

Terena put a hand to her mouth. Rydon continued eating, unfazed by this world-altering news.

"Whoever killed the prince orchestrated their escape," he said after a long pause.

Terena felt ill. She had thought Duke Ovenno was the one being set up, that it was the diversion for whoever was behind Lerek's murder. But the diversion was the murder itself.

All so the firstborns could escape the palace before the provinces broke from the empire.

"At least we can get our business done, then head north," Rydon said around a mouthful.

"Rydon," Terena said, shaking her head, "you don't have to stay with us."

He looked up at her and opened his mouth to speak, but she held up a hand to stop him. "Listen, I appreciate everything you've done for us, but it's only going to get worse. You've no obligation to us. Once Gabriol arrives with Croak and Orry, you should leave."

"I'm not leaving," he said with a quick shake of his head.

Terena narrowed her eyes. "Right. The money. You said the new king offered you—"

Rydon laughed and shook his head, tearing a chunk of bread with his teeth. Terena looked pointedly at him while she waited for him to finish chewing.

"It's not the money."

Terena blinked. "Then what?"

He stared at her, taking a moment before responding. He wiped a hand over his mouth to clear the crumbs from his red beard. "You know there are things in this world we cannot explain, aye?"

She nodded.

He gestured with the hand still holding the bread. "Let's just say... I was called."

"You were called," she said. He tilted his head in assent. "By whom? The northern king?"

"Aye."

"But who is he to you? Why is this more to you than money?"

Rydon dropped his gaze to his plate before looking back up at her. "I am sorry, Terena. I cannot say more. But," he said, lifting a finger as she opened her mouth to protest, "I promise you, you will have your answers. You will. It's not time yet."

"What does that even mean?"

He shrugged and took a sip of his ale. "Do you—"

The door to the inn opened and a young man came in, his eyes darting around the common room before he moved to the innkeeper. He looked as if he'd been traveling, his blue robes and light grey breeches coated in dust. His cheeks flushed and his ash brown hair disheveled, the man leaned over to speak quietly to the innkeeper.

Rydon looked over his shoulder at him, then back at Terena as she continued to watch while they exchanged some words before the innkeeper pointed in their direction.

Terena stiffened as the young man came toward them. She kicked Rydon under the table and he sat back, lifting his head when the stranger stopped at his side.

"Terena Luca?"

Terena's eyebrows shot up. "Who asks?"

"My name is David. I am an acolyte at the sanctuary here in Messene. The priestess has sent me to invite you to see her."

Rydon choked as he took a swig of ale. Terena gaped at the acolyte. She was silent so long the young man shifted uncertainly, his grey eyes moving between her and Rydon.

"How does she know I'm here?"

The acolyte smiled. He came a step closer and bent low so that he could speak quietly between the three of them. "The priestess is a seer, lady. She is the eyes of the gods and has foreseen your arrival." He gestured to the room behind him. "She doesn't invite you out now, of course. But I came to find you. I'll be back in the morning, at dawn. It will be a long day for you, so please eat something or bring it with you."

He bowed slightly at her and turned, striding for the door. He was gone before Terena could make sense of what had just happened.

"Huh," Rydon said as he picked up a hunk of cheese and smashed it into his bread. "One less thing."

CLOAKS ON AND HOODS UP, THE THREE OF THEM WAITED OUTSIDE THE inn the following morning, the chill dawn air creeping around their bodies and into any seam of clothing. Terena reached out to Sonah in reassurance as the girl shivered, the edges of her cloak pulled tight around her.

Rydon had done a quick walk around the inn and the surrounding buildings, watching for anything out of the ordinary. Terena lifted an eyebrow when he'd approached and the quick shake of his head had her relaxing her stiffened muscles.

A few minutes later, a lone horseman turned out from the street on their left, the dappled grey mare walking slowly toward them carrying the young acolyte from the day before. Terena moved closer to Sonah, one hand lifting toward the dagger at her hip.

"Good morrow!" The acolyte called out as he came to a stop before them and tugged his hood down. He looked at Terena first, then glanced at Rydon and Sonah.

"Rydon will fetch the horses if you tell us which way—"

"Lady," the acolyte said, clearly flustered as a wash of color stained his cheeks. "I am to take only you. Your companions—"

"They come with," Terena said, her tone brooking no argument.

"Terena—" Rydon started.

"Rydon, we all go."

"Lady, I cannot," the acolyte said, now so agitated, the mare danced uneasily. "The invitation is only for you. She's been waiting."

"Terena, you must go," Rydon said. "I'll stay with Sonah. Hopefully Gabriol meets us soon but we'll be here either way. Waiting for you."

Terena hesitated, glancing at Sonah, who gave her a quick nod.

"Fine," she said as she heaved a sigh. "I'll get Nyx and meet—"

"We must... that is, I...," the acolyte cleared his throat. "You are to ride with me, lady. It is the way."

"It is *what* way?"

The acolyte looked to Rydon for help. Finding none there, he looked back at Terena with a helplessness that almost made her pity him. "The way it's done, lady. It is the way everyone who sees the oracle gets to the sanctuary."

Terena froze, her gaze flying to Rydon, whose eyes were open as wide as his mouth as he caught it too.

"The oracle?" Terena asked softly.

The acolyte, David, looked at her with confusion. "Aye, lady, the oracle."

Fuck. Of course.

"We're in Messene," Rydon laughed as he shook his head.

"So?" Sonah asked, looking between the three of them.

Terena looked up at the acolyte. "This is the same oracle that advises King Altos?"

"Oh, not only King Altos," David said excitedly, a smile breaking across his freckled face. "Many kings seek her out. Emperor Solon himself came to her—" He halted, his face coloring once more. "That was inappropriate. My apologies. But, aye, she is the oracle that has counseled many great men, if that is your question."

Terena turned to face Rydon, considering. He did the same, their gazes locked for a few seconds before Terena turned back to the acolyte. "Thank you, David."

Before he could respond, she grabbed hold of the saddle and mounted behind him. She set her hands at his waist and David shifted, his cheeks flushed once more.

"Take care of her, Rydon," Terena said with a wave as they turned away.

"Bring us back good news!"

CHAPTER TWENTY

They rode for an hour through the western part of Messene, eventually coming to a clearing before a tall formation, sheer rock rising to a flat top mostly hidden by clouds. As they neared the base, the acolyte announced they'd take a brief break as the ascent was difficult.

Terena dismounted and stepped back, stretching as David jumped down, rummaging in his saddlebags.

"I have a water skin if you—" he said, but Terena waved him off.

"I'm fine."

The acolyte nodded and pulled his horse behind him as he walked to a tree a few feet away. He tethered the horse and pulled some food out of the saddlebags, offering some to Terena as he moved to sit on a nearby log.

Terena thanked him for the cheese and small piece of bread he'd torn off and given her. She ate while pacing in front of him, taking in the woods and looking up to see how far up the rock formation she could see.

"I've heard of the oracle, of course, but how long has this temple stood here? I feel like I should have known about it being here," she asked.

David chewed for a few seconds. "The original temple was built right before the Immortals War. One of Zeus's bolts struck it when he fought Calix. When the Olympians were banished, King Leander had his best craftsmen sent to rebuild it, to honor Leto, Apollo's mother."

"And how long has this oracle been... prophesizing? Is that what you call it?"

The acolyte grinned and shook his head. "No. No, we call it counsel. No one knows how long this oracle has been counseling. No one serving the temple has ever seen her. And anyone who does only sees her once in their lifetime."

Terena glanced at him, eyes wide. "Truly? You all serve her, but have no idea what she looks like?"

"She is not," he stopped and looked down, pensive. "She speaks for the gods, and only by invitation. Many have waited years to be granted one, while others have died without. We serve her and the gods. We do not seek her divination. We only serve. It is enough for us."

Terena arched an eyebrow and folded her arms at her chest. "That sounds," she shook her head, "that sounds pretty selfless. I can't wait to meet her."

He nodded, flashing her a quick smile before he popped a piece of cheese into his mouth.

"I wasn't even in Messene for an hour before I got an invitation. What's that about?"

David looked up at her again and tilted his head. "As I said, lady, she knew you would come."

"I guess so. Being the oracle and all."

"Aye."

"But I'm sure she's seen others who sought her out, as well. Right? I mean, before they came to Messene. She foresaw their journeys out here, too?"

The acolyte shook his head and stood. He brushed some crumbs off his tunic. "No, lady. The others have had to seek one of us out. There are acolytes in the temple who come down every first Monday of the new month to receive requests. They take requests back to the oracle and she decides whom she will invite. That's when I get sent down to the city," he gestures at Terena.

Terena shifted her weight to her right and narrowed her eyes at him. "So, what was different this time?"

He looked at her as if she was daft. "She saw *you* coming. I came down to find you as soon as I received word you were here."

"I get that. I get she foresaw my coming. I'm confused why *my* arrival would warrant a break of your standard, you know, invitation protocol."

He stepped closer, fishing something from the small pouch at his waist. "This is something perhaps the oracle will share with you," he said as he lifted his eyes to hers. "Rest assured that, for now, you know everything you need to know."

David opened his palm and blew in her face.

Startled, Terena stumbled back a step. Her vision blurred and her knees went weak. Black edged her vision and she fumbled for her sword, her hands thick and ungainly. She fell to one knee, blinking in vain as her vision faded, the acolyte's figure a blur as she lost consciousness.

THE SMELL OF INCENSE FILLED HER NOSTRILS BEFORE THE FOG FROM Terena's brain dissipated. She blinked, her eyes heavy and slow as she tried to focus. A golden blur edged her vision, slowly becoming clearer in the shape of pendant lights suspended from a high, domed ceiling covered in colored tiles. As her vision cleared, the tiles focused into a picture, a mural of people, surrounded and within clouds. Light edged the far left side over a giant of a man, his thunderous face in profile as he held a golden bow aimed at a group of people on the right. There were three bodies in the middle of the mural, dead or sleeping, Terena couldn't tell.

Gazing at the beautiful rendering, she realized she'd never seen anything so vividly alive captured by any artist. The paintings she'd seen in the castles or palaces she'd been to throughout her travels were all of ordinary life, of ordinary people. Even the temples and monasteries in Heylisia only depicted the mortal heroes; never any of the gods.

Somehow, Terena knew the man was no mortal.

Her eyes narrowed. Was this Apollo, then?

"Yes," a soft voice sounded from her right. Terena jerked, nausea lancing through her belly up to her chest as bile rose in her throat. She closed her eyes for several seconds before she shifted onto her elbow.

When she could, she opened her eyes and realized she was lying on cushions soft as air, arranged in a semicircle in front of a large altar. What seemed like hundreds of candles burned, and she thought might be where the smell was coming from.

A gorgeous white marble statue of a large man she'd never seen before, heavily muscled and wearing armor and greaves, stood in the center atop a large square plinth. Words below it were in a language she did not know but resembled Ancient Greek.

Terena turned her head slowly to look at the person who'd spoken, stiffening before she could stop herself. The woman sat on the pillows, her legs bent beneath her flowing white and grey dress, a rope of gold around her belly and up over her shoulders to cross at her chest. She had a head of hair so black and shiny it glinted silver in the light from the flames, coiled up in a tight bun atop her head.

What initially caught Terena's attention were her eyes. They were black, filling in the space where the irises and whites should be. A chill slid slowly down Terena's spine as she edged further back on the pillows.

The woman seemed familiar, and strangely beautiful, despite the harsh lines and angles of her face. Her thin lips disappeared when she smiled. She looked like she could murder without an ounce of regret.

Terena noticed the woman's comforting smile and wondered if she could see her.

"I can."

Terena startled. "You can read my thoughts?"

The woman's smile deepened. "Some."

Terena put her hands behind her as she scooted her butt, moving further away from the unnerving woman. The woman did not move or show any signs she was aware of Terena's discomfort.

"How are you feeling?" she asked, again in that soft voice at odds with her appearance.

"How did I get here?" Terena countered.

The woman moved her hands to her lap. "You were invited."

Terena snorted. "I was drugged."

"Yes."

Terena leaned her head forward. "Not denying it, huh?"

"It is how this is done."

"How *what's* done?"

The woman tilted her head. "Is this the question you came here to ask?"

Terena looked at her as if she'd sprouted a second head. "Of course not!"

"I understand you're disoriented—"

"And pissed!"

The woman pursed her lips, her odd eyes looking somewhere near Terena's forehead. "And angry. But you waste time."

She rose, her movements fluid and graceful, and Terena wondered again if her eyes worked. They looked like obsidian marbles, unnerving for Terena to look at for long.

"You were sent here," said the woman, "and so I will do my part."

"What part is that?"

"Is this the question—"

"NO!" Terena rubbed a hand over her face.

"Everyone who comes to the oracle has a million questions they want to ask. But there is one question, only one, whose answer they *need* to know. So Apollo allows one to be answered."

"Apollo," Terena said, her voice barely above a whisper as a shiver, something... strange shifted inside her. "You speak of a god long dead."

The woman smiled. "Apollo is not dead. He and the other Olympians are just... not here."

Gods, what the hell does that even mean?

Terena's head pounded, whether from what the woman was saying
—and not saying—or from the drug, she wasn't sure.

"How—"

"Is that the question—"

"Stop. I get it already," Terena sighed.

"Good," the woman said, clasping her hands in front of her.

"You're very patient with me," Terena said grudgingly as she tried
to stand.

The woman held out her hand to stay her, and Terena stopped,
thankful as another wave of nausea hit her.

"You are important," the woman replied, taking a few steps closer.
Terena craned her neck to look up at her, carefully avoiding those
weird eyes.

She opened her mouth to ask why, but then remembered. One
question only.

"Would you like some water?"

Terena nodded. "Aye, thank you."

The woman turned and Terena heard steps coming from her left.
She looked up and started, grabbing for the sword at her hip that
wasn't there; the dagger on her left was also missing. She got to one
knee, every fiber of her body ready to fight the man who approached,
a glass of water in his hand.

"Who the fuck are you?" she snarled at him as he handed the glass
to the woman. The man wore clothes similar to the Magi who'd
attacked her in Agraboda. But his tunic and leggings, the scimitar at
his hip and the scarf draped across his neck were all much finer than
that of the three Magi they'd bested in the ruins.

Was he the one watching?

"Is that the question—"

"Let's assume that, for the time being, I'm not asking the question I
came here to ask," Terena bit out, never taking her eyes off the man.
He did not move to leave, his scarred hands settling at his waist as he
watched her, his face impassive.

"That works for me," the woman said pleasantly as she bent down,
offering Terena the glass of water.

"I'll assume it's not poisoned, since you invited me here, and probably could've killed me when David blew the drug in my face."

"I could've had you killed in Agraboda if that was what I had wanted," the woman replied.

Terena's eyes shot to her. "You sent the Magi?"

The woman arched an eyebrow.

"Are you staying?" Terena asked the silent man, who continued to watch her.

"He is not."

Terena looked at the man expectantly. He stared at her a few seconds longer, then exchanged a look with the woman before pivoting, striding off to some exit Terena could not see.

David had told her no one had ever seen the oracle. Was that a lie or did he not know about the Magi?

When they were alone, Terena turned on the woman.

"You sent him and his men to attack me? And before you ask, no, that's not the fucking question I came here to ask. I'm annoyed I have to keep saying that, too."

The woman's mouth pinched and Terena could see from the narrowing of those weird eyes the woman was not happy with her.

"I will make allowances for your behavior because you are confused, and because—as I said—you are important. Never use that language in this room, in the presence of Apollo. You will anger him."

"How is he going to be angry if he's not even here?"

"He sees through me."

Terena opened her mouth to say something, but the woman raised a hand to stop her. "First you will listen. And then once you've understood, you will ask your question."

Terena heaved a sigh and gestured to the woman to continue.

"I am Pytho. I am the last oracle in this realm of the great god Apollo. I am here to guide you, Terena Luca."

Pytho took a few steps closer and dropped down until she sat next to Terena. "I am telling you this because I want you to know you are not alone. You will be the one to usher in the golden age of mankind.

Or you will not. The Morai—the Fates—are watching, but your choices are your own."

Terena looked as if she might speak, but Pytho reached out and laid her hand on Terena's forearm. "Before you ask your question, I want you to think about what I tell you."

She opened her mouth and closed it, then opened it once more before looking Terena in the eye. "It is not the question you think you want answered. Not that which started you on this journey, Terena. You may believe it is, but there is another question that drives the dreams you have at night. The visions you have are not what you think. They've led you this far, but they come from within you.

"You already know how to find your parents. The knowledge has always been inside you. I want you to look within yourself now and ask the question you've come to me to have answered. The question that sits deep within, creating the reality that seeks treasures and secrets long buried."

Terena's mind was a whirl of thoughts overwhelming her for a few minutes. The silence stretched as she thought on Pytho's words. She sensed the truth of them.

She turned away from Pytho and looked at the marbled Apollo. Realization dawned on her slowly, and when it did, her eyes stung. She *did* know how to find her parents. That's why she wasn't worried about them being dead. She wasn't even worried about when she'd find them.

And the Shroud of Faybhen was the key. That's why she'd been drawn to Agraboda and why she'd given Duke Aurora a fake. Her visions—

Her visions...

What had the Magi at Agraboda said about the shroud?

If you take it, it begins again.

She looked up at Pytho and for the first time in her life, she understood. Her visions were not some external force guiding her to clues.

"The visions are memories," she whispered.

Pytho smiled. "What is your question, Terena Luca?"

Terena became lightheaded. She'd done all this before. Her visions *were* breadcrumbs, but ones she'd left for herself. But why? Why was she doing this all again? To what end?

To what end...

Terena's lips parted, the blood roaring in her ears as she looked at Pytho and asked, "How do I break this cycle?"

Pytho's shoulders jerked and her eyes widened. She opened her mouth, pausing a second before she composed herself, once more folding her hands together in her lap.

When she spoke, her voice was not her own, but a terrible, powerful voice frightening Terena. The ebony leeched from her eyes like veins, surrounding the skin of her lids to her cheeks in inky black.

"Seven circles complete and the eighth is aligned at last. False death betrays love, forging Athena's Weapon. From the ashes of gods, the Heir of War rises, leading the gods to glory. The fate of man is for the Weapon."

Terena's mouth hung open. She waited for Pytho to say more and when she didn't, Terena sprang up. "That's it? Are you fuc—are you kidding me? I came all this way—I have lost—"

She shook, her hands balled at her sides, and she wanted to scream. "So I ask you a question, and all I get is a riddle?"

Pytho stood up, facing Terena as she watched her, but did not respond.

"How many more times? How many before it ends?"

Pytho did not answer.

Terena wanted to choke the woman. "You are useless to me," she hissed, springing forward. Pytho started and Terena's smile turned nasty. "I came here in good faith and this is all I get? Death, betrayal and weapons? That's your fucking answer?"

Pytho scowled, "Do not use—"

"Oh, I'll fucking say whatever the fuck I want!" Terena raged. "Why should I even bother to find my parents now? What's the point?"

Terena covered her face. She hadn't felt this kind of despair since she'd lost Lerek. It couldn't have all been for nothing. Everything she's gone through. Her mind spiraled, her hands shaking so hard she clutched them together. The ground beneath her trembled.

Terena heard Pytho back up a few steps. Behind her, the sound of someone running. She looked up to see the Magi, hand on the hilt of his scimitar, stop next to Pytho, his eyes wide in horror.

Heat flooded behind her eyes and Terena panicked for a moment, thinking they might turn to ash in her skull. She looked down and saw white light beneath her skin, racing back and forth over her veins.

Pytho lunged for her, grabbing hold of Terena's arms. Terena shook her off as if shooing away a fly and the woman went flying into the altar at her back. The Magi yelled and turned to attack, but Pytho screamed at him to stop.

She held out a hand, pleading with Terena. "You have lost your beloved and you are being hunted," she said desperately. "I know, and I am sorry for it! But you have a destiny, Terena, and like all heroes before you, you must earn it. This is your burden. Terena, I want to help you, but I am afraid that if I say too much, they will punish me. I will tell you what I always tell you: go to Sparta and seek King Altos. He has something belonging to you. It is your birthright."

"Am I a hero then? Is that why I have these powers?"

"You are a god, Terena. You know this," Pytho hissed at her.

She rose and took a few tentative steps closer. As the heat in her eyes subsided, Terena's veins continued to pulse with a radiant white light.

Pytho put a hand on Terena's cheek. "What I've not told you before is you have already found your sister."

"Priestess, no!"

Terena twisted her head, her eyes narrowed on the Magi who'd spoken, his face paling beneath his dark olive skin.

"She travels with you," Pytho continued, as if the Magi had not spoken. Terena shook, her mind not processing fast enough. "She travels with you and already this time is different because of it. *You changed it!* That's why there's hope; that's why I'm telling you this. This is the last circle, Terena. The very last. But there is so much more for you to do and you must harden yourself and keep your sister and your friends close. You have the power to save mankind and that is the point, Terena. That is why you must keep going."

Cradling Terena's face softly with her cool palms, Pytho smiled wistfully, her eyes glassy with unshed tears. "How long I've waited to see you again." She shook her head as Terena frowned, confused.

"And do not let his betrayal break you," Pytho whispered, her face so close to Terena's she could not look away from the depthless pure black of her eyes. "You will need his love. You will need his strength and his sword for what is coming."

Pytho brought her lips to Terena's, softly laying them over her mouth as she whispered something Terena didn't understand.

She moved away, slowly, and Terena exhaled, her body feeling heavy until she felt nothing.

CHAPTER TWENTY-ONE

M ist swirled around Terena as she walked. She did not know where she was going or where she was coming from. Echoes whispered around her, some words growing stronger, others unintelligible mutterings. Terena turned, looking for the source of the voice, but the echoes filled her head until she crouched down, covering her ears.

Take the Twins
You will lead them
Find—
Lead them
Athena's Weapon
Destroy him before he destroys you
Athena's—
Destroy him
Find—
Find—
Athena's Weapon.

TERENA BOLTED UPRIGHT, HER CHEST HEAVING AS SHE GASPED FOR AIR. She didn't know where she was for a moment. She looked down and saw the bed in the dim light of dawn coming through the small window.

Was she back at the inn? Was she still in Messene?

Terena's eyes darted right and saw the lump of Sonah's body huddled beneath the covers. Wiping her hand over her face, she exhaled. She threw off the covers, rising and dressing as quietly as possible.

Before leaving, she paused and turned back to Sonah.

Terena took a few steps closer and gazed down at the girl. She could not see her face, her mass of blonde hair covering most of it.

My sister.

Still coming to terms with what the oracle had told her, this at least was something she did not question.

Her breathing hitched as she reached out a hand, pulling back quickly when Sonah moaned and shifted, burying her head even more within her pillow. There'd be time for them to talk, but it was enough now for Terena to see her.

Turning to pad softly across the room, Terena glanced over her shoulder at Sonah before unlocking the door, lifting the latch as she pulled it open ever so slowly and ducked out.

The innkeeper was at his desk, nodding at her as she passed. Terena paused when she saw Rydon sitting at the back table in the common room. He was holding a mug, steam rising from the rim. As she neared, he looked up, his eyebrows shooting up to his hairline when he saw her.

"Where'd you come from?"

Terena's brow wrinkled. "What do you mean? I was upstairs sleeping."

Rydon stared at her as she sat. He glanced over her shoulder as the innkeeper came around the bar toward them.

He leaned in before the innkeeper reached them. "The fuck you were," he hissed at her. "You left yesterday with the acolyte, remember?"

Startled, Terena whipped her gaze to him. The innkeeper asked if she'd like anything for breakfast and she blinked, looking back at him as she searched for words.

"Get her the eggs with bread. And coffee," Rydon said when she didn't answer.

The innkeeper waited a moment, possibly to see if Terena would say something different. When she nodded, he turned and strode toward the door leading to the kitchen in back.

Terena looked around to ensure they were alone before she leaned closer to Rydon. "That was the last time you saw me?" she whispered. "When I left with David?"

Rydon nodded. "Aye. How did you get back? And when?"

Terena lifted her eyebrows and shook her head. "Fuck if I know. This has been the strangest few days of my life."

A corner of Rydon's lips crooked up. "Only the last few days?"

Terena pulled a face.

"Not sure how we missed you getting back, unless we were already abed," Rydon said, his eyes searching her face. "So? How was it?"

Terena let out an enormous sigh. "Honestly? Still trying to process. They drugged me."

Rydon choked a bit on his coffee. He stared at her. "What the fuck?"

She lifted a shoulder. "Even before we got there. One minute we're having a snack—me and the acolyte. The next he's blowing shit in my face and I wake up…" Terena shook her head. "It was all very weird."

"Did you see the oracle?"

"Aye. Maybe. That's what's weird. All of it feels like a dream. There are parts I remember vividly. And parts that are…," she motioned with her hands in circles around her head.

"Well, did she say anything useful?"

Terena shook her head again as she rubbed at her eyes. Rydon had proven himself to be an ally, and she was even beginning to think of him as a friend. But as she'd told him, there were things about what Pytho had told her she still needed to process and didn't feel now was the time to share all with Rydon.

At last, she looked up at him. "Sparta. She said we need to go to Sparta. That King Altos has something I need. Something that is mine. Didn't say what, though. Or if she did, I honestly don't remember."

"Do you speak Greek? Because I don't," Rydon said as he took another sip of his coffee.

"I understand a bit. Hopefully, they speak the common tongue. They speak it here and they're Greek."

"Aye, you're right," Rydon said with a nod. "So now we travel even further south. Looking for something that's yours but, of course, what that is, you do not know. Any thoughts on how long all this will take? Because we're no closer to heading north than the day we rescued you."

Terena sat back as the innkeeper emerged with a plate of scrambled eggs mixed with tomatoes and thick slices of buttered bread in one hand, a mug of steaming coffee in the other. He placed them both in front of her, then fished out a knife and fork wrapped in a linen napkin, which she took as she thanked him.

"Are you expected in the north soon? Did your king give you a time limit to fetch me? Because, according to the oracle, we can't go north without whatever Altos has of mine."

Rydon's lips peeled back. "No, there's no time limit. But I recall getting yelled at for suggesting taking a longer route to get to the north."

Terena snorted. "The Fates have other plans, I guess."

Rydon watched her beneath his lashes. "If it's even them driving you."

Terena frowned, flashing him a look before returning to her eggs. "What does *that* mean?"

"Did she say anything else?"

Terena noted how he'd ignored her question, but left it alone. "Aye, but I'll wait until the others are with us."

"Mmm," Rydon said, his eyes widening as if a thought struck him. "I forgot to tell you—"

"May the blessings of the gods shine upon—Ren! When the fuck did you get back?"

CROAK GRINNED AT THE LOOK OF SHOCK ON HIS SISTER'S FACE A SECOND before she bolted up from her chair and threw her arms around him. He laughed and caught her, stumbling a step.

"Happy to see you, too, sis," he murmured into her neck. He grabbed hold of her ponytail and tugged.

Terena pulled back, her expression soft, her hazel eyes bright as she scoured his face. She put her hands to his cheeks and laughed. "When did you get here? Gods, I am so glad to see you!" She pulled him close for another fierce hug.

"Late last night," he answered as Gabriol moved around him and clapped Terena on the back before taking a seat beside Rydon. "Luckily, Rydon was still up."

"How's Orry? Is he still sleeping?" Terena asked, finally letting go of Croak. She took her seat again once he'd taken the one next to her.

Croak glanced at Gabriol before dropping his gaze to the table. Terena frowned and was about to speak again when the innkeeper reappeared, two more mugs of steaming coffee in his hands he set on the table.

When Gabriol and Croak had finished ordering their breakfast, Terena looked pointedly at Croak.

"So?"

Croak twisted his lips and shifted his gaze back to her. "He's gone ahead to Seleste," he said at last. He lifted his coffee and before he took a sip, he muttered, "And then he's heading north."

"What?" Terena demanded, her mouth dropping open. "Alone? Why—"

"We had some trouble in Villadelle," Gabriol said, his face dark as he glanced over at Croak. He turned back to Terena. "Heylisian soldiers. We got caught up in a skirmish."

"He's fine," Croak said, laying his hand on top of Terena's when she looked like she might surge out of her seat. "He thought it might be better if he traveled alone with the shroud. No one's going to be looking for a cleric traveling alone. I gave him the last of my orichalcum so he'll be fine."

Terena scowled at him and snatched her hand back, crossing her arms over her torso. "And you both let him?"

"It makes sense, Terena," Rydon said with a sigh. "We're bound to run into more soldiers. Now we have to head even further south, it's best he's gone with the shroud than traveling with us and possibly getting caught with it."

"Wait, where are we going? Why south?" Croak asked.

Terena dropped her chin and Croak imagined the wheels turning in her head. After a silence in which Croak shared looks with both Rydon and Gabriol, Terena pushed her chair back and rose.

"Take a walk with me," she said to Croak. He lifted his eyebrows but stood, following her out of the inn.

When they were well enough away from the inn, he caught up to her and nudged her with his shoulder. "What's going on?"

"I didn't want to talk in front of the others," she said, her eyes darting around. "There are things the oracle said I don't want to say in front of Rydon and Gabriol. At least not yet. Rydon's still not telling all when it comes to that northern king of his."

Croak nodded. "Fair enough. What did the oracle say?"

They walked for a bit before Terena responded. "Something about someone's death and two souls. A betrayal. The Heir of War rising and Athena's Weapon being forged."

"Sounds like *she* was drugged."

Terena snorted. "Aye."

"What else did the oracle tell you?"

"That I need to go to Sparta. King Altos has something of mine, although she conveniently forgot to mention what that was."

"Fucking oracles," he said with a shake of his head. "Always so vague."

Terena couldn't help but smile at his grumbling. "Yeah. They're all the same."

Her brother winked at her and threw his arm over her shoulders as they started walking once more.

"Think we'll ever get to the north? I bet fifty silver we'll find someone else telling us we have to do something else to get something else and then go see someone else who will guide us to something else. We'll be old and grey before we ever set foot in Seleste at this rate."

Terena laughed. "I get that sense as well. Hopefully, this northern king will have more answers for us. But first, another detour."

"Well, what else would we be doing if we didn't have this legendary quest to go on?"

She grunted.

"And," he said, squeezing her shoulder, "how many people in this day and age can say they went on a hero's quest looking for the Olympian gods? Just saying that gives me chills."

Terena grinned up at him. "So, off to Sparta?"

"Off to Sparta! And if you're lucky," Croak wagged his eyebrows at her with a wicked grin of his own, "maybe you'll see a certain dashing commander."

Terena gasped and pulled back to hit him, but he anticipated her and jumped away, laughing.

As their laughter died down, she looked up at him with a hesitant smile.

"One more thing," she said, her voice low.

Croak looked down at her, waiting.

"Sonah's my sister."

CHAPTER TWENTY-TWO

The line to enter the city of Sparta was ridiculously long. They lumbered along with merchants, farmers, mercenaries, or anyone else having business in Sparta. Two hours later, they made it through without a hint of awareness from the guards posted there and along the western wall.

The region was mountainous, and Sparta took advantage of the landscape. From where they entered, the city spread out, white buildings with red-tiled roofs climbing the mountainside. Terena's eyes rose to the structure crowning the city. It appeared as if Arestia Castle had been built into the mountain, although it was difficult to make out from where they stood.

When they neared the city center, Terena blinked, her mouth falling open at the sight of the enormous statue before them. The man depicted was even larger than the stone statues of Calix and Alexandros in Metilai. This man was a warrior, wearing armor and a plumed helmet, hiding most of his face. In one hand, he gripped a spear, and the stone muscles of his other flexed as he held his shield. The ground beneath him was a mass of rubble, as if the man had landed on this spot and split the earth. He stood tall and menacing, his gaze overlooking the city as if he alone would protect it.

Icy awareness overcame her.

This must be the Olympian god, Ares.

Sparta was one of the last Greek kingdoms not swallowed up after the Olympians were defeated. Their heritage was proudly on display, with no fear of punishment for worshiping the ancient deities. There was no one who'd dare.

"Gabriol and I will scout around, get our bearings," Rydon said. Terena looked over at him. He sounded exhausted. He *looked* exhausted.

She looked at the others. Everyone looked wrecked.

"We shouldn't split up yet," Terena said, turning her gaze back to Rydon. "Let's find somewhere to stable the horses. Then we need to find an inn. The sooner we're rested, the faster we can plan our next steps. That includes reconnoiter."

"Aye," Rydon grunted, and they set off on foot, walking the horses slowly through the shifting crowds. Rydon and Gabriol stopped every few feet to ask someone a question, Terena assumed to the nearest stables.

"The best inn that might have enough rooms for all of us is a mile away, but it's also close to Arestia, the castle. And they have their own stables," Gabriol said as they sauntered back to their group. "We paid a couple of boys to take them there for us."

Terena shrugged. "Good. Get something to eat on the way?"

The others grumbled or grunted their agreement. Terena motioned for Gabriol to lead and they followed, Sonah next to Croak, Terena walking alone, and Rydon at the rear.

Ever since she'd told Croak about Sonah, he'd been much more attentive to her, staying close to her as they travelled and making a point of getting to know her better. Terena ducked her head, smiling, thinking of how cute he was with her; it made her heart happy to see them together.

She had said nothing to Sonah about it, yet, wanting to wait for the right moment. Maybe now they'd be sharing a room again...

A few minutes later, a roar went up around them and Terena and the others turned as the earth beneath them trembled.

Terena watched as a company of warriors thundered past. Their warhorses would have given them away if the men riding weren't already legendary.

"Fuck," Croak breathed as he slunk down a bit. Terena, too, tried to hide, lifting her hood as she ducked behind a tall man carrying a bushel of potatoes.

"The Liodari," Rydon said in an awe-filled whisper.

"We knew they'd be here," Gabriol said, resigned.

Terena and Croak exchanged a look.

"Come," Gabriol said when the warriors had passed. "There's a tavern across the way."

"We shouldn't eat all together," Rydon said.

Terena glanced over her shoulder at him. "Agreed."

"I'll go with Terena," Rydon said. Terena looked at him and shrugged.

"You two, let's go," Gabriol said to Croak and Sonah.

"We'll get the rooms, too. Yours will be under the name Lorence."

Sonah flashed Terena a look of panic, but Terena squeezed her hands when she stepped close to the younger girl. "You'll be safe with Gabriol," she reassured her. "And Croak. For whatever that's worth."

That earned her a smirk from Sonah.

Terena watched them until they reached the tavern doors, turning when Rydon hit her shoulder.

"There," Rydon said a few minutes later.

Terena looked to where he pointed. "You go in first. I'm going to get the rooms. I'll be right back," she added.

Rydon looked as if he would protest, but then gave a quick nod and strode off toward the tavern.

Terena bumped into a woman holding the hand of a much older man, apologized and moved around them. She walked in the direction she thought the inn was, about to give up ten minutes later when she spotted the sign for public rooms written on a wall to her right. She went inside and secured a room for herself and Sonah, then asked for rooms for her 'brothers'.

Satisfied, Terena walked out into the waning sunlight, lifting her head to catch the last rays with her eyes closed. A moment later, she sensed the shift in the people around her, their excitement in the way they moved and spoke. Opening her eyes, she saw Commander Daris Antonius pass not twenty feet away with ten of his men. The way they moved as if they were all of one mind and body fascinated her, and she stood rooted to the spot, her mouth hanging ajar.

There were shouts of praise and homecoming to the men, but they ignored it. Terena arched an eyebrow and scoffed.

The ones closest to Daris Antonius started chanting something in Greek she didn't understand except for the name of the goddess Athena.

Terena ducked to her right, hoping to stay hidden while she watched the commander.

Daris Antonius was almost out of sight when she turned to the woman next to her and asked what the words meant.

The woman grinned at her and sighed. "Athena's Weapon."

RYDON PUSHED THROUGH THE DOORS OF THE TAVERN AND HELD IT SO IT wouldn't bang shut behind him. He pushed back his hood and strode to the bar, motioning to the barkeep and ordered an ale. After dropping a couple of coins on the counter, he grabbed the tankard and moved beyond the bar to one of the back tables. With a satisfied sigh, he settled onto the wood chair and leaned back, stretching his legs out under the table.

He glanced around the room, his green eyes taking in the patrons, the stairs, the doorway to the kitchen on his left. A barmaid made her way toward him and through to the kitchen, returning a few minutes later to stop at his side.

"Get you anything, lord?" she asked, her voice slightly winded as she smiled warmly at him.

"Another ale. And food. Whatever you got," Rydon answered.

She nodded and strode off to the bar. Rydon shifted his gaze from her to the room at large once again.

Twenty minutes later, Terena came into the tavern, casting a cursory glance around the room until she spotted him. She wound her way slowly to his table, taking the chair to his right, facing the rest of the room.

"Stew's good," he said by way of greeting. Terena grunted, her face shaded by her hood.

Rydon passed her his tankard of ale. "I'll get more," he said as he rose and went for the bar. He leaned on the counter after he'd ordered more drinks and asked for another bowl of stew and bread.

The barkeep had set the drinks on the counter when the doors behind him opened, a gust of wind rushing in. He glanced over his shoulder, then froze. Five men—five big men—strode in, one peeling off from the right and heading toward a large table. Another followed, grabbing a chair from a table he passed and bringing it to the table they'd chosen.

Rydon turned back slightly so it wouldn't be obvious he was watching.

He picked up the tankards and turned slowly, all the while watching the rest of their party. They all wore the same colors, although the clothing varied, as did the armor. They were not in their uniforms from earlier, having replaced the bronze breastplates for leather armor, but they still wore the colors of the order they represented.

Liodari.

The man closest to him turned to another, said something before the other man dipped his chin and walked toward Rydon.

Rydon moved, taking the drinks back to his table. He placed one carefully in front of Terena, then took his seat, his hand wrapped around his tankard, and brought it to his lips.

He glanced over at the bar, then looked at Terena. She'd taken off her hood and now sat hunched forward and stiff, arms braced on her knees. She, too, watched the man who now walked back to his friends. Rydon stared as the man sat and his gaze naturally lifted.

To them.

Or more specifically, to Terena. Rydon peeked at her and saw she, too, had her eyes locked on the man. Rydon shifted his gaze between the two, noticing how still the man had gone.

"Food's coming."

"We need to leave." Terena said, not taking her eyes off the man.

"They don't know—"

"I'll go first," she said as if she hadn't heard him. "You follow five minutes behind."

"What's that gonna do?"

Terena tilted her head to him. "It'll look like I'm leaving because I'm done. And then you leave. Did you forget you ordered food?"

"But we're sitting together. Who would leave their companion behind? That's suspicious."

Terena turned her chin slightly toward him, her lips scrunched up, and glared at him. "We cannot stay here. So when you leave, be as natural as possible so we don't draw any of their attention. Especially *his*," she hissed at him.

Rydon glanced back at the man who was now speaking with his men. They looked to be sitting companionably, their limbs loose, conversing in twos or across. He shrugged. "Hate to break it to you, kid, but you've already drawn that man's attention."

"*That* man," Terena said, her voice pitched low, "is Daris Antonius. Commander of the Liodari."

Rydon's eyebrows shot up. He was saved by the barmaid placing a steaming bowl in front of Terena. She sat back as the woman then placed a plate of bread.

Terena mumbled her thanks and took the spoon in her left hand. Without looking up, she blew on the stew and said to Rydon, "He's seen me before. And if he sees me now, he'll remember me and I'd rather not have to outrun four Liodari and their commander."

"You've met Daris Antonius?" he asked, huffing in disbelief. "Where?"

"What's it matter?" she ground out and shoved a big spoonful of meat into her mouth.

"Well… I mean, what's he like? I never thought I'd run across him. Gods, the stories don't do him justice."

Terena rolled her eyes. "Stop it. We're fucked."

"Oh shit," Rydon said.

"Hmm?" Terena looked up at him while she chewed.

"Absolutely, do not—do not!—turn to look," he said and then kicked her under the table as she went to do just that. "*Don't!* He's heading right for us."

Terena froze, then said quickly, "I don't think I can take him, but I might be able to take two of his men before—"

"Terena Luca," the man's—Daris's—deep voice said. Not a question, either.

Rydon looked up in feigned surprise.

A second passed and Rydon shot Terena a look.

Terena had no choice but to look at the commander now, her expression such a believable mask of polite surprise, Rydon choked on his ale.

"Commander," she said after a long pause.

The commander smiled. It was polite but genuine. Rydon looked back at Terena and blinked to see the flush in her cheeks.

"It's a pleasant surprise to see you again. I wanted to stop and say hello," Daris Antonius said, his eyes never leaving Terena.

"Very kind," Terena said, her smile not reaching her eyes, but Rydon watched her as he folded his arms at his chest. She wasn't entirely unaffected.

Daris Antonius inclined his head, then turned to Rydon.

"Oh!" Terena said after an awkward silence, and waved a hand at Rydon. "This is my Rydon—my *worker*! That is to say, he works with me. In tracking." She cleared her throat and gestured again at him. "It's Rydon."

Rydon could not believe what he was seeing. "I'm Rydon of Decu," he said and stood, thrusting out his arm to the man. Only a moment's hesitation before the commander clasped it.

"Decu," the commander said, his light blue eyes assessing. "You're far from home."

"Aye," Rydon said with a grin. "It's been a long time since I've been there. I make my living in Heylisia. With Terena."

Rydon swore the man's eyes narrowed, looking at him now as if he was a threat.

"Well, thanks for stopping by," Terena said in a high voice. "Good to see you again."

"Would you care to join us?" the commander asked, his eyes on Terena once more.

Terena blanched, but Rydon quickly answered, "Alas, we were about to leave. Done with supper. Thank you, though."

Rydon looked over at Terena pointedly, his eyes widening slightly so she'd take the hint. Her face was bright red.

She shot to her feet and stepped away from the table, mute.

Daris Antonius stared at her a moment longer as Rydon rounded the table and clasped Terena's shoulder. "Again, fantastic to meet you, an honor, truly," Rydon said as he squeezed Terena's shoulder and tugged so she'd follow him.

He strode toward the door, feeling her at his back. When she stopped, Rydon turned back to look. The commander had taken hold of her arm. Rydon stiffened and took a step but stopped, watching as Daris Antonius said something to Terena as he bent close, something Rydon couldn't hear. He took another step, his hand drifting to the pommel of his sword.

Terena's back stiffened, and she nodded. Without another look at the commander, she strode for the tavern door ahead of Rydon.

Rydon looked at the man one last time, their eyes locking for a second before Rydon dipped his chin and turned to walk out after her.

When the door shut behind him and he caught up to Terena, Rydon spoke at last. "What the fuck was that about?"

TERENA WAS GLAD OF THE COOL EVENING BREEZE, AS IT BLESSEDLY encircled her overheated body, her face so hot she pressed her palms to her cheeks.

"Oh gods, that was... that was," Terena muttered as she gulped in air. Even her lungs seemed on fire.

"What is wrong with you?" Rydon asked, his lip curled in disgust. "A man—a fucking hero—says hello to you and you act like he's got the plague."

Terena scoffed and lifted a finger to point at Rydon. "That, that—"

"What did he say to you? As we were leaving."

If possible, Terena's face turned a deeper shade of red. "Nothing! It was nothing."

"By how you're acting, that's the worst nothing I've ever heard of."

"I don't even know what that means," Terena muttered and strode away.

Rydon caught up to her quickly. "Bullshit. Why won't you say then, if it was nothing?"

She groaned. "He asked if I'd be staying long in Sparta because he wanted to see me again. I said we were."

Rydon's brows shot to his forehead, and his lips parted. "Oh, shit. Do you..." he shook his head, "do you have a thing for him? I thought you and the prince—"

Instantly, the color bleached from Terena's face and her stomach fell.

She pivoted, tears pricking at the backs of her eyes as she fought to keep them in.

"Hey, I didn't mean—"

"You know what? I'm going back to the inn. Stay, if you like," Terena said, her voice overly loud to her ears. Rydon stopped following her a few seconds later.

Sleep. She needed sleep.

It was the only reason she could think of why her skin was clammy and her pulse raced. Her body was trying to tell her she needed rest.

That had to be it, because she didn't want to think it had anything to do with the commander's powerful body standing so close to her. Or the way those blue eyes looked at her as if he was starving and she was dinner.

And when he'd whispered to her, she wanted to rip the clothes from his body.

Terena choked back a sob because her mind chose that moment to flash an image of Lerek's smiling face behind her eyes.

Ducking her head, Terena marched inside the inn.

She took the stairs two at a time and opened the door to her room. Sliding the door closed, she turned, making out Sonah's outline in the bed closest to the window. Terena stopped and watched Sonah for a minute before she moved to the other bed.

Sliding off her cloak, she unhooked her sword belt and unfastened the sheath at her thigh. Sitting on the bed with a sigh, she lifted her right ankle and took off the sheath for her last dagger before unlacing and kicking off her boots.

She groaned over the amount of buttons on her leggings before she finally shoved them off. She kept her stockings on but chucked her tunic to the floor beside her leggings and boots. Stifling a groan, Terena bit her lip as she settled beneath the cool sheets.

She was out within minutes.

CHAPTER TWENTY-THREE

S onah's eyes flew open. She turned onto her back and lay there, blinking up at the ceiling as she strained to hear whatever had awakened her. Only silence answered her for a few seconds. She frowned and turned back to facing the lone window in their room when she heard it again.

Was that... a moan?

Sonah sat up slowly, trying not to make a sound as she sought any movement in the room that could alert her to someone's presence. She looked over at the mound in the other bed and stared while she waited.

Terena moaned. Longer and louder this time.

Sonah's eyebrows shot up and her mouth dropped open as Terena shifted, moaning again, and this time she groaned out a name.

"Daris."

Sonah's mouth stretched into the biggest grin as she moved the sheets aside and crouched on the bed, looking over at her friend.

"Yes. Oh *yes! Daris!*"

Sonah's hand flew to her mouth to stop the laugh bubbling up.

But this was too good.

Terena Luca sounded like she was having a *sex* dream!

She bit her lower lip, thinking. Should she wake her? Should she let her… finish? Oh gods, could she even be in the same room while—

Terena thrashed violently, her legs kicking out beneath the sheets and her arms flailed out. The armoire beside her bed caved in on itself and Sonah jumped with a yelp as a chair from across the room flew to the door.

"Please! No, don't—"

Sonah flew off the bed and flopped onto Terena's just as her right arm jerked out and slapped Sonah across the head. Stars burst behind her eyes and she shook her head once before she reached out to grab hold of Terena's arm.

"Terena! You're having a nightmare! It's only a dream, Ren! Wake up!"

Terena grabbed hold of Sonah's nightshirt at the neck and pulled her close to her face, a dagger raised in her other hand.

The door burst open. Sonah flinched but didn't look up, fearing any movement might be her last.

"What the fuck?" Rydon gasped when he took in the scene. He strode in, Croak right behind him. Gabriol stood guard at the door.

"Terena, it's all right," Sonah squeaked. "It's just a dream."

Sonah watched as Terena's eyes focused, blinking as she came back to awareness. She yanked up the sheet and let go of Sonah. Her hand trembled and she stared at the dagger in shock. Rydon moved and Terena jolted back on the bed, her eyes wild.

Rydon put up his hands after he sheathed his sword. "It's me."

"And me," Croak said as he came out from behind Rydon, mimicking his stance.

Rydon shot Croak a look before turning to Sonah. "We heard something crashing in here. Are you all right?"

Sonah had her hand to her chest as she stood beside Terena's bed. She nodded. "Aye, sorry. She was having a nightmare, I think, and I tried—"

"I'm sorry, Sonah," Terena said from the bed, her voice shaking, her legs pulled up so she rested her head on her knees. "I'm so sorry. I didn't mean to hurt you."

"Are you all right?" Sonah asked, taking a tentative step toward her.

Terena shook her head. Her sable hair slid forward to hide her face.

Sonah looked over at Rydon with a shrug, her hand out as if to ask what they should do next.

"Do you want to talk about it?" Croak asked, edging closer to the bed.

Terena shook her head again.

Rydon and Croak both looked at Sonah, who shrugged again, mouthing the words, "What do you think?"

"Do you want us to go?" Croak asked, stretching out the last word.

Terena lifted her head, but only to push the heels of her hands against her eyes. Rydon took a step back, his chin dropping as he turned away, and Sonah noticed the flush rising on his neck.

Sonah looked back at Terena and saw she was all but naked at the same time Croak must have realized it because he began stuttering and shuffling back, one hand curved over his eyes. He grabbed Rydon's tunic and started hauling him along.

"What happened to the armoire?" Rydon called, eyeing the ruined chest as he walked backwards.

"We're next door if you need us!" Croak yelled out before slamming the door shut behind them.

Sonah put her hands to her face and shook her head once, then tilted her head back and closed her eyes.

She was silent for a few minutes, letting Terena have her space. She dipped her head and opened her eyes, then quickly averted her gaze as Terena let the bedsheet drop and leaned on the other side of the bed to grab her shirt. Sonah sat back on her own bed, then moved onto the middle of it and tucked her legs beneath her.

"Are you feeling any better?" she asked softly, in case Terena had fallen back asleep.

"Aye," she said at last, and Sonah arched a brow. She settled further into the covers, the room annoyingly cool now she was wide awake.

"What... happened?" She ventured to ask. "When you started to moan... I thought it was, you know. A *good* dream."

Terena lifted her head slowly, piercing Sonah with a narrowed gaze so sharp, Sonah's face heated.

"I mean, good for you, right? If you were getting some in your dream," she mumbled.

"I was not *getting some*," Terena bit out. "I was fighting for my fucking life!"

"Oh!" Sonah said, propping her pillows up and scooting further back against them. "Right. Of course you were. That would explain... the broken furniture."

Terena stared at Sonah a second before she turned to look out over the rest of the room. When she saw the wreck of the armoire and the chair tossed near the door, she swore.

"Who's Daris?" Sonah asked.

Terena whipped her head around so fast, Sonah moved back reflexively.

"Where did you hear that name?"

"Uh, heard it from you," Sonah replied. She waved a hand in Terena's direction. "You called out for him. Or her? Anyway, when you first said it, I thought... well, it sounded like a good thing. Like, 'oh, Daris.'" Sonah's voice was higher and breathy.

Terena choked. "I did *not* sound like that!"

Sonah nodded. And nodded some more, her left eyebrow arched so high it hurt. "Aye. You did. It sounded like—"

Sonah had only a split second to put her hands up as Terena flung a pillow at her. When it fell, Sonah giggled. A few seconds later, she threw her head back and laughed harder, then looked across at Terena's red face as she struggled to look mad.

"Stop!"

Sonah made a face and laughed even more, earning her another pillow to the face.

"Oh! Daris!"

"I'm going to kill you!" Terena growled as she launched across at

Sonah, who shrieked as Terena landed on top of her, shoving her face into the pillows at her back.

The two women erupted into fresh peels of laughter, Sonah laughing so hard she had to wipe away tears. Terena's face was red. Sonah wasn't sure if it was the laughter or embarrassment.

When they finally calmed down, Sonah reached out to push back a lock of Terena's dark hair from her face. "I was mortified there for a second," she said, looking down at the bed. "I was like, oh, she's having one of *those* dreams and I swear—" she grunted as Terena slapped at her hands, "I swear I was going to leave the room, but then the dream changed, I think."

Sonah watched as Terena's face fell, her eyes downcast. She worried she may have pushed too far.

"He tried to kill me. I think he *did*, or he was close to it when you woke me," Terena said at last, her voice soft.

"Was it… was it that Daris person?"

Terena nodded, still not looking up.

Sonah had no response ready. She had no idea who he was, and she certainly wasn't worldly enough to be giving out relationship advice, especially to someone as well-travelled—and beautiful, let's face it—as Terena Luca. But if sitting here and listening while Terena talked helped her, Sonah was here for it.

"Maybe it was just seeing him today. I don't know," Terena said, mumbling more to herself than to Sonah.

Sonah tilted her head. "You saw him? When?"

Terena lifted her head, looking at Sonah as if she'd forgotten she was there. She puffed out a breath before setting her lips in a thin line. "He—well, he was with those soldiers coming through the city when we first arrived. I saw him again at the tavern where Rydon and I had dinner."

Sonah perked up. "Really? They were going fast, but I did manage to get a look at a couple and—oh my goodness, Terena! Those were… *men*."

Terena's lip curled up as she looked at Sonah fanning herself and nodding knowingly.

"Men?"

"Men," Sonah agreed as she tilted her head. "I've been around boys enough to know the difference."

"So the male nobles you've been around for the past seven years at the White Palace are not what you consider men?"

Sonah gave her a look. "Those are boys."

Terena laughed.

"Aye, well. Daris Antonius isn't only a… man. He's the commander of that group of warriors."

"Fancy," Sonah said with a nod, earning her another grin and a slap on the hand from Terena.

"You have to set a high bar," Sonah went on and Terena swore. "You're a god, after all, you can't have just any man in your b—"

Whack.

Sonah grunted when the pillow hit her.

"I'm sorry I woke you," Terena said after a while, her smile fading.

Sonah shrugged. "I'm sorry he tried to kill you."

Terena groaned as she sat up, pushing herself off the bed to stand and stretch. "Well, there had to be a flaw, right?"

Sonah sat up. "But, before he tried to kill you…"

"Stop."

"It—"

"Stop."

"…sounded—"

"Seriously?"

"Tell me one thing," Sonah said, holding up a finger as Terena grabbed one of the pillows she'd tossed at Sonah.

"Was the sex good?"

Sonah shrieked as the pillow landed on her face once more.

CHAPTER TWENTY-FOUR

"We need money," Rydon said the following day as they all sat for breakfast.

Terena had wanted to separate as they had the night before, but Rydon had informed them he and Gabriol had gone around the city looking for news the night before and had not heard of anyone looking for Terena Luca or Sonah Yahn.

In fact, the only news was about the latest battles breaking out all over the eastern continent. Heylisia was fighting Ravos, but Ovenno had come to their aid. Elis, home province to Empress Adanna, had not seceded from the empire and had sent a legion to retake Tursk. They were currently embattled near the border, but Aurora sent soldiers against Elis's army.

So basically, Emperor Solon had more important worries than Terena.

"How much do we have left?" Terena asked, sopping up some egg yolk with her bread.

"Maybe a week," Rydon replied.

Terena shoved the bread in her mouth and sat there, thinking.

"I can juggle," Croak said.

"Shut up, Croak."

"You know what?" Gabriol asked as he leaned back in his chair. "This city is huge. Let's find some fights. Two or three of them and we're good for some time."

Terena nodded as she chewed.

"Good with me," Rydon said. "Ask around, would you?"

"Aye," Gabriol said as he flashed a grin beneath his blond beard.

"So no one's looking for us?" Terena asked Rydon after she'd taken a swig of ale.

"Maybe some random squad," he said with a shrug. "I can't imagine they'd have anyone here, though. The Liodari would have killed them by now."

"Unless they're working with Solon," Terena said. Sonah's head shot up, her eyes meeting Terena's.

"Why would you think that?" Rydon asked, leaning his forearm on the table.

"They were in Aurora," Croak said, his glance shifting to Terena before turning back to Rydon. "We saw them—well, Daris Antonius and a couple of his men, anyway. Meeting with the duke, same as us. When was that, Ren? The spring sometime, maybe a month before all this shit."

"And you think it means what?" Rydon asked, arching an eyebrow. "Aurora's an enemy to Solon now. If anything, Daris Antonius and Lakonia would be allied with Aurora."

Terena shot Croak a look, but quickly dropped to her plate. "Something seemed off about it all. Why would he be that far north in the first place? Croak's right. Solon was on the brink of sending his legions from Elis to Lakonia before all this happened." Terena shifted as she warmed to the topic. "Think about it. Someone drugged Isher and... Lerek. But whoever did that, also let Isher live. And whoever that was also knew Sonah—"

Fuck.

Terena bit the inside of her mouth.

She sensed Sonah's panic as if it was a living thing, surrounding her and her stupid runaway mouth.

"Would need to be kept away. That's why they made sure you were in the courtyard, right, Sonah?" Croak said loudly.

Oh, gods, I love him. Terena swallowed as she nodded, chancing a glance at Sonah. Sonah grunted her assent, the color high in her cheeks.

"That's right, you were in the courtyard," Terena said.

"So if she's in the courtyard, then they can drug the princes, kill Lerek and the guards, and blame it on Sonah," Croak finished with flair as he held his arms out.

"Why would they blame it on the poor girl?" Gabriol asked.

Croak shrugged. "She's his Royal Taster. They think she was in on it. And she is the daughter of Duke Ovenno. Not a stretch to believe the duke is the one who started this whole shit."

"And keeps Solon from attacking Lakonia," Gabriol said with a nod. "That makes sense."

"If she's his Royal Taster, wouldn't he have waited to drink until she arrived?"

Terena frowned and opened her mouth, but once again Croak jumped in. "Lerek didn't always wait for Sonah to drink first. Only when others were around, right Sonah? The Tasters are all daughters of the dukes, sent to the White Palace as another way to control the royals. Stop them from moving against Solon. If he controls their kids, they won't rebel against him. No one took the Taster thing seriously. They mostly did it for the benefit of the servants."

No one spoke for a long time while they continued to eat.

"Well, at least that leaves us in the clear, for now," Rydon said at last.

"Now that we're here... why are we here?" Gabriol asked, his elbows on the table as he leaned across, glancing between Terena and Rydon.

"We're going to steal something from the king," Croak said with his mouth full.

THE PUBLIC HOUSE WHERE THE FIGHTS WERE HELD WAS LARGE, LIKE A barn, but made of stone. Two tiers overlooked the fighting pit, with people hanging out over the railings and shouting down at the spectators below. It was so loud, Terena cringed as they entered.

Terena looked over her shoulder at Croak eyeing the crowd. Next to him, Sonah clutched at her cloak but kept her head high. Terena caught her gaze and Sonah gave her a tight smile. She smiled back and turned to the fighting pit.

Ahead of them, Gabriol stopped next to a short, heavy man with a balding head already sweat soaked, his limp mustache not matching the soft skin of his large cheeks in a complementary way. Terena stopped behind Rydon, half turned to Sonah as she looked out over the room. From the look of the spectators, these fights were a great equalizer. Every class of citizen was present and pressed together.

Gabriol walked back to their group and leaned close so they could all hear over the pressing crowd.

"I'll be fighting third after this one," Gabriol said loudly, then pointed to Rydon. "You're the fight after me."

Terena looked at both of them, then over at Croak, who shrugged like he couldn't care less.

"What about me?"

Rydon looked over at her, an auburn eyebrow arched. "What about you?"

"We need money," she said, glancing from Rydon to Gabriol. "I'll fight."

Gabriol ducked his head as Rydon put a hand on her shoulder. "I know you can fight, but do we want to risk people getting curious about who you are?"

Terena looked around. He had a point. Heylisians weren't welcomed in this kingdom, and technically, they were Heylisians. Even if she was believed to be the one who'd committed treason and murder against the empire.

Her eyes caught on Croak.

"Give me your scarf," she said, holding out her hand.

Croak looked at her with a blank expression. "I don't have a scarf."

She snapped her fingers at him and pointed to the scarf around his neck. "That scarf."

"It's not a scarf," Croak said as he looked down at himself. "It's the top sheet from my bed. I took it when we left. It's cold out."

"Fuck's sake," Rydon scoffed, and even Gabriol smothered a smile.

"Fucking weirdo, why? Save it—I don't care. I'll take it anyway," she said, snatching it from his shoulders. She folded it twice, then wound it around her neck and over her head, wrapping the last bit over her mouth and tied the ends at the back.

She shoved down the cover from her mouth and nodded to Gabriol. "Better? Can you set one up for me now?"

Gabriol tilted his head. "Aye. But you know, they match the fights randomly," Gabriol said, tilting his head.

Terena shook her head. "Doesn't matter."

Rydon did laugh then. Loudly. She shot him a look as Croak reached over to grab her shoulders from behind, squeezed them and gave her a shake. "That's my sis!"

"All right," Gabriol sighed and turned back toward the short, bald man. Terena watched with the others, not hearing a word but gauging the conversation based on Gabriol's face. He looked up and over at her, a second's surprise at having caught her gaze before he gave a quick nod. He turned back to speak with the man, then walked back a few seconds later.

Gabriol exhaled loudly when he reached their group. "You're after Rydon."

She nodded. "Thanks."

He passed a hand over his mouth, then held it out toward her. "It's not a fist fight. It's knives or daggers. First cut wins."

"All right."

"All right?"

"Seems fine," she answered, bouncing anxiously on her feet and looking around at the others. "Any rules?"

"Those *are* the rules."

Croak made a weird, grunt noise, his lips pealed back. Terena frowned over at him before turning back to Gabriol. "Then it'll be over quick."

Rydon shook his head, but she saw a small smile tug at the right corner of his lips. "The arrogance of youth."

They wandered around, stopping every once in a while to watch the fights while they waited.

Twenty minutes later, the bald man motioned Gabriol over. Rydon jerked his head for the others to follow, and they lined up near the edge of the pit, the iron bar barrier at Terena's waist. The fighting pit was empty, the gravel on the ground decorated in sweat and blood spatter.

The fight announcer stood on the other side of Gabriol, and Terena watched as he made his way to the barrier, noticing for the first time there was a gate there. Someone pulled open the gate and the announcer stepped in.

Another man, slightly taller than Gabriol, with a scar marring his head from the right temple through to his hairline at the back of his neck, stepped into the pit. He wore a thin black shirt, his breeches cut in the style of the Offeni from across the Black Sea, wide through the thigh but fitted around the calves, with straps crisscrossing above his boots.

Gabriol stood near the gate and Croak moved to his right side while Rydon went to his left, each of them leaning in to say something to him as Gabriol shook out his arms and bounced on his feet. Terena moved to stand close to Croak, pulling Sonah along.

All around them, people were placing bets.

"He's big, but he looks fucking stupid," Croak was saying as he eyed Gabriol's opponent. "Run around a bit and he'll tire real quick. Then stab him a few times in his side."

"Don't get close to the barrier," Rydon said, ignoring Croak.

"Now go get our fucking money!" Croak yelled with a punch to Gabriol's shoulder before he lifted both arms and hooted. The assembled gave an answering roar as Gabriol rolled his shoulders and entered the pit.

Gabriol made quick work of the man, finishing the fight a minute later after a feint to the left had the bigger man lumbering past him. Gabriol merely flicked his right hand out and caught the other fighter in the side with his dagger. The crowd groaned, and only a few cheered loudly as money exchanged hands.

Gabriol stretched out his arm to his opponent, who grasped it in a quick shake before they both turned to exit the pit. Rydon was next to fight, standing at the gate as Gabriol passed. He thumped him once on the back and Croak jumped on top of him. Gabriol stumbled and pulled Croak under his arm, dragging him back toward where Sonah and Terena waited further down near the front.

While Rydon was fighting, Terena looked around, her gaze falling on a trio with the same uniform.

Liodari.

Terena straightened, watching them a moment more while she pulled on the sheet to cover more of her head. A cheer erupted, and she turned to look at the pit. Rydon's opponent was on the ground with Rydon atop, one knee on the man's sternum and his dagger poised at the man's throat. Rydon straightened and in a move so fast all Terena saw was a blur, he swiped his blade across the man's shoulder, leaving a thin cut in its wake as he moved away from the man.

Money exchanged hands again, and the patrons became more frenzied.

Terena looked across to the right where she'd seen the Liodari, but they were no longer there. She turned and headed toward the gate to the pit.

Rydon reached her side, his hand sliding out to grip her left arm.

"Don't react," he said, his voice low enough only she could hear him. She looked up at his narrowed green eyes. "Your opponent is a Liodari."

Terena froze, and Rydon's hand squeezed her arm. "Listen," he whispered. "They haven't seen you and no one knows who you are. You can leave right now and no one will care."

Terena looked over his shoulder, seeing one of the Liodari waiting at the gate to enter. He looked neither left nor right, as if who he was to fight was of no consequence to him. It irked her.

Shouldn't. But it did.

"I'm fine," she said to Rydon in a hard voice and pulled her arm from his grip. "Might not finish as quickly as you two, but I'll be back before you know it."

Terena pulled up the sheet to cover her mouth, securing the back so it was snug to her head. She patted the sheath at her thigh and made her way through the gate and into the pit, following behind her opponent once the announcer gestured their way.

As they gained the center of the pit, the Liodari turned to face her at last. Terena smiled to see the look of surprise fly across his face before he schooled his features into an impassive mask.

Was it her size or the mask, she wondered as she unsheathed her daggers. He did the same, giving a brief nod before getting into his fighting stance. Terena returned the nod then dropped into her stance, her legs braced and hands raised slightly, daggers gripped tight.

As soon as the announcer's bell rang out, Terena surged forward, feinting right, then left as she danced in and out of his reach. He moved with her, his blades lashing out in deadly response. Terena moved, her body reverting to the Mummer's Dance her father had taught her all those years ago, the fluid movements designed to confuse and anger the opponent, the swift arm motions making his own jerk reflexively as she teased in and out of his line of sight.

He grunted, whether in exertion or frustration, Terena didn't know. But she saw the change in him. His attacks became stronger, quicker, and more lethal. He spun, his sandy blond hair sticking to his forehead. His eyes narrowed and Terena moved to the side.

He stepped forward and twisted, snapping his elbow into her nose. Terena's head snapped back, and the blood soaked the cover over her mouth. She tugged it down quickly. With no time to recover, she watched as he flipped the dagger in his right hand, catching her eye, and then slashed out with the one in his left. She barely moved in time to avoid it. He leaned forward and roared, his right arm striking out, catching the end of the bedsheet and twisting. For a second, it tightened at Terena's throat. She reached out and tugged the other end, letting it fall forward, and stepped back to let it drop.

When it fell to the ground, she had a moment's satisfaction at the surprise on her opponent's face before she sprang backwards onto her hands and kicked him in the jaw as she flipped. The people roared, pressing against the pit barrier. The Liodari spat out blood and came at her in a series of moves so fast Terena stumbled back, each one harder and harder.

Her arms tired.

Buzzing built inside her chest, in her ears, slowly drowning out the crowd. Terena blinked, seeing her opponent slow, then stop as if suspended.

The Liodari's eyes fixed on her face, his lips screwed up and his face tight with tension.

But he just... stood there.

Terena moved from where he was about to strike. All at once, he lunged forward, his jaw dropping, eyes wide as if surprised Terena wasn't standing where he'd expected her to be. She moved then and he turned, his face flushed as he pounced forward once, twice, his arms quick—and long!—and she barely jumped back enough to miss the tip of his dagger as she dropped to her knees and rolled behind him.

Feeling a bubble of excitement, Terena sprang to her feet, only to cry out when something hot lashed her back. She stumbled a few steps.

The spectators erupted, bodies surging forward so fast Terena was sure they'd break the barrier. She took a couple of deep breaths, trying to slow her heart rate and erratic breathing. Blinking against the hissing sting at her back, she reached a hand up to find it as the Liodari came forward and clamped a hand on her shoulder.

Terena spun and saw the Liodari had raised his hands. The dagger in his right hand was red with blood.

Her blood.

Buzzing pounded in her ears, and she took a few more breaths.

"You fought well," the man said as he sheathed the dagger. He held out his arm to her. She looked at it for a few seconds, then took it. He nodded, his lips twisted in a half smile.

He held on to her arm a moment longer than was customary and pulled her close. "What's your name?"

"Ren," she replied, giving him the nickname Gabriol had given the fight master.

The man tilted his head, his lips pursed. He said nothing more as he squeezed her forearm once before dropping it.

The man strode past her and Terena looked over her shoulder to see him file out with the other Liodari, both of whom were looking at her before they disappeared into the crowd.

Terena's shoulders drooped as she made her way toward the gate. Rydon stood there with his arms folded over his chest.

Her face burned. She knew what he was going to say before he said it and it galled her she'd lost in such an idiotic way.

Never turn your back, Lorence had told them repeatedly. More than once, he'd caught her butt with the flat of his sword when she'd failed to learn the lesson.

"Let's go drink," Croak said, throwing his arm over Terena's shoulders.

CHAPTER TWENTY-FIVE

The city offered so many diversions, it wasn't hard to find one suited to their mood. The first tavern they stopped at was good for drinking, but the people were reserved and definitely gave them all side eyes or outright scowls whenever they became too loud.

They wandered down a few streets afterward, still giggly and buzzed, their spirits high.

Terena grinned as she meandered behind the others, laughing when Croak did a cartwheel. She recalled another time when his antics had gotten them kicked out of a tavern in Metilai, and Terena sobered a bit. Thoughts of Lerek crashed down on her cheerful mood. Sonah grabbed her arm and twirled. Terena smiled at her, glad she was feeling comfortable enough to let loose.

"I want to dance!" Sonah shouted as she did another twirl in front of their group.

"Oh!" Croak called out, his hand flying to his ear. "I hear music!"

And then belched.

They all let out a chorus of disgusted outrage and pleas for him to stop. Croak ignored them, grabbed Sonah around the waist and spun her around and round before crashing into a group of bystanders walking in the opposite direction.

"Another round?" Gabriol asked. "There's a tavern right there," he added, pointing to their left.

Rydon and Terena followed, Sonah and Croak skipping along behind them.

A group of soldiers from the City Watch—hopefully, off-duty—held court near the front doors, greeting every newcomer with a boisterous cry and salute with their drinks.

Gabriol flinched, his hand shooting to the hilt of his sword. His lips cracked a grin when the men began serenading Sonah and Terena.

Every citizen on this side of the city seemed to pack the tavern. Terena lost Rydon and Gabriol in the thickness of the undulating crowd, catching up with them a minute later. Looking at everyone to see if they were looking at her, Terena relaxed her shoulders. No one cared or knew who she was.

Gabriol motioned to her when she caught his eye, a tankard of ale held up over his head. Someone jostled him and his hand sloshed ale on the person in front of Terena. The man's only response was to scream, "Again!" as he tipped his head back.

Gabriol grinned and poured ale into the man's mouth and the crowd around them cheered.

By the time Terena got close enough to grab the tankard from Gabriol, the bartender turned it into a game, pouring ale into the mouths of those closest to the bar.

"Hey, hey!" Croak yelled at the bartender, cupping his hand around his mouth as he leaned in. "Where can we find some music around here? My lady's desperate to dance!"

Terena turned her gaze to Sonah. Instead of cowering low with a deep flush staining her cheeks, as was her typical reaction to anything obnoxious Croak did, she was grinning and hopping up and down. Terena smiled to see the grip she had on Croak's arm.

"Music, aye!" The man called back with an enthusiastic nod. "Give me a minute. I have just the boys we need."

The bartender went to the far end of the bar and leaned down to another man, whispering something in his ear. The man nodded and ducked under the counter, disappearing somewhere in the crowd.

"A toast!" Rydon yelled, his voice booming over the crowd. They all crowded close with glasses raised. "Gabriol—never doubted you, brother. You," he winked at Terena, "of course we knew you were a badass from the beginning. But to almost best a Liodari with only daggers? Fucking *goddess!*"

Terena flinched at the word, but the others all cheered so she joined in, holding her tankard up and slapping it against the others.

"How did you move like that? You were a blur!" Gabriol yelled over the noise after taking a swig of his drink.

Terena shrugged and took another drink. "Wasn't fast enough."

"You were plenty fast," Rydon said with a chiding look. "You turned your back on him. That's what cost you."

She was spared answering when the bartender jumped onto the bar, and whistled so loud Sonah squealed at her side.

"Listen up, you degenerates!" he called out in the common tongue.

The crowd erupted with joyous agreement.

"Live music out back! And get ready to dance!"

If possible, the roar from the patrons became even more deafening. Sonah and Croak jumped up and down, sloshing their ale all around them and Terena shrieked as some of it landed on her head. Rydon wrapped an arm around her shoulders and tugged her along as they headed out the back, along with half the crowd.

Two men seated to their right were playing instruments resembling small guitars, their fingers flying so fast over the strings Terena was transfixed as she watched.

A woman was singing in Greek, although Terena couldn't see her through the crowd already in the large open space, people lining up and dancing in one giant circle. Croak pushed past her, tugging Sonah along as the two separated dancers so they could join in.

They didn't know the steps, but quickly picked it up from the dancers on either side of them, and Terena's heart squeezed to see Sonah's shining face laughing up at the woman to her left. Rydon pushed Terena in front of him and she let him pull her into a line a few people down from where Sonah and Croak had joined. Gabriol joined on her left and Terena turned to smile up at him.

She was already dizzy from drink, and the dancing—how fast they moved!—had her breathless. She didn't know how long they danced; one song bled into another. Soon, people were jumping into the center of the circle, dancing in a way too intricate for Terena. And there was no way she was sober enough to do it.

She laughed in surprise as Croak jumped into the center, his dramatic leap making everyone cry out with encouragement and laughter. He pushed back a lock of sweat-soaked brown hair, then tried to copy the last dancer but tripped over his feet and fell in a heap, making Terena double over in a fit of laughter. Gabriol missed a step and fell on top of her. Since she was holding Rydon's hand, she pulled him down with her and he pulled down the poor woman on his right.

Terena couldn't stop laughing as they all sat there for a moment in a mess of limbs. It took them forever to rise, overcome with giddiness. The line of dancers reformed around them until it was only Terena in the middle.

The dancers began to clap and Terena twirled, arms up in the air as she spun. Terena closed her eyes and let the music fill her world as she moved. The crowd sang the song, and soon the voices of those dancing and watching made her heart soar.

She was carefree in that one moment. She wanted to freeze it, and stay in it forever.

Just one night without nightmares.

One night without thinking of him.

Terena opened her eyes and sighed, stumbling as a heady dizziness overtook her. Ready to rejoin the dancers, she moved to the people in front of her, smiling as they made room for her and lifted her smiling face to the dancers across the way.

Her smile slipped.

Daris Antonius stood in the line between two women, one of them smiling up at him as if he hung the moon himself.

Heat rushed to her face as their gazes locked. Surprise and something else on his face she couldn't name crossed his features, but instead of looking away, Terena grinned across at him before looking around the circle of dancers. She spotted Sonah and Croak singing along with the others, Croak's head thrown back as he belted out what Terena was sure were the wrong words, Sonah playing along at his side. Terena's gaze shifted to Rydon, who saw her at the same time and moved across the center to come to her side.

There were shouts from the other dancers as he passed the center, but his only concession to the unspoken rule those in the center of the circle must dance was to raise his arms up and snap his fingers as he came quickly to claim a spot next to her.

"I think I need another drink!" he yelled over at Terena as they shuffled first to the right, then back a step, then right again.

"Same! I want wine, this time," she called back, leaning closer to his ear so she didn't have to shout. He nodded and tugged at her hand. She pulled the woman's hand on her right toward the man standing on Rydon's left as they left the circle, then trotted after Rydon, weaving her way through the crowd around the dancers and back inside.

Gabriol, too, had had the same thought as them and Rydon yelled when he spotted him at the bar. Gabriol lifted his chin in their direction, then leaned over the bar so his face was obscured by the other patrons nearby.

When they were beside him, he held out a tankard. Rydon shook his head. He leaned in to say something to Gabriol, then the bartender, who nodded and placed a cup on the bar top as he reached for something below.

Terena grinned at the bartender when he handed them the wine and she raised her cup to Rydon and Gabriol.

"Let's go find somewhere to sit, I'm fucking tired," Gabriol yelled over the crowd, and Terena nodded. She followed behind Rydon as Gabriol led them through the crowd toward the front right corner.

He leaned over a table nearby and after some nods from those at the table, he grabbed a chair and brought it over to an empty one behind them. He set it down and moved to the one in the corner, Rydon taking the seat at his side and Terena the remaining one looking out over the rest of the room. Not that she could see over the sea of bodies, but she was grateful for Rydon making sure she was seated where she could see everyone.

"Gods, Terena, take it easy, or we'll have to carry you back," Gabriol said with a grin, watching her drain the last of her wine. Rydon clapped him on the back and rose.

"I'll get another round," he said, then strode off, disappearing through the crowd.

A minute later, a woman came over to their table carrying a tray filled with tiny glasses. She bent over and placed three of them on their table and said in a loud voice, "This is from Jason, the gentleman at that table." She gestured with her head over her shoulder.

Terena looked over, her eyes landing on a man holding one of those tiny glasses, his brown eyes holding hers as he lifted his glass and nodded at her.

She blinked, her mouth dropping open in recognition. He was the opponent she'd fought earlier. Terena looked back down at the glasses in front of them, then up at Gabriol. "What is this?"

He shrugged, picking up one of the tiny glasses, the clear liquid inside sloshing at the lip. He put it to his nose and sniffed.

Terena picked one up, then looked back over at the man—Jason, the woman had called him—and he lifted the glass and tossed back the contents in one motion. Terena watched as he grinned, then set the glass down on the table.

"I think you drink it all at once," she said to Gabriol when she turned back. Rydon came back then and sat down with a big sigh. He saw the glasses they were holding, another on the table and looked at them.

"What's this?"

"We don't know," Terena said, then glanced over her shoulder at the Liodari, Jason. Rydon looked over, too, frowning when he saw all four men looking back at them. She saw the moment he recognized them, too, from the fights.

"But I think we're supposed to drink it all at once," she added, drawing his attention back to her. "That man, Jason, did that. So maybe we should?"

"Smells strong," Gabriol said.

Terena looked over at Jason again, who was trying to seem like he wasn't watching her, but failing. She lifted the glass to her lips and tipped it back, letting the liquid pour into her mouth.

It left a trail of fire down her throat, eyes bulging and watering. She coughed and Rydon clapped her back and she chanced a look at Jason. His entire table was laughing, heads thrown back like her death was the funniest thing they'd seen in an age.

"Gods that's disgusting," she said hoarsely when she could speak. She wiped at her eyes, still feeling the liquid slowly sliding down into her belly.

Rydon and Gabriol drank theirs at the same time. Rydon did much better than Terena had, coughing only a couple times, but Gabriol's eyes watered like hers and he wiped at them several times before he could even speak.

They looked at each other at the same time and laughed, Terena's chest protesting a bit as it still burned from the drink.

Rydon leaned back in his chair and shouted across at the men, "What the hell was that?"

Jason grinned, looking at Terena before shifting his eyes to Rydon. "Ambrosia," he said, "the drink of the gods."

Gabriol lifted his empty glass to him in salute.

"Did you like it?"

Surprised he'd spoken to her, Terena turned back to Jason and nodded with a smile. "After I got over the almost dying part. Aye, I liked it very much."

He winked. "Good, you're Spartan now."

Terena laughed. "Is that all it takes?"

He shrugged. "We're a welcoming people."

Gabriol leaned across the table and muttered, "I think he's flirting with you, Terena. You fighting with him turned him on, I guess."

Terena flushed and swatted at him. Before she could reply, Sonah wedged through a few people in front of their table and smiled wide when she caught Terena's eye. Croak came up behind her, looking green.

Terena caught sight of the woman who'd brought them the drinks and quickly stood, grabbing hold of her elbow before she disappeared. She ordered a round of Ambrosia drinks for their table, and ordered one for Jason's table as well.

When she sat back down, Sonah was excitedly chattering about the dancing and the friends she and Croak had made.

Croak brought back two chairs, dragging them to their table between Gabriol and Rydon as the barmaid came back, setting the glasses down carefully on their table, then moving off to Jason's table.

"This is something the Greeks call Ambrosia," Terena said to Croak and Sonah. "You drink it all at once but—wait!" She reached across to Croak to stay his hand as he was about to toss back the drink. "It burns like fucking crazy. Just a warning."

"Hey!" Jason yelled from his table.

They all turned, and the men were all holding their small glasses up high as they looked at them.

"In Sparta we say 'Yiamas!' And then you drink," Jason said with a grin. "To our health!"

Terena looked around at her table, all of them lifting their glasses at the same time and yelling "Yiamas!" She waited half a second, watching the others toss back their drinks before she drank hers. The same burning sensation tore down her throat and through her lungs; she felt like she could breathe fire.

Sonah sputtered, coughing hard and stood up in panic, fanning her face. Gabriol surged to his feet, pounding on Sonah's back.

Croak puked on the table.

Rydon and Terena swore as they shot to their feet to avoid the mess. Terena saw movement to her right and looked up as Jason went to Sonah's side, offering her something in a large tankard.

"It's water," he said as she looked at him through bulging, tear-filled eyes. She tried to suck in air, taking the tankard from him and took a quick sip. She took a couple more and seemed to calm as she started muttering to the gods.

"It's not for everyone," Jason grinned, a dimple flashing in his cheek, once he'd made sure Sonah wasn't going to die. The barmaid had come back, yelling something in Greek and wiped up the mess, shooting dark looks at them.

"What the fuck?" Croak squeaked, wiping his mouth when the barmaid finished and stalked away.

"It'll grow on you," Jason laughed as he moved back to his table.

"Thank you," Terena yelled to him, impulsively reaching out to touch his arm as he passed.

He nodded, the movement causing strands of blond hair to fall over his right eye. He was about to say something when the other men at his table rose abruptly. Jason's head swiveled to his right, his body going rigid beneath Terena's hand.

A second later she realized why.

Daris Antonius appeared, standing behind one of his men at their table. He held a tankard in his right hand as he looked over at Terena and her friends, curiosity in his sky-blue eyes.

Terena's stomach dropped when his gaze finally met hers and she turned, dropping her hand from Jason's arm to retake her seat.

Jason moved back to his table. The men spoke with their commander, and Terena looked over at Sonah, who was once more breathing normally.

"Gods, Terena," Croak said with a belch. Rydon cursed and shoved at Croak's shoulder. "You undersold it."

"I kinda like it," Gabriol said.

Terena sighed, a smile flashing on her lips. Warmth spread through her body, sliding down her limbs. "I feel... good."

Rydon had his head tipped back, but he grunted. "Same."

"Another?" Gabriol asked.

"I don't—"

Before she could protest, Gabriol rose and left.

"Who is that?" Sonah whispered loudly, her fingers digging into Terena's wrist.

Terena winced and tried to pry Sonah's fingers away as she asked, "Who?"

"The one who came to my rescue!" Sonah said in a breathy voice and leaned forward, her head close to Terena as she peered over Terena's shoulder. "He's beautiful, and did you see that dimple?"

Terena grinned and folded Sonah's hand in hers. "That's Jason. He's the man I fought in the pit earlier."

The look Sonah shot her was priceless and Terena threw her head back and laughed.

"And which one is your Daris," Sonah slurred, a smirk on her face when she turned her narrowed green and brown-eyed gaze to her.

Heat crawled up Terena's neck and face. "He's not *my* anything! And he's the one that came to their table just now."

Sonah snapped her gaze back over to the other table and her eyes widened when she spotted the man in question. "Oh. Aye. That's... that's a man. A gorgeous man."

Terena chanced a look at Daris Antonius and caught him staring at her. She turned away quickly, but Sonah was merciless. "Oh, I think he likes you, too," she said, her smirk turning wicked as she shifted closer to Terena. She flicked another glance at the commander before turning back to Terena. "Do you think he has sex dreams about you, too?"

Terena shrieked and lunged for Sonah as the girl flung her head back and guffawed, the two women embracing and cackling like idiots.

Gabriol came back with a tray filled with more of the miniature glasses. After he'd plunked down enough for their table, he took the few steps over to Jason's table and dropped the tray with the rest in front of him. "Yiamas!"

Terena watched out of the corner of her eye as Jason smirked, but she shifted to look at Daris, seated across from Jason. She cursed under her breath to catch him watching her still.

"All right, one more, then more dancing," Sonah screeched at them and they agreed with much laughter. They lifted their glasses and screamed out the toast, earning them laughter from Jason's table.

They stood almost at the same time, Sonah slower as she tried to control her coughing again. Terena pushed out her chair and rose, ready to follow the others, when a wave of dizziness rocked her and she pitched back. Rydon shot forward to grab her, but Jason, sitting just as close, had a hand tight around her elbow. She thanked him breathlessly, then laughed as her friends began wending their way through the crowd toward the back and the music.

Terena shot a quick glance at Jason's table as she followed and saw they, too, had all finished their Ambrosia.

All except Daris.

Terena didn't know if it was the drinking making her bold, or that she felt alive for the first time in a long time, but she stopped in front of the commander and arched an eyebrow as she looked down at him.

He watched her, a wary look on his face.

A slow grin spread across Terena's face. "Not taking any drinks from us?"

She saw a corner of his full lips rise in a small smile as he regarded her. "I don't drink."

Her heart thudded, her body languid as she looked at him and the way his mouth moved. She thought again of how beautiful this man was.

Dangerously so.

But she was carefree right then. Instead of doing the smart thing and walking away, Terena's smile turned wicked and, without taking her eyes off him, she lifted the glass of Ambrosia to her lips and tossed her head back. The drink once more burned a path down her insides, and she closed her eyes for a second before looking back at him.

She turned the glass over and set it softly down on the table near his hand and whispered, "Yiamas," as she walked away.

CHAPTER TWENTY-SIX

I t was close to dawn before they finally set out for the inn. The streets were quiet, only a few others about at that time of day: the ones starting their day and others—like Terena and her friends—just finishing.

They were a few streets away from the inn when Terena turned her head to laugh at something Croak had said and almost fell over. The others laughed at her, thinking her clumsiness a result of her drinking. When Terena fell against a cart and slumped over, Rydon lunged for her, grabbing her around the waist to steady her.

"Easy," he said as he held her. "We've all been there."

"No," Terena whispered, her head pounding. She looked around and saw the street, but differently. It was much darker out in this new perspective, and the streets were alive with crowds looking for merriment. Terena opened her mouth, clutching at Rydon's hand, her eyes darting around to take in this new reality, when her gaze settled on a small, one story building ahead of them on the left.

She was having a vision. The vertigo was so strong she held on to Rydon as the vision superimposed over the street where they were stopped. Terena narrowed her eyes at that building and took a few steps forward.

"Whoa, easy, Ren," Rydon said, but she took another few steps, her eyes fixed on the building where people only she could see stood outside.

"We need to go there," she said, her voice strong despite still feeling dizzy.

"What, another tavern?" Croak said over a belch. "I mean, I'm good for one last round if you are, Ren."

"I'm so tired," Sonah whined. "Let's save it for tomorrow."

"I don't think it's open, regardless," Gabriol said, his eyes on the building Terena had indicated. He turned back to her, his arms akimbo. "Do you know it?"

Terena stared at it another moment before glancing at Gabriol. "Aye. I've seen it before."

"Another vision?" Rydon asked, his gaze narrowed as he watched her carefully.

"We need to go now," Terena said softly. She looked over at Sonah. "You can go back to the inn, I'm fine alone."

"The fuck you are," Croak said, sauntering over. "I'll go with you."

"I've got her," Rydon said with a quick glance at Croak. "You go on, get to bed. We'll see you anon."

The others hesitated but Terena started walking, feeling stronger now as she neared the building. Rydon kept a hand at her back as he continued at her side. He turned to the others to see they were walking back slowly toward the inn, Croak looking back every few steps, a concerned look on his face.

The place looked closed, as did every other building around them. No one was about.

"Looks closed, whatever this place is," Rydon said in a low voice. Terena scanned around, walking to the side of the building. She frowned and turned back when she heard a door opening. She jogged back to Rydon, who looked at her in question.

As Terena took a step, dizziness assailed her again and she stumbled toward him. He reached out and grabbed her arms before she fell.

"I have something that will help with that," a voice said behind her. Rydon cursed, scowling at someone over Terena's shoulder.

"Bring her inside," the female voice said. The vertigo overwhelmed Terena as she tried to turn her head, making her lose her balance and pitch to the right. Rydon grunted and wrapped an arm around her waist. Terena closed her eyes as he guided her inside the now opened door.

As quickly as it had come over her, the vertigo subsided as they went deeper inside. It smelled of incense, and Terena recalled the oracle and the temple sanctuary in Messene.

But this smell was different. It was just as strong, but not as cloying. Terena relaxed, straightening and looking around at her surroundings. A woman stood before them, a shawl wrapped around her thin shoulders. She was old, an octogenarian with a full head of grey hair. Wrinkles around bright black eyes mapped her face. Terena had the uncanny feeling she knew this woman. She smiled at Terena as if she knew exactly what was going through her mind.

"Thank you," Rydon said.

"Bring her through, Eudaemon," the woman said, motioning to Rydon to follow.

Terena looked up at Rydon, her nose wrinkled. He stiffened and she noted the red creeping up his neck to his cheeks.

The room beyond was empty, with old, faded furniture the only decoration. Even the walls were bare and stained with age. The only light in the room came through the threadbare curtains over the windows. Terena was about to say something when the woman's smile changed, her eyes narrowing as her lips turned down. Rydon swore and unsheathed his sword a moment before five men came out of the corners of the room, their faces hidden beneath black hoods.

"You've grown strong since we last met," the woman said, no longer the frail looking woman from earlier but closer to Terena's age, her hair now dark like Terena's and her hateful eyes a strange burnt orange. "But you'll die, all the same."

The hooded figures attacked a heartbeat later. Terena jumped back, unsheathing her sword clumsily as Rydon blocked the two in front of her, the clash of their swords ringing loud in her ears. She turned and quickly parried the man at her side.

He was strong.

Terena grunted at the force of his attack. His sword moved to a new angle, a different thrust as he forced her to step back until she hit the wall. Rydon yelled at her from across the room, engaged now with three of the attackers as another came forward from her left. This one had a short sword and another blade slightly larger than a dagger, both of them wielded expertly until she was down on one knee from the force of both her assailants.

Slowed down by drink, Terena's parries were weak. She thrust her sword at the man on her left, catching him on the inside of his thigh instead of his gut. He grunted but otherwise showed no sign of pain or slowing down. Terena's breath came in quick bursts and she panicked. She knew she'd be dead in minutes if Rydon didn't help her soon, because she was outmatched and drunk. A low buzzing beneath her skin started as the man on her right caught her with an overhead swing, the tip of his sword slicing into her shoulder, and she almost dropped her blade. She cried out, stumbling back, and then it happened.

Time slowed, the buzzing in her body turning to heat and her eyes hurt. She swallowed and looked up, her attackers frozen in place, the one on her left in a move sure to be fatal. Terena stepped to the side and glanced to her right, searching for Rydon, when she caught sight of the woman. Her face was screwed up in concentration, her hands out and her fingers halted with the tips of her middle fingers and thumbs touching. She was chanting something and Terena sprang at her. Coming up behind her, Terena put her sword to the woman's throat as her other arm wound around the woman's waist.

Terena blinked and time resumed, her attackers stumbling forward, confused as they looked down to where she had been, then up to see her holding the woman.

"Stop!" she screamed, pulling the woman back with her. Terena looked to Rydon and saw he'd defeated one man, the other two wounded, now still as they all watched her.

"Whatever you're doing, stop it," she hissed at the woman.

One man took a step toward her and she dug the sword into the woman's neck and cut her. When he saw the blood trail down her neck, the man lifted his hands and stopped.

"That wasn't very nice," Terena said to the woman as she sucked in a breath. "Why'd you attack us?"

"Kill her!"

Three of the men jerked into motion. Rydon caught one of them with a sword thrust to his belly. He yanked his blade free and the man fell to the floor, writhing for a few seconds before he was still.

"Call off your dogs," Terena warned, "or I'll have my friend cut them down."

"I'll do it anyway," Rydon growled, his sword at the ready.

The woman reached down, making a grab for Terena's dagger. Terena shoved her forward. Falling to a knee, the woman looked up, brandishing Terena's dagger.

The woman panted, her lips peeled back in a victorious sneer as she looked at Terena.

"Aye, much stronger than last time," she said.

"You'll forgive me if I don't remember you," Terena said, swinging her sword arm out to the men on her left. Rydon circled closer to her, standing at her side as the three attackers moved to stand at the woman's side.

"Oh, you remember," the woman said. "Why else would you come in here?"

"Remind me again why you want to kill me?" Terena asked.

"Oh, I'm not here to kill you," she said, as if they were having a cup of tea. "I'm here for your sister. *You* keep getting in the way."

Rydon's eyebrows shot up in surprise. Terena's blood went cold. She moved, her steps so fast the two men on her left had no chance. Before they could react, she swung, slicing the man on the far left across the throat, the gash opening and bleeding out before he dropped. Terena spun, thrusting her sword back into the other man's stomach.

She pulled her sword out and he fell to his knees. The woman's eyes flew open wide as Terena turned and narrowed her gaze on her.

The woman touched the pendant hanging between her breasts and began chanting; the man at her side instantly snapped out his short blade. Terena watched in horror as he struck Rydon in the chest.

She roared, heat flashing through her body and she reached out, a pulse of power bursting through her hand, throwing the man hard against the wall at his back. His skull caved and he dropped to the floor like a rag doll. Terena turned to the woman, this time lifting her up with invisible hands, like she'd done to Isher, only this time she was more controlled, stronger. She snapped the woman's neck before she could scream.

Terena gasped and ran to Rydon. She slid to the ground at his side, her hands shaking as she moved him to his back. Tears stung behind her eyes and she impatiently blinked them away, her mouth dropping open when she saw the blade still in his breast.

"Rydon, oh please no," she whispered. He groaned, and she gasped, her hands an inch from the blade.

His eyes blinked open slowly.

"How are you still alive?" Terena squeaked. She didn't want to remove the blade because he'd surely die. But honestly, how was he still alive?

As she sat there trying to figure out what to do, Rydon reached up, his face screwing up in a grimace. Jaw tight as he gripped the hilt of the dagger, he yanked it out. Terena sat back on her heels, mouth wide as she exhaled raggedly.

Rydon sighed and closed his eyes, dropping the blade with a loud clatter at his side.

She sat in stunned silence, her eyes searching his face.

"What the fuck, Rydon?" She shuddered, feeling lightheaded.

Rydon swallowed, the column of his neck dripping sweat as the tendons worked and he tried to speak. He opened his eyes and looked at her, resigned.

"It's as she said," he replied, his voice rough, barely above a whisper. "I am a Eudaemon. A Guardian. I am sworn to protect you."

Terena opened her mouth, then scoffed, her hands splayed. "So… so… so you can take a fucking blade to the heart and live?"

He had closed his eyes after he'd spoken and it took him a few seconds more before he opened them again to stare up at her.

"I can't die unless you do."

Rydon winced at the pain from the wound in his chest. Terena seemed dazed, her eyes unfocused. They sat in thick silence while their assassins lay dead nearby. Rydon moved to stand and Terena reached out reflexively, helping him as he made his way slowly to his feet, her arm strong around his waist, her feet sure and stable when a bit of lightheadedness had him swaying.

"You're unusually quiet," Rydon said gruffly. He took a few slow, deep breaths and covered the wound with his hand.

Terena watched him warily. "Lots to think on just now," she said at last.

He nodded. "I expect you have questions."

She snorted.

Terena took her arm from his waist, slowly, as if expecting him to fall down dead. He worried she was right to fear, but when she took a step back, he was fine on his own.

"We should leave," he said, glancing around at the bodies.

Terena said nothing, so he took the lead, walking carefully out of the room and into the entryway. He glanced over his shoulder to make sure she followed.

When they were outside, he slowed, waiting for her to catch up.

"How did that woman change her appearance so drastically? So quickly?"

Rydon's eyes widened as he eyed her. He walked a few steps before answering. "Do you remember when I first asked if you're a god? I told you some people in this world were also given powers, those favored by the gods. They are not divine, they are still mortal, but they have some… special abilities often confused with divinity. I confess, I have never seen one. I assumed they'd all been killed off, mistaken for gods."

Terena nodded. "That makes sense."

"Those men of hers; she must have been using some sort of enchantment to strengthen them. Or they drew strength from her somehow. Either way, we will never know for certain. What's more important—and something else we can't know now she's dead—is who sent her? And why did your vision lead us to that place if you were to be killed?"

Rydon saw her drop her head, her steps slowing.

"When I spoke with the oracle, I realized the visions are memories," she said. Terena lifted her gaze as she frowned. "Apparently, this isn't the first time I've done... all of this."

Rydon's lips twisted. "Aye. I had that feeling as well."

"Truly?"

"Aye," he said, catching her look of surprise. "When Her—when the king made me Eudaemon, it was," Rydon shook his head, recalling. "I can't explain it. An uncanny sense of having been there before. In that exact moment. I wasn't frightened."

"I wish you would have said something sooner." Terena frowned up at him.

"And I wish you would have said something about having a sister."

Terena stopped and turned to face him, arms folding and she hunched her shoulders. "I only found out myself, Rydon. I'm not trying to keep secrets from any of you. I wanted to tell Sonah before—"

"Sonah!" Rydon laughed. "Sonah's your sister? Now things are making sense."

Terena ducked her head. "Aye, Sonah's my sister. According to the oracle. But I haven't told her yet."

"We all need to sit down and speak openly about all this... shit," Rydon said.

Terena nodded and began walking.

They walked in silence until they reached the inn. Terena put a hand on his arm to stop him, the gloomy predawn light enough for him to see her pensive expression.

"I trust you with my life," she whispered. "I know that that's your mandate, or whatever, but I want you to trust me as well. I've been unfair to you, Rydon. For that, I can only apologize and promise you that ends now."

Rydon held her gaze a few seconds more before giving her a curt nod. She smiled tightly, patted him awkwardly on his arm, and preceded him inside.

CHAPTER TWENTY-SEVEN

After a few hours of fitful sleep, Terena finally gave up. She dressed and went downstairs to find something to eat. Spotting Rydon sitting at their usual back table, Terena smothered a smile. He took one look at her and kicked out the chair opposite.

After the sleepy innkeeper brought her a plate of stale bread and butter, Terena stared across at Rydon.

"Does Gabriol know? About you being a Eudaemon?"

"Aye," he said with a sigh. "He was there when it happened."

Curiosity made her halt her hand midway to her mouth. "Will you tell me?"

Rydon glanced over her shoulder and shrugged. "Someday. Not here."

Terena nodded and took a bite of the bread. "Did you tell them about last night?"

Rydon nodded. "Hard not to when I had blood on my clothes. Your brother took it as well as you'd expect."

Terena twisted her lips.

"Have you told your sister yet?"

Terena turned her head to look over the empty room, then turned back to Rydon with a shake of her head. "She was asleep already. And I didn't want to wake her yet to tell her."

"Are you worried?"

"No," Terena said hesitantly. "Maybe."

"She needs to know," Rydon chided.

They sat in silence for a long time before Terena pushed her chair back and rose.

"I'll go talk to her. Hopefully she's awake."

Climbing the stairs, Terena flexed her hands, her steps slow as she breathed in and out slowly. The room was awash in greys from the light filtering in through the curtain behind Sonah's bed. Terena closed the door softly behind her and made her way to Sonah's bed.

When she sat, Sonah stirred, mumbling sleepily. Terena smiled and put a hand on the girl's hair.

"Sonah?"

Sonah remained still. Terena bent close and whispered her name again.

She stirred and Terena sat back, waiting.

When the girl's eyes fluttered open, she smiled.

"I'm sorry to wake you, but I need to speak with you."

Sonah's brow furrowed, then she shifted up onto her elbow. She rubbed at her eye. "What's happened?"

"Nothing, everything's fine," Terena whispered. "But I need to tell you something before we meet up with the others."

Sonah regarded her for several seconds, then sat up. "All right."

Now that she was about to tell her, Terena's heart raced. She cleared her throat. "When I went to the oracle, she told me something else I... I wanted to talk to you about."

Sonah stared back at her, waiting.

"She told me... she told me you are my sister."

Sonah continued to stare at her, and Terena worried she hadn't understood. She opened her mouth to try again when the girl moved back against the headboard, her face screwed up.

"What?"

Terena's mouth seemed stuffed with cotton. She licked her lips.

"The oracle told me I travel with my sister. That *you* are my sister, Sonah."

Sonah's face paled, then reddened, and her mouth opened and closed. Dread washed over Terena, squeezing the breath from her lungs, and she inhaled sharply. Sonah's eyes misted and Terena looked away.

The girl covered her face with her hands.

"Sonah, I'm sorry," Terena said, placing her hand awkwardly on her forearm. "I wanted to tell you so many times. But—"

Sonah's shoulders shook as she sobbed.

Terena's heart broke. Her eyes stung and she went to rise, intent on giving Sonah some space when the girl launched herself at Terena, throwing her arms around her. Terena froze, then hugged her back fiercely. She buried her face in Sonah's hair, taking a shuddering breath as she willed herself not to cry. They sat like that, wrapped in each other, and Terena had a strange feeling of homecoming. She tightened her arms and Sonah did the same as her sobs quieted.

"I knew it," Sonah whispered. "I knew it."

Terena sniffed, letting the tears fall.

Sonah pulled back and looked at Terena with her beautiful, mismatched eyes. "I knew it. I don't know how, but I always... there's something... I always *felt* different around you. I always wanted to be near you and I thought it was because, well, look at you! You're amazing. Of course I'd be drawn to you, right?"

Terena laughed and Sonah's face blurred as fresh tears gathered. "I feel the same about you. And I'm glad you are with me now, and you are never getting rid of me."

Sonah giggled and hugged her again.

Then she pulled back with a frown. "Wait. Does that mean Croak is my brother now?"

"Whether you like it or not," Terena said with a wink.

"Does he know?"

"Aye," Terena said, smoothing back Sonah's hair. "I told him."

"So," Sonah swallowed, "he's all right with it?"

Terena furrowed her brows. "Of course. You hadn't noticed?"

Sonah's smile was radiant. "He's been different, aye. But I thought he had finally warmed to me."

"I know he has," Terena said as she rose. "There's more to tell you, but I'll wait until you're dressed. We'll go downstairs and have breakfast. All of us. We need to figure out how to get an audience with the king."

Sonah nodded and flashed her a smile. She jumped from the bed and grabbed her leggings from the end of the bed. Hopping to slide the pants over her butt, Sonah looked up at Terena with a frown.

"I wonder why we were separated," she said.

Terena paced the room as she waited for Sonah to dress. "Another thing we can ask them when we get north."

Sonah nodded. She sat on the bed to put on her boots, lacing the first one quickly. Then she flicked a glance at Terena. "Will we leave once we have what you need from the king?"

"Aye," Terena said with an exhale.

"Does Rydon and Gabriol know about me? About us?"

"Rydon does. When we were attacked last—"

"Attacked!"

Terena cringed. She held up her hands when Sonah bolted to her feet. "We're fine! He's fine. But afterwards I had to tell him about you because of what the woman who attacked us said."

"What'd she say?"

"Never mind that," Terena snapped, then smiled to take the edge off her words. She wouldn't tell Sonah the woman had laid a trap for her that Terena had stepped into instead.

Sonah studied her for a moment more, then bent to finish lacing up her boot. She grabbed her leather corset and put it on over her tunic.

"Ready," she announced with her arms held out.

Terena cocked her head and strode for the door.

As they reached the bottom of the stairs, Terena turned and stopped abruptly, her hand flying back to grab hold of Sonah's wrist.

Standing in the main room of the inn, Daris Antonius turned toward her, his hand on the hilt of his sword.

Behind him, four Liodari stood in front of Rydon, Gabriol, and Croak.

"What is this?" Terena asked in an icy voice.

"Lady Luca," Daris Antonius rasped. "The king would like a word with you."

"What about?" Terena asked. Her heart thudded against her ribs. Stepping closer, she flicked her eyes to her brother. His eyes darted between the Liodari in front of him and Terena. She saw the way his hands trembled as he held them up, but his face didn't betray him. Rydon's face was red, and she knew from the way his chest rose and fell heavily he was a second away from engaging the soldiers.

Terena caught his eye and shook her head slightly. He pursed his lips but relaxed his stance. Gabriol edged closer to Croak.

"The king has... heard of your arrival in Sparta and sent me to bring you to him." The commander's face was impassive. Terena saw by the slight tightening of his mouth something was off.

She stared at him a long moment. He seemed stiff, uncomfortable. *Good,* she thought. She would not make this easy for him.

"How'd you find me?"

Daris parted his lips. A few seconds passed before he said, "This is my city, lady."

Terena and Rydon shared a glance before she turned back to the commander. True, she needed to see the king anyway, and this was much better than wasting time trying to figure out a way to gain an audience. But she didn't like the fact he'd been aware of where they'd been staying.

Nevertheless, she intended to make good use of this opportunity.

"Very well," she said, feigning nonchalance. "I'm at your service."

Daris Antonius didn't move, and as the seconds ticked by, Terena became uneasy. He dropped his gaze to the floor, then looked back at her again.

"The young lady, too."

Rydon and Gabriol moved then as Croak protested loudly. The Liodari stopped them with swords up. Terena's pulse ratcheted up and her grip on Sonah's wrist tightened.

"Why?"

The commander pursed his lips, his face dark. "I do not question His Majesty," he bit out, his eyes boring into hers. "I'm commanded to bring you both to the castle. Please. Do so peaceably."

Heat suffused Terena's neck, rising to her face. "Or?"

A quick flash of exasperation crossed his face before his indifferent mask fell back into place. "There is no 'or.'"

"If it's all the same to you," she said, her voice low, "I'd rather not endanger my friends, so I'll come at your king's command. But I'll come alone."

"Your friends are only in danger if you refuse to let us take you both," he said, before looking over his shoulder at Rydon. "Or if they do something foolish."

Terena heard the frustration in his voice before he pulled up to his full height.

He stepped closer, looking down his nose at her. "This is not a request."

A few tense moments passed as she stared back at the commander. How blinded she'd been by this man's face to see the brutality beyond. She'd forgotten he was a famous warrior for a reason.

Terena fumed for a moment longer before giving him a malicious smirk. "Well. Since you asked so nicely."

She turned her gaze to Rydon and Gabriol. "You and Croak stay here. I'll be back as soon as I can and then we'll leave the city. The sooner the better." This last she directed at Daris Antonius, putting as much loathing in her expression as possible, so he had no doubt she wanted nothing more to do with him.

Damn those moments of weakness when she had allowed herself to be flattered and excited by the idea a man like him might be attracted to her.

Idiot. Serves you right.

The commander thinned his lips and looked over his shoulder, giving a quick nod to his men. The others waited until Terena had turned, still holding on to Sonah.

When they reached the door to the inn, another Liodari opened it, an apologetic look on his face.

Terena started, realizing it was the man she'd fought in the pit. Jason.

He looked away, his head ducked as he held the door open for her and Sonah.

CHAPTER TWENTY-EIGHT

Terena had refused riding with Daris Antonius or any of his men, insisting on taking Nyx instead. She rode with Sonah sitting behind her, her thin arms wrapped tight around Terena's waist. The commander rode at her side, his men flanking them.

He had tried several times to engage her in conversation but she'd ignored him. She could feel his frustration by the way he sat stiffly on his stallion, his jaw tight and his brow furrowed as he gazed straight ahead.

Long hours of drinking and then fighting that witch and her men with little sleep left Terena agitated and twitchy. A fierce headache throbbed behind her eyes. She cursed Daris Antonius as she cast death looks at his back.

Why hadn't he approached her last night? Or even at the tavern when she and Rydon were having dinner?

It was as if he'd calculated the moment she was most vulnerable to come for her.

They wound their way up steep streets toward Arestia Castle, and Terena looked up, marveling again at the spires piercing the sky and blending seamlessly, matching the jagged stone of the mountain it was built into. A waterfall fell on the left, creating a veil of mist to hide all but the outline of the left side of the castle. On the far right, closer to the bottom, was a stunning glass and gold-framed structure that, at that time of morning, reflected light refracting in the mist from the falls.

It looked to Terena like a castle the gods themselves might live in.

If she hadn't an asshole of a hangover, she'd have enjoyed the view more.

As they neared a large arched gate leading up to the castle, the commander called a halt and he and his men dismounted. Frowning, Terena watched them a moment before Daris Antonius held out his hand to her.

"What?"

"We walk from here," he said, his face placid.

Terena balked, once more looking up at the castle. "You're serious?"

He did not respond. With a grunt of frustration, Terena sprang down from her horse. She reached up to help Sonah, but the girl dismounted clumsily on her own, with only a hand at her back from Terena to steady her.

Terena eyed the commander warily as she once more took hold of Sonah's hand, watching as one of his men came and took Nyx's reins. Daris Antonius motioned for her to follow.

The gates opened to reveal wide steps branching off; one led away from the castle and into a cave where some of the Liodari led the horses.

"We're walking?" Terena scoffed and lifted a hand. "All the way up there?"

The commander didn't stop walking as he turned to glance at her over his shoulder. "Aye."

Terena smothered a curse. Narrowing her eyes at the commander's back, she fumed. "And this could not wait until later in the day?"

No response. Terena stopped walking and folded her arms. Sonah stopped by her side as well but looked over at her with apprehension.

"Terena, perhaps—"

"You did this on purpose," Terena spat at the commander's back.

He stopped. A few seconds later he turned to face her, his back stiff.

"We are on the king's schedule," the commander said. "And that is why you are here now."

"He is not my king," Terena said quietly.

The other Liodari had stopped as well, regarding the two of them in this standoff. At her words, they put their hands on the hilts of their swords and waited.

Terena smiled.

The look the commander gave her was somewhere between exasperation and anger. She quite enjoyed it.

"You are in Sparta now," the commander said as he walked toward her. "He is your king now as much as mine."

"And you'd bet your life on that?"

The sounds of swords leaving their scabbards filled the air. A buzzing burn coursed through her skin and she welcomed it this time.

She was sick of being at the whim of men.

"Please!" Sonah shouted, lurching between Terena and the commander. Terena's eyes widened in alarm. "Please, stay your swords! We will come!"

She turned beseeching eyes to Terena. Sonah stepped closer and whispered, "We need to see him either way. Why are you being like this?"

Terena shut her eyes and counted to five. When she opened them again, she shot a look at the commander over Sonah's shoulder. "Because I had a horrible night, Sonah, and I've barely slept. I'm hungover and I've got a lot on my mind and the last thing I needed was to be dragged before the king by this overbearing—"

"Terena," Sonah begged, laying her hands on Terena's shoulders. "The only way we get out of here with whatever he has that's yours, is by seeing the king. We can leave directly after, if that is your wish. But you said it yourself. We need to see him. Come," she added, grabbing hold of Terena's hand. "We'll walk together."

Terena stood still a few seconds more, then walked. As she passed the commander, she shot him a venomous look.

She didn't miss the grateful look he shot at Sonah.

Two Liodari preceded them up the other path winding around and up toward the main entrance: a large, curved entry surrounded by stone pillars.

Before they entered, Terena was disarmed, forced to remove her sword belt and daggers. She stared mutinously at Daris Antonius as she did so.

The doors opened as if by their proximity alone and Sonah's other hand settled over their clasped hands. The commander strode forward, no longer worried about whether they'd follow. They had nowhere else to go.

The foyer was as grand as she'd expected, with gleaming marble floors and a high, domed glass ceiling. There were courtiers, nobles, merchants and servants all milling about or—in the case of the servants—remaining as unobtrusive as they could while going about their duties.

Terena turned back to the commander as he made his way to the left and down a series of wide hallways filled with more people, then right to a set of doors guarded by four men wearing uniforms different from the Liodari.

Armored in bronze and leather, with red and gold capes and helmets bearing red plumes, Terena eyed the guards warily as Daris Antonius strode forward.

They did not bother to glance at Terena and Sonah. Without a word, the men on either side of the doorway reached out, opening the heavy gilt doors. The commander marched through. Terena hesitated a moment before following him inside.

The room was large and windowless. Two walls on either side looked to be whitewashed stone adorned with tapestries and paint-ings. The back of the room was rounded, and it was there the king's throne sat at the center of a large marble dais. Two guards flanked King Altos with two more at the foot of the dais.

King Altos sat forward, one arm resting on the side with his chin propped on his hand as he watched their progress through the room.

Terena had a moment's surprise as they neared. The king was

younger than she'd expected, around the commander's age, with a short beard complementing his full lips and firm jaw. He wore his brown hair short like the Liodari and had bright brown eyes, watching her with curiosity.

The commander motioned for Terena to stop while he continued on, pausing before the king to bow, then turned and clasped his hands behind him, his back stiff as he looked at the space behind Terena and Sonah.

Terena did not bow.

The silence gathered while Terena stared back at the king, her face hard. She hoped he saw her displeasure. She also wondered what he'd heard about her. Terena assumed he'd heard the rumors of her being a god. His enemy had, after all, arrested her and had been about to execute her, not only for the Crown Prince's murder, but for being a god.

"I thought you'd be taller," the king said at last, his voice unnaturally loud in the cavernous chamber.

Terena cocked her head and narrowed her eyes.

"And older," he mused, seeming unbothered by her silence.

He rose abruptly, taking the two steps off the dais and sauntering over to stop a foot away from her and Sonah. Terena saw the commander shift and look at her. She slid her gaze back to the king.

King Altos pursed his lips, his eyes searching her face before turning to Sonah.

"You must be Prince Lerek's Royal Taster," he said, and Terena stiffened. She saw Sonah's lips part and Terena squeezed her hand, hoping she'd keep quiet. She did, a tremor passing through her at the king's regard.

"Do neither of you speak?" The king asked in a light tone with a slight lift of his lips.

"You have something of mine," Terena replied. Her voice was harsher than she'd intended and she cursed herself for showing any emotion.

Intelligent brown eyes turned to her in triumph. "Do I?"

Terena gave herself a few seconds before she lifted her lips in a mock smile. "I'd like it back."

King Altos regarded her for a long moment, his handsome face pensive, before he tipped his head and clicked his tongue. "I'll be honest," he said, pacing away from her, "I expected... more. When word reached us of your treason, how you'd attacked the princes, killing one and almost killing the other, I thought, 'this must be the most cunning of assassins'." He clicked his tongue again, moving back to his throne.

He sighed when he sat. "I admit to being disappointed." He motioned to the guards closest to Terena, and they strode forward. She moved, intent on shielding Sonah, and failed.

Two guards held her while another grabbed Sonah's arm. Terena struggled against the guards, her blood roaring in her ears as she cast a desperate look at Daris Antonius.

Sonah screamed and thrashed, calling out Terena's name.

"You're making a big mistake," she said, jerking again at the hold the guards had on her.

The king lifted his hand and the guards moved away from her. Terena shot a look first at the commander, then silently to the king at his back. Her eyes filled with rage.

"Insurance, if you will," the king said, almost bored. Sonah stood shaking at his side.

"For what?" Terena ground out.

"Compliance."

Terena waited.

"You came here looking for something," the king said a moment later, his shrewd eyes narrowed as he waved a hand to her. "But I need something as well. I can, of course, simply use the... what you came for, as assurance, but I'm inclined to think you might find a way around that, so... here we are."

"Speak plain."

He laughed, and she saw the guards shift. Terena knew speaking like that to the king—any king—would likely earn her a physical rebuke but she was beyond caring at that point. The man had her sister as a hostage.

He clearly had no idea who he was dealing with.

"All right," he said with a heavy sigh, resting his chin in his hand once more. "I'll speak plain. Do you know the story of Bethana and Melanos?"

Terena blinked in confusion. After a few seconds of silence, she nodded. "The myth of the demigod and his lover. Poseidon killed him and turned the woman into a serpent. Aye. I know it."

"Good. I don't need to explain then." He shifted, lacing his fingers together while his arms rested on the sides of his throne and shrugged.

"I need you to find Bethana and bring me her fangs."

Sonah watched Terena. Her face slackened at the king's words.

"What?"

The king turned out his laced fingers and looked at her expectantly. "Too much?"

Terena scoffed. She glanced at the commander, then back at the king as if he were mad. "You asking me to bring back fangs from a mythical sea serpent? Aye. I'd say that's a bit much."

King Altos grinned. "You know, I am starting to like you," he said offhandedly. "I'm still going to need you to get me those fangs, though. If you want me to give you what you came for. Oh, and the Royal Taster, of course."

Terena's face reddened, her lips pursed in a way Sonah knew did not bode well for the king. Sonah tried to take a step, but the guard on her left tightened his grip until it hurt. As if sensing her pain, Terena's eyes shot to her.

"Stay your men," she seethed, "or this will not end well for them. Or you."

The guards all unsheathed their swords; even the commander had his hand on the hilt of his as he watched Terena.

Sonah swallowed.

The king lost his smile that quickly. He shot up from his throne. "How dare you? I've indulged your rudeness because I need your cooperation, but I can force your compliance, with or without Sonah Yahn. And if you persist, I will make sure you never see the Twins."

Sonah started. The twins?

"You don't want to do this," Terena said, her tone almost pleading. She looked between Sonah and the king and raised her left hand, as if to placate him. "I don't want to hurt you. Just give me what I want. Let go of my... friend, and I'll leave your city today."

The king's mouth dropped open, staring at Terena in disbelief. He turned his head and shared a look with the guard holding Sonah. She gaped, her eyes wild, and locked on Terena as the guard put a blade to her throat.

Clearly, this man had a death wish.

Terena's eyes and face went blank as she stared at King Altos.

Sonah chanced a look at the king and swallowed when he smirked in triumph.

Then his face flattened. He grabbed for his neck, his hands clawing at the skin there. Sonah's mouth dropped open and her eyes flew to Terena. She stood with her left hand up, fingers arced as if she were gripping something, her face so cold, it chilled Sonah deep in her bones.

Daris Antonius swore.

Steel rang out as he unsheathed his sword. The guards all yelled at Terena, threatening and cursing. Daris looked at the king and yelled for Terena to stop. Sonah almost felt bad for him.

"I warned you," Terena said, her voice sharp and without emotion. She ignored Daris as he took another step toward her.

"I dare you," she whispered to Daris when he stepped in front of her. Sonah saw the way her lips trembled as she stared down the commander. The king's face was turning purple and his eyes bulged. He flailed his left arm, turning his head enough to look at the guard holding Sonah, and the man lowered his dagger and stepped away.

Sonah stepped off the dais.

Daris raised his sword at Terena. "Don't do this, Terena," he said, his voice pleading. The scars on his left cheek and ear were stark white against his tanned skin. "Please."

Sonah thought she might ignore him. Then Terena dropped her arm and the king fell to the dais. Guards moved within two feet of Terena, swords lifted. Terena continued to stare at the king, who had gotten to one knee as he took deep gulps of air.

Daris turned back to Terena and, though he was still angry, there was something else in his expression Sonah thought looked much like how Lady Tollis had stared at Prince Lerek when she thought no one was watching.

With longing.

"The rumors were true," King Altos whispered, staring at Terena in awe.

Rising to his full height, the king's face still showed traces of red as he rubbed the sore flesh of his neck. It was so awkwardly quiet in the room, the pressure moved Sonah to break it.

"Your Majesty," Sonah said in a voice she thought was soft but, in that room and with the quiet so loud you could hear a mouse scurry, she winced at how loud—and meek—she sounded.

All eyes turned to her. She blushed and cleared her throat to try again. "Your Majesty," she said in a stronger tone, "Please, if I may suggest a... solution, to this stalemate?"

The king turned his head to her. After a long moment, he nodded.

"I will stay with you—"

"Sonah!"

Sonah held up her hand to Terena, pleading with her eyes before she turned back to the king. "I will stay with you while Terena goes to look for this... Bethana?"

"Sonah," Terena begged.

King Altos did not reply. Instead, he continued to regard her silently. She took that as permission to say more.

She clutched her hands together and took a step toward him, only to freeze when she heard movement behind her. Sonah's chin trembled. Hated the show of weakness in front of everyone.

"In the meantime," Sonah went on with a lift of her chin as she straightened, "You give Terena what she came for."

The king looked as if he might protest, but Sonah hurried to forestall him. "I'll still be here, as a guarantee Terena will return. She'll come back with your... teeth. Or whatever. She'll come back for me."

King Altos stared at her as the color returned to normal in his complexion, the olive skin only slightly red in the cheeks. Sonah waited, holding her breath, not daring to look at Terena.

"No," Terena groaned, defeated. She ducked her head and Sonah winced against the stab of guilt.

But she had no choice. She would do this to save her sister.

At last, the king shifted his eyes to Terena, then back to Sonah. "And why should she do so if she has what she's come to Sparta to retrieve? I understand from Commander Antonius you are friends, but even friendship has limitations."

Sonah saw Terena take a step forward, as if she knew what Sonah was about to do.

"You're right to be cautious," Sonah said, her voice strong. "You don't know her, and you've only my word for it, but she will come back for me. As she would come back for any of her friends."

"I cannot—"

"But she would definitely come back for her sister."

CHAPTER TWENTY-NINE

Terena exhaled, and her shoulders slumped.

What have you done? she thought as she gazed at Sonah in resignation.

No one spoke after Sonah's revelation. She watched the stunned expressions on both the king's and the commander's faces as they swiveled their eyes from Sonah to Terena.

Sonah shifted, breaking the spell.

"Your sister," the king said, his voice soft as if speaking to himself.

"Aye," Sonah said, and Terena looked at her again, noting the proud lift of her chin as she stared across at Terena. "Now. Do we have an accord?"

Terena looked to the king and waited. He stared back, thoughtful, then nodded absently. Daris Antonius waited another heartbeat before going to his king, the royal whispering in his ear. The commander stiffened, but gave a brief nod. Walking away, he motioned for a guard to follow him as they went behind the dais. Terena watched them as they exited from a concealed door in the curved wall.

"You *are* a god," the king said, snapping Terena's attention back to him. He hadn't moved, his back straight as he fully recovered from her assault.

Terena said nothing as she regarded him warily.

"And if she's your sister," he said as understanding dawned. He shifted and turned his gaze to Sonah, his brown eyes narrowed.

"I will kill you if you touch her," Terena snarled, hands balled at her sides. "Bargain or no, you will die."

"I believe you," the king said, his voice sincere. Terena relaxed a fraction when he turned back to her, his expression almost reverent.

The silence settling while they waited for the commander to return was tense. Terena thought her nerves might snap. At last, the door opened, and the commander strode into the room, carrying two short swords. He glanced over at Terena, his lips pressed tightly, as he stopped before his king. The royal motioned for him to give them to Terena.

As he neared, Terena glanced at her sister. Sonah's lips opened and she let out a shuddering breath.

The commander did not speak as he held up the blades in front of Terena, his eyes hard as he stared at her. Terena stared back, taking the short swords from his hands without breaking eye contact. The Liodari stepped back and walked to the king's side.

As soon as she held them, a jolt coursed through her hands and arms. Power surged under her skin, racing through her veins. Terena heard a gasp and looked down at the swords. Light flashed back and forth across the blades, illuminating symbols and letters, disappearing when the light faded. The swords appeared normal once more.

The king laughed and Terena lifted her eyes. He gazed at the swords with wonder.

"What you hold," the king said in a rough voice, "are what the man who sold them to my father over twenty-one years ago called The Twins. When I came into power, I went to see the oracle in Messene. She told me one day, a woman would come to claim them, and I was to give them to her, for they are her birthright." The king laughed in disbelief and Terena looked up at him to see him shaking his head at her. "I was angry at her, because I had wanted what every king wants when they go to see the oracle. I wanted to hear her tell me how to secure the safety and prosperity of my people. I had hoped to hear her speak of my destiny. Instead, she had instructions for me on how to help *you*."

Terena snorted. "There's a surprise."

"What?"

Terena arched an eyebrow. "That she was not helpful. I went to her as well. I left more confused than when I'd arrived."

The king flashed a grin and ducked his head. He lifted his eyes to her again and said, "She told me you would bring me Bethana's fangs. So that's why I asked it of you."

Terena looked down at the swords, then up at Sonah. "My sister has made a bargain with you," she said and turned her gaze to the king. "I will honor it and bring you the serpent's fangs. I trust *your* honor, Sonah will be safe in my absence." Then she hardened her expression. "But know she is not without her own resources. She may be young, but she is strong."

Terena looked over at Sonah, who was smiling at her even as a tear tracked slowly down her cheek.

"I would not do her, or you, the disservice of thinking otherwise," the king said. "And to honor your sister's bravery, I will lend you my aid in your endeavor." He gestured to the commander. "Daris will accompany you on this quest with two of his men."

"I don't need—"

"Your Majesty—"

Terena scoffed and looked at the commander, who was protesting as she was. She looked back at the king. His mouth was set firmly.

"I don't need his help," Terena bit out.

"Nevertheless, you have it."

Commander Antonius hung his head for a few seconds before he turned his gaze back to her. His eyes burned, his lips pressed so tightly together they were white. "I will serve, Your Majesty," he said to the king. He shifted back to Terena and added, "We leave tomorrow at dawn."

TERENA, CROAK, GABRIOL AND RYDON ARRIVED AT THE EASTERN GATE ten minutes late.

As they walked up, horses at their sides, Terena sensed Daris's displeasure, even before she saw the frown on his face.

She didn't care. When she'd returned from the castle without Sonah, the others were understandably upset. Terena had told them of King Altos's demand in return for the swords and the bargain Sonah had made with the king. She'd told them, too, she had revealed their relationship, and Terena had lost control, angered into displaying her powers.

"Any other family secrets you told them about?" Croak had grumbled.

Terena knew he was upset about Sonah. And Terena was angry with herself at how quickly the audience with the king had devolved. She had punched Croak a tad too hard on his shoulder. He had stumbled back, a hurt look on his face that had nothing to do with the punch. Rydon had suggested they get some food, which turned into too much wine and ale.

Terena was in a lot of pain from the overindulgence, having only slept for three hours before dragging everyone else out of bed so as not to be late.

Terena shifted her tired eyes to the two men at the commander's side. She knew Jason, the man she'd fought in the fighting pit and celebrated with at the bar that same night. The other she didn't know, although she'd seen him as well that night.

Turning back to Daris, she lifted an eyebrow, expecting him to make introductions. Instead, he looked over at the others with her, and his frown deepened.

"You and your friends don't look well."

She loosed a sigh, stopping a few feet away from him.

"A little softer, please," she said and closed her eyes, her own voice barely above a whisper.

Daris shifted on his horse, narrowing his light blue eyes and glared as he leaned over the pommel.

"Are you drunk?"

"No," she answered, drawing out the word. Not convincing, apparently, by the way his lips curled back.

He didn't speak for a long while. Terena opened her eyes and looked up at him. He glared at her friends.

Daris turned to Terena. "They cannot come."

She shook her head, then winced. Sighed.

Loudly.

"We can waste time," she replied, as patiently as she could muster, "or we can go. We're *all* going. I'm not leaving my friends behind."

Rydon move closer to her as she watched Daris decide.

"This is *my* quest," Terena added. "Stay if you want."

She clicked at Nyx, turning to move past the commander. He shifted his much larger stallion to block her. His horse snorted in a not-friendly way above her.

She lifted an eyebrow at Daris.

"It's a long way to Pyrgos," he bit out. He lifted his chin, motioning behind her. "They'll slow us down."

"Why would we be riding to Pyrgos?" she asked.

"Because that's where—"

"We're going to Ibros," Terena cut him off, her patience snapping. "To Thuria."

Jason snorted behind the commander.

Daris stilled. Terena shrugged and made to move around him once more.

"A word," the commander bit out, dismounting in one graceful motion. "Please."

She swallowed the curse she was about to hurl, pursing her lips as she whispered to Nyx, rubbing her neck once before she handed the reins to Rydon.

Terena followed the commander as he moved a few feet away from the others, steeling herself against the rebuke she was sure he was about to give her.

She put her hands on her hips and shifted her weight as she glared up at him.

Even scowling, he was striking.

Unfair.

She wished she'd bathed before they'd left. Terena was sure she smelled of cheap wine and Ambrosia. She could smell it coming out of every pore in her body.

She took a couple of steps away from him. Just in case.

"I'm leading this party," he hissed, bending closer as he pointed a finger at the ground.

"Aye, fine," she said. "But lead us to Ibros."

"And why would we go there?"

"Because that's where Melanos is from."

"What's that matter?"

Terena cocked her head to the side. "Hey—out of the two of us—which one does this for a living?"

He straightened. No response, though.

A terrible headache was creeping up on Terena, making her more surly than she had intended. "That's right. Me. And we go where *I* say. I'll let you know when it's time for whatever you're here for."

He jerked forward a step, his face tight. "Tell me why."

Terena startled, but... gods. He looked good. Even angry. Then she remembered she was angry as well. Angry he'd ambushed her yesterday, taking her to his king for an audience ending with Sonah staying behind as hostage.

The gods must be punishing her.

Terena held out a placating hand. "Do you know the myth?"

He gave a curt nod.

She sighed. "Right. The thing is, no one knows where exactly the serpent was when it slew Melanos. There are different versions. A lot of it was lost because it was mostly word of mouth. But if we go to Thuria, where Melanos was born—he was a demigod, right?—we might find something, giving us an idea of where to look. He's their hero. They'd know that story inside and out and in ways you and I do not."

Terena waited a few seconds for him to speak. When he didn't, she bowed her head, sweeping her left arm out. "So. We start in Thuria."

She took a step forward to head back to their group, but he stopped her with a hand at her elbow.

"You're right," he said, surprising her. Terena's gaze flew to his face. He was looking down, his face so tight a muscle jumped at his jaw. "You are the expert. I apologize for overstepping."

She huffed a laugh. Terena hoped she sounded as unaffected as he seemed; his touch sent a spike of lightning down her belly.

"I'm sure it won't be the last time."

A corner of his mouth curled up, and he gave a quick nod before letting her arm go.

"We good?" she asked breathlessly.

His eyes stared into her, and for a second she was sure he could see inside her head.

Daris straightened and nodded curtly. Terena stared at him a moment before moving to step past him, then stopped.

"How is Sonah?" she asked softly.

The commander didn't respond. She looked up at him. He sighed and his expression softened.

"She's fine," he said. "King Altos is a good man. You need not fear for her."

Terena searched his eyes, deciding at last he was in earnest. "Thank you."

She turned to leave, but he grabbed her elbow again. "I am sorry for what happened yesterday," he said, his tone urgent. "I had no time to send a warning, and in front of my men I..." He dropped his head and shook it, then lifted his eyes to her. "She'll be well cared for. You've no worry on that account. But I am sorry for my part in the affair."

Terena frowned and mumbled her thanks. She knew that wasn't something he'd control. If Altos had ordered him as Commander of the Liodari, Daris had had to obey without question. That didn't mean she had to like it.

But she could be more gracious toward him, she decided.

"Mama and Baba are done arguing," she called out to the others. "Let's get this quest started!"

Croak whooped in excitement. Even Daris's men were grinning.

Daris choked on a cough behind her.

Rydon and Gabriol both grinned at Terena before mounting. She mounted Nyx and glanced over to check on Croak.

Croak hocked and spat on the ground before mounting his horse so smoothly she was impressed by his constitution that morning. He seemed to be the only one of them not hurting after last night's bad decisions.

Maybe it was the anticipation, but Terena was excited as well, her lips widening as she turned her gaze to Daris. He watched her with an unreadable expression.

She gave him a pointed look, and he rolled his eyes.

He turned his horse to the gates and rode off, Jason and the other Liodari falling in behind. Terena and the others followed.

THEY RODE UNTIL AN HOUR AFTER SUNSET, UNTIL THE MOONLIGHT WAS the only thing to light their way. Daris steered them toward dense woods off the Greek road they'd been traveling.

As they neared a clearing, Daris called a halt. Terena dismounted and handed the reins to Rydon. He and Gabriol led the horses to the edge of a creek. Terena set off with Croak to gather wood. They found berries in a thicket further away from where the others set up camp and picked some to bring back.

Once they'd eaten, they sat in silence around the fire Daris had built with Rydon and Jason. Croak sat next to Terena, his legs pulled up to his chest as he stared into the glowing embers.

"I feel like we should be singing," Croak said, his voice a shade too loud in the peaceful silence.

Rydon grunted, tossing a twig into the fire. Jason looked over at him from his right.

"Sing away, if you know any," Jason said.

Croak shrugged. "I—"

"Don't," Terena warned, her hand grabbing his wrist. She looked over at Jason wryly. "The only songs he knows are dirty ones."

Jason and the other Liodari, Michael, chuckled. Even Gabriol was grinning from his place at Croak's other side.

"Sing one," Jason goaded.

Croaked loosed a loud sigh. "Terena will turn bright red if I do that."

Terena scoffed. "I've heard your songs before, idiot."

"There once was a man with a very big c—"

"Stop!" Terena yelled, and the others laughed.

After the laughter died down, Michael asked, "How did you become a tracker?"

Terena looked across at him in surprise. It was the first time the warrior had spoken to her, to any of them.

She ducked her head and lifted her right shoulder. "I," she cleared her throat. "I was maybe eight or nine, when I find out my father and mother—the people who'd raised me—weren't my actual parents. I was... devastated. To learn the only parents I had ever known, my family, were not my blood."

"She beat the shit out of the boy who told her," Croak added, his eyes boring into Terena's and she ducked her head. This was the story they had concocted, because to share the truth would be to reveal too much.

"He started taunting you with it and you wailed on him, remember?"

Terena nodded. "My father was horrified when the boy's father approached him, dragging me along. Screaming at my father about what a heathen I was."

"He was so pissed," Croak muttered.

"Did you two... grow up together?" Daris asked.

Terena started, her gaze jumping to his across the fire. "Yes, of course." She looked over at Croak and jabbed her elbow into his side. "He's my brother."

Terena glanced back at Daris, a look flashing on his face she couldn't decipher.

"What'd your father do?" Jason asked. "I hope he gave the man a good beating, too."

"No," Terena answered, shaking her head as she dropped her gaze from Daris to her hands. "He spoke calmly to the man, diffusing his anger."

"I thought you said your father was the one who taught you to fight?" Rydon said.

"I didn't say he didn't know how to fight," Terena clarified. "He was the best fighter I've ever seen. But that was only his profession, not his passion. Books. Knowledge. That was what he lived for, and what he gave me—us—along with the gift of how to defend ourselves."

"Your father was a soldier?" Jason asked, his voice soft.

"Our father was the Captain of the Imperial Guard to Emperor Solon," Croak said proudly, his eyes on the fire.

She heard the murmurs from the Liodari.

"Aye," Terena said, clearing her throat once more. It hurt still to talk about him, even though it had been five years since his death. Croak leaned closer and Terena calmed. "He taught us how to fight, but he also taught us about the gods and the wars, the myths and the heroes." Terena rubbed at her forehead.

"When I asked him if… what he—what that boy had said was true, about me not being his daughter, I'd never seen such devastation on his face. I knew right then it was true, and I cried. Cried so much it took him forever to calm me down."

This part of the story was true. She'd been shattered.

Croak slipped his hand into the crook of her arm. Terena blinked furiously to clear her eyes of the tears that threatened.

She didn't speak for a long time, but no one said anything to push her.

"He told me," her voice cracked, and she swallowed a couple times before trying again. "He told me he would always be my father. That we were family, no matter how I'd come to them. And then he told me the story of how he'd found me. How he'd been on his way home from

Olympia with a company of soldiers. They had stopped at Hekate's temple to leave an offering, and he'd wandered off to relieve himself," Terena laughed and Croak shot her a grin. "And then he heard me crying a few feet away. He walked until he found me. When he came over to grab me up, he found a man beside me, face down. Lorence, my father, said he'd gone to the man, but he wasn't moving. When he flipped him over, he saw the man was dead.

"A few years later, I asked him for more details." Terena wiped her nose with the back of her hand and sighed. "I asked him if the man had any wounds. If he looked like me; did he have the same black hair or hazel eyes?" Terena shook her head. "And when I started asking more questions about the man, he told me if I wanted to know more about who I am and who my parents were, he would help me. He gave me some things he'd found when he rescued me: my blanket, a gold armband the man wore, a gold necklace he'd had in his pocket." Terena lifted a hand to touch the necklace she wore at her neck.

"We poured through books to see if we could find any mention of either, anything similar that might lead us to the city-state or region I might have come from. Of course, we started in Olympia, where he found me. Lorence told me about people called trackers and how they made their living finding lost treasures left behind by the gods. That we could hire one to find my parents. I told him I wanted to be a tracker, and that was that."

"Have you found your birth mother?" Jason asked, his voice soft as he looked at her, his eyes shining.

Terena dropped her head, but did not speak.

The silence thickened around them.

"*There once was a man with a very—*"

They erupted in laughter as Croak began singing in the fraught silence. Terena's laughter was sharp as tears stung her eyes and she hung her head. The others howled as Croak's bawdy song got worse.

Terena looked up at last.

And met Daris's heated gaze.

CHAPTER THIRTY

They traveled for a week, camping in wooded areas far from any villages or towns they passed. Daris wouldn't risk questions or prying eyes seeing their sizable group passing through.

After Croak had grumbled about a warm bath, Daris had told them to get used to their situation, for he wouldn't let any of them be seen by someone who might take back word to their enemies.

He did, however, send Jason and Michael into one of the first villages they'd come across for provisions. Croak had tried to tag along, but was vetoed rather quickly by both men. When they'd returned with only the food and supplies Daris had sent them for, even Rydon and Gabriol had added their voices to Croak's loud complaints about the lack of alcohol.

So the next town they'd neared, Croak had gone along with the others to bring back appropriate provisions.

They were a few days away from Thuria when Daris called a halt for the night. Jason and Rydon had gone off to scout for a suitable place to camp while the rest of them stretched their legs or sought privacy to see to their needs.

Terena let out a groan and rubbed at the back of her neck as she paced away, tugging Nyx along as they neared a small pond close to where they'd stopped. She crouched at the edge and cupped her hands into the cold water, lifting it to her face, and drank. Nyx dropped her head and lapped at the water beside Terena, sending gentle ripples across the still surface.

The moonlight cast a pretty glow over the pond and surrounding trees, a soft melody of night filling the silence. Terena lifted more water and splashed her face, sighing as the cold bit into her skin, waking her.

After that first night with Daris and his men, Terena had remained wary, unwilling to fully fall asleep.

"You're exhausted."

Terena stiffened, glancing over her shoulder to see Daris standing a few feet away to her left. Rising, she wiped her hands on her pants.

"We're all exhausted," she replied.

He shook his head once and took a few steps closer. Terena turned slightly toward him, her hands at her sides.

"Truth. But you haven't been sleeping much."

Terena lifted her shoulder. "I doubt any of us have been sleeping much."

He looked at her a moment longer, his brow furrowed. "I've seen you. When you're close to drifting off. It's like... you *will* yourself to stay awake. At first, I thought maybe you were uncomfortable around me, around my men. Understandable. But we've been traveling for over a week now and you haven't let down your guard."

"Have *you* let down your guard?" Terena countered. It was bad enough he'd noticed. That he'd been watching her that closely. For him to try to figure out why was something she would not allow.

He lifted a corner of his mouth but said nothing.

Seconds passed, neither of them breaking the silence. Terena turned to leave, feeling awkward, when he spoke.

"I didn't realize he was your brother," Daris said.

Terena turned back with a frown. "Croak?"

"Aye," he said. He took a couple steps closer and Terena braced herself. She wouldn't give him the satisfaction of thinking she was unnerved by him and wanted to keep as much distance as possible between them. The tension she'd experienced around him ever since the fiasco at the castle was unnerving.

"Well. He is. I mean... you know. He is, though."

Terena cringed, hoping it was dark enough to hide her face.

Daris crossed his arms, his face guarded. "I had thought..."

The moment stretched while she waited for him to finish.

Then realization hit her.

A burst of laughter escaped her mouth before she could stop herself. She clapped a hand over her mouth but couldn't hide the grin stretching her face to the point of pain.

"Sorry," she said, her voice shaky with laughter. "Not laughing at you. Just..." She shook her head and gestured at him. "You thought he was my—you thought we were together?"

He shrugged, a small smile on his face.

Terena's heart skipped.

"I wasn't sure," he said, his voice low. It rumbled through her. She wrapped her arms around herself to keep from shaking. "I didn't think so when I first saw you. In Aurora. Thought maybe he was a colleague. Danilos didn't bother to say, and I didn't bother to ask."

He raked a hand through his hair.

Terena watched him like a hawk.

"And in Sparta, when you were all out together; the way he's always near you. Or how he touches you..."

"Oh gods, gross!" Terena cringed as the words escaped her mouth with such force she almost leaped toward him to stop them from coming out of his lips. "No, *not* a lover. Just my brother. We're only a year apart, so we're close." She shook her head and loosed a sigh that was half laugh. "I'll make sure he touches me less. Gods."

Daris's smile widened and he dipped his chin. "That's good to know."

Awareness filled her and her heartbeat ratcheted up. Terena's pulse throbbed in her ears. "Why?" She cleared her throat. "Why is that good?"

His smile slipped but a look crossed his eyes that made her shiver.

A predator watching his prey.

"I'm curious about you," he said, his voice almost a purr. He took another step closer. Right then, she wished so badly she didn't reek of horse and sweat and a week's worth of riding.

But she didn't move away.

"Truly?"

He nodded.

"What," she swallowed. "What would you like to know?"

He took another unhurried step closer.

She didn't move.

Danger.

"What were you doing in Aurora?"

The fire in her blood winked away.

"I delivered something the duke had contracted me for," Terena said, her voice cool. "Anything else?"

He eyed her for so long, buzzing roared in her ears and beneath her skin as his eyes narrowed on her.

"Was Prince Lerek your lover?"

Fuck. *Fuck.*

The words cut her like daggers. His name on Daris's lips hitting her heart hard. It broke open as she struggled for air.

"Gods, what you must think of me," she laughed sarcastically. "First, Croak. Now you ask me about Le—"

Her lips clamped shut and she made to move past him when he shot his hand out and grasped her arm. His clear blue eyes searched hers, a look like sorrow or pity filling them before they flashed with something else.

Something that looked like guilt.

Terena had no desire to have him feeling anything for her. Especially not guilt.

But Terena was guilty herself. Because his presence had made her forget—every time—that she had lost Lerek. That she loved him. That she ached and mourned him, the guilt tearing at her whenever she stopped thinking about him.

And thought about the man in front of her, instead.

"Terena—"

Terena was cold, so cold she shook, the blood gone from her face, pooled low in her belly.

She became dizzy and sick. The bile rose in her throat and she turned, looking around wildly.

Her eyes landed on Nyx a split second before she jerked her arm from Daris's grip and launched forward, grabbing hold of the bridle as she leaped onto the saddle and thundered off. Nyx's head tossed back, her agitation matching Terena's as she tried to distance herself from Daris and the guilt she couldn't escape.

Terena thought she heard him shout out her name, but she did not stop.

THEY TRAVELED IN SILENCE MUCH OF THE FOLLOWING DAY. IT HAD BEEN awkward when they'd broken camp, Terena and her friends keeping separate from the Liodari, the battle lines drawn. When she happened to catch Jason's eye, she only offered a tight smile before looking away.

As dusk settled around them, Croak broke the silence.

"Do you hear that?" he said, tilting his head as he slowed his horse to a stop.

Rydon turned to him, then looked over his shoulder.

"I hear it," Gabriol said, his voice low.

They all stopped and listened.

Ahead of them, Michael glanced back and called out.

Rydon held up a hand for him and motioned for silence.

Michael whistled at Jason and Daris, and the three of them stopped and turned their mounts back when Michael gestured with his head.

A scream reached them just then.

"It's coming from there!" Gabriol yelled out and rode off. The others were only a moment behind.

They reached a ravine and Terena leaped from Nyx, pulling her bow over her shoulder as another scream—pitched high like a child's —pierced the quiet gloom around them.

Terena ran to the ravine edge and dropped to the ground to peer down.

Rydon and Gabriol crouched at her side. Croak cursed over her shoulder as they saw the boy at the bottom, his right leg at an unnatural angle. He was small—from this distance all Terena could tell was he was young, maybe five, and from his ragged screams he must have been down there awhile.

"Get the rope from my bag," Terena called over her shoulder to Croak as Daris and the Liodari came up behind them. She made to put her bow back over her shoulder when Rydon gripped her wrist and motioned with his chin.

"Shit," Jason said, as he looked down at the ravine at the same time Terena saw it.

Saw *them*.

Three wolves slunk toward the boy, their low growls making the boy's cries more urgent. Desperate.

Terena's heart raced. She bolted upright, pushing past Rydon and Gabriol as she ran along the edge of the ravine, her eyes on the wolves as she nocked an arrow.

The wolves turned their heads in unison when the men shouted after her. Terena's mind cleared as she dropped. Pulling the bowstring tight, she loosed it on the wolf closest to the boy.

A second arrow was already in flight before the first reached its target. Swiftly flying through the air, the third arrow hit the back leg of the second wolf with a thud.

Terena heard more arrows and glanced back long enough to see Rydon and Michael with their bows raised, arrows flying at the wolves.

Croak ran to her with the rope coiled in his fist and flung it at her. Terena dropped the bow and wrapped one end of the rope around her waist, tossing the other end at Croak. She turned and looked over the edge again, trying to find a way down the ravine that wouldn't kill her.

At last, she found a path and dropped down. Daris raced forward and dropped to his belly, grabbing the strap of her shoulder guard when she slipped. Terena's eyes shot up and blinked up at his face, flushed red and tight as he clenched his jaw, his eyes flashing.

Terena exhaled roughly and looked around to find another spot for her hand to hold on to. She peered over her shoulder. Her right foot found a rock to support her as Daris released his hold on her.

She looked up again and saw he'd taken up the front spot of the rope Rydon and Gabriol held. Croak was on his belly, hanging over the edge as he watched her, terror in his eyes.

Terena reached the bottom, heart thudding painfully against her ribs. Untying the rope at her waist, she heard the others call down to her, Croak's voice loud in protest.

Pushing back a lock of hair, Terena unsheathed her sword. She swallowed, glancing over to where the wolves had stood, two of them dead.

The third wolf was nowhere in sight.

As if sensing her thoughts, Gabriol called down. "He ran off. We're watching for him, don't worry. Get to the boy!"

Terena nodded, not bothering to look up. Holding her sword loosely at her side, she strode forward, the boy watching her through tear-filled eyes. His chin wobbled and his face was streaked with tears, dirt and blood from a cut on his temple.

"You're so brave," she crooned, hoping her voice sounded reassuring. She held out her free hand to him. "So brave, sweet boy. So brave. I'm going to help you. Is that all right?"

His small head bobbed once, and he whimpered.

"You're okay now. I'm here. We're all here to help you. Don't you worry. You'll be free soon."

Terena glanced over her shoulder one more time before she sheathed her sword and dropped to the boy's side. As she moved her hands closer to his broken leg, she asked, "What's your name, sweetheart?"

She touched the break at his shin, and he jerked it back, a small cry escaping his lips before he started sobbing again.

"You're all right, you're all right," she whispered, moving her hands slowly over the rest of him to check for other breaks or sprains. "What's your name, brave one?"

He winced when she glided her hand gently over his left hip, but didn't cry out. "Nikos."

"Nikos," Terena said and flashed him a big smile as she moved closer. "That's a fantastic name for such a brave boy."

His only response was another whimper, but he tightened his tiny mouth, trying to stop the wobble of his chin.

"I need you to be brave for me again," she said, moving her hands slowly under his body. "I need to pick you up, all right? But it might hurt. Only for a second, Nikos. And then I'll carry you out of here. Can you be brave for me a bit longer?"

He nodded, shifting as she moved her hands under him and lifted him. He cried out sharply, his broken leg dropping as Terena pulled him up and close to her chest. She made to rise, crooning more soothing words at him when she heard the shouts from the top of the ravine. She turned and saw the wolf racing at her, dodging the arrows her friends were shooting at him.

Terena froze.

Her eyes widened, then she turned and ran, feet pounding against the uneven ravine floor as the wolf gained on them. She heard the shouts from above and more arrows zinging in the air.

She turned and saw the wolf leap. Terena dropped, intending to shield the boy with her body. Instead, a roar ripped from her chest as she fell to one knee. Her hand shot out and everything stilled.

No more shouts from her friends.

No wolf snarling.

No boy crying.

Just the deafening sound of silence.

Terena turned her head. It was heavy, as if she was underwater. The wolf was frozen mid-leap, close enough she could see the arrows protruding from his hide. His jaws were wide, saliva suspended from sharp fangs. Terena stretched forward and wrapped her hand around its throat and squeezed.

She blinked and exhaled. Sound returned in a rush and the wolf's body dropped to the ground, Terena still gripping its throat.

The boy, Nikos, squirmed in her arms, trying to twist to see. She heaved another breath, looking at the wolf in horror.

Terena opened her hand. Flexing her fingers, the wolf's head dropped against her ankle. Panting, she stared at the dead animal, its vacant eye glazed. She shifted and looked up at the ravine edge. Her friends stood hunched over, mouths agape as they stared back at her. Terena's eyes snagged on Daris, his eyes wide in shock as he stared back.

Terena turned when Nikos moved, his small arms wrapped tight around her neck. She pulled at them to keep him from choking her. She whispered soft words to him again, letting him know they were safe, and rose.

Nikos squirmed against her chest. Terena took a step and her legs wobbled. She stood still for another minute, letting the adrenaline fade from her body long enough for the strength to return to her legs.

She started walking back toward the rope, stepping carefully around the dead wolf when she heard Nikos's inhale.

"He's so big," the boy said, wonder filling his voice.

"Aye," Terena said, her voice shaky. "Don't look."

"You killed him," he said, pulling back to look at her face. She glanced at him with a tight smile, seeing the awe in his pretty brown eyes.

"See?" She gave him a wink. "I told you I'd help you, that you'd be all right."

He said nothing as they reached the rope. Terena set him down carefully, leaning his weight against her side as she hunched down on one knee. She held his waist and used her right hand to pull the rope around his middle.

"I need you to be brave again, Nikos," she said in a hard voice as she looked him in the eye. He nodded solemnly. "Do you see my friends up there?" Terena looked up at the others huddled above. Daris and Rydon crouched down, holding the rope, their faces tight.

The boy nodded. Terena turned back to him and said, "Those are the bravest men on the continent. That man there," she lifted her chin at Daris, whose eyes never left hers, "He's the Commander of the Liodari. In Sparta. Have you heard of them?"

Nikos's eyes widened comically as he looked up at Daris with another nod, awe filling his face.

"Good. He's going to pull you up now. And when you get to the top, they're going to pull me up. All right? It'll hurt, because your leg is broken and you're bruised from falling, but I promise you, we'll take care of you and take you to your family."

The boy nodded again, his eyes never leaving Daris.

"Are you ready?" Terena didn't wait for his nod this time before she looked up and motioned for the men to pull the boy up.

When he was halfway up, Terena rose and dropped her head back, her hands falling to her hips, and then she bent over, bracing her hands on her knees.

Fucking gods.

That was close.

That was so close.

Calm down. Calm down. Calm.

Terena looked up in time to see Daris grab Nikos's arm and lift him up, wrapping a big hand around the boy as he hefted him up to his hip and rose. He moved back to put him on the ground where Terena could no longer see him.

The rope dropped back down and she grabbed it, climbing back up. When she neared the top she turned her face up. Daris was there, gazing down at her. He grabbed the rope and heaved, pulling her up so fast her legs fell away from the wall and she was suspended for a second before he hauled her up and wrapped her in his powerful arms.

She stiffened and pushed away. As she turned, Croak enveloped her in his arms, crushing her tightly and stealing her breath away. Terena clung to him fiercely, burying her face in his chest. He shook, and Terena squeezed him tighter, her eyes stinging.

He let her go at last and she stumbled a step before turning to see where Nikos was. Jason held the boy cradled in his lap on the ground.

When he turned his head and saw Terena, the boy held out his arms to her and she dropped to the ground to hug him.

"Fucking gods, Terena," Croak said behind her, his voice shaking. "Does it have to be so fucking dramatic every gods damned time?"

"Language!" Terena hissed over her shoulder at him.

The others grumbled their agreement and Terena looked up to see Gabriol walk away, his hands on his head and Michael crouched on his haunches, his head bowed to the ground.

Rydon stood near the ravine edge, head tucked to his chest. Jason gathered up the rope, his lips tight; she caught the glance he shot at her and the wariness in his eyes.

Terena cradled the boy's head and stood.

Croak jogged up to her, her bow in his hand. He walked to Nyx and attached it to the saddle. Terena handed him the boy, who moaned in protest, but went to Croak when she assured him he'd be riding with her.

She mounted, then reached down as Croak hefted Nikos into her arms and settled him in her lap, being careful of his leg. Michael came to her side, a piece of wood and cloth in his hand. Terena nodded when he caught her eye and he efficiently bound the boy's leg, splinting it as best he could without hurting him.

Terena thanked him. He nodded once and strode off.

She looked up. The others stared at her for long seconds before they launched into motion, moving to their horses and mounting.

"All right, Nikos," Terena said, her voice loud so the others could hear. "Now, do you know where your family is? Where we can find them?"

The boy thought for a few seconds before his brows shot up. "My father lives in a cave!"

Croak snorted behind her.

Terena looked down at Nikos with a smile. "He does? Do you know where it is?"

He nodded emphatically.

She smiled. "Brave boy. Can you show me how to get there?"

He nodded again and pointed to their right. Terena looked around at the others before prodding Nyx to walk, conscious of Nikos's leg and the fading light. "Let's go find him then!"

CHAPTER THIRTY-ONE

"We're about an hour's ride from Thuria," Daris said, pulling up to Terena's side. She nodded without looking at him.

When she didn't reply, he said, "Let's find the boy's father quickly and secure rooms in town."

"You and your men should go on," she said, proud of the steel in her voice. "We'll find his father."

She dared a look at him. His face was impassive, but she saw the surprise in his eyes. He dipped his chin and pulled on his reins, his large stallion moving left as he pealed away.

Terena rode off in silence with Rydon, Gabriol and Croak. She looked down after a moment to see Nikos fast asleep in her arms, his head resting on her chest with his lips parted.

She hoped she was going in the right direction, as she was loathe to wake the boy. He'd said earlier they had to keep going this way, assuring her the cave would be ahead 'in a long time'.

Terena didn't know what 'in a long time' meant to a boy his age.

The path he'd told them to take led them down, and Terena looked back the way the others had gone to see she was much lower, about the level of the base of the ravine.

A black shape appeared ahead and Terena frowned. "What is that?"

Gabriol squinted. "Do you see that?"

"Should I wake him?"

"I think—"

Before Rydon could finish the thought, the dark shape resolved into a sheer cliff, the shadow of it falling to a foot in front of them as Rydon and Gabriol dismounted. Terena stayed on Nyx and pulled to a stop.

The men walked forward slowly until they reached the wall of rock. Rydon looked back at Terena but she couldn't see his face.

The boy stirred in her lap at the lack of motion, blinking up sleepy eyes at her. "Are we there yet?"

"I don't know," she said honestly. "It's dark and we can't see."

The boy looked around, his face brightening. "Aye! That's it!" he said, pointing right at the cliff wall where Rydon and Gabriol stood.

Just then, Gabriol gave a shout, waving his arm. Terena urged Nyx forward and the boy wiggled in her arms, excited.

She pulled on the reins as Rydon jogged over, holding his arms up to take Nikos when they stopped. The boy went easily, so excited he squirmed in Rydon's arms. Terena dismounted and followed Rydon. Croak and Gabriol fell into step behind her.

"Here!" Nikos squealed. He wiggled and Rydon cursed. The boy dropped from his arms and raced forward. Terena shoved at Rydon and bolted after him.

"Your leg, Nikos!"

The dark enveloped them, the void pressing all around her. She willed herself to calm and a moment later, Terena came out into a large cave.

And froze, eyes wide in shock.

Rydon and Croak appeared on either side of her, Gabriol exclaiming softly behind her as he shoved Croak aside and moved up next to her. Croak protested, but Terena didn't dare take her eyes off of the scene before them.

Terena's mouth slackened. She stared at what looked like hundreds of people, bodies writhing to sultry music filling the cave. Smoke wrapped around their ankles like wraiths.

Terena took a tentative step forward, her hand grabbing hold of Rydon's wrist when she saw couples engaged in public sexual acts. Some didn't even bother to find furniture to take advantage of. Chandeliers heavy with crystal and dripping candles hung from invisible cords, suspended in the air above the orgy unfolding in front of them.

Terena cast a side eye at Gabriol, who gawked at the scene.

"Are you seeing this?" she whispered to Rydon, her eyes darting around at the half-naked and—*yes, that is a naked man; oh there's another.*

"Where are we?" Gabriol asked.

"Paradise," Croak sighed.

Terena squared her shoulders and took a few steps forward, grateful she wasn't alone. As they passed people, Terena nodded and smiled, hoping she looked unaffected as she caught sight of a woman greedily sucking on a man's—

"Who are you?"

Terena jumped at the booming voice.

The people around them vanished. Gone were the countless bodies, the music, the smoke, replaced by stalagmites jutting up from the ground in patches around the edges of the cave.

And a man—an enormous man looking like he had muscles on his muscles—was standing on the far side of the cave. His blond hair hung in braids to his shoulders and he had gold bands on both his arms like belts that would fit Terena's waist nicely. He wore no breeches, only a long tunic belted at the waist and sandals laced up his ankles.

Terena swiveled her eyes to Rydon before she held up her hands to the man and took another step forward.

"My name is Terena Luca. We saved a boy in the ravine back there, and he brought us here."

The man looked at her as if she'd grown a second head. After a moment of awkward silence, he took a few steps forward, his eyes shifting to Rydon, then Gabriol, and finally Croak.

"And these three? They were with you?"

Terena looked at Rydon from the corner of her eye, then back at the giant man. "Aye."

"Who saved the boy? Was it you?"

"Uh…" she frowned at him. "Aye. I mean, it was a group effort."

"Who killed the wolves?" he demanded, stopping close enough Terena craned her neck to look up at him.

"She did," Rydon said at her side.

She glanced at him and then back at the stranger with her hand splayed. "Aye, but," she motioned with her finger encircling all of them, "…group effort."

The man looked at her so long Terena fidgeted.

What is happening? How did he know about the wolves?

"So… where is Nikos? Are you his father? Where did all the people go?"

The man's stare never wavered. "You look like him," he whispered in awe.

A chill slid down her spine. She blinked up at the man.

"Who?"

The man took a step back. "Your father. Ares."

RYDON'S JAW HURT FROM HOW FAR IT HAD DROPPED. WHILE THE revelation she was a god was still fairly recent—and something they'd suspected anyway—he was stunned to hear her father was the god of war.

Ares.

From the way Terena's body stiffened and her face leeched of color, Rydon thought she must feel the same. He eyed her, watching the emotions chasing across her face, a stab of sympathy for the woman pierced his chest. She had spent much of her life searching for her parents, and having the greatness of who she was thrust upon her like this was a heavy burden for anyone, much less for someone so young.

"Ares… is my father?"

The stranger tipped his head as he regarded her. "You did not know?"

Terena shook her head.

"Do you know who her mother is?" Rydon asked.

The man arched a blond eyebrow at him. "No."

"How do you—"

"If you were a boy, you'd look just like him," the man said. Then added with a smirk. "Not as pretty as him, though."

Poor Croak looked like he was close to passing out. Gabriol clapped a large hand on the boy's shoulder to steady him. Croak glanced over at the others, his eyes wide.

Rydon made a noise, and the man turned his gaze to him.

"Eudaemon," the man said with a nod at him. Not a question, Rydon supposed, but a confirmation.

"Aye," Rydon said, shifting closer to Terena. "And you, Stranger? Who are you?"

This close, the man's light grey eyes seemed unnatural. He turned away, dismissing Rydon as his gaze sharpened on Terena.

"I am Melanos," he said, his voice booming through the empty cavern. "I must say, I never expected to see you."

Another shock.

This man is a myth!

"You're...?" Terena couldn't finish her thought.

The man—Melanos—cocked his head. "It certainly took you long enough. I've been here for centuries."

Croak found his tongue at last. "You're Melanos? The demigod?"

Melanos turned those strange eyes to him and scowled. "I'm no demigod, boy."

Terena made a sound and Melanos whipped his gaze back to her.

"You're... but all the stories..."

"I don't know what stories you've been told," he said, his voice rumbling through Rydon's bones, "but I am no demigod. I am the son of Helios and Clytia."

"Clytia!" Terena exclaimed.

"Enough of this," the god said as he drew himself up straighter. Rydon and the others backed up a step.

"You've come for Bethana."

Terena nodded. "Aye. But how—"

"As I said, I've been expecting you."

"Wait," Terena said, holding up a hand. "Have I done this already?"

"Not this," Melanos said.

"I've not been here before?"

Melanos looked at her, concern flashing in his grey eyes. "Are you simple?"

"What?"

The god turned to the others, his gaze landing on Rydon as he frowned and pointed at Terena. "Is something wrong with her? She doesn't seem to understand."

"I'll be honest with you, lord," Rydon chuckled. "We're all having trouble understanding. It's been a strange few months."

Melanos looked over at each of them, then crossed his gigantic arms across his chest and sighed. "This is the first time you've been here, child."

Terena scowled at him. "The oracle said 'seven circles completed'. Does that mean anything to you?"

Melanos pinched his nose. "You've spoken to the oracle and you don't know? If the oracle told you you've completed seven circles and you're only now coming to me, then," he clicked his tongue as he regarded Terena, "I am worried about the fate of mankind."

"How many do I have left?" Terena asked.

"This is the last circle. Whatever happens in this one will determine the fate of the world, regardless if you live or die."

Rydon balked. He did not know what that meant, but it couldn't be good. Judging from the look on Terena's face, he knew he was right.

"Why... why are there eight circles? I don't understand any of this."

Melanos quirked an ashen brow. "Every new god is given eight circles. Time loops. You die, it starts a new one. It's an initiation from the Fates to prove our worthiness. Usually, if a god fails at whatever task the Fates set for them," he shrugged, "they fade into obscurity. The Fates have a different plan for you, it seems."

The god looked at Terena a moment longer before he dropped his head and snapped his fingers. Behind him, a sitting area appeared, with beautifully upholstered plush chairs, a matching couch and a large table filled with fruits and delicacies Rydon couldn't fully pick out from that distance. Melanos turned and motioned for them to follow.

Rydon looked at the others, who turned their dazed faces to one another before Terena walked off after the god. Croak jogged forward and stayed near Gabriol.

When they sat, Croak leaned forward, his expression of awed eagerness worrying Rydon.

"Any chance you can bring back the scene we walked in on? I mean, just for background noise," Croak said, shooting an apologetic look at Terena as Gabriol slapped him across the chest.

"They're not real. Those are Relics. Mortals I can bring back from memory for short periods of time. They look and feel real, but are essentially a figment of my mind. That is how I amuse myself sitting in here waiting on the Heir that was promised. The boy is a Relic, too. Another test for the Heir."

"The Heir?" Rydon said, his eyes widening. He glanced at Terena, her gaze already on him.

"Aye," Melanos said. He reached out and plucked a fig from a plate before them. "Athena came to see me once, long ago. Before they were banished. She said the Heir of Ares would come find me. And when that happened, the Heir would free me, but only if I helped the Heir take Bethana's fangs."

Terena put a hand to her head. "I'm sorry. What?"

"How did Athena know she'd come?" Gabriol asked.

Melanos shrugged. "She's smart."

"And how does Terena free you, exactly?" Rydon asked. He was concerned about Terena. She clearly looked more shaken than he'd expected.

Melanos stared at Rydon while he chewed. "That I do not know. Hoped you would," he said with a glance at Terena.

When she didn't respond, Rydon nudged her arm. Terena blinked at him, then looked up at Melanos.

"I will do it if I can," Terena shrugged.

"Fantastic," Melanos clapped his hands, startling Croak. With a wicked grin, he leaned forward. "Let's get started then."

"WHAT IS THE REAL STORY BEHIND THE MYTH OF MELANOS AND Bethana?" Gabriol asked.

All eyes pivoted to Melanos.

He chewed thoughtfully as he regarded them. "By the looks on your faces, I can only imagine what you've all been told and believe as truth."

"The story I know," Terena said after it became apparent no one else would speak up, "is that you and Bethana fell in love after she saved you. You'd been fatally wounded in battle. Though we all thought you were a demigod, so mortal, and that your love for each other saved you."

Melanos snorted.

Terena went on. "But Poseidon was in love with her, found you two together and killed you. And then turned Bethana into a serpent."

"He was in love with her," Melanos agreed softly into the thick silence that followed. "And he did find us together. But I am immortal and he could not kill me without risking my father's wrath. So he cursed me to this cave. It wasn't until Athena found me that I had any hope of leaving. Of course, you took your time about it."

"Right," grumbled Terena, twisting her lips. "So I have to kill Bethana?"

Melanos spit something at Croak, who flinched back.

"Well," the god said with a big exhale. "Technically, you only need her fangs. I've had a long time to think about it. She's my lover, after all, and since I'd be very upset over her death, perhaps there's another way to fulfill this part of your labors without killing her."

"My labors?"

Melanos gave her a flat stare. "You're not yet two and twenty, are you?"

"No," Terena said, her brow furrowed.

"You're destined to bring back the Olympian gods," Melanos said, pointing a finger at her as he leaned toward her. "This is the test the Fates have created for you. You think they're just going to let you bring them back? They almost destroyed this realm."

"The Fates don't want the gods to come back?"

Melanos only stared back at her.

"What does my being twenty-two have to do with it?"

"That's when you come fully into your powers. And when you're supposed to start your trials. For some reason, you started early, which is why you keep failing." He popped a piece of cheese in his mouth and chewed. "How do you not know any of this?"

"I don't know I'm *supposed* to know any of this," Terena grumbled. "I went to the oracle and—"

"Psh!" Melanos waved a hand dismissively. "Pytho? She's useless."

"Ha!" Croak guffawed and Terena glared at him. "What? I knew she was full of shit."

"Hmm," Melanos said, smirking at him. "Smarter than you look."

"What happens when I come fully into my powers?"

Melanos spread his hands. "I honestly don't know. Hasn't happened yet. I only know when you do, this one will no longer be tied to you. He'll be mortal again," Melanos said with a glance at Rydon.

Surprise widened Rydon's eyes, and he sat back. "In truth?"

"Aye," Melanos grunted. "But be careful. The closer she is to her majority, the closer you are to mortality. It'll take longer to heal if you're wounded. Once she's immortal, she won't need you."

Terena pitched forward, her hand reaching out to grasp Rydon's wrist. "I *will* need him. I will need you, Rydon."

Rydon grimaced. "I appreciate the sentiment, Ren. And I'll continue at your side, if it is your wish."

"Not that anyone's asked," Gabriol said as he puffed out his chest. "I will be with you as well."

Croak snorted. "You're only staying because of Rydon."

Terena shot him a dirty look before she smiled at Gabriol. "Thank you, Gabriol. I definitely need you as well. We don't know what will happen in the next six months until that time, and I will need all the help I can get."

"So?"

Terena leaned back in her seat, confused. "So…"

"Do you want to hear my plan or not?"

"Huh?"

Melanos hung his head, then shook it and sighed. He lifted his gaze to Terena again and motioned with his hand. "Bethana?"

"Oh. Yes, of course."

"Well," Melanos said as he looked out over the selection of food in front of him, "since you only need the fangs, you don't need to kill Bethana. You just need to take her fangs. You'll need something large, like, I don't know, a branch or something. Get her to attack you and then," he slammed his fist down on the table, crashing plates onto the floor.

Croak jumped onto his seat, holding the chair arms as he shrieked in fright.

Melanos roared with laughter.

"She sinks her fangs into the wood," Rydon said to Terena, "and you can pry the fangs from her mouth."

"See? Even the Eudaemon gets it." He pointed at Croak and laughed. "That was funny, boy."

"Where can I find the serpent? Bethana."

Melanos regarded her in silence for a minute. "There's a warren of caves beneath the falls where she and I first met. That's where Poseidon imprisoned her after turning her into the serpent."

"And imprisoned you here."

"As you see."

"So, do I free you now or after I get the fangs? How's that work?"

Melanos chuckled. "Your guess is as good as mine, Heir. Come see me after you've acquired the fangs, to be safe."

CHAPTER THIRTY-TWO

The journey to Elis, where the waterfall Melanos had told them to find, was much quicker than Terena had expected. They'd rested in Thuria for the night before riding off at dawn, heading northwest from Ibros and crossed into Elis by nightfall.

The Liodari had understandably been suspicious when Terena shared the story of their meeting with the god Melanos, but they'd followed her the next morning without protest. Daris opined more than once that traveling to Elis was not safe. He'd peppered her with questions about the god and what had transpired in the cave.

"Listen," she said at one point, annoyed with all his questions, "if we survive meeting this serpent, you'll see him yourself."

Melanos had told them the falls were about an hour's ride beyond the southern border, so they made camp near a small stream once they'd crossed the border, leaving the Greek road and traveling on a worn, rough path where the horses could only ride in single file.

The food was plentiful, as Melanos had conjured three sacks full of provisions for them before they left his cave. Croak sat on his bedroll, digging through one sack and pulled out apples and grapes, and a wheel of cheese he kept for himself despite protests from Gabriol, who had tried more than once to snatch it from Croak's lap. The other two sacks were similarly investigated. Gabriol, the more judicious traveling companion, gave the provisions he revealed to Michael, who passed them along to Jason and Daris.

Terena slapped Croak on the back of his head and while he yelped, she passed the wheel of cheese to Rydon. When he was still rubbing at the hurt, Terena grabbed the loaf of bread peeking out from the bag and split it evenly amongst their group.

While they enjoyed their food, Croak pestered Daris and his men with questions about Sparta, about how he'd become the Commander of the Liodari. Terena tried hard not to seem overly interested, although she did lean in closer, cocking her head so she could hear better across the low crackle of the fire.

"When I was twenty, the Commander of the Liodari took an interest in me. Spartan boys train from an early age to be soldiers, but Liodari are the best of those soldiers. Only those who have distinguished themselves in battle ever receive an invitation to join. Because I had not, they tested me against Magi."

"What?" Croak scoffed and flicked a hand at Terena. "We fought Magi! We beat them too! Make us Liodari, Daris."

The others laughed and Terena dropped her chin as she grinned.

When she looked up at Daris, he looked bemused. "When did you fight Magi?"

Croak blew through his lips. "Seems forever ago now. Back in Agraboda."

Terena glared daggers at him. His smile faded when he saw it.

He ducked his head.

She could feel the heat of Daris's stare. Her face burned from it.

Terena schooled her face and turned to him. "Long time ago."

Daris continued to stare at her. He turned his head when Jason leaned over and said something to him. She watched as he nodded before turning to gaze out at the fire.

"What happened next?" Croak asked.

Daris looked over at him, startled. His expression turned thoughtful. "Our commander fell after a small incursion from the Ibrosians five years ago and I succeeded him."

"The youngest commander in Liodari's history," Michael said with pride.

"I feel like you skipped a lot," Croak said, his eyebrow lifted. "That battle you speak of? Even in Heylisia we'd heard the Ibrosians had you cornered when you went to retrieve your commander's body. You slew twelve men before more Liodari could get to you. Or that a bear once attacked you when scouting near the Gulf of Heroes. That's how you got the scars along your left ear, aye?"

Daris shrugged. "We are a warrior society," he said in a low voice. "We do not boast of our deeds. We make ourselves ready for the next ones."

Terena couldn't help the smile spreading on her face. She ducked her head as Rydon nudged her with his knee.

"Something amuses you," Jason bit out.

Terena shook her head once. "Not at all." She looked up with a quick glance at Daris. "I've not known you long, but that is... that's exactly what I'd expect you to say."

Daris watched her across the dying fire, his eyes sparkling in the flickering light. She kept his stare a moment longer before she shifted.

"Why do they call you Athena's Weapon?" she asked, her lips twisting when his face shuttered, his eyes narrowing for a split second before he dropped his gaze to the fire.

"He's the hero of Sparta," Jason said defiantly. "It stands to reason he'd be the hero that was promised to help the Heir of Ares upon his return."

Terena's pulse quickened. She glanced between Jason and Daris, noting Daris was frowning at Jason. She saw the quick shake of his head.

"Heir of Ares, huh?" Croak said with a sly grin and she snapped her eyes to him. He winked back at her. "You think *he* needs help from a mortal?"

Jason opened his mouth to reply, but Daris tilted his head again and Jason quickly shut his mouth.

Croak wasn't deterred. "Maybe *he* already has Athena's Weapon."

"Croak," Terena said in a low voice.

"What?" he shrugged, then held out a hand to Daris. "No offense, Daris. You could definitely be someone's weapon, obviously. But... how would you even know the Heir? What if the Heir was sitting—"

"That's enough," Rydon said.

Croak looked over at him and shrugged.

"We've had a long day," Terena said into the silence. "I'm to bed. I wish you all a pleasant sleep."

With that, she turned on her side, her back to the fire as she pulled the edges of her cloak tighter around her and closed her eyes with a deep sigh.

"I'll take first watch with Michael," Daris said in answer, and Terena heard the others mutter their assent as they bedded down.

Croak bent over Terena's hip and whispered loudly, "Are you sure you don't want to switch places and take the watch with the handsome commander?"

Her only response was to jerk her elbow back sharply, a satisfied smile on her face at Croak's yowl of pain.

Terena bolted upright, thrashing against something heavy, her chest heaving with fear so potent she lashed out wildly.

"Stop! It's me! Stop—Ren!"

Her blood roared in her head, her ears rang with it, dissipating enough she heard Croak's words, heard him hissing at her to stop. Her eyes focused finally and she saw his face, tight with concern and pain. He exhaled, his breath heating her face.

"Gods," Terena said, her voice hoarse. "Your breath is rancid."

A scoff sounded behind her as Croak's mouth tilted up in a smirk. "I'll breathe on you again if you don't stop fucking hitting me."

Terena held onto his forearms, her grip easing as embarrassment washed over her. She glanced around and saw the others watching her with varying degrees of concern and wariness. Terena sat up.

"The prince again?" Croak whispered so only Terena could hear.

She nodded.

Croak pulled back and kissed Terena's forehead before he stood. "All better now," he called out and winked at Terena. He groaned as he rose, his knees cracking. "Yikes. I'm too old for this. Promise us a soft bed tomorrow, Daris."

Daris and the others seemed inclined to ask about the nightmare that had Terena thrashing so violently, but they remained silent and took their cue from the others as they went about the business of breaking camp.

Rydon and Gabriol strode to their horses, hoisting their saddle-bags in place. Croak muttered about visiting Gaia for his morning prayers—which was Croak for taking a piss—while Terena gathered her bedroll, shaking out her cloak and tossing it over her shoulders.

They reached the falls a short while later. From there, they had to search for the caves beneath the falls Melanos had mentioned, so they dismounted to search. They looked for ten minutes near the base of the falls. Croak and Gabriol stayed with the horses while the rest wound their way up to the top of the falls.

As they walked further on, their group separated. Daris and his men were a hundred feet ahead of where Rydon and Terena walked. Somewhere in that area was an entrance to the cave system where they would find Bethana, the serpent.

The water ran swift, rapids dragging the rocks beneath, pulling along tree branches and other debris from the banks on either side. Terena crouched, setting her bow down, and cupped her hand in the cold water. As she drank, she looked around and spotted Rydon meandering further north, keeping close to the edge.

They were a few hundred feet from the drop to the falls when the first arrow landed near Rydon.

Terena snapped up, turning toward where the shot came from. Rydon ran to her, his sword out. Another arrow whizzed at her back and Terena spun, eyes wide, when she saw the riders on the opposite bank, arrows trained on her. She pulled off her bow and reached for an arrow as Rydon yelled out.

"Rivermen!"

They were on either side of the river, the ones on their side charging straight at them. Terena nocked an arrow and let it fly, her left hand snatching up the next arrow and nocking it as Rydon shot past, engaging two men behind her.

Terena heard more yelling from her right as she turned to shoot at the men on the other bank. Daris and his men thundered toward them, their swords lifted as they engaged more attackers at her back.

She had just fired another arrow across the river when a jolt of pain on her left thigh made her stumble forward. Terena cursed, her right hand shooting out to stop her momentum, but she slipped on the riverbank and fell in.

The rapids grabbed hold of her and sucked her under. She fought to emerge, arms digging against the current. As the rapids dragged her down again, Terena opened her mouth in a panic and swallowed water. She flailed her arms, her chest tight and throat burning. Pushing against the water, the rapids pulled at her, taking her further away.

The river roared around her whenever her head emerged, and she gasped for air. Terena swung her arms some more and was able to keep her head above water for a few precious seconds. Turning her head, she took several deep breaths as she hurtled toward a large rock near the center of the river. Her eyes darted around, landing on a thick tree branch clinging to the side of the river.

She thrust her legs down and for a second had enough momentum to push toward the branch as she rushed past. Grabbing it, she pulled herself up enough to keep her head above water. Terena coughed, retching up water and air as she clung to the branch.

Shouts sounded, and she turned her head. Rydon and Daris raced toward her.

The tree snapped, and she screamed when the rapids whipped her away, pulling her toward the falls. Terena yelped and tightened her hold on the branch, hugging it as she tried to lift herself atop it.

The branch collided with another rock, allowing her enough time to twist her leg and hoist herself up. It turned and the rapids carried her along once more.

Terena looked up when she heard Daris shouting at her. Looking around, her terrified gaze landing with surprise on Daris and the others, now in the middle of a wood bridge she was careening toward. She had a second to register Daris hanging over the bridge, with the others holding him as he extended an arm down.

Terena's heart jumped to her throat.

She lifted her right hand, screaming as pain shot up her leg when the branch hit another rock. It snagged and caught, but Terena was now on the other side of Daris. She looked up again and saw he'd scrambled to the other side, so close now she whimpered, trying to pull herself up.

"REACH!" he screamed at her, his hand shaking.

Terena inched her hip up higher on the branch, crying out against the pain in her thigh and gritted her teeth. She reached up again, her fingers glancing off of Daris's when she heard a crack.

Her eyes widened, glued to his when she realized what was happening.

A primal scream ripped through her as Terena jerked violently. The roar of the falls drowned out all sound as she fell.

CHAPTER THIRTY-THREE

Water engulfed Terena, spinning her around like a child's top. Her lungs screamed, her body falling
falling

She landed and was immediately swept up again and tossed. The burn in her lungs overwhelmed her and darkness edged her sight. When she began to succumb, she was jerked backwards. Her body spun, rocks and dirt biting into her, and she fell.

Landing on her side, Terena's right shoulder smacked into the ground hard enough she heard the pop before the pain hit. Stars exploded behind her eyes and white hot pain ripped through her as she lost consciousness.

Sleep was so good.

No.

She hated sleep.

Sleep was filled with pain jabbing at her shoulder, her hip, her leg.

Everywhere.

Terena moaned.

She was moving.

She hated the movement.

She squirmed. Cried out when pain lanced through her leg.

A voice.

Someone held her.

Moving.

Someone was moving her. Terena didn't want to move. She wanted to be still. She begged for stillness.

The voice spoke again.

What was it saying?

"Please," she whispered. Even that hurt. Her mouth and throat seemed lined with grit and she dropped her head.

Something hard.

Wet.

"Don't speak," the voice said.

Terena blinked, her eyes heavy, achy. She moved her head back and saw his face at last.

"Daris."

"Shh," he said. Soothingly. That made her settle.

"Your shoulder's out," Daris said, his voice short but not unkind. He had set her down on the ground. Terena tried to curl up, whimpering, when her body protested.

"You went over the falls," he said, his hands probing the rest of her body gently. She opened her eyes, watching him as he methodically moved his hands over her, feeling for other hurts he could not see.

Terena sighed.

"My leg," she whispered, her hand reaching out to touch his as it came to her hip.

"I see it," he said. Daris rose and walked a few feet away. His head lifted to the sky, and she turned her head to see where he was looking. A hole, with meager light filtering down. The dull roar of the falls surrounded them.

"She's down here!" Daris shouted.

Terena inched back, trying to sit up. When she cried out, Daris was at her side.

"Don't move," he murmured as he placed a hand on her shoulder.

"It hurts," she whispered through gritted teeth.

"I know, I know," Daris crooned. She blinked up at him. His face softened.

"Listen," Daris said firmly, "I need to get your shoulder back in. It'll be quick, I promise, but it will hurt."

Terena nodded, not taking her eyes off him.

His lips thinned, and he moved to her right side. Daris put an arm under her, bracing her against his chest and, with his right hand, held her wrist lightly.

"I'm going to do it on three," he said, his eyes boring into hers. She nodded again.

Daris moved his hand up an inch. "Ready? One, two—"

Terena didn't have time to brace as he pulled with one quick snap of his wrist. Her brain seized as pain seared through her shoulder and down her arm. She gasped and blinked rapidly against stinging tears, rolling down her cheeks unchecked as she panted.

"What the fuck happened to three?" she squeaked. Her arm shook. Cradling it against her chest, she shot him a mutinous look.

"Don't be a baby," he muttered, moving back to her left. The arrow piercing her thigh had snapped during her fall, but was still in her leg.

Daris pushed her hip gently. "Can you lay on your right a bit more? I need to push it out through the front."

Terena's head bobbed, teeth gritted as she shifted her hips. She hissed when the movement made her leg throb. Daris's hands moved over her leg, and she stifled the urge to laugh. This was not the situation she'd imagined when his hands moved over her body. She'd much rather they'd been in a big, comfortable bed. Maybe a—

"*Fuck!*" she screamed when he pushed the arrow further into her leg. Her body shook, and she lifted her left hand to push his hands away. Dropping her head back, she closed her eyes, biting her lip hard enough to taste blood.

"Terena!"

Croak's shout from above made Terena whip her head up. She panted.

"She's fine," Daris called out, his eyes hot and mouth pinched as he stared at Terena. "I'm getting the arrow out!"

"Don't you fucking hurt her!" Croak yelled back, his voice breaking.

A muscle jumped in his throat, but Daris only replied, "Jason! Move everyone back!"

He turned back to Terena. "Ready?"

She wasn't coherent enough to speak. Her mind had seized, paralyzed by the excruciating, fiery flame searing her from the inside. She kept her eyes closed, the tears falling freely. Her shoulders trembled.

A few moments of quiet settled around her, and Terena thought the worst was over.

Then Daris yanked the arrow out. Black spots crowded behind her lids and the void enveloped her.

Terena awoke to Daris shouting in her face, his hand gripping her chin.

"I didn't even get a warning?"

Daris hung his head. When he looked back at her, his face was pale, but he managed a smirk.

"You didn't die," he said gruffly. Daris looked back at the wound. Blood pooled and her leg shook violently.

Daris sat up straight and took off his leather armor, then lifted his tunic.

"We don't have time for that," Terena joked, a tiny laugh escaping her lips. She sobbed again, ruining the effect.

The corners of his lips tugged up. Daris tore the bottom of his shirt, setting it under her leg, and put one of his hands between her legs. "Believe me," he said as he wound the strip of cloth around her leg. "When we get back to Sparta, I'll make time."

Terena's heart seized. Did he know what he was saying? She'd been teasing.

Was he?

"Good for now," he said, more to himself.

"Hey!" a voice called down. Jason?

Daris shot her one last look before he pivoted, rising to stride over to the hole, and looked up.

"Don't bother," he said, "she can't climb with her shoulder."

"Tie it around her waist. We'll lift her up."

Terena looked up at Rydon's suggestion. Daris looked over at her with an arched eyebrow. She shook her head. "We found the caves. Let's see if we can find Bethana now."

"We can try to come down," Jason called back.

"No, don't," Daris yelled back. He waved a hand. "There's a path down here. I'll find another way out."

"You sure? Croak is going nuts up here," Jason said, his voice echoing around the small chamber.

Terena shifted, groaning against the pain trying to keep her rooted to the ground.

"Tell him I'm all right!" she bellowed.

Daris glanced back at her, then turned back to the hole. He held a hand to his mouth and called out, "You hear that? I'll get her back to him. I'll get her back to you, Croak!"

"All right," Jason's disembodied voice called down. A second later, the rope hanging down was pulled up.

Daris walked back and hunched down at her side. He frowned, moving to her right. He put his arm under her shoulders again and she whimpered, holding her injured arm close to her chest.

"Easy now," he said in a low voice and she shivered. He lifted her up as if she was as light as air and shifted to tuck her closer.

His face was close to hers now. Heat stung her cheeks as he looked down at her.

"Good?" he asked, his voice a caress.

She nodded. Didn't trust herself to speak.

"Aren't you supposed to be a god?" Daris chided. "You seem to get hurt often. And easily."

She gave him a sour look.

Daris's lips twitched. He turned to look around, and Terena watched him out of the corner of her eye. The strong column of his neck was inches from her lips. The thought kicked up a corner of her mouth.

"Right," he said. "This way."

He began walking further into the cavern, further from the light filtering down. The deeper they went, the darker the cave became, and he cursed. "This isn't going to work. I can't see."

He paused, looking around.

Terena shifted. "Put me down," she said. He turned his eyes back to her.

"I can—"

"We need a light, which we don't have," she said and hissed as another sharp pain shot through her arm when she moved. "I'll be fine to walk, but we need you free to feel where we're going and, you know, in case there's anything in here wanting to eat us."

"Like a giant snake?" he asked. She could feel the smile on his lips. Something hot moved in her chest that was definitely not pain.

"Exactly," Terena snapped. "Put me down."

Daris held her for a few seconds more. Long enough she arched an eyebrow at him. He set her down gently, still holding his arm around her back as she steadied herself.

"I'm good now."

He dragged his arm away, letting his hand slide down to her lower back. Terena shivered at the trail of tingles his fingers left behind. Arching her back, she moved a half hop away.

Terena let out a low noise as her leg protested. Daris's arm shot back out to steady her, but she batted at it with her left hand, mewling when the motion only jostled her bad shoulder.

"Just... go. I'll be right behind you."

Daris stood at her side a moment before he started walking. Using his right hand to feel along the rock wall, his left hand stretched back to Terena. He glanced back at her, then switched positions, holding his right hand back to her. He waggled his fingers and she huffed, giving him her hand.

"What happened up there?" she asked after a few minutes of silence. His hand gripped hers tight when she put weight on her bad leg.

"Rivermen," he ground out. He glanced back at her before turning back. "When you fell in the river, we'd already cut down the ones on our side. Michael grabbed up your bow and took care of the ones on the other side while Rydon, Jason, and I chased after you. Rydon wanted to jump in, but you'd gotten to the branch. Thought we could grab you then, but right when we got to you..."

Terena squeezed his hand twice. "And?"

He was silent for a few moments. "We got to the bridge in time to grab you, but the current's fast near the edge and when you went past me, I thought we'd lost you." He was silent again before he added in a gruff voice, "Then we *did* lose you."

"How'd you find me?"

A long pause. Then, "We ran down to the bottom. Rydon and I jumped in. Croak ran at us like a lunatic. It was chaos. I don't know about the others, but I went under and swam. Saw there was an entrance behind the falls and went in. Found the hole."

"And the handsome hero jumped in to save the lady fair," Terena said, her voice rough as she grimaced against a fresh stab of pain down her leg.

Daris looked down at her with a smile. "You think I'm handsome?"

She twisted her lips at him. He winked.

"Fucking Rivermen," she said into the dark. His only response was a grunt.

"Hey," he said after a few minutes of silence. Terena looked up. "It's lighter up ahead."

As if his words conjured the light, the corridor became brighter as it narrowed. Terena sensed the decline and her feet faltered. Daris turned and stepped closer, pulling his hand—and hers—closer to his side as they stepped slowly down and into another large cave.

"What happens if we find Bethana?" Terena asked, slightly light-headed from holding her breath to navigate the last few steps into the opening.

"Hopefully, the others will find us before then," he said roughly. She looked up and yelped when he wrapped his arm around her waist, swinging her up and over some uneven flooring. Terena mumbled her thanks. He slipped his hand down until he had hold of her hand again. She sucked in her lips to hide the smile blooming.

"Or, we find a way out."

"Right," Terena replied softly.

The sound of the river surrounded them as they moved through the cave. Daris stopped to get his bearings. "This way," he muttered.

Terena followed, her stilted steps annoyingly slow. "Do you mind —oh *gods!*"

Daris whipped around as she gasped, biting down hard on her lip as another wave of pain tore through her leg when she'd stepped on a rock and her ankle gave.

His hands grasped her waist, digging in until she was steadied.

"Thank you."

"Are you all right?"

Terena nodded, her hands on his forearms. She let out a half sob, half laugh. "Fucking pathetic."

"Why don't you use your powers to heal yourself?"

Terena scowled at him. "We're doing that now?"

He arched an eyebrow.

"What?" Terena asked.

"Can you?"

"Can I what?"

"Heal yourself."

"Aye! Of course! Why didn't I think of that? Thank the *gods* you're here to remind me to heal myself!"

He pulled back with a smirk as he shook his head. "Who knows? Maybe you like faking injuries to get my attention."

Terena's eyes threatened to bulge out of her face. "Are you kidding me right now?"

Daris's grin was so disarming, her lips opened, momentarily forgetting she was angry with him.

"You're playing with fire, Commander," Terena hissed, and yanked his hands off her hips.

"So. To be clear, you don't have the power to heal yourself."

Terena snarled at him. His grin widened before he took her hand once more. She tried to shake him off, causing another streak of pain to rumble through her body.

"I only want to get you to that rock over there. See it? You can sit and relax a few minutes while I look around. I think the light is coming from over there."

Terena mumbled under her breath but let him guide her to the rock he'd indicated. It was not so low she'd have trouble lowering herself on it. Terena gritted her teeth, tightening her hold on his hand as Daris brought his arm around waist and helped her sit.

When she was settled, Terena gave him a quick nod as he watched her. After a moment in which his hands lingered at her waist, Daris moved off toward the far side of the cave where a thin stream of light wavered.

Terena tipped her head back and closed her eyes. When she opened them again, she glanced around the cave. He was gone.

And she was alone.

Perfect.

Terena lifted her hand to her hair, brushing back the black strands plastered to the side of her face. She groaned, thinking how disastrous she must look.

She wiped her nose on her forearm and loosed a long sigh.

Something slid behind her.

She stilled, holding her breath as she listened.

There it was again. Closer.

Where was Daris?

"Who are you?"

Dread buzzed through Terena's body at the silky voice coming from behind her.

That sliding sound came again, and Terena slowly turned her head to look over her injured shoulder.

"I smell the other one on you," the voice said languidly. "Is he your lover?"

Gods.

Terena shifted on the rock as she tried to find the source of that voice. She didn't have to see it to know who it belonged to.

"Bethana," she whispered.

The sliding stopped. A second later she heard the hissing voice near her left ear and jumped.

"I haven't heard that name in a long time," the serpent said, her voice edged in steel.

Terena willed her body to stop shaking.

"You smell different," the serpent said, closer still. Terena sensed her over her shoulder, but did not move. "You smell like him, but beneath that…"

"Over here!"

Terena's eyes snapped up, finding Daris as he stepped back into the cave, his sword out.

The serpent hissed and Terena held up a hand to stop him from moving closer.

"The lover returns," Bethana hissed, drawing out her words. Terena shuddered at the brush of the serpent's forked tongue near her ear.

"There's no glory in killing an injured warrior," Daris called out angrily. "Come for me instead."

The serpent remained at Terena's side. "She's much more interesting."

Terena's gaze locked with Daris's. "Go," she whispered loudly. "Please, go."

Daris shook his head once, ignoring her plea. "Come for me, Bethana."

"Willing to die for your love?" The serpent crooned.

"No one has to die," Daris said. "If you move away from her now, we'll leave you in peace."

The serpent let out a hoarse laugh. "That's not a very enticing offer," she said, her voice seductive. "I want to know more about your lover. There's something fascinating about her."

Daris took another step closer, earning him a hiss loud enough to reverberate through Terena's body.

He stopped, holding up his free hand. "What's so fascinating about her?"

The serpent, Bethana, moved, and Terena could see her out of the corner of her eye. She shifted her gaze back to Daris.

Daris looked between Terena and Bethana.

"You know," the serpent hissed.

"No, I don't. What is it?"

"She smells like *them*."

Terena quaked. She sensed the rage emanating from the reptile. She turned her head a bit more and winced when she saw its eye focused on her.

"Who do you mean?" Daris called out, his voice loud as if to force the serpent to keep its focus on him.

"He was jealous," the serpent hissed at Terena, its tongue darting out to flick Terena's cheek. "He found us. Turned me into this!"

"Do you speak of Poseidon?"

The serpent snapped forward, hissing angrily at Daris. "DO NOT SAY THAT NAME TO ME!"

Terena let out an involuntary sound as the serpent raged. She caught sight of its body and closed her eyes.

Bethana was much bigger than Melanos had led them to believe.

"She smells like him." Bethana turned her head and Terena's blood drained from her body, terror squeezing her heart as she beheld the face of nightmares.

"She's not like him!" Daris shouted.

"DO NOT LIE!" The serpent snapped forward again, this time at Daris. To his credit, he did not flinch.

"I am *this* now. My love killed. Because of *him*!"

"Melanos lives!" Terena cried out, her voice breaking. She swallowed.

The serpent whipped its head back to her. It crept close slowly and Terena froze.

"*Lies!*"

Terena shook her head quickly. "No. No, in truth, he lives. We just saw him. We dined with him last eve. He lives."

Bethana watched her with those unblinking eyes. "Where?"

Terena exhaled and swallowed again. "Nearby. Half a day's journey. He was... when Pos—when you were turned, Melanos was cursed to live in a cave near here, forever. Never to leave. Never to come find you."

The serpent regarded her for so long, Terena's lips trembled as she exhaled.

"You look familiar," it hissed, twisting its head.

"Melanos lives," Terena repeated, an edge of desperation in her voice.

"Lies," Bethana said at last, her face resuming its slow progress toward Terena. "You smell like him and you lie!"

Terena raised her hand to shield her face as Bethana struck. She heard Daris's roar behind the serpent as its mouth widened and clamped down on Terena's forearm.

Terena screamed and time warped. The serpent had its fangs deep in her arm; they went through the other side. Terena yanked on her arm with a cry, renting the air around them, rattling the cave. Time sped up and Terena stumbled off the rock as the serpent screeched, slithering off to the far side of the cave.

Terena looked up. Daris lunged, running toward Bethana as she reared up for another attack. Daris launched onto the rock Terena had been on, pushing off with such force he flew. Terena blinked, slack-jawed, and got to her knees. Daris brought his sword up with both hands and landed, slamming the blade down, severing her tail.

Bethana's scream shook the cave and Terena fell back, hitting her head on the ground.

Daris was in front of her a moment later, cursing loudly as he gawked at the fangs in her arm.

"What the fuck?" Terena cried, holding out her arm as she stared at it in disbelief. Her breath heaved in panicked waves.

Daris grabbed her around the waist and lifted her over his shoulder. Snatching up his sword, he ran toward the pathway where the light was coming from.

Terena's head swam. She looked up in time to see Bethana slithering toward them fast. Terena screamed at Daris to go faster.

They made it into the passageway as the serpent lunged for them again.

She closed her eyes.

When she opened them again, her vision swam. She was still bobbing on Daris's shoulder.

She closed her eyes again.

Pain ripped through her and she cried out.

She blinked against the blinding sunlight. How long was she out? Where were they?

Daris began shouting, calling out for his men, for anyone.

Shouting so loud her ears hurt.

When next she woke, she was on a horse.

Her eyes drifted shut.

CHAPTER THIRTY-FOUR

Rydon rushed into the cave, Daris at his back carrying Terena.

"MELANOS!" Rydon roared, his eyes wild, searching for the god through the mass of naked bodies before them.

He heard the others skid to a stop behind him and he glanced back to see the Liodari gawking at the scene.

Daris dropped to his knees, cradling Terena in his arms. "Help! We need help!"

Just as it had when they'd first found Melanos, the scene before them winked out and the god strode toward them, a scowl on his face.

"Please," Daris begged, his voice barely a whisper. "Please help us. Please."

"Give her to me," the god said, bending down.

Daris gasped, startled when he saw the giant god pull Terena from his arms. He resisted but Rydon put a hand on his shoulder. "It's Melanos!"

When Melanos stood, Daris rose as well, only to be pushed roughly from behind.

"Where the fuck were you?!" Croak screamed at him. Daris turned, his eyes bleak. "You fucking let it—"

"Peace, Croak!" Jason yelled, pushing Croak back.

Gabriol snarled and grabbed Jason's cloak. Rydon sprang forward and Michael intercepted.

"Enough!" Melanos bellowed as he turned, Terena's limp body in his powerful arms.

Daris raked a hand through his hair and surged toward the god. "What can we do?"

The god ignored him as he walked toward a sitting area much the same as the night they'd first met him. Rydon yanked his arm out of Michael's grip and strode after him, Daris close to his side.

Melanos set Terena on the largest couch—almost a bed, by the size of it—then lifted Terena's arm.

"Well, shit," the god said, scowling down at Terena's ashen face. "This wasn't what I meant, but," he shook his head, "I get why you keep failing. Came all this way just to die on me? Not now, goddess."

"Please," Croak was moaning, "Don't let her die."

Rydon's chest tightened.

Daris moved to the side of the couch where Terena's head rested and stroked her hair with a shaking hand.

"Move back," Melanos said, his voice harsh as he motioned with his free hand. "I need room!"

Croak and Rydon moved back a few steps but Daris stayed where he was, glaring at the god.

"What are—"

"I'm going to remove the fangs."

Melanos frowned down at the them, his hand hovering. He grasped a fang and yanked.

Terena bolted upright, screaming.

Daris sprang forward, grabbing her shoulders. Croak fell over and Rydon cursed, barely grabbing him before he hit the ground.

"Ready this time?" Melanos asked Daris sarcastically. When the commander nodded, his hands firmly pressed to Terena's shoulders as she thrashed and cried, Melanos grabbed the other fang and pulled it out. This time, Terena gasped and passed out.

"Eudaemon," Melanos said. He looked up and his gaze landed on Daris. Rydon stepped into his line of sight.

"Aye, I'm here."

Melanos narrowed his eyes at Daris and scowled. Daris scowled back, his stare menacing. Rydon caught the look of confusion on the god's face before he looked up at Rydon.

"What can I do?" Rydon prompted, edging closer to Terena's side.

"Switch places with this man," said Melanos. He flicked another glance at Daris.

Daris protested but Melanos glared at him until he stepped back enough for Rydon to sit on the couch near Terena's head. He scooted closer, lifting her head onto his lap, and looked up at Melanos.

The god looked over at Daris again and ran his hand down over his mouth. He dropped his eyes and pulled one of the short swords at Terena's hip. He flipped it over and extended the hilt to Rydon. Rydon looked at Melanos, uncertain.

"That's—"

"You need to give her your blood."

"What?" Daris shouted, aghast.

Rydon did not hesitate. He grabbed Terena's sword and sliced his wrist. Handing the weapon over to Daris, Rydon held his wrist over Terena's slightly parted lips.

"Drink, girl," Melanos whispered. Rydon watched Terena's face. A few beads of sweat dotted her forehead, her face pale. She seemed lifeless.

Rydon's blood dripped into her mouth, and he heard someone moan behind him. He glanced over his shoulder to see Croak huddled on the ground, watching them with huge, haunted eyes.

He turned back to Terena. She was so still. Rydon squeezed his wrist, more blood pouring onto her lips. "Come on, Ren," he muttered.

His pulse thundered in his ears as he repeated those words, over and over until despair wrapped around his heart. His hands shook and a sharp sting behind his eyes made him gasp.

She was dying. He knew it.

He would die now, too.

Melanos reached out and snatched Rydon's wrist, bringing it to

Terena's lips. Daris shouted again and grabbed hold of Rydon's wrist, too, when Rydon's eyes widened in shock.

Terena's eyes fluttered open.

Melanos pushed Rydon's wrist away from Terena and leaned close enough to block out Daris.

"Terena?"

Terena looked up at him and blinked.

Melanos winked at her and patted her knee before standing.

Croak rushed forward, looming over Daris as he looked down at Terena. "She's alive?"

"Wipe your snot, boy," Melanos said and slapped Croak on the back, sending him stumbling forward into Daris's back. "She'll live."

"Is she dead?"

Croak had taken a seat on the couch by Terena's legs. From the gasps around the room at Melanos's question, the god quickly added, "Is Bethana dead?"

Daris stood and scrubbed a hand over his face. He looked exhausted, his face haggard. It was the first time Croak had ever seen him looking less than handsome, the scars on his face pinched and standing out even more against the pallor of his skin.

Terena continued to sleep soundly, cocooned in the plush couch with several furs thrown over her from a snap of Melanos's fingers.

"No, she is not," Daris answered. "As soon as she was free of Terena's arm," he said this with a wince, "I severed her tail. She chased after us, but we lost her. My only thought right then was of Terena and getting us out of there."

"And where were you that you couldn't stop what happened?"

Daris looked over at Gabriol, standing next to Rydon with his arms crossed as he glared at Daris.

The commander's jaw tightened, the color high in his neck and cheeks. "I was looking for a way out. Terena was tired from walking on that leg and I set her down for a moment's rest. I was on my way back when I heard their voices."

"What were they saying?" Rydon asked.

"The serpent—Bethana—said she smelled like *them*."

Croak made a noise and looked over at Rydon, who was watching Daris through narrowed eyes, his arms crossed at his chest.

"What's that mean?" Michael asked, his eyes moving from Daris to Melanos. The god was stroking his chin, looking off into space.

"What did Terena say?" Croak asked when Michael's question was met with silence.

Daris stared at him a moment. "She saw me then and told me to leave."

"Why?" Michael asked, swiveling his head from his commander to the others.

Daris dropped his chin. "I think she was resigned. Wanted me to have a chance, at least."

"But you didn't, of course," Jason said, pacing closer to the couch.

"No."

"Did Bethana say anything else?" Melanos asked. Croak wondered again if the god could still be in love with the nymph after centuries apart.

"She was insistent Terena was like 'them'." Daris shrugged. "I asked who she meant, but she kept saying 'them'. So I asked if she meant Poseidon and she went a little…"

"That wasn't wise," Melanos chided.

Daris arched an eyebrow. "No, it was not. She spoke of you, though. Of what Poseidon had done to you both." He swallowed. "Terena told her you live. I think she did so because the serpent looked close to making me her dinner and Terena… she turned its attention back to her." He ran a hand through his hair. "She saved me."

Silence settled around them for a few minutes and Croak turned his gaze back to his sister. Her face was slack, but the color was once more in her cheeks and her breathing was steady. They had wrapped the wounds and only a faint bit of blood now marred the cloth.

"It worked, too," Daris said, jarring Croak's attention back to him.

"Bethana was so enraged, thinking Terena was lying to save me, save herself, that the serpent just... struck." Daris crossed his arms. "It was so fast. I blinked, and she struck. If I live a thousand years, I'll never forget Terena's scream."

"She must have been in tremendous pain," Melanos said and frowned when he saw Rydon's eye roll. "Terena is not yet fully into her powers and still mortal," he said with a scowl at Croak."How did you extract her from Bethana?"

Daris stared down at the ground in silence. The silence stretched, broken up by the shifting of the men as they waited for the commander to reply.

"That's the part I don't understand," he said at length. "It was like what happened with the wolf."

Daris looked up and stared hard at Melanos, then at Rydon. "You cannot deny it anymore. Not with the things we've seen. The things we've seen her do."

Rydon's face reddened, his face tight but otherwise he did not speak.

Melanos looked between the men in surprise. At last, he looked at Rydon.

"They do not know?"

The color on Rydon's face deepened, his eyes locked on Melanos, but still he said nothing.

"Why should they?" Croak spat and curled his lip. He motioned to Daris with his chin and sneered. "They hold Terena's—*our*—sister hostage so she can bring them back some fucking teeth that almost killed her! They don't deserve to know anything!"

Melanos scoffed. "I think you'll find, boy, she was always fated to bring back these fangs. Whether these men deserve to know more," he shrugged, "I cannot say. But their lives are in as much danger as yours or your sisters, if they travel with you. Best to be open."

"Why?" Croak asked, exasperated. "So they can kill her? Do you know—"

"Croak," Rydon warned.

"What are you saying?" Daris demanded. "You think I—"

"We don't fucking know you," Croak yelled, shooting up from the couch. His face was hot and his breath was ragged. "You pretend friendship and then you kidnap Sonah—"

"We didn't kidnap her!" Daris yelled back. "*She* volunteered to stay with our king, who is a good man and would never harm her! And I *saved* Terena when I could've easily let her die and take the fangs myself if that was my aim!"

"You wouldn't let her die," Melanos scoffed. "I don't know why there are two of you, but—"

"You stay away from her," Croak snarled and launched at Daris.

"Enough!" Rydon roared, lunging between Croak and Daris. He had a hand on Daris's chest the commander slapped away. Gabriol moved a few steps closer.

Melanos laughed.

"You're afraid the Liodari will kill her?" he asked in amusement. "They are Spartans. Sworn to Ares. If there's anyone besides you she should trust, boy, it's these men."

Daris's face was thunderous, his chest rising and falling rapidly as he stared back at Croak.

"What?" Daris asked, his brow furrowed as he looked between Rydon and Melanos.

Melanos sighed. "She is the daughter of your god. She's a child of Ares."

Croak's hands drifted to his hips, his lips twitching at the look on the commander's face. Daris went three shades of white, his mouth dropping open like a dead fish. His men were no better. Michael blinked rapidly, gaping at the others, and Jason had his hands on his head as he tipped it back, eyes closed.

"What?" Daris whispered. "That's impossible."

Melanos was genuinely amused. "You've been traveling with her for how long and you've seen her do the things she's done, and yet you doubt? You were the one insisting the other Eudaemon tell you—"

"Why do you keep calling him that?" Daris snapped.

Melanos blinked. "Huh?"

"You keep calling this man," Daris stabbed a finger toward Rydon, "Eudaemon. Why?"

Melanos's face scrunched. "He is."

"I am her guardian," Rydon said quietly, his eyes narrowed on Daris.

"Eudaemons are myth," Jason grumbled.

Melanos laughed. When he caught sight of their expressions, he laughed longer, his head thrown back with his hands at his belly.

At last, he looked over at the Liodari, his smile softening as his laughter died down. Then he turned to Rydon with a raised eyebrow. "After all they've seen, they still... unbelievable." He shook his head and waved a hand at them dismissively.

"If she's who you say she is," Daris asked after an awkward pause, "how is she hurt? Why does she even need a Eudaemon?"

This time, Melanos's face shuttered. "She is not yet twenty-two. Which means she's still mortal and doesn't have control of her powers."

"She had a dream about you killing her, " Croak snarled at Daris.

At this, Rydon swore and glared at Croak. Croak didn't care. He was savoring the look of horror on the commander's face.

"What?"

Melanos's eyes shot to Daris and to Croak's satisfaction, he looked like he might hurt the commander.

"Was I wrong, Liodari?" Melanos asked in a low, soft tone.

Daris gaped at the god. "I would *never* hurt her! I—" He swore and hung his head. "She is... it was only a dream. I would never kill her. That's absurd."

"Her dreams are memories," Rydon said, his face grim as he stared at Daris.

Croak felt the first stirrings of sympathy toward the commander. He pushed them back, reminding himself this man allowed his sister to come to harm while in his care. So far, the commander wasn't living up to his legendary reputation.

Daris rubbed his forehead, his lips thinned. His eyes darkened as they rose to stare at Rydon. "I don't even know how that's possible.

But if you continue to doubt my word, I won't give you a chance to regret it."

"Croak."

Terena's soft voice cut through their argument and Croak leaned forward, his face splitting in a shaky smile as he knelt at her side.

"Hey, you," he whispered, squeezing her knee. She frowned, then flicked her eyes over to Daris and Rydon.

"What's going on?"

"Nothing," Croak said quickly with a wink. "We're sitting here waiting for you to wake up. How are you feeling?"

She groaned and closed her eyes. "Like shit."

Melanos sauntered over. "You're weak," he said. "You should rest more. With the state of you, you should remain here at least for the night."

"I'm staying too," Croak said quickly.

Melanos grumbled but did not object. He looked pointedly at the others.

Only Rydon took the hint.

"We'll... be back in the morning, then," he said and moved closer to the couch. He bent over and squeezed Terena's left shoulder. "I'm glad you're alive."

She snorted and opened her eyes. "I bet you are," she said with a weak smile.

The others turned to leave.

"Daris," Terena called out, then winced and shifted her head on the pillows.

Croak curled his lip as the commander came closer.

"Aye, Terena," he said awkwardly.

She looked up and held out her hand. Daris hesitated a second before he reached out and took hold of it.

Terena looked up at him and Croak turned away.

"Thank you," she said.

The commander stared at her for so long, Croak turned back to see his sister gazing at the man with her heart in her eyes.

Gods help us.

THE INN WAS QUIET AND DARK WHEN THEY ARRIVED. JASON WENT INSIDE to get rooms while the rest saw to the horses.

No one spoke.

Michael cast furtive glances at the others as they left the stables. Rydon caught his eye and arched an eyebrow.

"Something on your mind?" he asked, not unkindly.

Michael frowned. "Quite a lot, in fact." But he looked away and Rydon did not press him.

They walked back to the inn slowly, Daris alone up ahead of Gabriol, Michael a few steps behind, with Rydon trailing them all.

Gabriol fell back, waiting for Rydon to catch up. "What a mess, lord," he muttered.

Rydon only nodded.

When they reached the inn, Jason was waiting for them in the common room, alone, a pitcher and five tankards on the table.

Of the innkeep there was no sign.

"Do we have rooms?" Daris asked, strolling over to join his man.

Jason draped an arm over the back of his chair and smiled tiredly at them. "Aye."

Daris grunted, then sighed loudly as he took the chair beside Jason. Rydon was loathe to sit, not because he disliked them. They had turned out to be decent men—honorable men. But he was bone tired and not in the mood to be tricked into answers by the commander.

Gabriol took his indecision as participation, taking a seat across from Daris and his men. Rydon scowled, but took the seat at his side.

Jason pushed a tankard toward Daris. "Water."

The commander muttered his thanks.

The others reached out and took a tankard each, waiting patiently as Jason poured them ale. Rydon sat back and took a long drink, closing his eyes and savoring the bitter brew.

All of them were quiet, lost in their own thoughts and nursing their drinks. Rydon was thinking of taking his leave once he'd finished his ale, but Jason leaned forward with the pitcher, refilling his tankard in silence.

"It will be some time before we can return to Sparta," Daris said at last.

No one argued against this.

"Poor girl," Michael said, and Rydon looked at the man from beneath his brows, alert. But Michael looked genuinely upset, his head hanging, his hand shaking slightly as he twisted his tankard.

"Aye," Gabriol agreed.

"That night at the fighting pit? I knew there was something about her," Jason said as he stared off into space. "There's no way she would've been that close to beating me otherwise."

Rydon's bark of laughter surprised him. The others looked at him, grinning, and broke into laughter as well. Rydon lifted his tankard to Jason, the Liodari grinning at him as he raised his own tankard in salute.

"What will you all do when we return?" Jason asked. "If she is truly the daughter of Ares, then you must stay in Sparta."

Rydon saw Daris tense. He sat back and crossed his arms. "Once we have Sonah back, we'll head north."

"Why not stay in Sparta?" Jason urged. He looked at his commander for support. "It must be why the Fates guided you there. Now we all know she's the Heir, Daris—"

"And what awaits in the north?" Daris interrupted.

Rydon narrowed his eyes. "Opportunity."

"We hear the new king is gathering an army," Michael said after he took a drink. "For what purpose, I wonder."

Gabriol leaned forward, cradling his ale in both hands. "To defend against the tyrant Solon, I'd imagine. As any sensible sovereign."

"Solon has his own problems just now," Michael replied. "I don't see him looking north anytime soon when his own nobles are rebelling against him."

Rydon looked over at the three men. "We've only heard rumors."

"Makes sense," Jason said, glancing at Daris. The commander

shook his head almost imperceptibly. Rydon wondered if he'd imagined it.

"How did the two of you come to be with Terena and Croak?" Jason asked before Rydon could respond. "I know Sonah was at the palace. That she grew up with Croak and Terena when they were in Metilai. But Sonah didn't mention how you joined their ranks."

Rydon stared at Jason so long the man stiffened, but he didn't turn away.

"You know much of Sonah, Youngblood," Gabriol said as he eyed Jason across the table. "When have you had occasion to speak with her?"

Jason reddened. "We spoke when we met you that night in Sparta."

Rydon and Gabriol shared a look.

"We met Croak in Laurica," he said after an awkward pause. "He asked us for help in rescuing his sister when word reached him of her capture."

Well, it was as much truth as he was willing to offer just then.

Jason grunted.

Rydon wasn't finished. He leaned over the table, his eyes holding Jason in place. "She is too young for you."

Jason blinked. Michael snorted, and Gabriol smothered a smile.

The color in Jason's face deepened until it covered him to the roots of his blond hair as Rydon sat back.

"How old do you think I am?" Jason demanded, his brown eyes narrowed as he pointed to himself.

"Too. Old."

"I'm twenty-three!"

Rydon leaned forward again but said nothing as his gaze narrowed at Jason.

The others laughed, breaking the tension. Daris clapped Jason on the shoulder, a smirk on his face.

"Is she..." Jason paused, casting a quick look at Gabriol. "Is she with Croak?"

Gabriol choked on his drink, coughing and laughing at the same time. Even Rydon's lips tugged up.

"Is she promised? Betrothed?" Jason pushed, warming to the topic now as the others smiled.

"No, Youngblood, she is not," Gabriol sighed.

Jason sat back with a satisfied smile which quickly dissolved at the warning on Rydon's face.

"Did you know of the king's visit to the oracle? Terena said she's the reason we're all here." Gabriol asked after a companionable silence.

None of them responded for a long time. Daris looked up at him, then at Rydon.

"Aye."

"Do you know what Pytho told him?"

Daris blinked. Whether from the fact Rydon had used the oracle's name so casually or because of the impertinence of his question, he did not know. Neither mattered to him.

"He told me," Daris answered at last, his voice soft.

"Did you know before or after you saw her in Aurora?" Rydon pressed. Gabriol stiffened.

Daris's smile was no longer friendly.

His silence was answer enough.

"What were you doing in Aurora?" Rydon asked, his voice deadly soft. The others at the table tensed.

It was a long time before Daris answered. "That is Spartan business."

"Of course," said Rydon with a nod, his eyes never moving from the commander. "Does Terena know?"

Daris did not respond.

Rydon registered Gabriol leaning over, yet did not break contact with Daris's cold blue gaze.

"Does she know you have a battalion of Liodari there?"

Jason swore, shoving back his chair just as Daris's arm slammed down on his wrist to stay him. After a few tense seconds, Jason settled. Rydon flicked a glance at the man's scowling face before raising an eyebrow at Daris.

"Again," Daris said softly, "that is Spartan business."

"And what of the Spartan prophecy your man spoke of?" Gabriol asked. "Now that you know of Terena's paternity, perhaps you'd like to share?"

Daris's face shuttered. "That is between the king and Terena."

"Funny," Rydon said, his hand raised as he looked at Daris over the lip of his tankard. "I thought that might be between you and Terena."

Rydon watched him, but the man gave nothing away. The commander and his exploits were well known, and Rydon had seen the way he'd torn into the Rivermen at the falls, making quick work of them before racing after Terena when she'd fallen into the river. And to have survived the serpent...

Being commander of the elite Liodari legion known throughout the continent—and one reason Emperor Solon had not immediately invaded—should have been enough for Rydon to see this was not someone to be trifled with. But somewhere along the trials and tribulations of this journey, Rydon had become protective not only of Terena, but of Croak and Sonah as well. Whatever the prophecy he spoke of, if the man was unwilling to confide in them after all they'd shared, then Rydon must remain vigilant around him.

He admitted to being a bit awed by the man upon first meeting, but now, after enduring the past month with him and seeing his eyes on Terena whenever he thought no one was watching...

Rydon was watching.

"I can't keep my eyes open anymore," Michael groused and stood, groaning and stretching. He left with a wave and the others grunted in response. A few minutes later, Gabriol reached out and squeezed Rydon's shoulder as he too stood, draining his tankard. He set it down and muttered his good wishes for pleasant dreams before he went off and up the stairs.

Jason left shortly after, leaving Rydon and Daris alone.

Rydon looked at the commander from beneath his brows as he stretched his legs out. Daris was lost in his own thoughts, hunched over with his arms braced on his thighs.

A long silence descended and Rydon's eyes became heavy when Daris spoke.

"What is your issue with me?"

Rydon started. He looked up to see Daris's light blue eyes watching him askance. Rydon rubbed a hand over his mouth to stifle a yawn. "I've no issue."

"Is that so?" Daris snorted.

Rydon stared back at him. "Aye."

"All those questions earlier? And why do you scowl at me whenever I mention her name? Or ask anything even remotely having to do with her? You also insert yourself whenever I go near her." He cocked his head. "You're either interested in her or me. Which is it?"

Rydon scoffed. "Neither."

"I don't believe you."

Rydon opened his mouth to protest but then jerked forward, bracing his arm on the table as he leaned across, his face thunderous.

"I don't like the way you look at her," he growled. "I don't like the questions you ask about her and I don't like the way you watch her; the way you always seem to be right by her side when she's in trouble. You find reasons to touch her, her cloak, her hand, her hair when you think she doesn't notice. But I notice."

"Oh, this is a pissing contest, is it?" Daris asked, his smile cold.

"This is a warning," Rydon snarled. "That girl has been through too much for someone so young, and she's still a good person. Her heart is so big, her compassion so strong, she throws herself into trouble just to spare the rest of us." He arched an eyebrow and a muscle spasmed in his neck. "Did you know she was in love with Crown Prince Lerek? When he was murdered, *she* was the one to find him."

Daris blanched, but Rydon forged on. "If that wasn't bad enough, the emperor saw fit to accuse her of conspiring with the prince's murderers and had her beaten, *tortured* and then sentenced her to death. By drawing and quartering!

"She has the power of the gods in her blood," Rydon seethed, uncaring he should probably stop, but the words had built up in his chest for too long to be held back any longer. "If she wasn't already wanted for treason—for murder!—she would definitely be hunted if anyone outside our circle found out what she is. She suffers from these visions that are, more often than not, terrifying nightmares, all the while mourning her lover and trying not to die at every turn!"

Daris sat back, his face pale, looking as if Rydon had slapped him.

Rydon took a long drink, draining his tankard before slamming it on the table. "And on top of that pile of *shit,* I see how the guilt eats at her, how confused she is because she can't reconcile how she felt about her dead prince with how she feels about *you,*" he fumed, spittle landing on his beard. He wiped his mouth. "So, do us all a favor and leave her the *fuck* alone."

Rydon rose abruptly, catching his chair before it toppled back and woke the entire building.

He muttered a curse and left, his heart racing. He put a hand to his chest and closed his eyes for a second, knowing it'd be a long time before sleep found him.

CHAPTER THIRTY-FIVE

Pytho sat on a cloud of pillows, her spine straight, her arms out in front of her with her palms up as she muttered words Terena couldn't hear.

The room was hazy from the burning incense and the smoke made her want to sneeze. She took a few steps closer, calling out to Pytho.

The next moment, Pytho stood before her, holding Terena's face between her ice cold hands as she continued to mutter in a language Terena did not know.

"I don't understand," she said, but Pytho's hands squeezed, her nails biting into Terena's jaw.

Pytho's muttering became more forceful. Those strange black eyes stared back at her as if she hadn't heard.

"Pytho," she said.

Terena's eyes widened as she watched a line of red appear at Pytho's throat. The wound gaped and Terena screamed.

But Pytho's hold on her face hardened.

"They've found me," she hissed.

"Who?" Terena asked as she sobbed. Her hands clutched at the oracle's arms.

Come find me come find me come find me come find me

Terena's scream echoed in the smoky chamber as blood covered her hands and raced up her arms.

"...your father's blood." Pytho gurgled, blood now seeping from her mouth.

the heir the heir the heir the

"FIND ME!"

TERENA JERKED AWAKE, THRASHING AWAY FROM ARMS TRYING TO pin her.

Was she drowning?

Was that blood coating her throat?

What were they doing?

Why—

"It's me," a familiar voice said. "Terena stop, please! You'll reopen—"

She flailed again when someone forced her mouth open, slapped at hands too close and cried out when the movement sent an arc of fire racing down her arm and through her bad leg.

"It's me, Ren, it's me. It's Croak. Stop. Stop!"

Her body shook and she blinked furiously as bile rose in her throat, the liquid poured down her mouth now coming back up.

She lashed out again but someone had hold of her arms. They were like vices.

When she finally focused, she saw Melanos, his enormous hands bracing her as he stared back with concern in his eyes. Croak was on the couch at her side, panting, his face pale and eyes bloodshot. He was holding a glass away from her.

Terena willed herself to calm down as she looked between the two.

"Was it—was it another dream?"

"Where am I?" Terena mumbled, her voice raspy.

Croak sat back. "We're in Melanos's sex cave."

Melanos flashed him a flat look.

"How do you feel?" Melanos asked her.

Terena closed her eyes and leaned back onto the pillows as he slowly released his hold.

"What happened?" she asked.

"What do you remember?" Croak countered.

She pursed her lips. Then, as if recalling something important, she shot back up, her hand wrapping around Croak's wrist tightly.

"Daris! What happened? Is he all right? Where—"

"He's fine," Croak groused, waving his hand as if she'd asked something stupid.

Terena looked at him a second longer before lifting her left arm up, looking at it even as she winced. The bandages hid the wounds the serpent had left, but she did not forget the feel of the fangs in her arm. A ghost of that pain returned as her memories flooded back.

"Fucking gods," she swore, her body shaking. She looked up at Melanos. "She was bigger than you said." Terena's eyes narrowed accusingly.

Melanos shrugged, his face blank. "Well. It's been a millennium."

"Drink this," Croak said, shoving the glass in her face. Terena's stomach curdled. She tried shoving the drink away, but Croak swatted her hand. "It will ease the pain, idiot."

Terena eyed him, then took the glass from him and took a sip. She immediately spewed it out.

"What... is that blood?"

"It's mostly wine," Croak mumbled, wiping the spit off his face. "But there is some of Rydon's blood—"

"Oh gods," Terena whined and put a hand over her mouth. She closed her eyes and waited a few precious seconds. When she could speak again, she held up a finger. "Why the fuck would you give me Rydon's blood to drink?"

"His blood will help you heal faster."

"Ugh. Being a god is not fun."

"It should've healed your wounds by now. At least, the pain in your shoulder," Melanos said. He regarded her a moment, then shrugged. "Well. At least it saved your life."

"How'd I get here?"

"Your lover brought you," Melanos answered, and she and Croak answered at the same time.

"He's not my lover!"

"He's not her lover!"

Turning to Croak, she asked, "So how'd he find the rest of you? We were looking for a way out when Bethana found us."

"He probably led it right to you," Croak grumbled.

Melanos grinned. "He didn't say."

"We were all walking around looking to see if there was another entrance we could find and then we heard him yelling," Croak said. "Then he was just... there. Running right to us with you in his arms." He shook his head. "Gods, Ren, you had those fucking things sticking out of your arm and I thought I was going to faint."

"You *did* faint," Melanos snorted.

"Has he—" Terena started to ask when a shout from the cave entrance drew their attention. Croak shot to his feet and Terena slapped at his leg for him to move out of the way.

When she caught sight of Rydon, his face lit up when he saw her. Next to him, Gabriol grinned and slapped a hand on Rydon's shoulder.

Terena smiled and propped herself up higher. Rydon bent over when he reached her side, giving her a kiss on the forehead. Gabriol squeezed her shoulder and moved back, pulling Croak into a hug that morphed into him holding Croak's head in his armpit, hauling him away while Croak yelped.

Daris stopped a few steps away. Terena reached up to smooth her hair. Her smile became reserved when she looked at Daris, who smiled back at her with as much affection as he would give a tree. She raised her eyebrows but looked past him to see the other Liodari, who were both smiling in relief.

"You're looking much better," Rydon said, moving to the end of the couch when Terena motioned for him to sit. Gabriol moved in closer and perched on the arm. Daris remained standing near Gabriol as he watched her, his face unreadable.

"I feel a thousand times better," she said, looking at Rydon. "They gave me a tonic made from your blood, so that was weird."

He threw his head back and laughed. "Aye, it was weird for me when it revived you." He patted her knee. "But I'm glad you feel better."

Daris shifted, his eyes moving to Rydon. Terena saw the tension between the men and shot Rydon a quizzical look. He shook his head imperceptibly.

"Oh!" she exclaimed and laid her hand over Rydon's as she recalled, "What happened to the fangs? Did you—"

"I have them," Daris said in a soft voice.

Rydon snorted. "Of course you do."

Terena shifted her gaze to Daris then. Heat crept up his cheeks, and he looked at Rydon like he wanted to rip his head off.

"I was asking Croak what happened after Bethana tried to eat me, but maybe I can get the actual story from one of you?" Terena asked with a grin, looking at the three men.

"Not much to tell," Daris said, and Terena saw Rydon scowl. "I grabbed you and ran the hell out of there. Found everyone else shortly after and we rode like the Furies were after us. Melanos took care of your wounds."

"Well, thank you for getting me out of there," Terena said sincerely. Daris ducked his head.

Rydon snorted. Again.

Terena looked between the two. "What's going on with you two?"

Rydon looked confused. Daris shrugged. Terena looked to Gabriol for help, but his only response was to widen his eyes.

"Fine," Terena murmured. "Help me up," she said to Rydon.

"Are you sure you should?" Gabriol asked, waving a hand at her. "You were almost Bethana's dinner."

"I need to get up," she said with a shrug. "My body's too stiff lying in bed so much."

Rydon gave Daris a look, and the man moved back. Gabriol stood and backed away as well.

"Hey," she whispered to Rydon when he bent close, "did he say anything about what happened in there? In the cave, with Bethana."

Rydon nodded tersely. "Aye. And then Melanos told them everything."

Terena cringed. "Great. Now everyone knows, right?"

He nodded again.

Terena sighed. "Do I need to worry?"

Rydon sat down at her side again and leaned in, his face earnest. "Not from us, Ren. And if he tries anything…"

Terena shook her head. "He won't. I know he won't. But I'm not worried about him, so much as I worry about his king. Altos might try to use the knowledge for his own purposes if Daris or the others tell him." She leaned closer. "We need to get those fangs back to him and get Sonah so we can head north as soon as possible. It'll take us months as it is, so we're already losing time."

"I know it," Rydon snarled.

He made to stand again when Terena stopped him. "What's going on with you?"

"Just watching your back," he said. Then he looked over at Daris and dropped his head.

"Listen," he said as he turned back to her. "We need to talk. When you're feeling up to it."

"About?"

"We'll talk later."

Daris pretended to be interested in the food in front of him as he stole glances across the table at Terena. While his men and Terena's friends pestered Melanos with questions, Daris kept to himself, preferring to listen while he kept a surreptitious eye on Terena for signs of pain or discomfort.

Melanos had manifested a table with enough chairs for all of them and food enough to feed the Spartan army. It was surreal to be sitting at a table with a god—make that two gods—and yet Melanos behaved much like any man Daris had ever met. He laughed, and he made jokes. He shared stories with them about the Immortals before the war and listened with rapt attention, leaning in close to the others as they shared their own stories.

Daris glanced up as laughter erupted at the other end, and he found Rydon watching him. He held the man's gaze a moment before turning away dismissively. The revelations of the past few days sat heavily with him.

A tingling sensation crept over his scalp and he raised his eyes again to catch Terena watching him this time.

"You're quiet, Commander," Melanos called out, his booming voice startling Daris. He looked over at the god, then at the others who were now watching him. The barely concealed dislike on Croak's face made him duck his chin.

"He's always like that," Terena said. His gaze shot to her and he blinked, his eyes widening at the smile she gave him.

Melanos twisted his lips at her. "I thought you've not known each other long."

Terena started, a pretty color rising to her cheeks. "We haven't."

"Well," Jason said before swallowing something he'd been chewing on, "You have the right of it, lady."

Daris frowned and Jason looked away.

Melanos regarded Daris in silence, his hand stroking his chin, then he pointed a finger at him. "There's something about you, Commander. I cannot put my finger on it but something seems…" He shrugged and picked up a hunk of bread, tearing it with his teeth.

"Off? Aye, that's murderous intent you're picking up on." Croak snarked, then cried out when Gabriol slapped his arm.

Melanos turned to Terena. "The Eudaemon's blood should have healed your wounds by now. Maybe you should try the other."

Croak gagged. Daris flicked his gaze to Terena and saw her lips twist.

"I don't know what to say to that," she laughed.

"You healed enough you didn't die," Melanos went on, still

watching Terena thoughtfully. "Curious you're still not healed, however. If you try—"

"Godhood hasn't gone well for me so far."

Melanos grunted but continued to regard her in silence.

"Do you think she's well enough to travel?" Rydon asked.

"Should be," Melanos said, "but again, she's not healed yet, so take it slow if you can."

"I'd like to be back soon," Terena said with a glance at Rydon. "I want to get Sonah."

Croak threw Daris another dirty look from across the table. "And offload some of this dead weight."

Daris leaned back in his chair, his face blank as he held Croak's hard gaze.

"Stop," Terena muttered. She gave Daris a wan smile. "Would you mind walking with me, Daris? I'd love some fresh air."

Daris's eyes widened, and he sat up slowly. His eyes darted around at the others before settling back on Terena, her lovely eyes sparkling. "Aye."

The chair scraped along the rough stone floor and heat flooded his face. As he saw Terena begin to stand, he strode toward her side, only to have Rydon's big body block him as he, too, stood and looked him square in the eye, his chest puffed out. Daris frowned at the man and shifted his gaze to Croak who also stood, his eyes dancing.

"Really?" Terena murmured at Croak, pushing him aside as she hobbled closer to Daris. He shot out a hand to grip her good arm and his stomach bottomed out at the smile she flashed at him.

"There's a cave off to the left on the path just outside," Melanos called out, pulling everyone's attention back to him and breaking the tension. "It's closed off, so no need to fear another encounter with Bethana," added Melanos with a smirk as he caught Daris's scowl. "We used to meet there in better days. You'll see why, when you find it."

"Thank you, Melanos," Terena said as she smiled at him.

Turning to Daris, she twisted her hand so her fingers threaded with his own. Terena called out to the others they'd be back soon and hobbled toward the entrance. Daris stared down at her and saw the tight set of her jaw. He moved closer to her, locking his arm to take more of her weight.

"I wanted to talk to you privately," she said when they were outside. The sun was setting to their right, and when she turned her face up to smile at him, his breath caught as the last rays of the sun picked out the gold in her eyes.

He let her choose the direction, uncaring of where they went. It was quiet out and he was glad to be away from the others at last.

"I'm sorry for the way Croak is treating you," Terena said at last. They followed a path away from the cave. "And Rydon. In case he didn't apologize for whatever he said to you last night, I'm sorry. He can be a bit," she scrunched her face up and waved her bad arm, then winced.

"I don't mind," Daris replied.

Terena's brows pulled together. "You are not like any warrior I've ever known," she mused. "What's wrong with you?"

Daris laughed.

"No, truly. You're quiet, you don't drink, you're the youngest Commander of the Liodari in history." This last she said in a deep voice, mimicking Jason. She gasped when her foot slipped on the dirt path and he released her hand to wrap his arm around her.

When she was steady once more, she laughed. "Thank you. Clumsy."

"May I ask you something?" he asked, his heart hammering beneath his ribs. "Do your visions..."

When her fingers tensed on his arm, he apologized.

"It's all right," she said after a pause. "What do you want to know?"

Daris pursed his lips, his eyes searching for the words. "Are your visions premonitions? Can you see the future?"

Terena laughed. "I wish. Actually, for the longest time, that's what I thought they were."

"And now?"

She shrugged. They walked in silence as he waited for her to continue. When she didn't, he didn't press her.

"Oh!" she exclaimed, tensing. She grabbed his forearm, staring off at something ahead. "Is that the cave Melanos spoke of? Let's look."

Daris's brow furrowed as he stared at her, then off to where she was looking and saw a faint light in the distance.

Terena walked toward it, the sun so low on the horizon they were surrounded by a dark blue and russet colored sky. Daris saw the mouth of a cave with dim blue light dancing at the entrance. Terena flashed him an open-mouthed smile and reached for his hand at her waist, threading her fingers once more through his and tugged him toward the cave.

Daris dug in his feet. "Absolutely not."

"What?"

"We're not going in there. Come on," he said and tried to turn her back. "We've been gone long enough. I'm sure your brother will come looking any second now."

"Don't be a baby," she teased and pulled on his hand again. "What's the worst that could happen?"

"Uh, we run into a crazed giant serpent?"

Terena laughed, and the sound did funny things to his insides. "Melanos said it was closed off. Come, now."

The cave was not as dark as he'd feared. The antechamber opened up into a larger cavern with a hole in the ceiling opening to the sky, a small pool of standing water beneath reflecting the blue light glowing along the cave ceiling and walls. Terena stared, her mouth slack and eyes blinking slowly, her grip tight in his hand.

"Glow worms," Daris murmured as he watched her wide-eyed stare taking in the tiny insects lighting up the cave.

He had to admit the effect was beautiful. The tiny pinpoints of light haloed translucent strands hanging from the ceiling.

Daris moved his thumb across Terena's hand as he stared down at her. Thunder rumbled in the distance and Terena sighed, stepping closer to the water's edge.

A minute later, rain poured in through the opening in the cave and she laughed. She let go of Daris's hand and hopped to the center. Turning her face up to the rain, Terena closed her eyes.

Mesmerized, Daris watched her joyous expression as the rain fell all around and he walked toward her, his heart pounding unevenly. The rain flattened his short hair, and he pushed it back as he looked down at her, stopping a foot away.

Terena opened her eyes and looked at him. For a second, he thought he saw her eyes reflecting the same wonder that must be in his own.

Daris reached for her. Her lips trembled. She tilted her face up to him and he lowered his head. His hands went to her waist and she stiffened, backing away a step as her mouth opened. Raising her hand to her lips, her nostrils flared.

"I saw this," she whispered, and Daris leaned closer to catch it. "I saw all this."

Terena looked up at him, her eyes wide. "You were standing right there. And then you... and then you kissed me."

Daris started. He opened his mouth to reply and she gasped, her hand stretched out as if to touch him.

And then she ran.

CHAPTER THIRTY-SIX

Terena stumbled only once as she ran, adrenaline fueling her body. He might not have been expecting it, but Daris was fast and she sensed him a step behind as she spurred her body faster, fear seizing her chest.

He grabbed her arm, wrenching her around. She cried out as he wrapped his other arm around her waist. Terena bucked against him, slamming her foot down on his. He swore and loosed his hold enough she whipped her hand up and punched his nose.

She turned, but he was still there, hauling her back until her back pressed against his chest, her momentum forcing him to lift her and she kicked wildly at the air.

"Stop!" he roared. Her foot connected with his shin, but still he held on. "You're going to hurt your—Terena, for the love of the gods, stop!"

She didn't. The fear engulfing her when she'd realized this was what she'd seen in her dream—what she'd thought was a dream—had, in fact, been a vision.

A memory.

But it had been different, too. Subtle ways that pricked at the back of her mind. Different enough she had paused. At the least, that might mean something had changed.

"Please, Terena." He pleaded with her to stop, but now his voice was soft, desperate.

Terrified.

"Let me go," she whimpered and hated herself for it, but she was desperate, too.

Incredibly, he complied, his arms falling away. Terena stumbled, her mind registering him backing up, and she turned. Holding her hands up in a defensive stance, Terena's wild eyes watched him warily. Daris held his hands up in defeat, his face flushed, the hurt in his eyes almost unbearable.

"Please," he said, wiping the blood from his nose, his voice low. The way it broke at the end made tears sting the back of her eyes.

She blinked rapidly, watching him as he panted. Her chest heaved as she gasped for air.

"I don't know what you're thinking," he said, "but I will not hurt you. I would never hurt you."

A tear slipped from her eye. He flinched at the sight of it and backed up a step.

"I don't—" He stopped, dropping his chin and shaking his head before looking back up at her. "Go. You don't have to run from me. If you want to leave, just... go."

Her blood roared in her ears. Terena watched him as he backed up a few more steps. Her heart squeezed, and she wanted to cry. More blood slid from his nose and he wiped it away, shoving his other hand through his wet hair.

Her whole body shook with the need to cry, and she didn't know why it seemed like her heart was breaking as she looked at him.

"I have... visions," Terena said, swallowing. She had no idea why, but she wanted—needed—to explain. *He deserves to know why*, she thought.

"I know," he mumbled.

Right, Terena thought.

She raised a hand, lamely gesturing at him. "One of them," she swallowed, "it was just like this. This cave. You and me standing here. But we were different." She wouldn't tell him how it had felt when they'd embraced. How it had seemed the most natural thing in the world.

Daris remained silent, his gaze fixed on her, cautious yet filled with a heartbroken expression that pained her.

"You tried to kill me," she whispered.

He winced and turned his head away. She could see from the way he took a step back she'd hurt him. Again.

She didn't—couldn't—speak for a long time.

Daris was still looking away when he spoke, his voice hoarse. "I would never hurt you. I cannot."

There was a pause, but she didn't speak.

He looked back at her and started toward her. She stiffened. He dropped his arms at his sides, defeated. "I've had many chances, Terena. I could have let Bethana do the job if that was what I'd wanted."

Daris leaned forward, his face a mask of despair and passion; the power radiating off him should have scared her. The glowing blue light around them limned his pale face, and the scars across his left cheek and ear moved as he worked his jaw.

Considering everything in the past few minutes, that slight movement should have made her run as fast and as far as she could get from him—indeed, it had been her first and only instinct when realization had hit. She had power, too, but she hadn't used it against him. Even in the dream, she hadn't used her power and now she thought about it, she wondered why that was.

Emboldened, Daris took another step closer, his jaw tight as a muscle ticked. He narrowed his eyes. "Since I saw you in Aurora, I can't," he held a hand up to his chest and exhaled. "I can't stop thinking about you."

Her mouth opened and her heart slammed into her ribs.

"I don't know what your vision showed you," he said through gritted teeth, "but it couldn't have been me. I know it. When Bethana attacked you, I swear to the gods, Terena, it was as if I was dying. I don't know how I even breathed, seeing her mouth on your arm, the pain on your face, I—"

He turned his head. Closed his eyes and took a breath. "I know it couldn't have been me in your vision because I would give my life for you."

Terena exhaled raggedly.

When she'd seen him at the duke's palace, she had experienced it too. At the time, she'd thought it was an attraction simply because he's handsome. But she remembered that feeling of... knowing him. Deep in her bones.

In her soul.

Since she'd fled Metilai and come to know Daris, the guilt ate at her for what she was feeling for him while she should have been mourning Lerek. Whom she'd loved. The man she had wanted to spend the rest of her life with.

And a voice in her heart plagued her, telling her maybe she hadn't loved him at all.

Terena looked at Daris, vulnerable and overwhelmed. They had spent little time together, but she somehow knew more about him, who he was as a person, than she ever did about Lerek. There was no rationalizing it, and she had the sudden thought that if she had done this before, that if she was reliving this life somehow, she had, in fact, known him in that past life.

Had loved him.

That thought hollowed out her insides, and she became dizzy.

Her mind screamed at her to stop, to turn and run, but she took a step closer to him.

"Me too," she said. "I mean, I can't stop thinking about you, either."

His head snapped up, his eyes blazing. But still wary.

She swallowed and waved a hand at him. "Obviously," her laughter hitched, and she took a deep breath, "since I have dreams about you."

That acknowledgment unlocked something inside her. The pain in her chest eased and her mind settled.

Terena wasn't sure which of them moved first. Daris crushed her in his arms, and she wrapped hers around him, grasping, finding his head, and threading her fingers through his hair. Their kiss was wild and desperate.

Liberating.

He consumed her, greedy, her mouth opening, wanting to taste more of him, all of him. He slanted his mouth and swept his tongue inside, finding hers, teeth clashing, mouth devouring.

His hands slid to her backside, molding, caressing. Terena dropped her hands to his shoulders, to his back, and groaned.

He shuddered as he tore his mouth from her, but she leaned in, hungry for his lips, for more.

He gripped her hips and set her away, his forehead dropping to hers as they panted. Her hands moved to his chest, flexing against the muscles under his leather, wanting to feel his flesh.

"Ren," he gasped, his eyes closed as he shook his head against hers. "You're hurt. We should stop. I don't want—"

Terena pulled back and nodded, closing her eyes. She opened them again to see his eyes searching her face. Those beautiful eyes she couldn't stop looking at every time he was near. She gasped out a laugh and his lips twitched up in answer.

"I don't... there's no pain." She laughed again. "At least, not there."

His smile widened and the heat in her chest dropped low in her belly.

"All right, but," he said, closing his eyes for a few seconds. "We can't... here. Not here and not now with you... and your leg. Your arm."

"Some god I turned out to be, huh?"

Terena tipped her chin up and kissed him again and for a minute she thought she'd won that argument, but he pulled back with a grimace. "And as much as I want to, as much as I'm dying to, if Rydon shows up and sees us like this, it'd be a pity to kill him."

Terena threw her head back and laughed.

Daris, too, chuckled, hugging her close as he buried his head in her neck. She closed her eyes and savored him here, with her.

"You can't kill him, remember?" she teased and stroked the back of his neck.

They stayed like that for a long time.

Forever.

And not long enough.

As if he'd conjured him, Terena heard Rydon and the others shouting from above, their voices faint. Daris groaned and pulled back. Terena lifted her hands to his cheeks, her eyes devouring his face, the powerful lines of his jaw, his brow furrowed over those gorgeous eyes narrowing on her as if she was the only thing that existed.

She pulled away slowly, his hands tightening at her waist for a moment before he let go. Daris ducked his head as he took a step back, then lifted his gaze as if bashful. The giddiness sweeping through her made her lightheaded, and she tossed her head, her wet hair slapping the side of her neck.

Terena frowned at how much of her hair had come loose from the tie, some strands stuck to her cheeks and neck. She undid the hair tie and lifted her arms to pull all of her hair up and retied it securely below the crown of her head.

"Ready," she said.

"I need a minute," he muttered. Terena laughed and put a hand to her mouth, even as her cheeks flamed when he shifted uncomfortably.

A long time later, he offered her his arm. She took it, hugging close to his side as they turned to leave the cave. Her leg didn't bother her at all and neither did her arm, even after all that activity. Terena marveled again at the blood tonic Melanos had made for her. Glad Croak had made her drink it.

Terena looked up at Daris with a shy smile he returned.

"Say nothing," she said impulsively as the voices of their friends became louder, singsonging her name or Daris's. "Not about—I mean, about the vision. I don't want them knowing. Especially Rydon. Or Croak. Gods know what he'd do."

Daris scowled. "They know already. Croak... mentioned it yesterday."

Terena swore. "Is that why Rydon looked like he wanted to murder you?"

"There you are!" Croak exclaimed, then frowned at Terena, arms crossed, when he saw how close Daris stood.

"You're okay? Not hurt?" he asked her, his eyes searching her face. Gabriol and Rydon ambled over, but the natural beauty of the cave captivated their eyes, a sight she was sure they'd not seen before if the looks on their faces were any indication.

Rydon cast a wary glance at Daris, but had only smiles for Terena when he turned back to her.

"All good?" he asked.

"Aye, I'm fine," she reassured them. "We went for a walk, not to slay any serpents."

"Ha. Ha." Croak said with thick sarcasm.

"I feel tired, though," Terena said, although she was anything but. She was exhilarated, her smile wide enough to hurt. She caught Rydon's eye and her smile slipped. "We should go back. You stay, if you want. Daris can walk me back."

Rydon and Croak both vetoed that option, and they all turned to walk back to Melanos's cave.

Terena took Croak's proffered arm, listening as the others chatted around her. A million thoughts chased each other in her mind.

What did it mean that her vision—a memory—had been different? She should have asked Pytho more about—

Pytho.

Terena stopped, the blood draining from her face.

"Pytho!"

Terena told everyone of the vision she'd had of Pytho, and her fear something had happened to the oracle. They'd all agreed to leave in the morning and talk to the king as soon as they had returned.

Standing near the cave entrance, Terena had tried to pull Melanos through the cave but it hadn't worked. Whatever she needed to do to free the god, she either didn't yet have the power or she needed something else to make it happen.

A thought had popped into her head. "Perhaps the oracle knows of a way to free you. On our way back north I'll come back and try again."

Melanos had looked at her with a frown and a shake of his head. She hadn't the time to try to convince him of her word but she vowed she would return. Whether or not he chose to wasn't something she had time to worry about.

The trip back to Sparta took the better part of a fortnight. Terena had not healed enough despite having another round of the disgusting drink from Rydon's blood. A part of her had almost felt weird drinking it in front of Daris, so she'd snuck away for some privacy and taken the drink with her. While it helped her recover much of her strength, it still hadn't healed her wounds as quickly as Melanos had claimed it should.

Something else she needed to ask Pytho about.

The late morning sun beat down on them when they finally made it to the city. The day promised to be beautiful, a cloudless sky with the sun bright, but with a bite in the air that spoke of autumn. As they crested a hill overlooking the city, Jason called out.

Below them, four soldiers on horseback thundered toward them and Terena shifted her eyes to Daris. He was frowning, looking not at the soldiers, but beyond. Terena followed his gaze to the city walls and squinted. She could see movement on the wall walks.

"What's going on?" Croak asked.

Daris urged his horse on, and they all followed. The soldiers slowed when they neared. One man pulled off his helmet and bowed his head at Daris.

"Commander, one of our scouts caught sight of your return. The king is asking to see you at once."

"What's happened?" Daris asked as the others reined their horses a respectful distance away.

The soldier looked at the others and pursed his lips. He dismounted and a second later, Daris did the same. While they conferred, Terena shot a look at Rydon, who looked back at her, his mouth pinched.

Daris strode back to his horse and mounted. "Heylisia attacked from Elis," he said. His face was tight, and Terena could see a muscle in his neck jump. He flicked a glance at her before he addressed his men. "They captured Messene and took the oracle."

Everyone spoke at once. Or rather, shouted. Terena surged forward on Nyx, her hand clasping Daris's forearm. He spared a glance at her, patting her hand with his before he roared for silence.

"Terena and I will go to Arestia Castle," he said, then turned to Rydon. "I need you and your men to gather your things. We'll meet you at the Champions Gate and then we ride for Messene."

"Wait, what?" Terena demanded. She shook her head, casting a look at Rydon, then Croak before turning back to Daris. "No. No, I can't do that. We can't do that, Daris."

"What are we even going to do in Messene," Rydon asked, his arms wide. "Is the oracle even there still?"

"We're wasting time," Daris snapped. He turned his mount and Terena's hand slid away. "You need to come with me, now, to the king."

There was no speaking to him after that. Daris spurred his stallion and his men followed, leaving Terena to gape at his retreating back. She swiveled her wide-eyed gaze to Rydon, her mouth slack.

"What the fuck?"

"Fuck!" Rydon slammed his hand on his thigh.

"Let's get our shit and meet them at the gate," Croak said, his voice shaking. "We can leave them in Messene and head north from there, right?"

"We can't!" Terena yelled, then swallowed. She turned in the saddle to face Croak. "Pytho's in this mess because of me, I'm sure of it. And then there's my promise to Melanos I'd get him out of that fucking cave!"

Terena threw her head back and screamed, her hands on her head. Nyx shifted uneasily beneath her. "Gods! Give me a break already!"

She opened her eyes and huffed, glancing around at the others. "Let's go. Fuck!"

Terena turned Nyx and raced after the Liodari.

CHAPTER THIRTY-SEVEN

Sonah paced in her room, the smell of jasmine and thyme drifting in from the open balcony behind her. Since she'd only had the clothes on her back when she remained behind after Terena had left weeks ago, the king had sent the Royal Seamstress to her with some dresses she and her servants had quickly altered for her.

Smoothing her hands down the silk skirt of the dress she wore, the soft lavender accented with a simple gold belt, Sonah turned when she reached the end of the room and paced back the other way.

An hour ago, one of King Altos's guards informed her Commander Antonius and Terena had been spotted, and Sonah waited anxiously, her nerves stretched taut. While the king's hospitality had been generous, Sonah had no desire to remain in the castle.

For one, she swore it was haunted.

The king allowed her to move freely during the day—well, with two armed guards and only in the east wing of the castle—and locked in her room after dinner. The first night she had protested—not much, if she was honest—but the king had said it was for her own protection. Shortly after she'd retired, Sonah heard a noise. She had bolted upright in bed, clutching the bedspread to her chest and stilled, listening for whatever had startled her awake.

A few minutes later, ready to settle back down, she'd heard it again. This time, Sonah had gotten out of bed, padding softly around to the edges of her room, listening with her ear to the walls when she heard scrapping coming from somewhere on her right. She had scuttled closer to the wall, pressing her ear against the cool stone and was rewarded with scraping and a loud bang.

Sonah had jumped back, her hand clapping over her mouth, then bolted for the door. She had pounded on the wood until a guard shoved it open, knocking her in the forehead. She'd been shrill, her words incoherent—according to the guard—and the guard had sent another for the king.

As she'd stood outside in the hallway, her arms folded at her chest while shivering in her thin nightgown, a door at the end of the hall opened and a man walked out, flanked by three guards. Sonah had turned, watching as the man walked in the opposite direction, only glimpsing him before they turned the corner at the end of the hallway.

After telling the king what had happened, that it must have been the man who was staying next to her, the king had blanched, his reaction so unexpected, Sonah hadn't time to think on it before he had called for servants to have her moved to the west wing of the castle.

No longer plagued by strange noises or unruly neighbors, Sonah also had the added benefit of being closer to the Royal Conservatory. The beautiful structure was where she'd spent most of her time while she waited for her sister's return.

A cough sounded behind her. Sonah turned, smiling at the servant standing there.

"Aye?"

"Your presence is requested, lady," the man said with a slight inclination of his head.

"She's here," Sonah whispered and shoved past the startled man to find a guard waiting outside her room to escort her.

Heart racing, Sonah bounced up on her toes as they neared the doors to the king's throne room.

The king usually dined with her in the evenings, but hadn't done so for the past two days. And there had been a flurry of activity as well, but Sonah had received no answers from the guards when she'd asked.

Maybe now she'd get some answers.

Either way, she was excited to see Terena and the others again.

The king stood below the dais, his hands clasped behind him. He looked at the ground while his advisor—Sonah forgot the man's name —spoke to him. The Captain of the Royal Guard and two of his men flanked King Altos, who looked like he'd not slept, his eyes heavy with dark shadows and his lips pulled down. Commander Daris Antonius stood close to his king with his head bent and arms crossed at his chest. Her sister stood a short distance away.

Sonah darted into the room and squealed, throwing up her hands as she bounced over to Terena. When she heard Sonah, her face lit up and she laughed, catching Sonah as she stumbled back a few steps. Sonah buried her face in Terena's neck, squeezing her so tight Terena's laughter choked off.

Several loud gasps sounded around them, but Sonah paid no heed. Pulling back as she stared up at Terena, Sonah's smile stretched so far her cheeks ached.

"Gods, where have you *been?*" she whined, unmindful of the exaggerated throat clearing on her right, her eyes never leaving Terena's face. "I thought I might end up living here! You took forever!"

Terena grimaced when Sonah leaned back, yanking on Terena's arms, and her smile slipped.

"What's wrong?"

Terena glanced over her shoulder at the king and Sonah shifted her eyes to the men. The advisor man was glaring at them, the Royal Guard and their captain watching with wariness. The king only looked distracted, and Daris had a smile on his face as he watched them.

Sonah turned a knowing look at her sister. "Well. I sense you have much to tell me."

Terena chuckled and tugged Sonah further away. Her smile faded. Lifting her hands to cup Sonah's face, Terena said, "I missed you. Have they treated you well?"

Sonah nodded. "Aye, of course."

"You look beautiful," Terena remarked, her eyes falling to Sonah's dress as she stepped back. "It's been a while since I've seen you in anything but plain shirts and leggings."

"Ah, but I still have my favorite boots," Sonah said, wiggling her eyebrows.

Terena grinned. She glanced back at the men, who continued to converse in low tones, and Terena pulled Sonah close. "Have you heard what's happened?"

Sonah wrinkled her brow and shook her head. "No. I mean, I know something has, but no one told me anything. Why? Do you know?"

"Solon's men have captured Messene and taken Pytho," Terena said, her grip tightening on Sonah's hands when she gasped.

Sonah's eyes widened as the blood drained from her face. She opened and closed her mouth a few times before Terena continued.

"The king is sending Daris and his men to Messene to reclaim it but, basically, they're at war now with Heylisia."

"But Heylisia is already at war with... Heylisia," Sonah finished lamely.

Terena nodded. "Aye, but Elis is still with the empire and now Altos has heard from his allies in Aurora that Solon has reinforcements coming in from Rois."

"Altos is friends with Aurora?"

"Apparently," Terena said, casting a quick glance back at the king. "Rydon said he sent some Liodari there to help against Heylisia. I think that's what Daris was doing in—"

"Lady Luca," the king called out, his voice booming across the room. Terena stiffened and pulled her hands away from Sonah. They walked back toward the men, Sonah a few paces behind her sister.

"Aye, Your Majesty?"

"Daris tells me you had a... vision? That you knew the oracle was in trouble."

Terena shifted and glanced at Daris. Her lips thinned, and she gave the king a curt nod.

"Aye."

The king walked toward her, stopping a few feet away. "General Peleon has her," he said, his voice rough. "And he knows you're here."

Sonah became lightheaded. She reached out a hand to Terena, her vision blurring.

Terena swore. "She must have told him."

"Aye," the king said, his gaze unfocused as he looked off into the distance. "That was my thought as well. He's looking to trade."

Sonah balked. "What? No!"

Terena held up a hand to her, her eyes on the king. Sonah turned to Daris, his face tight as he stared at Terena.

"I've told him you weren't here," the king sighed, "but it wasn't you he wanted to trade for."

Terena's hand shot out and grabbed Sonah's forearm. "He can't have her."

The king shook his head. "No, he didn't ask for Lady Yahn." He lifted his eyes to Terena at last.

"He wants the Shroud of Faybhen."

TERENA LAUGHED.

The sound echoed throughout the otherwise silent room, everyone watching her as if she'd lost her mind.

"Good! Give it to him," Terena said at last, waving her hand.

The king scowled at her, then glanced at Daris, his brow furrowed.

"I gave it to Duke Aurora," she added, when the king didn't respond.

"I know," said King Altos, "and the duke gave it to me."

"Ha!" Terena laughed. "Even better!"

"How is that better?" The king glared at her. "Do you know what the shroud is?"

"Of course I know what it is," she scoffed. "That's how I make—made—my living. That shroud is worthless."

The king crossed his arms at his chest. "That shroud—"

"Is fake."

Terena had a moment's satisfaction at the way the king's mouth dropped open, his face turning several shades of red. She winked at Daris who also looked like he'd been smacked in the face.

Terena shifted her weight and planted her hand on her hip while she waited for it to sink in.

"What do you mean?" the king asked slowly.

She gave him a knowing look. "Who do you think gave Duke Aurora the shroud?"

He frowned, annoyed. "I know it was you," he said. "You gave him a fake?"

"Aye," Terena said, preening. Then a thought occurred to her. "Wait. Why do *you* have it?"

"Never mind that," the king spat, his face thunderous. "You're telling me the Shroud of Faybhen is fake?"

Terena twisted her lips. "The one *you* have is fake, aye."

Daris wiped his hand over his mouth and looked up at the ceiling as he turned away.

"I need—" the king began, then stopped abruptly, hanging his head. Taking a quick step toward Terena, he jabbed a finger at her. "I needed that shroud! You do not know—"

"Why do you need it?"

The king's face became even more mottled. Terena glanced behind the man to his advisor, who watched them all with wide-eyed panic. The Captain of the Royal Guard shifted, his eyes on Terena.

"Would you leave us?" she called out to them. The advisor gawked at her while the captain ignored her. King Altos shifted his hard, dark brown eyes to them both and gave a quick wave of his hand. The advisor bolted for the doors. The captain stared at his king with a scowl before motioning to his men to follow, and they all quit the room.

When the loud thud of the doors closing faded, Terena shifted her gaze between the king and Daris and frowned. "You haven't told him?"

Daris cocked his head, his brow wrinkled.

Terena's head fell back. When she looked at King Altos again, it was through narrowed eyes.

"I think you know, or have suspicions, I am a god," she started. She saw the second she had his undivided attention. "I've learned my—our," she said with a wink at Sonah, "our father is the god of war. Ares."

The change in the room her words caused unnerved her. At first, the king looked at her as if he hadn't heard. Then his eyes rounded, his mouth going slack. He looked like someone had dumped a large sack of jewels at his feet.

His hand trembled as he lifted it first to his mouth, then, as if he didn't know what to do with it, smoothed it over the hair at his forehead. King Altos swiveled his eyes to Daris, who confirmed with a brief nod.

"So," Terena continued in the silence, "I, more than anyone, know what the shroud is. And I say again, the one you have is fake. So trade it for Pytho. Please."

The king did not speak, so Terena was compelled to add, "I'm assuming you needed the shroud for whatever Spartan prophecy you believe in. Hopefully, it had to do with me?"

"But... but..."

Terena was genuinely concerned now for the king. He seemed so out of sorts, she looked to Daris for help.

"You're the Heir?"

At his softly spoken question, Terena smiled thinly at him.

"The oracle—"

"Did he say anything about us?" she asked.

"What?"

Terena walked a few steps closer to the king. "Did Solon say anything about us?"

"Aye. But he's..." King Altos shook his head. "The messenger wanted to confirm the rumors he'd heard about you being here. I told him you were but that you'd left. And that's when he asked for the shroud."

"When do you need to respond? I'm assuming the messenger is

still here."

Altos nodded. "He's still here and I have until tomorrow to reply."

Terena turned to Daris. "Give him the shroud. Duke Aurora must have also given you the letter of authentication he'd drawn up and the only way to guarantee it is for him to take it north to open the portal which," she laughed and rubbed at her forehead before she looked over at the king with her hand out, "I don't think he'll ever do."

"There's something else," Altos said with a grimace. "We've received word from our allies in Heylisia the emperor is rounding up trackers. He's holding three of them so far. No one knows why."

Sonah gasped and Terena's heart skipped. Rydon had told them a while back the northern king was looking for trackers as well. That they were supposed to have powers like Terena. But whether or not they were gods or had powers gifted to them wasn't clear.

There was still so much she didn't know, but she wasn't going to volunteer the information to King Altos. Not until she was certain of his own motives.

That got her thinking about Bethana's fangs, and she pulled them out of her pocket.

Terena held up the pouch and tilted her head. "We'll have to worry about that later. For now, I have the item you requested, Your Majesty," she said with only a hint of a sneer. "But I'll need something else from you first."

She saw Daris stiffen.

The king folded his arms and waited.

"Why do you need them?" she asked.

Daris straightened as the king glanced at him. "They are said to have powerful magic," he hedged.

Terena waited for him to continue but he stared back at her, his face impassive.

She closed her eyes and sighed. When she looked at him again, she motioned with her hand. "Aye? What king of magic?"

"That's Spartan business."

Terena grinned. "Unbelievable." A second later, she tossed him the pouch, and he caught it awkwardly at the last moment. "Our bargain is complete, then. I'll be taking my sister and my leave of you, Your Majesty." This last she said with a deep, mocking bow.

Striding back to Sonah, Terena took hold of her hand and walked toward the door.

"Wait."

Terena bit back a smile and ducked her chin, waiting until she'd schooled her face into a blank mask before turning back to the king.

He glared at her for a moment, then exhaled. "'Lightning turns to ice, the ground lies frozen and the skies weep. Twenty-four moons and the Heir wields Athena's Weapon, leading her army of undead from the mouth of the serpent.'"

The hairs on the back of Terena's neck rose. It was as if someone had whispered a secret to her soul.

She stared at King Altos for a long time; her pulse was the only sound in her ears. An odd feeling flashed through her; not dread, exactly, but similar enough she cast a glance at Sonah to make sure she was all right.

"That's what the oracle told me," King Altos said, assuming her lack of comment was due to confusion. Terena knew those words, although she swore a minute before he spoke them she'd never heard them before.

Terena nodded slowly, thinking. "It was more than a year ago the north was devastated by some freak storms; weather anomalies changing the whole of the continent."

"Aye," King Altos said as he walked toward her.

Terena worked through the rest of what he'd said in her head. Two years after that freak storm she was supposed to wield Athena's Weapon. But the short swords Altos had given her were called The Twins.

She looked over at Daris.

The Spartans had called him 'Athena's Weapon'. Is that what Pytho meant? Was she supposed to use him to lead an undead army?

"Army of Undead from the mouth of the serpent," she said, her voice barely above a whisper as she shifted her gaze to Altos.

"Aye," he said, his lips pressed in a tight line. "That is when the oracle told me it would be you that brought me the fangs from the serpent."

She pointed at Daris. "And he's Athena's Weapon? Not The Twins you gave me?"

"I cannot say for certain," the King said. He clenched his fists at his sides, his mouth pinched. "I was to give you The Twins and have you retrieve the fangs. Beyond that..."

"Well," Terena sighed and let her head drop back, her eyes darting over the empty ceiling. She looked back at the king. "We have time, I guess. It hasn't yet been two years since the north froze." Her eyes widened. Terena lifted a hand to her mouth before she caught herself.

"What?"

She didn't know if this was something she should share. Telling them both about how Melanos told her she'd come into her full powers when she reached the age of twenty-two made her insides twist.

"Nothing," she answered at length, ducking her head. "Thank you for trusting me with the counsel you received from Pytho."

"She said it is the Spartan prophecy."

"Spartan prophecy," she repeated. That seemed oddly specific. Why not just 'that's the prophecy'?

"What will you do now," Daris asked, jarring her from her thoughts.

"I will," Terena glanced at Sonah, then dropped her eyes to the ground. "I'll head north. That was my plan all along."

Daris stared at her a moment longer before turning his eyes to his king. When the king nodded, Daris said to her, "We'd like you to come with us to Messene. To help with the oracle."

Terena balked. "I am *not* putting myself out there for my enemy, Daris," she hissed, shaking her head. She motioned to Sonah. "What of my family? I did my part. I got the fangs for you and I warned you about Pytho." She waved her hands. "You're the Liodari. You alone are enough to get her back."

He cocked his head. "We'll escort you north once we've reclaimed her," Daris said, taking a step closer. "To Seleste."

It took a few seconds for what he'd offered to register.

"Heylisia and its provinces are at war, Terena," he added, taking another step closer. "We can get you there safely."

"Why?"

"Because Daris will stay with you once you get there," King Altos snapped.

"W<small>HAT</small>? W<small>HY</small>?"

"Your questions are beginning to annoy," the king said with an arched eyebrow. "Understand, it is because of who you are and what you mean to Sparta I am as patient as I have been. But even my patience has a limit, lady. I am sending my most valuable warrior to what could be a rival king, and that is *only* because of who you are."

Daris shifted his gaze between Terena and his king. Altos stopped a foot away from Terena, hands at his hips.

"Solon may be fighting his own provinces right now, but make no mistake. He will come for us, and when he does, he will have weapons made for gods in his possession. This invasion will not be the last. He has other trackers now, so he no longer needs you."

"He doesn't *need* me," Terena scoffed. "He wants to kill me!"

"And he will have his allies from Rois," the king added, ignoring her. "Daris will ensure you return when the time comes for you to help lead our army."

Terena balked. "Return? I—"

"Aye," the king snarled, lunging forward. His face was inches from Terena and Daris's skin prickled as if insects raced across his body. He moved close to Terena's side and stared back at King Altos when the man's shocked eyes swung to him. He realized with shock his hand gripped his sword. Something in his head was screaming at him he was close to drawing down on his sovereign. All because of how the king had leaned in too close, threatening her.

Daris's blood rose to flood his face as his hand slowly fell away. He dropped his hands to clench at his sides.

When the king finally turned back to Terena, Daris closed his eyes. He willed his heart to stop its erratic pounding, the need to spill his king's blood over the threat he posed to Terena still so strong Daris panicked for a second. Had his desire for this woman so overpowered his loyalty to his king? Is this what he'd been reduced to?

Years of loyal service now rendered meaningless because of this woman.

"You may be a god, the daughter of Ares, but all that means is you no longer have agency. You are not for yourself anymore, Terena Luca. You are for *us*. You were promised, you are the one fated to bring back the Olympians and if there's ever a time we need their help, *your* help, it is now."

"You think you can control me?" Terena asked softly.

Daris tensed, warring with his own body to keep his hands from unsheathing his sword.

What was wrong with him?

"Stop!" Sonah cried out, her voice shaking, yet strong. Daris took a step back, snapping out of the mind fog that had replaced his common sense.

She put a hand on Terena's arm and looked at King Altos. "Must I make another deal to get you both to calm down?"

King Altos cast a wry glance as he stepped away from Terena.

"I'm sorry," Terena said at last. Daris assumed she was speaking to her sister.

"I think it's a good idea to have an escort of the most powerful warriors in Elysium," Sonah said, her voice pitched low yet Daris heard. "Daris is right. If the entire continent's at war, how are we to make it to the north without help?"

"I made a promise, Sonah," Terena said, her voice as soft. "I have to go back for Melanos."

"We'll come with you," Daris said and both women's eyes shot to him. Terena looked annoyed but Sonah beamed.

"There!" she said, waving a hand at him. "We'll go together to Melanos and then bring him with us to rescue Pytho. Who is Melanos?"

"He is the god from what we'd thought was a myth," said Terena dryly. "I'll tell you later."

Turning back to King Altos, she frowned.

"If we have another god with us," Terena groused, "why would we still need the Liodari to escort us north? Melanos is plenty to frighten anyone with a design on us."

"You assume he'll go with you," Daris replied. "You wish to bring back the Olympians. One of those Olympians is why he was stuck in that cave for more than a thousand years and why his lover is a giant snake."

"So?"

"He's right, Terena," Sonah said, tugging at her sister's wrist. "What will it hurt to have them come with us north? We'll get what we need up there and come back." She tightened her grip on Terena's sleeve until she turned to her sister. "It's the right thing to do."

Daris watched the exchange between the women, his eyes resting at last on Terena's face, his chest tightening as her face relaxed and her beautiful eyes shone bright.

Terena groaned loudly and waved at King Altos. "Fine. But I have a promise to fulfill first." She turned to Daris and he straightened. "We'll meet you in Messene in a ten days."

CHAPTER THIRTY-EIGHT

Without the Liodari, Terena and the others returned to Melanos much faster this time.

The sun was high in the sky when they finally reached Melanos's cave. The wind whipped at her cloak as Terena hopped off Nyx. She called out to Croak to stay with the horses. Rydon came to her side as they walked off toward the cave entrance.

"What? Why always me?"

"I'm coming with you!" Sonah yelled and Terena turned her head in time to see Sonah racing to catch up.

"I'll stay with the whelp," Gabriol called out.

Taking her time, Terena cautiously walked through the dark entrance. Inside, she saw a much tamer scene than the one she and the others had initially witnessed when they had met Melanos.

As Rydon and Sonah came up behind her, she heard Sonah's gasp. White columns surrounded the large room, transforming the cave into a beautiful outdoor ballroom. Every variety of rose imaginable adorned the room, and thick garlands stretched across the columns. A canopy of sheer fabric covered the cave, concealing the starry sky above them. Guests took advantage of the many areas for privacy provided by large oak and black pine trees along the edges of the cave.

"Come on," Terena said with a smile as she tugged at Sonah's cuff. Sonah gawked a few more seconds before following Terena and Rydon, stumbling once because she was paying more attention to the people than she was where she stepped.

A few people were laughing, sitting on large pillows and plush ottomans beneath a willow in a far corner. As Terena drew closer, her eyes widened and she stopped, moving fast to cover Sonah's eyes with her hand.

"Melanos!"

The deity was reclining on the floor, kissing one woman, while another crouched near his stomach, her head bobbing in a rhythmic motion. When Terena bellowed his name, Melanos lazily tore his lips away from the woman and stared at them for a moment before recognition dawned. Sonah squawked at her side, clawing at Terena's hand.

The scene disappeared and Melanos strode toward them fully clothed, thank the gods.

Terena lowered her hand from Sonah's eyes and the girl got her first look at the enormous god. He stopped a few feet away, a huge grin on his face as he folded his arms at his chest.

"I knew you couldn't stay away," he laughed.

"I told you I'd be back," Terena snapped.

"Where did all the people go?" Sonah asked, glancing around.

"Would you like me to bring them back, little one? I can—"

"No!" Terena yelled, lunging with an arm out toward Melanos. His deep laughter rang through the cave, and Sonah moved closer to Terena's side.

"Can you please," she said with a sigh and closed her eyes for a second, "can you please not corrupt my sister? We came back to get you out of here."

At her words, the big man arched a sandy eyebrow at her, then shifted his gaze to Sonah.

"Another daughter of Ares?"

Sonah watched him silently, but Terena nodded. "Aye."

The god inclined his head and winked at Sonah. "It is a pleasure to meet you."

Sonah was too awed to say anything until Terena nudged her. Her lips formed an O and then she blinked at Melanos. "The pleasure is mine, Melanos," she said as she curtsied.

"None of that now." Melanos waved his hand, but Terena saw the color blooming in his cheeks. He turned his bright grey eyes to Terena. "And have you figured out how to do it correctly this time?"

Terena shrugged. "No. I mean, it's not like I have a bunch of divine advisors to help with this sort of stuff, but I'm hoping, now I'm fully healed, it might work."

Melanos stared back at her for a moment before giving her a sharp nod and clapping his hands. "Let's go then. I'm ready."

Rydon led the way to the entrance, followed by Terena with Melanos behind her. She reached back to take hold of his hand when he stopped before the dark passage, his body stiff.

Taking a few steps back, Terena saw the god's startled expression as he looked behind him. Sonah stood behind Melanos, and Terena strained to see what was happening. In the passage's gloom and with his enormous frame blocking everything behind him, Terena opened her mouth to speak when she heard her sister.

"Don't be afraid," Sonah was saying. "It's all right."

Terena stilled. The god turned back to face her and motioned her forward. Walking, she reached back to grasp his hand again, and this time, he didn't let go.

Her heart raced as she made it outside, the light blinding, and she raised a hand to shield her eyes. She turned to look at Melanos.

Sure enough, Melanos stood at the cave entrance, dropping Terena's hand to squint up at the bright sun. He hesitated, then took a step forward, and Terena's tears stung as she saw his face. A moment more and he was on his knees, tears falling freely as he stared in wide-eyed wonder at the world. Sonah stepped up beside him, pulling her hand from his and laid it on his shoulder. He turned his head up to her, laying his large hand over hers as he stared back at her, mute. Sonah beamed at him, laughter bubbling out of her and Melanos joined her, his laughter ringing out around them, boisterous and wet with choking sobs.

Melanos's joy filled the air and birds took flight. Terena's chest was so full she thought she might burst, so happy they had done something on this trip that had her feeling this good. She looked over her shoulder at Rydon, who had come up behind her and clasped her shoulders in his hands, shaking her. His jaw tightened as if he was holding back his own emotions while he watched the god laugh.

"It worked," Croak said in awe as he walked up to her left, and she turned when she saw Gabriol come up beside him. She turned back to Melanos and Sonah, the fullness in her chest threatening to burst her heart as she looked at Sonah's wide smile.

Melanos ducked his head at last, lifting his hands to cover his face, and Sonah gave him a quick squeeze before she skipped to Terena. Fresh tears blurred Terena's vision.

Impulsively, she grabbed her sister in a big hug, kissing the top of her head.

"Thank the gods something went right," Rydon said, his voice gruff.

"Looks like you were right," Gabriol said and smacked her shoulder. "You needed to fully heal. I'm glad we came back."

"So am I," Terena said.

"Big man," Croak taunted, "Ready to go or still crying?"

Sonah gasped and Rydon slammed his hand between Croak's shoulder blades. Croak yowled as Rydon and Gabriol walked to the horses. Sonah glanced back at Melanos before following.

Terena walked over to Melanos, crouching down at his side. "Do you need more time?"

Melanos shook his head, his face still hidden in his hands. At last he dropped them and exhaled, his face red and his eyes puffy, but he was still smiling. "No. I'm ready. Let's get away from this cave and never return."

A FEW MILES AWAY FROM WHERE THEY WERE TO MEET DARIS AND THE other Liodari in Messene, Terena slowed Nyx to walk. Rydon was at her side and he whistled, Gabriol looking over his shoulder at them before clicking his tongue and pulling on the reins to slow his horse. The others slowed as well.

They had no horse for Melanos, but Sonah had volunteered to ride with him. They looked ridiculous. Terena sympathized with Sonah's horse; the giant god dwarfed both the beast and Sonah. But Sonah had only smiled happily and rested her head against Melanos's back as they rode. Terena suspected she much preferred sitting back and letting someone else do the work.

Before setting off for Messene, Terena had filled Melanos in on where they were going and why. Melanos had volunteered to join them. Once more, he reiterated his opinions on Pytho, but even he could not stand by while a child of Apollo was so blasphemed.

"Rider," Gabriol called out, and Terena's pulse skittered. She tightened her hands on the reins, straightening as she spotted the rider wearing Liodari colors. They urged their mounts into a trot, meeting the rider as he slowed.

The sun sat low on the horizon, bathing the landscape in rich oranges and deep blues, limning the rider in gold and hiding his face from view. As he urged his horse closer, Sonah gasped behind her, a bright smile on her face.

"Jason!"

The Liodari grinned when he caught sight of Sonah, and Terena smothered a smile. She saw Rydon and Gabriol exchanging smirks while Croak made a retching sound.

"Well met," Jason said, his eyes crinkling. He nodded at Melanos and put his hand over his heart. "My lord. Looks like she figured out how to free you. Thank the gods you came, too. With three gods on our side, we won't be as easy to intimidate as Solon thought."

"He's here?" Terena's heart missed a beat.

"No, no," Jason said hurriedly, holding out a hand to her. "Apologies, that's not what I meant. Well... you'll see. Come. Commander Antonius awaits you below. We've camped outside of the city."

They crested the hill and saw the tents dotting the field, a large one at the center. More soldiers in Spartan colors stood in groups amongst the Liodari but Terena did not see Daris.

"How long have you been here?" Croak asked.

Jason shrugged. "We arrived last night. We've had scouts out this way, looking out for your arrival. Happy coincidence, it was my turn."

Terena was watching him when he winked at Sonah.

"And when are we making the trade?" Terena asked.

"The commander should've sent a messenger as soon as my arrow was spotted."

"Arrow?"

"Aye," he said as he glanced back at Terena. "One arrow to signal your return."

"Have you seen the oracle?" Rydon asked, nudging his mount closer to Jason.

"Not yet. We've sent scouts, though. The commander will update you."

They rode in silence until they reached the camp. Three men came forward to take their horses away to be cared for, while the rest of them followed Jason into Daris's tent.

The interior was sparse, with a cot to the side and a small collapsable table where four men stood, three of them with their backs to the opening. When Terena saw Daris, his usual impassive mask slipped and his lips tugged up in a smile before he schooled his face and he was the Commander once more.

"So this is where the party's at," Croak said, folding his arms as he stood with legs braced next to Terena.

"Melanos!" Daris's face lit up when he spotted the god. He came around the table to greet him. Melanos held out his arm and Daris clasped it with a grin. "You're out. How do you feel?"

Melanos made a sound and leaned back, his eyes landing on Terena. "Ask me in a few days. I might have recovered from the shock by then."

Daris made quick introductions and Terena and the others clasped each man's arm.

"Have you heard anything?" Rydon asked as he released the arm of the Spartan army captain, Linos Athanasi. He looked to be older than Daris but not by much. Ten years at most was Terena's guess as she took in the slight wrinkles at the corners of his mouth and eyes. He had thick brows atop deep-set brown eyes that made him seem angry even when he was smiling.

"No, not yet," Daris replied, "although I hadn't expected to hear so quickly. I sent a messenger earlier telling them we'd meet them at dawn for the exchange."

"You're not worried they'll just send troops in to take it from us?" Croak snorted.

Daris spared him a glance, then walked back to where he'd been standing when they first came in. "I'd love to see it. Especially with you here." He motioned to Terena and Melanos.

"Let's not forget this little spitfire," Croak said as he hooked an arm over Sonah's neck and dropped a kiss on her head.

"Have you seen her?" Terena asked.

Daris gazed at her for a moment before shaking his head. "My men haven't seen the oracle, no. But they've locked up her Magi. One escaped. We're not sure where he is, but he wouldn't leave his priest-ess, so he must be nearby."

Terena thought back to the Magi she'd seen in Pytho's temple; the same man who had stood off in the distance while she and Croak had killed his men in Agraboda.

No, she thought. *The Magi would not leave Pytho.*

"So, what's your plan?" Rydon asked, his arms stretching his tunic as he crossed his arms.

Daris shifted his eyes to Rydon before looking at Terena. "Terena, Melanos and I will—"

"And me," Rydon grunted.

Daris sighed. "We'll go make the trade. A guard of four will travel with us, and Captain Athanasi will have his men positioned here." Daris pointed at a spot on the map in front of them. "I'll have Gabriol join them," Rydon said as Gabriol moved closer.

"Fine," Daris said with a nod as he continued to regard the map. "Since they have most of their men posted here, the captain will ensure our archers target them." Looking up and around at the others, Daris's eyes landed on Sonah. "Sonah—"

"Sonah will stay back," Terena said firmly. Sonah did not contradict her.

"And when we have Pytho?" Rydon asked after a pause.

"We take Messene."

CHAPTER THIRTY-NINE

Messene differed vastly from their last visit. The legion of soldiers lining the streets as Terena and Daris led the way into the heart of the city was a big reason. Another was the fact none of the citizens so happily thronging the streets on their previous visit were anywhere in sight.

They neared the main square, soldiers watching them as they dismounted and brought their horses to a hitching post.

Feeling better knowing they'd have protection, Terena still worried for Sonah and Croak back at camp. Daris had assured her before they left that Jason and a hand selected group of Liodari would guard them.

Terena's stomach sank when they stopped in front of a group of Heylisian soldiers and they parted to reveal General Peleon.

He sneered at them, his hawkish nose looking even bigger than she remembered, his eyes like slits. Terena kept her face blank. Daris and Rydon flanked her, with Melanos a few steps behind and the Liodari at their backs. Peleon stared at her a long while before spitting on the ground. Without a word, he motioned with his hand behind him and the soldiers parted again.

Two people were brought forward, hoods over their heads, one of them struggling against the grip of a massive soldier while the other was hunched and broken. Terena knew right away from the soiled robes the smaller figure was Pytho, so different now from the ethereal woman she'd met months ago.

Terena's hands dropped to her sides, her thumbs tracing the pommels of her short swords. Her face heated, and she pinched her lips when Pytho was thrown roughly to the ground.

"Such a fucking coward, Peleon," Terena seethed, taking a step forward. The guards closest to Peleon reached for their swords.

"Can't say I'm surprised to see you here," Peleon spat again, his eyes narrowed so far she wondered if he could see her at all. "Hiding behind the Liodari isn't going to save you."

Daris stiffened at her side. She gave the general a nasty smile. "I'm going to enjoy killing you."

Peleon continued to sneer at her, but didn't rise to her taunt. He turned his head to the men guarding Pytho and the other prisoner. The guards removed their hoods and Terena cursed inwardly to see the young acolyte, David, with Pytho. He had a large bruise on the left side of his face and blood crusted his mouth. His clothes were filthy, like Pytho's, and Terena wondered if Peleon had even bothered to allow them to bathe or change their clothes since their capture.

Knowing what an asshole he was, Terena doubted it.

"Where's the shroud?"

"I'll give it to you after you release them," Terena said, feigning boredom.

"Oh, no, tracker scum," Peleon said and clicked his tongue. "Only this bitch is being traded. This bitch," Peleon said as he grabbed David by the back of his neck and shoved him to the ground, "is incentive."

"What?"

He unsheathed a dagger inside his cloak and Terena quickly pulled out her short swords. Peleon grabbed a fistful of David's hair and yanked his head back. The acolyte inhaled sharply as the general put the dagger to his throat.

Looking across at Terena, his face dark, Peleon roared, "Where is the shroud?"

"Fuck, there's no need to shout! I have your shroud," she said as she turned to Melanos, who produced a small rucksack. Taking the bag from him, Terena raised it, shaking it for Peleon's benefit. "See? Put the dagger away."

"Bring it here."

"Fuck that," Terena snorted. Her eyes sparkled as she gave him a flirty smile. "You come get it."

He stared at her, his face going slack.

Then he slit David's throat.

Pytho cried out, her shrieks drowning out Rydon's curse, and Terena lunged forward, ready to strike Peleon down. The soldiers on either side of them dropped to a knee, lifting shields as the row of archers behind them trained arrows on Terena. Swords unsheathed behind her, the Liodari readying for an attack.

"Understand now?"

"You fucking—"

"Enough!" Peleon shouted, his face mottled. Behind him, two men wearing cloaks and plain trousers, their black shirts opened at the throat to reveal a jangle of pendants hanging off of silver and gold chains, stepped forward.

"Cyphers," Melanos hissed as the cloaked men spread their arms. Their pendants glowed.

"What's that?" Terena asked, turning to look at Melanos over her shoulder.

"Mortals with powers gifted by the Olympians. Those pendants are runes imbued with those powers. And there are two of them."

Like the woman in Sparta that had attacked her and Rydon.

Well. Fuck.

Terena stared at the cyphers. She took a step forward. Daris's hand shot out, grabbing her elbow. "I'll take it," he said, pulling her close. His eyes were inches from hers. "I don't want you giving Peleon a chance to take you."

She was about to argue when Melanos's large hand gripped her shoulder. "I agree. Let the commander go."

Terena hesitated, then gave Daris the bag with the shroud. Daris stared at her a moment more before striding toward Peleon.

"Here it is," he said, holding the bag up when he stood a few feet from the general. "Now give me the oracle."

Peleon did not respond as he watched Daris step closer. He snatched the bag and Daris darted for Pytho, his hand outstretched.

Terena watched Peleon the whole time and saw the moment his face changed. Her hand shot out, and she opened her mouth to scream a warning, but no sound came out.

Peleon lunged, stabbing Daris in the face.

CHAOS ERUPTED.

Terena ran for Daris. Pytho crouched on the ground near him with Peleon screaming at his soldiers to attack.

Rydon dove for the men on their left, grunting as an arrow slammed into his shoulder. He roared, dropping to one knee. A soldier attacked on his right, and he thrust forward, snarling as he embedded his sword in the man's leg. The Liodari engaged as well. They fought fast and fierce, but the Heylisian soldiers were faster, stronger.

Another soldier approached Rydon from the left. He gained his feet and stumbled, yanking his sword free of the man's leg when the earth shook.

His eyes fixed on Terena, an eerie glow overtaking her eyes. Light arced back and forth over her short swords, revealing symbols etched into the blades he hadn't known were there. She moved like lightning, her swords invisible as they cut through the soldiers closest to her, the speed with which she attacked impossible.

He turned, intending to reach the oracle before Peleon. His steps faltered when he saw a man dressed in flowing black breeches and tunic with a matching hood raise his scimitar and cut down a guard standing behind Pytho. That must be the missing Magi.

Rydon heard a grunt behind him and he rolled to his left, spinning in time to block the blow almost taking his head from his shoulders. He blinked up at Melanos as he grabbed the soldier's head and twisted. The man fell to the ground. Melanos whipped a dagger at another soldier over Rydon's shoulder.

Melanos winked at him as he passed, his movements fluid and graceful for such a large man. Rydon gained his feet, running for Terena. She was hacking away at the men guarding Peleon, her swords an extension of her arms as she slashed and spun, dropping the soldiers with ease.

Rydon knelt at Daris's side. Pytho cried as the Magi cut at her bound hands as they reached for Daris. He lay unmoving in her lap. Glancing over at Terena, Rydon saw her stalking the general; her steps were slow and deliberate as the man stood behind the last cypher.

"Don't!" Peleon screamed, the sword he held up toward her shaking. "Let me go or I'll have the—"

Terena twisted her wrist, stabbing her sword in the ground. Her hand shot back out so fast Rydon barely registered the motion. The cypher rose in the air as Terena approached. She made a fist and yanked, tearing the cypher's throat out before he fell. Peleon made a strangled noise, his wild eyes darting from the dead cypher to Terena. His face shook and he whimpered, waving his sword at her.

Rydon turned to Daris and his heart stopped.

"No," he whispered as he shoved his fingers into the commander's neck. "No, no Daris, no, not now."

"He's dead," the oracle cried, her chest heaving as she slumped back, covering her face with shaking hands. The Magi hovered over her, his eyes catching Rydon's.

"Terena!" Rydon roared. He turned back to Daris. General Peleon had stabbed him in the eye, the dagger still embedded deep, and blood poured from the wound down his cheek and into his hair. Someone shoved Rydon from behind and he whipped his head up to see Jason bending over him, his face white.

"No," Jason said, shaking his head as his mouth opened and closed again and again. Out of the corner of his eye, Rydon saw movement and turned to see Terena running to them. He yanked the dagger out, not wanting Terena to see it, and rose unsteadily.

The sounds of battle died down, a few shouts or cries snuffed out as Spartan soldiers poured in, killing off the remaining Heylisians alongside the Liodari.

Rydon's shoulders were heavy as he watched Terena slow, her steps faltering as she stared down wide-eyed at Daris's lifeless body. A small circle of Liodari formed around them, the despair and shock on the men's faces reflected in Terena's eyes.

"What... why isn't he moving?" Terena asked, her voice shaking as she dropped to her knees beside him. Rydon looked away, his eyes aimless as he glanced at the surrounding carnage. He saw Peleon ride off with a handful of his men.

"Daris," Terena choked, her hands on Daris's chest, shaking him. "Daris! You can't die. You can't die!"

The cry torn from her was primal, and it scared Rydon. She'd already lost her prince. To lose Daris now...

Terena buried her head in his neck and sobbed. Rydon was helpless. Standing there watching her break all over again was gut-wrenching.

"I need you," Terena sobbed, "please don't leave me. Not when I just found you again. Please."

Rydon raised his eyes, finding Melanos, who watched the scene with a scowl.

"He's not dead," the god said, stopping a few feet behind Pytho.

"He took a dagger to his head," Rydon snapped.

"You took a dagger to the heart; you're not dead," Melanos scoffed as he motioned at Rydon with his hand.

There was movement near his foot, and Rydon looked down to see Daris's fingers twitch. Rydon jolted, his hand snapping out and catching Jason's arm as he stared down at Daris. The commander's head moved so slightly he would've missed it had he not been so focused on him. Then Daris's hand reached up to stroke Terena's hair.

Terena pulled back, her face streaked with tears and snot as she blinked at Daris, the lid of his good eye fluttering open.

"How?" she asked so softly Rydon barely heard it.

Melanos looked at her as if she'd asked something idiotic.

"He's Eudaemon."

CHAPTER FORTY

Terena's knee bounced as she sat next to Daris's cot in his tent. She could hear the murmur of voices around them, but her eyes never left his face while he slept.

The tent flap rustled, and Terena glanced up to see Sonah, her hands clasped around a bowl.

"You need to eat," she whispered as she inched closer. An owl hooted as the flap dropped. The lantern on the table cast a weak light in the tent, and for the first time since they'd gotten back to the camp, Terena wondered how late it was.

She gave Sonah a tired smile. Kneeling beside her, Sonah sighed and set the bowl on the ground.

"How is he?" she asked after a while.

Terena gazed at Daris. The army surgeon had tended the wound, dressing it with a bandage wound around his head, covering the damaged eye. Terena's breath hitched as she thought of how he'd looked. His beautiful blue eye gone and in its place a hole surrounded by ridged, angry flesh and blood. She had looked away as she lifted his hand to her lips, muttering nonsense to herself. Prayers and bargains to the gods.

"Pytho made him a potion that seems to help," she answered at last.

She reached out to brush his short hair back from his forehead. "He was in so much pain."

"I heard Melanos say Daris is like Rydon. A Eudaemon."

"Aye."

"How? I mean... did you know?"

Terena looked at her with a frown. "I would've told you, had I known."

Sonah dropped her chin and nodded.

They sat in silence for a few minutes, Sonah looking at her hands while Terena continued to stare at Daris, her eyes dropping to his chest to watch him breathing.

"Good," Pytho said as she poked her head inside the tent. She came inside and around to Sonah's side as she peered down at Daris. "He's still asleep."

"Pytho, how is it you didn't know he was Eudaemon?" Sonah asked, her tone curious.

Pytho shrugged. "I see only what the Fates allow me to see."

"How is it that Melanos knew?" Terena asked, her voice sharper than she'd intended.

The oracle raised her black eyes and stared at Terena with sadness. "He is a god," she said after a few moments. "He must sense it."

"Aye," Sonah said while shifting her legs beneath her. "He told Rydon he thought we knew, because we all traveled together. He knew when you were all at the cave."

"He must be your Eudaemon, then," Terena said. The pang of jealousy sparking in her chest making her feel like the worst sister in the world. She did not begrudge Sonah having her own immortal bodyguard, but she was still nettled Daris was hers.

"So it's a good thing then he's going north with us," she replied, cautiously excited. Terena gave her a look.

"I don't know he'll be fit to go," Terena said.

Pytho looked uncomfortable and Terena noticed.

"What?" Terena asked, her eyes narrowing.

Pytho started, her eyes widening before she whiffled her head. "What? Nothing."

Terena shifted, her eyes locked on the oracle. "What are you not saying?"

"Terena please," she said, her voice low. "I already told you more than I should have and look what happened. The gods punished me for overstepping."

"Well, can you at least tell me if he'll travel with us?"

Pytho looked wretched, her gaze swinging between Terena and Sonah, searching for words.

"No, he will not."

Terena's skin prickled. Something shifted inside of her. "Why?"

Pytho shook her head and splayed her hands. "I cannot say, Terena."

"If he's bound to Sonah," she bit out, "he should go with us."

The pained look on Pytho's face made Terena back down. She sighed, pulling her hand out of Daris's. She dug the heels of her hands into her eyes, hoping to bully her growing headache into going away.

"I have a potion that will help," Pytho said.

"Thank you, Pytho," she said. The poor woman had been through so much herself. She didn't deserve to be badgered into sharing celestial secrets. She was right. Look what had happened already because she'd shared more than she should have.

Pytho stood there for a long moment and Terena looked over. The woman was looking at Sonah with something like pride before she shifted her gaze to Terena. As soon as the oracle caught her gaze, she quickly left the tent. A few minutes later, Sonah stood, muttering to Terena about letting the food get cold before she, too, left the tent.

Silence fell when she was once more alone with Daris sleeping at her side, settling her. Terena sighed and dropped her head, then stood up, stretching and wincing as her body protested. Her muscles ached from sitting in one attitude for so long. It had been a while, too, since she'd eaten and she cast a longing look at the small bowl Sonah had brought her.

The sideboard off to her left near the foot of the cot Daris slept on held various tinctures and rolled up bits of cloth she'd used to wipe Daris's blood.

But it also held a decanter of wine.

Her steps were heavy as they carried her closer, and she sighed, exhaustion settling on her shoulders. She lifted the decanter and an empty goblet and filled it to the brim. As she lifted it to her lips, she paused. Terena glanced over at Daris, his chest rising and falling slowly.

Rydon's blood had brought her back from the brink of death, allowing her wounds to heal much faster than if she'd relied on healing ointments or poultices.

Maybe if she gave Daris her blood...

Before she could think more on it, Terena set the glass down and unsheathed the dagger at her chest. Slicing it across her palm, she winced as she fisted her hand over the wineglass, watching as the blood dripped and mixed with the wine. She swirled the cup and carried it over to the stool she'd been using all day, slowly settling herself on it as she stared at Daris's closed eye.

Not wanting to wake him, she set the goblet down beside her and took his hands in hers once more.

THE THROBBING IN HIS HEAD WOKE DARIS. IT WAS AS IF HIS BRAIN WAS on fire. He groaned, lifting a hand to his head, but soft fingers coiled around his wrist, and he stilled.

One eye fluttered open, and he blinked a few times to focus. His right eye wouldn't open.

"Terena?"

The smile she gave him sent a wave of warmth over his chest, and he exhaled.

"Aye," she whispered. A watery sheen blurred her eyes and her chin wobbled. "How do you feel?"

He groaned. "Like my head is splitting open."

She flinched, covering it with an unamused chuckle. "Well. Good thing I have just the remedy for it." She bent over, her eyes falling away, and the absence of them hit him in his gut. She lifted a goblet in his line of sight and he narrowed his eye. "Wine? Really? I thought you knew by now I don't drink."

"I know," she said with a rueful smile as she held it out once more. "Which is another thing I want to know about but right now, I'll need you to forget it's wine and just drink."

Still, he hesitated. "What's in it?"

The left side of her beautiful mouth lifted in a genuine smile. "Wine with some extra special medicine for the Commander of the Liodari."

Terena moved, her right hand tucking under his head as she lifted him enough to drink. She held the goblet to his lips, and he brought his hand up to cover hers as he took a sip.

He made a face and looked back at her.

"Ugh," he said, his lips twisted. "That's awful."

"Well, it's not supposed to be good. I don't know any medicine that tastes good, Daris. Now, stop being a baby and drink up."

He tried to scrunch his face, but the motion only made his head ache even more, so he drank the rest and sighed when she let his head lower back to the pillow.

Silence settled and Daris closed his eye again, then frowned.

"What happened?"

Terena's breath was shaky, and he opened his eye again to look at her. A tear fell and she quickly swiped it away.

"I mean… where do I start?"

"How about why the hell my eye won't open? Did something happen? I remember nothing after I gave Peleon the shroud."

Terena was quiet for so long, a strange sense of wrongness settled in his bones. Maybe it was the tincture she'd given him, but his gut roiled.

"Peleon," she started, then dropped her chin and sighed before she looked back at him. "Peleon stabbed you. In the eye. As soon as you reached for Pytho."

Daris jolted. He lifted his hand to touch the cloth over his ruined eye and tried to sit up too fast. He cried out at the sharp stab of ice hot pain that almost split his head. Terena put a hand to his shoulder, her grip firm as she leaned closer.

"Don't," she said, her voice pained. "Please. Can you please be calm?"

Daris's pulse raced, and his breath quickened. The nausea from a moment ago was back in full force, and he thought he might embarrass himself by retching in front of her.

"Daris," she said soothingly. "Calm down or you'll hurt yourself. I can have Pytho bring you the sleeping potion she made for you. Do you want that?"

He clutched her hand, willing his stomach to calm, willing his heart and his breathing to calm.

"No," he said. Daris swallowed, then took in a deep breath, letting it out slowly. "No, don't leave."

"Never," she whispered.

His eye widened and they stared at each other for a long moment before she smiled.

"What else happened?"

Terena blinked. *"That's* your question? I just told you that weasel stabbed you in the eye and you want to know what else happened?"

He frowned but said nothing as he waited.

Terena scratched at her nose and then lifted her hand. "Let's see. You died. A battle broke out. We killed these fuckers called cyphers—wait till I tell you about those guys—and we took back Messene. Oh, and Peleon got away because, of course, he's a snake and they always land on their feet... belly, I mean. You get it."

Daris stared at her for so long she fidgeted. "I didn't die."

She scoffed, but it sounded more like a choked sob. His eye narrowed as she wiped at her eyes again. Terena nodded, her eyes sad. "Aye, Daris. You died. I saw you."

Daris looked away, his heart squeezing tight at the look on her face. "I have to tell you something."

"What? That you're Eudaemon?"

Daris's eye whipped back to her and his mouth went slack. She smirked at his expression.

"Melanos told us."

"How does—"

Terena shook her head and laughed. "He's a god?" She shrugged. "He said he thought we knew."

Daris opened his mouth to say more when the tent flap rustled. A second later, Pytho appeared, carrying a cup.

Terena twisted to see, smiling when she saw the oracle.

"I've brought more of the sleeping draft," Pytho said in a low voice as she held out the cup. Terena stood, and as her hand slipped from his, Daris tightened his grip before her fingers left his.

Turning back, Terena smiled at him. "I'll let you get some rest." She walked past Pytho, laying her hand on the woman's shoulder as she did so.

The moment she was gone, Pytho turned back to him, uncertain. He watched as she looked at him, then turned away. He remained silent, letting her decide. She took a tentative step toward the stool Terena had vacated.

Setting the cup on the ground at her side, she gave Daris an awkward smile. "How are you feeling?"

He was about to remark about his head aching and the fact he'd lost an eye, but he paused, frowning. The sharp pain piercing back and forth across his head was no longer there. Even the tightness around the wound at his eye socket no longer bothered him. He was still tired, but every moment that passed, he became stronger.

Terena's tonic was potent.

"I feel much better, thank you," he said at length, smiling at the oracle.

She smiled back, but it was tight and her black eyes darted around. They were unnerving to look at.

"I will leave soon," she said, her words measured. He watched her but said nothing.

"I...," her mouth opened and shut until she exhaled loudly. "There are forces at work here that will do everything in their power to keep you apart," she said at last, and Daris stilled. He had a feeling from the way she spoke she was choosing her words with care. "When you are better," she turned to look at him finally, "you will travel north, with Terena and Sonah?"

At his nod, Pytho pursed her lips and dropped her gaze to her clasped hands. "Whatever happens, you need to bring Sonah back to Sparta."

Chills arced up his spine. A moment passed in silence and then he turned, inching his body up, and with a grimace and Pytho's help, he sat up. He let one leg drop to the ground and brought his other down before he looked back at Pytho with a frown.

"What are you saying? What have you seen?"

She loosed a shaky sigh and rubbed at her forehead, her strange black eyes hidden by an equally shaky hand. Dropping her hand, she said, "Just... bring Sonah back with you. It's the only way Terena will return."

Daris whipped his hand out, holding her wrist, and she gasped. He leaned forward. "Tell me."

The oracle stood and Daris had no choice but to drop his hold on her. She turned as if to leave, then turned back and held her hand out to him once more. "You'll know when. Whatever happens, you must bring Sonah back, or you will never see Terena again."

Without another word, Pytho darted out of the tent, taking his breath with her.

A FEW DAYS LATER, MELANOS LEFT WITH PYTHO AND HER MAGI. THEY had formed a semi-circle around them as they said their goodbyes. Pytho had held on to Gabriol longer than seemed appropriate, and Terena arched an eyebrow at Rydon, who shrugged. When Gabriol pulled back, Pytho whispered something to him that made him stiffen, then nod. The moment was forgotten when Melanos came forward to thump Gabriol on the back. Terena had asked Melanos if he'd like to go north with them, but the god had laughed.

"I do not wish to offend you, Terena," Melanos had said with a wry smile. "But I have no desire to see the Olympians return. For obvious reasons. Besides, after I see the oracle safely back to her temple, I've a mind to find Bethana."

"What of Poseidon's curse?" Croak had asked.

Melanos had winked at Terena. "Perhaps my new friend will figure a way to break that curse as well."

Terena wound her way through the tents, pondering Melanos's words. Could she break Poseidon's curse and return Bethana to her nymph form? Part of her wanted to test the theory, but she also knew finding the northern god king might help her odds.

The late afternoon sun was amazing on her back. A cool autumn breeze whipped her face and her eyes watered. Finding herself at the edge of the camp, Terena turned when she heard grunting a few feet away. Frowning, she walked toward the sound.

She paused when she spotted Daris swinging his sword. It had been days since she'd given him the blood tonic. When she'd gone to see him the following day, she had been turned away by two Liodari she didn't know. After tracking down Jason, she'd been shocked and hurt to hear Daris had left instructions he didn't want to see anyone.

Including her.

Terena watched Daris as he swung his sword expertly. Then he stumbled and Terena's breath caught. His balance was off.

"It'll take me some time to get used to it," Daris said, startling her. Terena had backed away, intent on leaving unseen. She hadn't known he'd even been aware of her standing nearby.

"I didn't mean to intrude," she said after a pause, her hands balled at her sides. Daris glanced over at her before going back to swinging his sword, his movements fluid and graceful. When he turned to his right, however, his shoulder dropped and his steps faltered.

Terena saw the way his lips turned down and shook his head. She warred with herself; part of her wanting to stay with him, but a part of her still hurt at how he'd refused to see her.

Making up her mind, Terena turned to leave when he called out to her.

"Stay," he said in a rough voice.

Terena stopped. She stood awkwardly for a few seconds. He went back to swinging his sword.

"I can see you're busy," Terena grumbled and turned to leave again.

"Terena, stay."

"Oh, now you want to see me?" She knew she sounded childish, but it still bothered her he hadn't wanted to see her.

He turned to face her fully, and she blinked. The bandage he'd worn that first day was gone, replaced by a scrap of leather held in place with ties winding behind his head. She schooled her face, not wanting him to misread her expression. Somehow, he looked more dangerous. Harder. So unlike the quiet, steady commander she'd come to know.

The man standing before her was menacing in a way Daris never was.

"I didn't want you to see me like that."

Blinking, Terena cocked her head. "I already saw you like that, remember?"

Daris didn't respond. He dropped his chin, swinging his sword idly. Long moments passed before he sheathed his sword.

"Do you remember when we saw each other in Aurora?"

The words startled her. She'd been expecting him to tell her he did not know he was Eudaemon and would she please forgive him for making her worry so much?

Instead, he brought up the first time she'd seen him, her chest squeezing when she looked up at him. A sense of something more, something like a memory. The first time she locked eyes with him and could not look away. The first time she knew, deep in her bones, this man was important to her.

The first time she doubted her feelings for Lerek.

"Vaguely," she said with a lift of her shoulder.

He shifted his stance, bracing his hands at his hips. "Fine. You're mad." Daris raked a hand through his hair. Terena willed her scowl to stay in place when several locks of his gold tipped hair stood on end. Even with the leather over his eye, he was still breathtaking. Somehow, it had the effect of making his good eye more intensely blue, like the clear blue of Obsidian Bay.

Daris stared at her for a few long seconds before he lifted a hand toward her. "When I saw you in Aurora, I...," he swallowed and stopped, pursing his lips. "I can't explain it. I saw you and it was like... I instantly knew who you were. In reality, I had no clue who you were. I'd never seen you before and I know I'm messing this up, but I sensed... in my soul, I knew you."

Terena's jaw loosened. Any anger or hurt she'd been feeling before now evaporated.

Because she knew what he meant. She'd felt it too.

"At first, I thought my heart had stopped because you were the most beautiful woman I'd ever seen. I even repeated that over and over to myself later that night, but..." He wiped a hand over his face. "It wasn't until I went to bed and I dreamt of you—"

"You had a dream about me?" Terena interrupted, unable to stop the smile growing on her face.

He frowned and nodded. "Aye, Terena. That's why I brought it up. I dreamt about you that night. But it wasn't the first time."

It took a second for his words to sink in. Terena's pulse stuttered, then raced and her eyes widened. "What?"

"When I was twenty, a bear terrorized a village nearby and our instructor thought it would be an excellent test of us in the Agoge, our training. Five of us went to that village, but I was the only one who made it back. The bear attacked us while we were bedding down for the night. The bear," Daris dropped his head back, his mouth open as if recalling. "That beast was unnatural. It was the biggest monster I'd ever seen, then or now. Well... Melanos might be the same size.

"We'd made spears out of branches and attacked it, but it killed three of our brothers-in-arms. We managed to hurt it bad enough we thought we had it. When one of my brothers, Artagos, went in for the kill, it roared and swiped him across the middle, opening him up."

Terena was chilled by his recollections, her heart hurting for these boys, barely men, having to endure this in order to become soldiers in the Spartan army. She approached Daris, but he remained lost in his memories.

"They were all dead within minutes and I stood there in shock, trembling, afraid as it stalked toward me." He looked over at Terena, his expression haunted. "I don't remember what happened after that. I woke up with this," he pointed to the three scars on the left side of his face by his ear. "I had gashes, too, on my shoulder and legs, and I lay on the ground knowing I was dying when I saw this woman walking toward me. She knelt at my side and whispered."

When he didn't continue, Terena asked, "What did she say?"

Daris's expression hardened as he stared at her. "Eudaemon."

Terena's skin sizzled at the word. It was an unlocking of sorts, her soul opening its eye in recognition. She dared not say anything.

"Aye. I knew before we got here I was Eudaemon, but I did not know what that meant. I'd only ever heard it that one time until Melanos said it again when we were in Ibros. I told Jason and Michael the story while you were recovering from the encounter with Bethana. It explained so much about why I'd been wounded in count-less battles, some mortally, and yet I survived."

"Didn't you tell your instructor or anyone else about that encounter? Or ask about what she meant?"

Daris shook his head. "I thought it a hallucination from blood loss. I didn't say a word about it to anyone." He looked up at her. "When I went to sleep that night, I dreamt of you."

Terena's mouth dropped open.

"It's true," Daris said ruefully. "I saw you, clear as you are standing before me."

"What... were we...," she coughed and shook her head, trying to appear unflustered. "What was I doing?"

"You were dancing," he whispered, his voice a caress, his good eye heated as he took a step toward her. "I dreamt of you dancing, holding hands with people on either side of you, and you looked up at me and you smiled and I... I swear my heart stopped. That was my dream."

Terena's chin trembled, tears filling her eyes. She quickly blinked them away.

"Daris…"

"But it wasn't a dream," he said softy, taking another step closer, now less than a foot away, his head tilted down to her. His eye was on her mouth as he lifted a hand, the pads of his fingers stroking over the line of her jaw. "Seven years later, you smiled at me while dancing that night in Sparta."

So many thoughts chased each other for dominance in her mind, she was stupid with the flood of them.

"When I saw you in Aurora, that's what I was feeling—recognition. Attraction. But then I dismissed it because, of course, I was attracted to you. Look at you. I didn't stand a chance. Then in Sparta, when I saw you dancing," he finally looked into her eyes, his smile resigned, "that was it for me. I was yours. I *am* yours."

A flood exploded inside her chest and she leaned up, her hands clutching his forearms as she pressed her mouth to his. She sensed him stiffen, then instantly coiled his arms around her, bending to pull her closer as he slanted his mouth over hers. She begged for entrance with her tongue across his lips and he opened with a groan, his tongue dancing with hers, tasting her mouth, her lips, teeth clashing, biting.

Daris pulled away, his breath hot on her face, his chest rising and falling against hers. He stared down at her, mouth open. Terena pulled his head back down but after a brief kiss he pulled back with a shake of his head.

"Not here," he whispered, dropping a quick kiss to her nose. Daris stepped away and slipped his hand into hers. Terena's stride lengthened to keep up with him. She didn't bother to look at the curious soldiers watching as they passed.

When they were inside Daris's tent, he turned. For a moment, he looked embarrassed and tried to step away.

"What is it?" Terena whispered as she clutched at his waist to keep him close.

"I don't," he cleared his throat as his face flushed. "I don't have anything to prevent—"

Terena grinned. "What? You don't want babies with me?"

If possible, Daris's face became a deeper scarlet. Terena laughed and decided to go easy on him.

"I'll talk to the surgeon later. I'm sure he can help with what I'll need. Now," she said with a wink, "speaking of what I need…"

He wrapped his arms around her and crushed his mouth to hers again. Daris shifted, walking her backwards until she was stopped by something at her back and she whimpered to get closer to him.

Daris moved his hands over her back, down to her waist, his fingers digging into her hips before he reached down, grabbing her ass and lifting her. Terena's mouth opened, her legs wrapping around his waist, and she had a second to revel in the hunger of his gaze before he slammed his lips back to hers. He moved, the muscles beneath her fingers shifting, and then he bent over, lowering her onto the cot. She kept her legs wrapped around him, unwilling to let him go as he growled at how little space the cot afforded him. He pulled back, grabbing the bedding and tossing it on the floor, then lifted her and spun before lowering her onto the blankets and furs.

"Wait!" she said, her hands flying up to his shoulders. He was panting, breathing as hard as she was, and it made something unfurl low in her belly as she gazed up at him. "Daris, we should stop."

He looked like he'd never heard a worse idea in his life, and she smiled. "I only meant… Daris you were dead a few days ago! You fucking lost your eye! You need to heal still and I—"

Daris growled and grabbed her wrist, pulling it to the laces of his breeches. "Does this feel like I need to heal?"

Terena shivered at the feel of his hard length beneath her palm. This was definitely a much different Daris than the one before he lost his eye. She looked up at him, her eyes heavy, but she had to try one last time. "Baby, I don't doubt your… strength. I'm worried about you, though. We should wait."

"If you want to stop, we'll stop," he said, and she thrilled at the frustration she heard in his voice. "But I am fully healed, I promise you."

"Good enough for me," she smirked and yanked his head back down, slamming her lips to his.

CHAPTER FORTY-ONE

"It was a memory."

Daris's eye drifted open, and he stared up at the canvas of his tent. He pulled Terena closer, letting his hand drift down to her thigh and up to her hip, drawing lazy patterns across her fair skin. He'd fallen asleep, sated and at peace for the first time in ages. Terena lay tucked at his side, her soft breaths on his chest. It was nice to fall asleep like this, even nicer to wake up with her snuggled against him.

"What was?" he asked, his voice sleep roughened.

"Your dream of me," she whispered. Gooseflesh rose on his skin from the movement of her lips. Daris ducked his chin to look at her. She moved her head to meet his gaze.

"Aye."

The quiet lengthened as she continued to stare at him, and he held her gaze. "Was that the only one you've had of us?"

He stared at her a moment more before nodding. "Aye."

She shifted, her gaze now following the path of her hand as it trailed across his chest, tracing old scars, and then around his nipple. His breath hissed as his nipple hardened, heat coursing slowly down his belly to his groin, and he gripped her hand. He folded his fingers around hers and brought it to his lips.

"If you keep that up, we won't be getting up for a long while," he muttered.

Terena stretched up, holding his stare as she straddled him. His face tightened as he dropped his hands to her hips.

"I wasn't trying to be subtle," she whispered, and he groaned when she rolled her hips.

The tent flap rustled and Daris bolted up, shielding Terena's body with his own.

"Messene better be under attack," Daris shouted when he caught sight of Jason. The younger man's face heated. He spun around, his back stiff.

"Apologies, Commander," said Jason. "Captain Athanasi and his men are moving out. He wants a word before he leaves."

Daris swore under his breath. "Tell him I'll be there shortly."

Jason moved to the tent flap and called back, "Good to see you feeling better, Commander."

Daris waited until the man had gone before looking at Terena. She was staring down at him with a small smile.

"Does 'shortly' mean we have time to play, or..."

Daris grinned and settled onto his back. "If you want to play, I will not stop you."

Terena lost her smile and her eyes glittered as she shifted again and his cock bucked at the friction. He hissed, his grip tightening on her hips when she lifted and moved her hand down to guide him to her entrance.

"I want you to have more dreams about me," she whispered, her gaze holding him captive until she took him completely. Her head fell back, and she sighed, tightening around him. Daris's breath came out ragged and he stared up at the beautiful woman who had captured his heart, his soul, his being. His pulse raced when she moved, languid at first, then faster, her breaths coming in quick, short pants as she rolled her hips, taking him deeper.

Daris gritted his teeth, his mind and body consumed by her. His hands slid up to her breasts, cupping the fullness of them as she rode him. When she looked back down at him, her eyes hooded and her mouth open, he was lost. Never in his life had a moment burned itself into his mind so thoroughly as the sight of her taking her pleasure from him.

Heat suffused his skin and he leaned forward, trying to regain control. Hooking a hand over her shoulder, he captured those pretty lips, swallowing her gasp as his tongue slid inside, dueling with hers. Holding her in place as he bucked his hips, grinding harder and harder against her soft wetness, Daris pulled back to stare into her gorgeous eyes.

The wonder he saw in them as she climaxed made him lose the last thread of his composure and he shouted, his own release barreling through him, and he clutched her to him as they shattered.

They stayed like that forever.

Daris felt her body calm, and she melted into him, her arms sliding over his shoulders as she leaned her forehead against his head.

"I'll dream about you for a lifetime," he said raggedly, recalling her words from earlier. "A thousand lifetimes."

She smiled against his head. Pulling back, her eyes searched his face. He wasn't sure what she saw. Her chin trembled, and she ducked her head.

"Daris," she said as he lifted her chin to see her eyes. "Promise me something."

He stared back at her and smiled. "Anything."

His hand moved to her cheek, pushing back a lock of her sable hair to tuck behind her ear. She licked her lip, and he was mesmerized.

"No more secrets," she whispered.

Daris's hand stilled. The vulnerability in her eyes made his stomach fall.

For a long time, he stared back at her, reveling in the feel of her around him, in his arms, a lifelong dream come to life.

Cold slithered through his chest, but he smiled, hoping she wouldn't see anything other than happiness on his face. The tension in her body faded as she relaxed against him, tightening her arms.

"I promise," he whispered. "No more secrets."

And hated himself when she kissed him.

Because of the lie he'd just told her.

THEY DEPARTED THE FOLLOWING MORNING, SHORTLY AFTER DAWN. Everyone was in high spirits, laughing and joking as they set off. Daris and the Liodari—Jason, Michael and another man by the name of Fane—leading them out of the city with Terena and the others filing behind. The rest of the Liodari stayed behind to hold the city.

At dusk, they veered off the main road and onto a less travelled path, one Daris said would take them into dense woods where they'd camp for the night. An hour later, Daris called a halt. Terena and Sonah walked off to gather wood for a fire while the others set about caring for the horses or laying out the bedrolls.

After dinner, they conversed by the fire, and Gabriol shared a story from the early days of their journey. How Sonah had dropped the firewood she'd gathered and run screaming when a fox had come darting out of the woods at her. Or the time Gabriol had been showing her how to hold a sword and almost lost a hand when she turned to say something to Croak with the sword still in her hands. Jason offered to show her some basic sword maneuvers, but Rydon had cut him off, letting him know they'd already been teaching her how to handle herself.

"But I would *still* like to learn all I can," Sonah said, shooting Rydon a pointed look. He smiled and scratched at his beard. "It's not every day one gets to learn something from the legendary Liodari."

Croak began to tease her about the things he thought this particular Liodari wanted to teach her.

Rydon slapped the back of his head.

Terena was grinning when she caught Daris's eye. He stared back at her for a second before gesturing with his head. She pulled in her lower lip and gave him a quick nod.

"I'll be right back," she muttered to no one in particular. The others were still engaged in teasing Sonah or making fun of Croak. Even Fane, new to their group, was laughing and joining in.

Terena walked a few feet away from their camp before she heard the crunch of leaves and twigs behind her. She turned, smiling when she saw Daris. He came close, taking hold of her hand and led her further away, neither of them speaking.

A few minutes later he turned, lifting his hands to either side of her jaw, his thumbs stroking gently as he bent his head to kiss her. Terena sighed, welcoming his lips, hungry for more as he flicked his tongue across her lower lip. She opened her mouth wider and his tongue swooped in, slowly at first, so slowly heat slid down her thighs. She stepped closer, pressing flush against him as she gripped his waist.

"I've wanted to do this all day," he whispered, breaking the kiss to move his lips down her jaw, feathering soft kisses on the underside of her ear to her neck and down to the hollow at her collarbone. She shivered and pressed closer. "I've been hard ever since you left my bed yesterday."

Terena moaned, tipping her head back to give him more access, his thumbs sweeping down to her neck, caressing lightly.

"I can't stop thinking about you," she said, her voice breathy. She ached to feel all of him. "Do you—we can't... can we?"

"What?" he asked as he moved his lips along her jaw, teasing the corner of her lips. He ground his hips into hers and she felt the hard length of him against her belly. She whimpered.

"I want to fuck you," she said, her face heating with her words, her embarrassment quickly fading as he took her lips again. His kiss was hot, urgent, his tongue deep in her mouth in long, achingly slow strokes.

"Please," she said when he broke the kiss, her hands on his chest, running over it as she tried to find a way inside his clothes.

"Not here, Ren," he groaned. She slid her hand down to his breeches, enjoying his hiss of pleasure as she put her hand over his cock. It bucked in her hand and she laughed.

"He says otherwise," she murmured, biting at his lower lip.

"He always does," Daris said through gritted teeth as she stroked him through his breeches. He put his hand on her wrist to still her but she kept it there while she traced his lips with her tongue.

"What if—"

"This is where we all piss, you know," Croak called out in a loud voice.

Terena started, whipping her head around when she heard others laughing softly. Daris swore, wrapping his arms around her.

Terena was about to tell them to leave them alone when she heard a trickling noise. "Gods! Are you really doing that now?"

"Can't stop midstream," Croak yelled. "We started pissing before we heard you two. Thought it was a couple of animals."

More laughter.

"Guess we were right," Gabriol said.

"Fucking gods," Terena hissed. She grabbed Daris's hand and pulled him behind her as they heard one of his men call out.

"Apologies, Commander." She thought it might be Fane.

More laughter followed, and Terena fumed. When they were far enough away, Daris reached out and wrapped an arm around her waist, stopping her as he pulled her against him. When she looked up, he had a big grin on his face.

"I don't know what you think is so funny," she said, pushing against him.

He tightened his hold and laughed. "It was a little funny."

She started pushing against him in earnest, but he laughed and bent his head to her neck. He bit her softly and when she stilled he soothed it with soft kisses.

"I promise," he said between kisses he trailed up her jaw and back to her lips. "The next village we come to tomorrow, we'll get a room."

She mumbled under her breath about shitty brothers and he chuckled.

"But," he said when she'd relaxed against him once more, "I'd like to sleep by you tonight, if that's all right with you. Watching you from across the fire isn't good enough."

Terena melted but threw him a sour look before she turned and started walking back. "Fine."

His chuckle as he followed her back was his only response.

CHAPTER FORTY-TWO

They rode all day before stopping at a village north of the border in Pyrgos. Daris assigned Jason, Michael and Fane to care for the horses while he went with Rydon to secure rooms. Terena, Gabriol, Sonah, and Croak walked to a nearby tavern Daris had pointed out. They were all to meet back there for dinner.

After they had pulled a couple of tables together, Gabriol shoved Croak toward the bar to get a few pitchers of ale, wine and one with water for Daris.

Croak drained his first tankard and was well into his second when the Liodari showed up. Jason frowned at the seating arrangements and shot Croak a scowl. As he grabbed a seat at the other end, Sonah jumped up and moved to sit next to him. Terena and Gabriol exchanged a look and Terena had to smother her smile behind her wine glass.

Gabriol was in deep conversation with Fane when Rydon strode in. Terena's eyes shot up and she barely glanced at him before her eyes shifted to the man behind him.

"Croak will be asleep before we finish dinner, I see," Rydon said with a grin as he took a seat next to Croak. He clapped him on the back as Croak finished his drink.

"Just getting warmed up, old man," Croak said around a belch.

They ordered food, and Terena's chest lightened as she looked around the table. She had her brother safe at her side, her newfound sister smiling and laughing with the handsome Liodari, and Rydon and Gabriol sharing tales with their new friends.

Terena looked up from beneath her lashes at Daris, who sat across from her, one hand wrapped around his glass of water as he listened to something Fane was saying.

"If you're happy, I'm happy," Croak said softly near her ear. Terena snapped her head around, her eyes searching her brother's face. His dark brows were furrowed as he gave her a wistful smile.

"What are you talking about?"

He tilted his head and gave her a knowing look. "Stop, all right? You think we're all stupid? I saw Jason when he tore out of Daris's tent the other day. He stood guard nearby and made sure the rest of us stayed away. And then half an hour later, you came out."

Heat crept up her face but she shrugged. "That's our business."

"I know," Croak grumbled. "And like I said, I'm happy if you're happy. But…"

"But what?"

Croak looked down at his nearly empty ale tankard and shook his head. He turned and pierced her with his dark brown gaze. "It's only been six months, Terena. I fucking miss him. A lot. I thought you did, too. That you can just…" Croak shook his head as he took a drink of ale.

Terena stiffened. Her mouth pinched, and she had to force herself not to smack her brother. Closing her eyes, she took a deep breath. When she looked back at Croak, she was glad to see he looked miserable.

"I do miss him. And a part of me will always love Lerek," Terena said after a long pause. She flicked her eyes to Daris, who was watching her with his good eye narrowed. Turning back to Croak she added, "But Daris is different. *We* are different together."

"He's not even your type," Croak whined, leaning back in his chair with a groan. "Lerek was going to be an emperor. Now, you're with

Daris? He's a soldier who lives his life with and for his men and his king." He scoffed. "Don't get me wrong. He *is* handsome, if you like men with half their faces ripped off."

Terena did smack him that time.

The table went quiet. She stood and leaned over, grabbing Croak by his tunic as she hissed in his face. "If you can't say anything nice, say nothing at all. Asshole!"

She turned and stormed out of the tavern, her chest rising and falling rapidly. Outside, Terena walked a few paces to lean against the wall of the building. Pressing a hand to her chest, Terena closed her eyes.

"Are you all right?"

Terena startled. Daris stood near the door with a concerned expression. She launched herself at him, kissing him with needy intent, drowning herself in the feel of him. She sighed when his arms instantly came around her, pulling her closer. The feel of his muscles beneath her hands as they moved and bunched made her shiver. Terena threaded her hands up at the back of his head, loving the feel of his soft hair in her fingers, and she sighed into his mouth.

"Terena," Daris groaned as he tried to pull back, but she refused to let him go.

"Daris," she whispered. "Take me to your room."

The way his mouth curved up was so wicked, fire sizzled down to her core.

"Whatever the lady wants," he answered with a wink.

It was late—or very early—before Sonah snuck upstairs, Croak behind her shushing her every two seconds. Gabriol and Rydon had retired much earlier, but she'd stayed longer with Croak and the Liodari.

Sonah paused in front of her door and Croak turned to look at her over his shoulder before he opened the door to his room.

"What?"

She turned to him. "Nothing…"

He turned to face her fully. "What?"

Sonah bit her lip. "What if… what if she's… not alone?"

Croak grunted. "I guarantee they're in *his* room."

"You think?"

"Trust me."

Sonah looked at him skeptically. Croak twisted his lips and moved forward, taking the key from her hands and unlocking the door. He pressed the latch; the door swung open to reveal the darkened interior.

Sonah sighed in relief.

"Thank you."

"My pleasure," Croak said with a smirk as he flicked her nose.

"Gods!"

"Good night, gorgeous," Croak called as he shut the door behind him.

Sonah slumped off her clothes and sighed as she slid between the cool sheets. As she lay back and closed her eyes, the world swam alarmingly. She snapped her eyes open. Sonah was so tired but too drunk to sleep. Did that even make sense?

She groaned, leaning up and punching the pillow a few times to make it more comfortable before settling on her side.

Nope. Worse.

She swore and sat up. Much too quickly. She had a second to aim before her dinner and all those drinks that seemed a good idea at the time came up. She groaned and wiped her mouth, looking at the mess she's made on the floor between the beds.

Sonah whimpered, thinking of how she had to get up now to clean it up.

As gently as she could, Sonah rose and put on her pants and shirt. She didn't bother putting her boots on as she padded across the cold wood floor and unlatched the door carefully. No sounds came from the hallway, so she ducked out and closed the door softly behind her.

Taking the stairs painfully slow, she strained to hear any noises from below. When she was satisfied, she moved swiftly across the main room on the first level, easing around the tables. The only light in the room came from the windows, the weak predawn light enough for her to see the bar counter. Sonah tiptoed over and went behind it, hands out to feel for some kind of cloth or hopefully a bucket she could fill with water to clean up her mess.

Ducking down behind the counter to search, Sonah heard a door open and several voices in low tones before the door closed again. Sonah froze, crouched as she was, listening.

"…make a move before we get to the north," a familiar voice said. Sonah blinked, recognizing Michael's voice. Soft laughter followed his remark. They were speaking in the common tongue. Probably because Fane—who was not Greek but Offeni from the east—did not speak it well.

"That's why I haven't," Jason replied, defensively. "I like her, very much. But I'm Liodari and she'll be gone soon." They were closer now, almost to the stairs. Sonah frowned and made to move, to announce herself, when Fane spoke.

"The commander doesn't seem to share that sentiment. I never knew him to be that cold-blooded. First, he kills her lover and then he beds her. Ruthless."

Sonah froze, the blood draining from her face. She became dizzy. Looking up, Sonah tried to get a look at the men as they ascended the stairs. There was a thud and Sonah jumped, clamping a hand over her mouth.

"Shut the fuck up," Jason hissed.

Sonah's pulse roared in her ears as she moved, slouching around the bar. She stepped closer to the stairs. The men had paused on the steps.

"*Never* talk about that. Don't say it again," he warned, his voice low, but she heard the anger in them. He said something in a whisper and she strained to hear, but this time Jason had switched to Greek and she only understood a couple words.

One was Lerek. The other was Terena.

She was ill again and feared she might give herself away by retching when they continued up the stairs.

Sonah took deep breaths, hoping to calm her stomach, but her mind raced.

What the fuck? she thought as she sat on the ground next to the bar.

What did he mean?

Why would Daris kill Prince Lerek?

He wouldn't.

Sonah wouldn't believe it. She must have misheard.

Sonah wiped her face with her hand. She rose slowly, her mission forgotten as she climbed the stairs, her feet leaden and heart heavy.

Her last thought as she pulled up the bedsheet and closed her eyes was whether or not to say anything to Terena.

CHAPTER FORTY-THREE

Terena cringed and put a hand to her nose at the stink in the room she shared with Sonah, grateful she wouldn't be there long. She was only there to change her shirt, wash quickly, and brush her hair. Sonah had still been asleep when Terena had left the room.

When they were readying their horses to leave, Terena had glanced over at Sonah. She was about to mount when she turned again, truly looking at the girl this time. Her face was pale, drawn.

She looked ill.

Terena had gone over, a hand on Sonah's shoulder. "Are you all right? You look sick."

Sonah had shaken her head and mumbled she'd been out too late and the drink had not sat well with her. Croak had caught the tail end of that comment and punched her in the shoulder, telling her she shouldn't hang with the big boys if she couldn't handle her drink.

Sonah heaved on his boots.

While the others laughed, Terena had shoved her brother away, cursing as he lamented the state of his boots. Terena had helped Sonah clean up, then asked Gabriol to help her get Sonah up in her saddle. The girl looked on the verge of tears and Terena felt for her.

They rode all day, Terena falling behind to stay near Sonah. The girl no longer seemed ill, but despondent. Terena grew more and more worried as the day wore on.

When the sun set, Daris called out to stop for the night. Terena silently thanked him.

While the others took care of the horses and setting up camp, Terena took Sonah off toward a small stream nearby, hoping some cool water on her face might help settle her.

Sonah crouched pathetically near the edge of the water while Terena tore a strip off the bottom of her shirt and soaked it in the water. She brought it to Sonah's head.

"A few weeks more and we'll be in the north," Terena said softly. "I know it's been rough, but you're doing so well. Next time, maybe don't drink as much. Those men are much bigger than you and can drink a lot more—"

Sonah started crying. Terena felt awful, thinking she was the cause because of what'd she said.

She tried to apologize, stroking Sonah's blonde hair. "I'm sorry, Sonah, I know you're—"

"I have to tell you something," Sonah said softly. Terena narrowed her eyes, uncertain.

"What was that, love?"

Sonah swallowed and raised tearful eyes at her, the soft brown and green of her eyes turning a beautiful smoky quartz through her tears. "I have to tell you something."

"All right," Terena said, a reassuring smile on her face as she stroked Sonah's hair again. "I'm here. What do you need to tell me?"

Sonah reached out and gripped Terena's wrists. The wet cloth fell on the ground between them. She opened her mouth, then quickly closed it on a whimper. She shut her eyes tight. When she opened them back up again, Terena braced at the look on the girl's face.

"I got sick in our room last night," Sonah began, swallowing before she could continue. "So I went downstairs to find something to clean it up. I heard the Liodari come in. I heard them talking."

Something oily slid under Terena's skin. She fought hard to keep her smile in place. "What did they say?"

Sonah's face crumpled. Then she seemed to steel herself. She wiped at her face and exhaled. "I heard Fane say something. He said... he said something about..."

Sonah paused. Terena sensed the air shift and snapped at Sonah, "What did he say?"

The girl winced. "He said Daris killed the prince," she whispered, her voice so low, Terena had to lean in to hear the words.

Even then, she wasn't sure she'd heard her. She couldn't have heard.

"What did you say?"

Again, Sonah lifted a hand to wipe at her face. "Daris killed the prince."

Blood thundered in Terena's ears. She was chilled to the bone, as if she'd fallen into the stream at their side.

"What prince?"

Sonah looked at Terena sadly. "*Your* prince."

Terena had a sense everything happening right then was a dream.

A nightmare.

Not one of her visions, but a nightmare, the likes of which had tortured her for months after Lerek's death.

Now, she was living one.

She stood slowly. Sonah scrambled to her feet, reaching out to clutch Terena's icy hands in her own. "I was drunk," she said desperately. "I probably misheard what they were saying. And then they switched to Greek and I for sure don't know what else they said."

Terena pulled her hands away from Sonah and took a couple steps backward. Her feet were heavy and she trembled.

"I'm wrong," Sonah was saying, her voice rising as Terena continued to back away. "I'm sure I am. I was so drunk and sick and I'm so sorry I didn't mean to say anything! I don't know what I'm saying!"

Terena turned and ran.

D ARIS WAS LAUGHING WITH HIS FRIENDS , ENJOYING THE FIRE AND THE company, his heart full and realized he was truly content. He looked up, and spied Terena coming toward them. His smile grew.

Terena.

She was the reason for this contentment. This fullness in his heart. He knew it now, looking at her as she neared.

He loved her. Was *in* love with her.

Had loved her long before he'd realized it. Had loved her since that night seven years ago when she'd crept into his mind, his dream, and ruined him for anyone else.

Daris rose, his lips widening as he made to greet her, but stopped when he saw Sonah running behind her, crying, screaming at Terena to stop. Croak and Rydon ran after Sonah. Gabriol went to Terena, but she pushed him away, her eyes on Daris. She unsheathed one of her short swords, pointing it at him.

His smile faltered when he saw the rage and panic on her face.

What is going on?

Terena turned the sword a bit, stiffening her arm.

"What—"

"Did you kill him?"

He stilled. "What? Who?"

"Who?" Terena's voice was shrill. "Lerek!"

The blood rushed down his body, his hands slowly rising in front of him. Around him, his men went silent, tense. Out of his peripheral, he saw Jason rise slowly.

Daris swore the air had paused.

"Ren—"

"You didn't, did you?" she whispered, her voice cracking as she swallowed a sob.

His heart shattered.

"Listen—"

"Gods," she hissed, the sword beginning to shake. She wiped at the tears falling with her free hand.

He didn't know what to say.

How to make it better.

He dropped his head. He couldn't look at her beautiful eyes, couldn't face her pain.

Coward.

"Did you kill Lerek?"

Daris's head shot up at the hard edge in her voice. His heart squeezed at the sight of that flat, icy stare, as if she had gone far away.

He took a step toward her. Her hand stiffened.

Her face…

"I can explain," he answered softly.

Her face crumpled and she almost fell. Then she lunged forward so fast he knew if he hadn't been wary of her, she would have struck him in the gut.

At the last moment, Daris dodged and grabbed her arm as she thrust at him, twisting her arm to disarm her. Terena twisted as well, sweeping a leg out and catching him behind his ankle and he let go as he fell. His men jumped back, weapons at the ready, watching in disbelief as Daris and Terena squared off.

Daris sprang up, crouched in a fighting stance as he watched her. His balance was still off. Sounds erupted all around, the rest of their party moving closer but on clearly opposite sides.

"Daris! What the fuck are you doing?" Croak roared behind Terena, his arms stretched out toward both of them, his face ashen.

Terena snatched the other short sword from its sheath at her hip and sprang at him again, her face a mask of pain and pure rage, lips pressed tight as she swung one sword a split second before she lashed out with the other at his left side. He moved right and under her left arm and paced backwards as he braced for another assault. She snarled, stepping forward, first right then left, moving so fast with the Twins he barely had time to move.

Behind her, Sonah screamed nonsensically at them, her face streaked with tears as Gabriol struggled to hold her while she writhed against him. Michael tossed his sword to Daris, and he caught it by reflex, twirling the sword once, deflecting another blow from Terena.

"Jason, make them stop! Please!" Sonah begged, screaming at Jason as he stood behind Daris, sword drawn. He made a move to go to her but Rydon stepped in front of her.

"Don't you dare move, Liodari!" Rydon roared at Jason, his gaze whipping over to him before going back to the fight between Terena and Daris.

"You said you'd never hurt me," Terena hissed at Daris, swinging first her left sword then the right at him. He parried, his face tight. "You said you'd rather *die* than hurt me," she continued, her voice pure venom, eyes wild with pain and rage. He deflected her next thrust.

"So die! Die like *he* did!" Terena raged, then spun, whipping out her left arm as she whirled, her right arm right behind it ready to open his stomach.

"What are you doing, Terena?" Daris roared as he fell back a few steps. "You can't kill me. You know this!"

"A girl can dream," she snarled with another nasty swipe at his chest.

He jumped back, panting. "Please listen!" he yelled, blocking another blow. "We need to talk, Terena!" Another thrust, low on his right side he blocked with some difficulty. "But I need you to stop! Will you please stop!"

She was a whirlwind, ducking, thrusting, snarling and cutting with the Twins. He parried—barely—meeting blow after blow as she dropped to a knee and spun, her hand flung out as he met the flash of steel again.

Daris fell back step after step after step, blocking and parrying. He had to do something to get her to stop and listen.

He jumped back as she thrust forward again, her momentum causing her to slip. She dropped to her knee, hard—a rare mistake— her left sword loosed from her grip. Quick as an asp, she swiped her hand along the ground, tossing dirt in his eye.

He swore, blinded, blinking furiously. Tears streamed and blurred his vision but he saw Terena pounce, his eye clearing barely enough to show him where to block her renewed offensive. Cold sweat broke out on the back of his neck. He was in trouble. One eye gone and the other almost useless now.

Around them, the others shouted at them, at each other, Sonah's screams piercing as she yelled at Daris; she yelled at Jason and the others to do something.

He had to get through to Terena somehow. No matter what, he had to try to get a hold of her, pin her long enough to listen to him. He had no time to think as he tried to anticipate her movements, tried to disarm her without hurting her.

Terena whirled, a dancer caught up in a deadly song, her face a terrible beauty carved in stone; her left hand pulled back as the right hand slashed down at his thigh and he barely blocked it as she instantly swung the sword in her left hand. She stepped back, spinning as she bent over, her left leg fanning up and out so her foot struck him in the jaw. He stumbled to the side.

His men roared behind him, and he saw Terena's friends surge forward, Rydon and Croak holding their swords.

Terena bounced forward but Daris swung down on her weapon until his sword had snared hers and pulled her in. They locked eyes, hers spitting fire.

"I love you," he said through gritted teeth, their faces so close he could see the sweat above her lip. Could see her nostrils as they flared, her eyes widening at his words. "I fucking love you, Terena. Please stop and let me explain—"

"I *hate* you," she said softly, her voice breaking. He saw the devastation in her eyes and wanted to give up.

She may hate him just then, but she hadn't used her powers on him. Neither had Sonah. That thought popped into his head as another quickly chased behind it.

Yet.

He had to hope she'd listen.

"Ren—"

He had barely said her name when she shoved at him and a second later something hot tore down his side. Terena stepped back as he fell to one knee, his hand going up to his side, blood seeping over his fingers. He looked at her in shock, saw the short sword in her right hand coated with his blood, and then looked back up at her. Her face was pale as she looked at him wide-eyed, her lips trembling as they moved wordlessly.

The silence was deafening. As if the world had slowed, he saw his men form a wall in front of him. Gabriol dropped his arms, releasing Sonah, who stood there in shock. Terena dropped her swords, her face crumpling as she sobbed.

She screamed, and it tore through his soul.

Rydon and Gabriol stepped forward, swords fanning out to protect Terena as she stumbled back.

Daris surged up, grabbing hold of Fane's shoulder as he pulled past him, trying to get to Terena. His men held him back.

Terena continued crying gut-wrenching sobs as her knees buckled. Sonah snatched up Terena's sword and pointed it at him and his men. She moved forward and threw her arm over Terena's shoulder, pulling her back. Sonah's scared face was pale and streaked with tears, still pointing that sword at them as she backed away. Terena all but collapsed in Sonah's embrace, shaking as she sobbed.

Croak eased forward, casting wary glances at Daris and his men as he grabbed up Terena's other short sword, then backed up slowly.

"Terena!" Daris called out, trying again to get her to listen to him, but it was no use.

Rydon jerked his sword at him in warning. Daris watched in despair as Sonah hauled Terena's limp figure further away, two hunched forms disappearing behind the wall of their friends.

"I fucking knew it," Croak muttered, his face tight with anger. "I *knew* you were bad for her."

"Croak—"

"Shut the fuck up," he whispered, and Daris swore he saw hurt in his eyes before he spat on the ground in front of him. "You never deserved her."

Daris ordered his men to stand down as he watched Sonah drag off Terena, who looked completely broken, followed by Gabriol and

Rydon. Croak stopped long enough to grab some food and supplies, stuffing them in a rucksack before he scrabbled after them.

Daris watched until they mounted their horses and rode off. The thundering of hooves faded long before he dropped his eyes from where they'd disappeared.

CHAPTER FORTY-FOUR

Terena clutched at Nyx's reins, blinded by tears and anger and a pain so sharp she thought she might die from it. She cried harder when she thought of the pain she'd experienced seeing Lerek's dead body that night.

This pain was different.

This pain broke her soul.

Made her want to rage at the gods.

Her breathing was coming so fast now, her chest hurt. Nausea roiled up in her belly.

"Hold!"

She heard Rydon yell at them to stop, but it sounded so far away. Someone grabbed her reins, and Nyx almost reared.

Terena didn't care. She slumped off her back, stumbling away a few steps and retched.

She dry heaved for what seemed like forever before someone was at her back.

Sonah.

The girl cried and beseeched her. To do what, Terena wasn't sure.

She didn't care.

Terena swung her right arm back, trying to swat away Sonah's hands as she rose, her legs weak and more tears blurred her vision.

She heard them speaking behind her, but she kept walking, not knowing—not caring—where she went.

Terena wiped at her face and then stopped. Throwing her head back, she screamed.

Screamed with everything she had.

The earth trembled beneath her, as if her cries had unleashed a response in the world. Her anger and pain a shockwave making her stumble.

She fell to her knees, sobbing, her heart and soul dying inside her.

"Terena," Croak said softly behind her. A moment later, he came and covered her back, wrapping her in his arms as he kissed her head. He whispered words meant to sooth but Terena was beyond hearing.

"That was… something," he muttered, moving to crouch at her side.

A long silence followed, broken only by her sniffles and ragged breaths. Croak stroked her back while he sat with her.

Much later, Terena wiped her eyes and sighed. "I feel like I'm dying," she whispered.

"I know," he said in a low voice. He moved away.

"Ren?" Sonah came over, hesitant. After a pause, she sat in front of Terena, crossing her legs.

Terena opened her eyes to see Sonah and her face crumpled again, fresh tears welling and spilling over. Sonah wrapped her arms around Terena, her sobs shaking the both of them. Croak moved, standing and walking away while she cried on Sonah's shoulder.

"Terena," Rydon said a long time later. He crouched next to her, his hand on her back. "I know you're hurting. We're all hurting with you. But we need to get moving. Solon's men are nearby, and I'm pretty sure Daris will come after us, too. There's no way what you just did wasn't felt for at least fifty miles."

"Let him come," she said bitterly, the effect spoiled when she wiped her nose on her arm bracer. "I'll fucking kill him this time."

"You can't, remember?" Croak snorted. When she skewered him

with her gaze, he held up his hands. "But, you know, a dagger to the heart might make you feel better."

"How could I be so fucking stupid? I'm such an asshole."

"You're not," Rydon said firmly. "You have history with him and it's all tangled up with what you're feeling now. Which is normal. I don't know what happened, but I promise the pain will ease."

"I didn't feel like this with Lerek," she whispered, swallowing as she wiped at her nose. Looking up at Rydon's kind expression she begged, "Did I not love him? I thought I loved Lerek, but this is so much worse, Rydon."

"I know, love. I know. But let's not sit around like easy prey, all right?"

Terena nodded and allowed him to help her up when Sonah let her go. They walked back to the horses, Nyx snorting softly as she moved to nuzzle Terena's arm when she came near. Terena whispered to her, "Such a good girl," and mounted.

"We should ride for Tursk. At least there, if we're stopped by soldiers, they won't be loyal to Solon. It'll take us a week to get to the Pass if we ride hard, and then another to reach Seleste. Only a few miles to the border from there. And we should probably start traveling at night," Rydon said, his voice firm.

"They know we ride for Seleste," Croak objected, his arms wide as he looked between Rydon and Gabriol. "They'll be waiting for us!"

Rydon waited until Terena settled in the saddle before he turned on Croak. "We've no choice. We can't go through Osta and we can't go anywhere near Aurora or Ovenno right now. If we go through Tursk, we can lose them in the mountains. Maybe wait it out for a week or more. He can't watch forever."

Rydon and Gabriol looked back at Croak. He raked his hand through his hair, a lost look on his face. He caught sight of Terena watching him, and he squared his shoulders, turning back to Rydon.

"All right," he said quietly, and walked to his horse and mounted.

Terena wiped her face one last time, then rode off after Rydon.

As soon as the sound of horses's hooves faded, Daris turned to face his men.

"Who talked?"

By the looks his men gave each other, they knew what he meant.

No one outside of his officers in the Liodari and King Altos knew about Prince Lerek.

And since that didn't include any of Terena's friends, that meant one of his men had been talking about something that would get them all killed.

His men remained silent.

Daris's eye twitched. He pulled his lips in to stop them from trembling. His mind raced, still thinking of the fight with Terena, but he was so despondent he latched on to any excuse absolving him of the blame she'd laid at his feet.

How could he have hoped to explain it to her when he'd lied to her for months?

And she was right. He *had* said he'd never hurt her.

But keeping this from her, after everything—

"It was me, Commander," Fane said, holding his chin up as he took a step forward. His blond hair looked mussed as if he had slept badly.

"I made a poor joke and mentioned it. It was only in passing, and although I had believed we were alone, I had no right to speak on the subject."

Daris lunged at him, grabbing fistfuls of the man's leathers in his hands. The metal plates at his shoulders rattled when Daris shook him.

His face a breath away from Fane, Daris asked softly, "What was said?"

Fane, to his credit, did not flinch. "As I said, it was a poor joke."

"I want to understand how a poor joke accounts for a state secret being spoken of so openly, people outside of Sparta are now aware of it?"

The other men stopped moving. Everything stilled around him as Daris's eye narrowed on Fane.

"Do you know what will happen if this gets out? If they want to use that against us?" Daris asked, pushing Fane back to look at every one of his men. "The eyes of the Heylisian Empire will turn to us once more and we will now not only have Solon at our throats but a unified Heylisia! And all for a *fucking joke?*"

The clearing remained awkwardly quiet as the blood roared in Daris's ears.

"Break camp and prepare to ride. We're going after them. Michael and Fane, ride for Messene and meet us in Seleste with a host of Liodari."

He strode off, needing some space, when the ground beneath him trembled.

Daris looked up and saw the looks of bewilderment on the faces of his men.

A moment later, they were knocked to the ground, and what sounded like the loudest clap of thunder Daris had ever heard rumbled over them.

CHAPTER FORTY-FIVE

"They're here."

Terena stiffened, bolting upright as Rydon strode into the stables. Sonah gasped. Her hands stilled as she was gathering the reins of her mount.

"They're here!" Croak said, coming in seconds behind Rydon.

Rydon turned and twisted his lips at her brother.

"Croak, you and Sonah take the horses out the main gate and bar it behind you. Wait for us on the west side."

Terena turned to Rydon, laying her hand on his forearm as she leaned in. "Can you and Gabriol cover me from the roof of the stables? I'm heading to the east gate. I'll start firing once I get there and you guys make your way to me."

Rydon gave a curt nod, turning quickly with Gabriol at his heels.

"How do I bar the gate from the outside?" Croak asked Terena as he lengthened his stride to keep up with her.

"Figure it out! You'll have plenty of time. They don't know we're—"

"Soldiers!" Sonah hissed as she came running back in.

Terena swore. Looking around, she motioned for Croak and Sonah to follow where Rydon had gone up to the loft.

They had reached Seleste the night before without trouble. No Heylisian soldiers or Liodari in sight. Now, it seemed their relief was a joke from the Fates as Terena eyed the soldiers outside.

As the others ran for the ladder, Terena hid behind a bale of hay and peeked out. She didn't recognize any of the soldiers, but they wore the Imperial uniform.

She swore again.

They didn't seem to be in a hurry, but she silently urged them to move away from the gate.

Gaia was smiling down on her. The soldiers moved further inside. She backed up and took the ladder up to the loft.

"New plan. Croak, you, Sonah and Gabriol take the horses to the east gate. Slowly!" Rydon cautioned.

He turned to Terena. "You and I will cover them, and once you see them safely outside the city, we'll make a run for the main gate and bar it ourselves."

"Still want to meet up at the west—"

"No," Rydon bit out, shaking his head. "Ride for the main gate and we'll head north from there. Fell River is only a few miles from here. We ride hard, we'll be in the north before they can reach us."

As the others went down the ladder, Terena peered down. "Hey, hey!" she hissed. Three sets of eyes looked up at her. "Take that cart in the back and dump some hay in it, please. Then push it out the back. All right? Just outside."

Croak pointed his finger at her as he turned toward the cart. Gabriol followed. A minute later, the three of them left the stables, leading the horses as quietly as possible.

Terena pulled her bow over her shoulder and looked back at Rydon.

"Ready?"

He nodded once and she turned, moving in a crouch to the window. Swinging her leg over the ledge, Terena ducked under the opening until she was out on the narrow lip of the roof. She edged along until she could clamber up to the top of the building, Rydon right behind her.

Thankful for the moonless night and snowfall hiding their movements, Terena watched the soldiers loitering in the square.

As she was about to turn her head to ask Rydon if he saw the others, she caught sight of Daris Antonius striding toward the soldiers.

Ice slid down her spine as she watched him. A cascade of emotions battled inside her, her heart thumping wildly as she watched this man who'd made her feel alive again, who had touched her heart.

Knowing the whole damn time he had lied to her. Had killed Lerek.

And destroyed her.

"Those are Aurora's men," said Rydon, crouched beside her.

"Aye."

"What are they doing in Osta?"

Terena cast him a side-eyed look. "Shall we ask?"

"Are they working with Sparta?"

Terena let out an exasperated sigh and stared at Rydon until he shrugged.

She pulled in a shaky breath and tore her gaze away to look back at Daris. Despite the leather patch across his eye—or maybe because of it—he looked more dangerous than ever. He had on dark armor unlike what he'd worn the last time she'd seen him. Atop the bronze plates at his shoulders, he wore a thick cloak snapping as he walked. From the stiff lines of his body to the way his gloved hands clenched at his sides, the anger rolled off him in waves she could feel even at that distance. The soldiers closest to him flinched away at whatever he was saying, and hastened off to do whatever he'd barked at them.

Turning to Rydon, Terena asked, "Are they clear?"

Rydon watched for a few more seconds before turning to her. "Aye." He nocked an arrow as he shifted beside her.

Terena pulled back on the bowstring as she lifted the bow, aimed—first at Daris—then swung to the soldier behind him and to his left.

And let it fly.

Rydon's arrow was a split second behind hers as she quickly nocked another and fired. Chaos broke out as the soldiers scattered, those unfortunate enough not to have outrun their arrows falling around them. Terena and Rydon kept shooting until she grabbed his arm. They both turned and ran in a crouch toward the lower roofline. Her foot slipped, and Rydon gripped her arm a split second later. She took off again, and they jumped onto the hay cart where the others had left it.

Rydon pulled himself out, then helped Terena. Surging forward with Rydon a step behind, they raced for the gate. Two guards stood huddled together near the gates. Terena caught both men across their throats with her dagger. Rydon had pulled one gate and Terena ran to help him pull the other until they shut with a bang.

Croak and the others rode toward them.

Rydon grabbed his sword and jammed it into the ground in front of one door and angled it so it blocked the other as well.

Gabriol leaned over his horse and tossed Rydon his own sword. Rydon slammed it into the ground across from his own before pivoting and running for his horse. Gabriol held the reins for him. Croak pulled Nyx forward and Terena ran to them.

"We can lose them in the storm," she said, panting.

"Stay close!" Rydon yelled at them.

Gabriol turned his horse and bolted, Rydon and Sonah close behind with Croak and Terena pulling up the rear.

They rode hard, Terena looking back only once as the snowfall closed around them.

They were safe for now, but Terena knew it wouldn't be long before the soldiers caught up. She hoped they'd be at least at the river before they did, and if they could get there first, she knew they'd be safe on the other side.

An unwanted thought invaded her mind. Would Daris be with them? Would he and his men follow them, too? And if they did, would he…

Terena shook her head. If Daris caught up to them, she had a feeling she wouldn't win a second fight.

"THEY'RE HERE."

Daris looked up from the letter he'd been writing as Fane came into the room. He dropped the quill and sat back. "Who is she with?"

"The merc from Decu and the girl. Her brother and the Roison I did not see."

Daris stood. "They'll be here too. Where?"

"Stables," Fane answered.

"Make sure none of the men are seen," Daris said as he strode for the door. The common room beyond was filled with his men, all of them turning their gazes to him as he appeared. "Tobias, take three and guard the eastern gate, Michael, you and three more get to the main gate, but make sure you stick to the wall. They're at the stables now, but I don't want to chance them seeing any of you."

He strode through the room, hearing the others rise as they all made to follow. "No one is to hurt any of them, understood?" Daris turned back, eyeing each of them. "Especially her. We're fucked if she uses her powers, and I don't want to have to do anything to hurt her to save any of you."

His men nodded and murmured their agreement. Daris turned, heaving open the door. He made to say something to Jason, who followed behind as the others peeled off when he froze, catching sight of something sending a shock of anger through him.

He swore softly under his breath as Jason said, "What are they doing here?"

A squad of Duke Aurora's soldiers had appeared near the city gates and were dismounting. Daris pinched his lips as he made his way toward them, the element of surprise he had counted on to get Terena to listen to him gone in a frenzy of shouting men and an overzealous captain barking out orders. It had taken him the better part of two days to clear out Osta's soldiers. How did Aurora's men even know to come here?

As he neared the captain, he saw the soldiers fan out, racing past him and his men in every direction.

"Captain," Daris called out, his face a mask of displeasure, "this isn't necessary."

The captain only flicked a glance at him before turning back to one of his men.

Daris caught the man's baldric, whipping him around so his face was inches from Daris's own. "Did you not hear me?"

The captain flinched but didn't back down. "I'm here on direct orders from Duke Aurora. Your King—"

"And I've just told you this isn't necessary. My men and I will take care of it."

"I'm not here to steal your glory, *Commander*," the man sneered, and Daris's eye widened. He heard a choked sound coming from Jason. "I have orders from—"

Daris hauled the man closer, as he hissed, "I don't care who gave you orders. I am taking her in, so you and your men can leave."

He pushed the man, satisfaction lifting his lips as the captain stumbled back, bumping hard into his man behind him. Flustered, high color rose in the man's face as he sputtered, "You have no authority! I demand you step aside!"

Daris didn't bother to respond as he turned to Jason. "Get—"

Shouts sounded across the square as arrows whistled through the air. Several soldiers behind Daris yelled, and he spun in time to see two of them fall. He roared for his men to find cover as he raced toward the nearest building and ducked. Leaning forward, Daris cursed as more arrows whistled past and caught soldiers not fast enough to hide. He motioned to Jason, who had sheltered behind a barrel next to a small house, to stay low. Jason nodded, then looked out at the yard as others scrambled to find cover.

Daris waited. Whoever had fired those arrows—and he had a pretty good idea who—seemed to have stopped. He leaned further out, sword in hand, then nodded to Jason as both sprang out onto the main thoroughfare, Daris calling out to his men. They raced to the inn, mounting their horses quickly without regard to the captain or his men as they rode for the main gate.

"Shit!" Jason swore as he jumped from his horse and ran for the closed gates. The two men posted there were dead on the ground, their throats slit.

"They're barred from the outside!" Jason called up to Daris as he mounted his horse.

Daris wheeled his horse around, and his men followed as they tore across the city to the eastern gate. He cursed again, their pursuit slowed by the terrified citizens running out of their way—or rather, into their way in their panic to get out of the path of charging horses.

When Daris saw the gates, he yelled at the people blocking their path, slapping the reins as he urged his horse into a full gallop. He turned his mount left after exiting the gate and hoped was the direction Terena had taken.

Behind them, he heard the captain's men close in. The snow let up enough for a few moments he urged his horse faster, his men riding in formation around him as he tore across the plains.

At dawn, the snow stopped. Daris pulled up, his men doing the same around him. He swore, turning his horse as he glanced around the snowy landscape. Mist swirled over the ground, the weak light of dawn making everything appear eerie.

The captain and some of his men finally appeared, drawing up when they caught sight of them.

"Did you see them?"

The absolute fucking gall. "No, I didn't catch sight of them, Captain," he bit out. "I wouldn't be sitting here, would I?"

The captain didn't seem to catch the sarcasm as he looked about. Like he expected to see them in the wide open space.

"Are you sure they went this way?"

Daris dropped his chin. His head snapped back up as Michael answered. "Must have. You can reach Fell River from here."

Daris shot his man a look that shut him up.

The captain didn't seem to notice. *Of course not.*

"Yes," he muttered, looking in the direction Michael had indicated. "Fell River is about a mile or two away."

"We're so close to where The Event occurred, the river's sure to be frozen enough to cross on horse," one of his men said at his side, his mount dancing beneath him.

Daris shot another death look at Michael, who ducked his head.

"Right," the captain said. "Listen up! Our quarry seeks to evade us, but we are men of Aurora and we will bring that traitorous bitch right to the duke's feet!"

He turned his mount and shot forward, his men following behind as they all roared their bloodlust.

"Follow behind, but do not engage," Daris said to his men. "If we get to the river and they are not there, we'll fall back to the city."

"And if they are?" Jason asked.

Daris looked up as the soldiers faded into the distance. He turned his mount in a tight circle. "If they are, we take out Aurora's men."

He didn't bother to acknowledge the shocked looks on their faces as they glanced at him, then at each other.

Jason nudged his mount close to Daris. "What do we do with Terena and her sister after we take out Aurora's men? They won't come easy."

Daris glanced at him with a frown as he tightened his grip on his reins. "We only go after Sonah. Whatever happens, she comes with us."

CHAPTER FORTY-SIX

Their horses thundered across the snow covered plains. Terena chanced a look back and saw soldiers gaining on them. Her eyes widened as she saw a few raised bows.

"Arrows!" she screamed, urging Nyx faster. Rydon caught up to her, his body low over his mount. A second later, Cerberus, carrying Sonah and Croak, reared back and fell, two arrows lodged in his flank.

Terena screamed as her brother fell back, Sonah dropping like a stone atop him. Ahead of them, Gabriol cursed as his mount buckled and he, too, slammed to the ground. Rydon swerved toward him, stretching out low over the side with his arm out to grab him but he jerked back as an arrow pierced his shoulder.

Terena unhooked her bow and yanked on Nyx's reins, leaping off her back. She sprinted for Croak, who had slowly gotten to his feet, but Sonah was still on her back in shock. Terena helped Croak mount Nyx, slapping her rump to take off. When they were a good distance away, Terena lunged for Sonah, wrapping her arms under the girl's shoulders and heaving her up onto her feet.

"Please," Terena hissed, panicked, knowing there was no way she could carry Sonah in time to outrun the soldiers. Sonah struggled and lurched forward, and Terena almost sobbed in relief as the girl regained her faculties enough to run.

Terena sprinted behind her, grabbing two arrows from her quiver and pulled the bow over her shoulder. Rydon and Gabriol had gained the river, Croak and Nyx a few steps behind. They didn't pause as they rode full tilt onto the frozen river.

Sonah slipped and fell hard on one knee as she got to the river but sprang back up, not once looking behind her.

Terena's feet pounded on the ice as they raced across, the sound of hooves behind her like thunder in her ears.

She dropped to her knees and slid, spinning as she brought the bow up. Terena reached back and grabbed an arrow, nocking it and pulling back on the string, releasing in one smooth motion. Another arrow nocked and fired as the first raced through the air. She fired again, bringing her right foot up and pushed up, gaining her feet as she turned and ran.

The hiss of arrows sounded on either side of her and she hunched her shoulders, hands up to her head as she ran first to the left, then cut back to the right.

Out of her peripheral, Terena saw horses on her right, and she cursed. The soldiers were trying to flank them and she'd failed to notice.

Her steps faltered as she caught sight of soldiers bearing down on Sonah.

Liodari.

Terena screamed, desperately reaching for an arrow as she veered right. Dread coursed through her. The bow shook in her grip as a Liodari grabbed Sonah and threw her over his saddle. In her haste and distraction, Terena slipped and landed hard. The Liodari pulled away, racing back toward the riverbank as Terena fired three arrows at them.

Gabriol roared from her left and Terena looked over her shoulder to see Croak drop short of the snowy bank on the other side of the river.

She stood rooted, closer to Croak and the others than the side of the river where the Liodari were now racing off with Sonah. Soldiers bore down on her from the right and Terena's heart lodged in her throat. Caught between needing to go after her sister or helping her brother, Terena's throat closed up in fear.

The world slowed.

Sound stopped.

The loud pressure of silence filled Terena's head. She watched her brother's body lying in the snow, Rydon down at his side, with Gabriol a step behind him. The soldiers bearing Sonah disappeared while others rode straight at Terena.

Quick as lightning, she unsheathed the Twins, flipping them once and lifting them high above her head. She brought them together and roared. Fire coursed down her arms when the swords joined, her eyes burning.

Terena slammed the swords into the ice.

For a few endless seconds, there was no sound except for an eerie silence filling her mind.

Sound rushed back in with a loud boom pulsing from the joined swords.

Ice exploded.

A wave of ice and water tore from the fissure and raced toward the soldiers.

They had no chance as an enormous wave crashed over them, obliterating them before they could even scream.

The river crashed and roared ahead of her. Terena looked out in horror a second before the ice beneath her feet cracked. She jumped back, bringing her hands back to her sides. Terena sheathed her swords and turned, bolting toward the shore.

Rydon screamed her name as she leaped. The ice buckled beneath her as she stretched out her arm. Rydon ran onto the ice and grabbed her as the ice collapsed and they both plunged into the freezing water. He tugged at her, dragging them both to the shore. Gabriol kneeled and wrapped his cloak around her.

Coughing and sputtering, Terena scrambled over to her brother, a whimper tearing from her throat. As she reached him and turned his face to her, his eyes fluttered open, a half smile on his lips.

"Always so dramatic," he said, his voice weak. Terena choked on a sob and dropped her forehead to his.

"Sonah," she sobbed as her body convulsed.

"What?" Croak said in with a crack in his voice. Terena cried harder.

"Where is she?" Gabriol yelled, falling to Terena's side.

"They took her!" she screamed in Gabriol's face. She shook her head in misery.

The sound of hooves made her spring back up, her sword in her left hand as she crouched over her brother. Rydon and Gabriol had daggers raised.

"That is quite the entrance," a familiar voice called out as the riders pulled up.

Terena tensed as she watched soldiers wearing unfamiliar armor stop a few feet from them. They moved their mounts aside so the man who'd spoken rode closer.

"*Orry?!*" Terena exclaimed. Her vision blurred and tears stung her eyes. He dismounted and rushed over to them, throwing his arms around Terena.

"He found us a week ago," the man beside him said. Glancing up, she saw he was tall—even mounted on his warhorse. His dusty blond hair fell over his forehead and down to his neck as he leaned forward and grinned down at them, his deep blue eyes locked on hers. "He had a marvelous story to tell about what delayed your arrival. He assured me you'd be here soon, though, and here you are."

Terena's mouth dropped open when she glanced to her right and saw both Rydon and Gabriol drop to one knee, their heads bowed.

"Your Majesty," Rydon said, and Terena whipped her gaze back to the blond man.

He dismounted and Terena shifted, unsure what to do.

The blond man grinned and sauntered over to them. He held out a hand to Terena as she eyed him warily.

"We meet at last, Terena Luca. I am Hermes."

Sonah stood with her arms crossed, staring out the window at the thick clouds obstructing her view of the city. King Altos had assured her more than once she was not a prisoner, yet she refused to leave her rooms.

After arriving back in Sparta a few days ago, the servants had put her in the same rooms she'd had the last time she'd stayed in Arestia Castle. The dresses King Altos had had made for her were still in the wardrobe, but Sonah had refused to wear anything other than the leggings and worn shirt and corset Terena had bought for her. Her boots now had holes in them, yet she'd refused his offer to have new ones made.

Sonah would rather die than take anything else from that man.

When Daris had brought her before him, the king had told her she was brought back for her own protection, but she knew she was leverage to use against her sister. Daris had said as much on their way back. He'd said having Sonah with him ensured Terena's return. Burning to ask why he wanted her back after how he'd betrayed her, Sonah kept silent. Daris was not the same man she'd come to know. The man who'd left her at her bedchamber door was cold and scary.

And very dangerous.

The doors opened and servants bustled in carrying pails of steaming water. Sonah looked over her shoulder with disinterest before turning back to the window. She could hear the sounds of water being poured in the room off to her right. Soon, she'd go through the ritual of taking her bath while the servants laundered her outfit, then wait patiently wrapped in nothing but a towel while she waited for them to return with her clothes. For some reason, that small bit of rebellion made her feel better.

When the servants hurried from the room, Sonah made her way to the bathing chamber. She had removed her corset when a thump sounded on the other side of the wall. Clutching the garment to her chest, Sonah stilled.

This again?

A minute passed without another sound, and Sonah resumed removing her clothes. As she settled in the bath, another thud sounded. Gripping the sides of the tub, Sonah's eyes widened. She strained to hear. Behind her, a scraping noise reached her and Sonah scrambled out of the tub, sloshing water onto the marble floor. Cursing as she slipped, Sonah grabbed onto the edge of the tub and snatched at the stack of towels beside it. Shaking one out and wrapping it quickly around her body, Sonah tiptoed out of the bathing room and into the bedchamber.

"There you are!"

Sonah's mouth dropped open, and she thought she might faint. The man standing before her had shorter hair than when she'd last seen him.

"*Isher?*"

Sonah's squeak made the smile disappear from the prince's face. She lifted a trembling hand to her mouth and took a step closer.

"No, Sonah," the prince said with a sad smile. "I'm Lerek."

CHAPTER 47

"So. King of Olympus, huh?"

Hermes didn't so much as flinch when Terena stopped at his side.

"It seemed wrong not to seize such a perfect opportunity to thumb my nose at my father."

Terena smirked. Leaning over the stone wall, her gaze ran across the Strait of Olympus to the land she'd known her whole life. The view from the battlements took her breath away. Everywhere she looked, the landscape shimmered as if covered in layers upon layers of diamonds. Terena shivered, pulling the furs they had given her after Fell River tighter around her body.

Hermes, standing in a plain white cotton tunic and leather pants, didn't seem to notice the cold. He folded his large arms across his chest and frowned.

"You've much to catch up on. Which is why I'm here."

"How are you even here? You were all banished."

Hermes gave her a weird look. "I'm a realm walker."

Still not understanding, Terena shook her head.

"I'm the messenger god. I can pass between realms," he drawled, as if to a young—stupid—child. "I am immune to the banishment the Titans decreed."

"But why?"

Instead of answering, he glanced back over the horizon at the pure white of Olympia below them and waved his hand lazily. "I cannot believe how much it's changed. This is no longer Greece."

Terena eyed him for a moment before shrugging. "You've been gone a long time."

He nodded absently. "Before the war, this was all ours. We created it. All of what you see here and more you cannot. And when we were banished, we recreated it in the new world. All of it, as it used to be here. Better, even, because we learned from our mistakes. Of course, part of our punishment was that we could no longer leave Mount Olympus. But Zeus found a way around that. We could join the humans, but only in animal form. It made us even more creative in how we interfere in the humans' lives."

"And you all want to come back? To this?"

Hermes smiled in a way that made her uncomfortable.

"We have plenty of time to discuss that later," Hermes said. "You asked me many questions earlier. Do you wish me to answer?"

Terena straightened, staring up at him.

"When we lost the war, Zeus agreed to banishment only if there was a way to come back. So he went to the Fates. They told us we'd return when the heir of Ares rises. Which is why you and Sonah are so important to us. Your destiny is tied to our return."

"Pytho told me something a little different," Terena said, looking at him askance. "She said 'False death betrays love, forging Athena's Weapon. From the ashes of gods, the Heir of War rises, leading the gods to glory. The fate of man is for the Weapon.'"

"Fucking Fates," Hermes said under his breath. He looked out over the Strait, his mouth pinched. Terena turned to the snow covered landscape as well.

Somewhere out there, Sonah was on her way back to Sparta.

With Daris.

Terena dropped her gaze, her nails scratching idly at the stone.

She would go back. She had to go back. For Sonah. And when she did, Terena wasn't sure what she would do about Daris.

As if reading her thoughts, Hermes turned to her, his big frame blocking out the bright morning sun.

"We must get your sister back."

"Aye."

"We cannot continue without the Heir, but it is you—"

Terena's body jerked hard at his words. She looked at him, unsure of what he'd said.

"The Heir?"

Hermes turned back to the view, his eyes on the horizon.

Terena waited, a slow buzzing building beneath her skin. She itched with it but did not squirm.

"You are the key, but she is the lock," he replied.

Terena hung her head for a moment. Frustration bit at her so hard hot tears pierced the backs of her eyes.

"Is that what godhood is?" she asked bitterly. "Just throwing us into bullshit, withholding information that could help us do better, *be* better? All in the name of whatever games the Fates decree?"

"You and your sister are different," Hermes said. "You had no one to guide you. But you're here now. You've cut it close, waiting until the eighth circle to find me."

"You assume I know of what you speak," Terena bit out. She stopped and took a breath, and her voice was stronger when she said, "I do not. Which is why I'm here. I need to know, Hermes. I need to know who I am and who Sonah is. I know Ares is our father, but who is our mother? Why is there a prophecy around us? How do I make sure I don't fail in this eighth circle?"

She hated the way her voice broke. The wind at the top of the castle was much sharper and stole her breath when she opened her mouth to breathe in deep. Terena had a brief panic that it might freeze her lungs.

She stared at Hermes a long time before he cocked his head, considering. "Your mother is a complicated answer. One I cannot share, as it would have unpleasant consequences."

At her rigid stare, Hermes sighed dramatically. "Believe me, if it would help you to know right now, I'd tell you. Besides, it would make the Fates angry and you do not want that." He grunted and turned away. "No one likes them very much."

"What *can* you tell me?"

"I can tell you that, in the prophecy the oracle gave you, you are Athena's Weapon. She claimed you in your Naming Ceremony."

Terena gaped. Several times she opened her mouth without saying a thing while Hermes watched her with amusement.

"*I'm* Athena's Weapon? What about Daris Antonius? They call him that in Sparta!"

"It matters not what they call him," Hermes replied and for a moment she swore something unpleasant crossed his features. "You are Athena's Weapon."

"And Sonah is the heir?"

He nodded.

"How?" she asked. Her throat was dry. "How is that possible? She's seventeen!"

Hermes frowned. "Huh?"

Terena waved her hand. "How can she be the heir if I'm older?"

Hermes's face lost some of its color. "No," he said, bemused. "She is the elder. By mere minutes, aye, but she is the elder child."

Terena's eyebrows hurt from how high they climbed. "Well, does age work differently with gods? Because I promise you, she is younger than me by four years!"

Hermes was still. The silence that stretched seemed pregnant, as if the world had stopped to listen in. Who knows? Maybe it had. Terena knew one thing after everything she'd endured.

And that was that she knew nothing.

Then Hermes laughed. It was a chuckle at first, and Terena folded her arms and glared at him. When he saw the look, he roared, his laughter shaking the ground beneath them, his head tossed back as he bellowed his mirth to the sky.

When he calmed enough that he was grinning at the ire in her stare, he said, "You and Sonah are twins."

Terena gasped.

"Aye," Hermes said with a smirk. "I don't know what happened this last time, but she's never been this young. The weather is new, too." This last, he remarked with some bemusement.

Terena grabbed a fistful of his sleeve, craning her neck to look him in the eye. "That's not possible!"

"Aye, she's your twin," he said as if to a dullard. "When you made it through the portal—"

"Wait, what?"

Hermes scowled. She'd made a god scowl. Terena backed up a step, letting go of his sleeve.

"We are not from here?"

Hermes's scowl faded, and his eyes turned sympathetic. "No, child. You are from the realm we were banished to. The new Greece we created. The new Mount Olympus. Your mother tried to hide you from Ares and made a bargain to keep you from him. Although, as the Fates will tell you, there's no running from destiny."

Terena's stomach flipped. The acidic taste of bile climbed her throat.

"When you and Sonah went through the portal," Hermes continued, "Zeus… was not happy. He threw a lightning bolt after all of you."

Terena's hand flew to her mouth.

Hermes looked around, considering. "Must be what caused all this."

Terena made a noise in her throat. "Zeus did this? It's been like this for almost two years now."

"And it's also the first time you and I have met in this realm."

"That's why I had no visions of you," Terena thought out loud, ducking her chin to stare at her nails. When she looked back at Hermes, her eyes were hopeful. "My mother came through as well? So she's here?"

"Careful," Hermes admonished. "Remember, you'll have to wait to hear about your mother."

"Gods," Terena groaned and lifted her hands to her head. "So we both get eight circles? Me and Sonah?"

"No, Terena," Hermes snorted. "You and Sonah are bound. Your destiny is bound. You share the loops. If you die or she dies, the loops reset. But this is the eighth and final. Whether you succeed in your labors or not, whether you live or you die, there will be no new loop. No more chances."

"But I have a destiny," she said with a sharpness to her voice that made Hermes's eyebrow arch.

"Aye. And whatever happens in this last circle is that destiny."

Terena squeezed her eyes shut tight. "This is hurting my head."

"Aye," Hermes said, almost sounding sympathetic. Then he clicked his tongue and Terena's eyes popped open as he hit her on the shoulder. "Cheer up, niece. You found me and now we can begin."

"Begin what, Hermes?"

His smile was slow as he bent over, his face so close to hers she could see something moving behind his eyes. It made her tremble.

"Taking back what's ours."

ACKNOWLEDGMENTS

It takes a village. And that village for me started with my mom. I wish you could be with me to share in it, but I hope you're watching over us and can see this. And for my father, who always wanted me to have an easier life with steady paychecks, I'm glad I stopped listening ;). I love you.

David, my love, my partner, my husband, you will never read this book, but that's okay because you heard about it a million times and still don't know what it's about. Thank you for knowing I'm crazy, but loving me anyway.

Colin (my soul) and Noelle (my heart): how fucking lucky am I to have you as my kids?

Antoinette Spyropoulos, you are the best sister anyone could ever hope for. You are my soulmate and I am not who I am without you.

Elena Mendez, you are my sister from another mister. You are the rock that we've been blessed to have in our lives since 1st grade.

Jen Curry, another one of my day-ones. Thank you for everything.

I'm grateful to have these bad bitches in my life: Megan Munster, Taylor Lavelle, Katie Murray, Ashley Kania, and Bethany Sage. Thank you for always being there. We may no longer work together, but you're always in my heart (and the group chat).

Laura Cashman, thank you for your friendship and support. You've lifted me more times than I can count.

Debbie Samoson, my amazing sister-in-law who read the book quickly and enthusiastically, thank you for the sympathetic ear whenever I'm unhinged.

Andrea Roberts and Verna Regier, I am so grateful that Debbie gave you my book to read! You both were so gracious and helpful with your feedback. Thank you so much. You are officially my betas for life.

Taylor Dux, thank you for loving the book and for the lovely note you left me in your feedback journal. I read it every day.

Courtney "Coco" Hale, you are my spiritual goddess, my mystical mentor, my friend and my sage. Thank you.

Jaqueline Kropmanns, thank you for the gorgeous cover and for your patience with me! I can't wait to work with you on the next one!

Shepengul - so so grateful I took the plunge to have a professional map done because yours is WAY better than mine ;). You're amazing.

Allison Wright, thank you for the fabulous blurb! You took a hot mess and made magic out of it.

And a special shout out to my little Carlos, who was with me every single day I wrote, hoping I'd drop a Cheeto. I love you and miss you so much, buddy.

ABOUT THE AUTHOR

Katerina Speers grew up in the Chicago area where she currently lives with her husband and children. When she's not writing, Katerina can be found reading a book, playing video games or enjoying movies at the theater.

instagram.com/katerina.speers
goodreads.com/katerinaspeers
tiktok.com/@katerinaspeers

www.ingramcontent.com/pod-product-compliance
Lightning Source LLC
Chambersburg PA
CBHW020649110726
47901CB00001B/107